P9-BZQ-222

Dead Days
of Summer

Also by Carolyn Hart

Death on Demand
Death on Demand
Design for Murder
Something Wicked
Honeymoon with Murder
A Little Class on Murder
Deadly Valentine
The Christie Caper
Southern Ghost
Mint Julep Murder
Yankee Doodle Dead
White Elephant Dead
Sugarplum Dead
April Fool Dead
Engaged to Die
Murder Walks the Plank
Death of the Party

Henrie O
Dead Man's Island
Scandal in Fair Haven
Death in Lovers' Lane
Death in Paradise
Death on the River Walk
Resort to Murder

Dead Days of Summer

A Death on Demand Mystery

CAROLYN HART

WM

WILLIAM MORROW
An Imprint of HarperCollins*Publishers*

This book is a work of fiction. The characters, incidents, and dialogue are drawn from the author's imagination and are not to be construed as real. Any resemblance to actual events or persons, living or dead, is entirely coincidental.

ISBN-10: 0-06-072402-1

To Eve K. Sandstrom,
aka JoAnna Carl,
with great affection

1

The moon broke free from the low-lying bank of clouds, revealing the white crests of breaking surf. Pinpoints of light sparkled at the water's edge, the bioluminescent glow of tiny zooplankton. Humid summer air lay over land and sea heavy as a funeral pall. Waves boomed and water surged around the pilings of the fishing pier. Footsteps echoed as a shadowy figure walked alone to the end of the pier, reached out to grip the railing. The grasp was tight, unrelenting.

Anger burned, scalding and uncontrolled. The thought came, words vivid as scarlet neon: *She had to die.*

Resolution provided release. Taut muscles eased. The hands fell away. *She had to die.*

Vanessa Taylor surveyed the dimly lit restaurant with satisfaction. Not a woman she saw could match her for beauty. Vanessa felt exultant. Everything she wanted was within her grasp. She looked across the table at her companion. Her richly red lips curved in a cat-in-the-cream smile.

He reached into the pocket of his blazer, pulled out two snapshots, handed them to her. His eyes were intent, though he managed a smile. "Think you can handle it?"

She glanced at the photographs. "Of course. I'll persuade him. You can count on it. And once it's done, we'll be together. Everything will be wonderful." She lifted her wineglass. "To us."

He raised his glass, dark head bent forward.

Vanessa drank every drop and laughed aloud.

The burst of laughter turned the head of a nearby diner, a tired single-mom real estate agent out for an evening with a chattering group of friends. She rubbed an aching temple. God, to be young again, to be happy and confident, to be triumphant. Not to be worried about the slowdown in house sales and the ugly whispers that real estate might be the next bubble to burst. Not to be frantic about her son Mike and his thirteen-year-old girlfriend who wore her blouses too tight and her shorts too short. Not to be fearful that her mom was making less and less sense. Not to be tired to her bones, yet wake up in the night scared and anxious, sleepless until dawn. Too beaten down for envy, she stared at Vanessa, admiring the raven black hair that curled in soft ringlets, the bold, forceful features, the voluptuous body in the low-cut crimson dress.

The older woman sighed. If she had a dress like that, it would hang from her thin shoulders, making her look like a bony hag. Her face bleak, she watched as Vanessa dropped two snapshots into a small silver purse. The man with her watched attentively. He wasn't smiling. He looked intense and determined.

The observer wondered what that look meant. Was he crazy about the girl who laughed with such delight? Probably. The single woman's face drooped. Nobody had looked across a table at her for more years than she wanted to remember. She felt a hot rush of tears, dipped her face until her hair swung forward. She was tired, so tired. She wished bitterly that she and the dark-haired woman in the beautiful red dress could change places. Just for one night.

Heather Whitman ignored the knock on her bedroom door. After a pause, the knock was repeated, soft, inquiring, yet subdued. Heather clutched her pillow with tense fingers. The knock didn't come again. The only sound was the rev of a motor in the drive in front of the house, the throaty purr of Jon's car. She glanced at the bedside clock. Almost noon. Her stepfather always took his own sweet time but he had no need to hurry to his office. Not since he'd married Mother. Of course, Mother always lauded him to the sky, said how lucky the island was to have a man of his caliber, inferring he was so successful. Successful at marrying a really rich woman, that was for sure. Damn Jon. She didn't like him. He was always snide about Kyle. How many times had Jon brought up the flagpole flap? For God's sake, it was years ago, a high school prank. Heather pushed away other moments when Kyle's daring and defiance had landed him in trouble. And now . . . Could she overlook his last wild escapade? Oh damn, damn, damn.

Thoroughly awake, Heather rolled from the bed. She stopped at the vanity, yanked up a brush to pull at her tousled dark hair. She didn't look at her face. She was likely pale as a ghost, with huge smudges beneath her eyes. Whenever she got upset, she looked like a wraith, all gray and silver, insubstantial as a ghost. She flung down the brush, walked to the French window. She pulled it wide, looked out at the familiar sweep of the gardens, brilliant with roses and hibiscus and bougainvillea. The wedding was supposed to be there at the gazebo. *I, Heather, take thee Kyle . . .*

Was there going to be a wedding?

3

———

Lillian Whitman Dodd paused at the top of the steps, looked down the hall toward Heather's room. Perhaps she should go back, knock again. Clearly, Heather was distraught. Lillian was surprised at her sudden feeling of dismay. That was odd. She should be overjoyed if this marriage didn't happen. She'd never tried to hide her regret at the engagement. She'd hoped Heather would outgrow Kyle, but she had never looked at another boy, not from the first moment she met him. Admittedly, Kyle was appealing with an impish charm and good looks, but he was a disaster waiting to happen. Why now did Lillian feel sadness for her daughter? Perhaps because passionate love is rare and when it happens it is worth fighting for. Just as she'd been determined to marry Jon despite Heather's opposition. Lillian had been certain Jon was the right man for her from the moment they'd met. He'd done such a fabulous job on the promotions for the Art League. He had such an eye for color and the charm of a successful public relations executive. How lucky she was that he'd chosen the island to start his own business. He'd spent so many years in much larger venues. Jon was enormously empathetic. He knew how troubled she was about Heather. It was too bad Heather disliked him. She needed a man's counsel. Not for the first time, Lillian regretted Heather's romanticized memories of her father. Howard Whitman, wealthy, cultivated, charming . . . Lillian stood stiff and still at the top of the stairs. As always, when she remembered Howard, she felt a curl of ice in her soul. How could she have been so wrong. . . .

Maybelle Whittle carried her tray of cleaning supplies with an edge resting on one hip. She walked slowly across the room. Summer nights were good nights for the ha'nts. That's what Dr. Fox said. Maybelle's mouth opened. She gulped in air. She always had trouble breathing when she thought of the wizened old man who lived in a dark tumbledown shack at the end of a twisty gray road on the other side of the island. Dr. Fox talked in a silky voice as whispery as a cougar rustling through the forest, about people who went against what was right and who treated people bad. Dr. Fox could make a root bag and then those folks would do what you wanted. If they wouldn't do good, you could fix them where they'd never trouble you again. Her mind shied away from what he meant. That kind of talk could lead you into hell, that was what Aunt Esther claimed. But Maybelle knew there was truth in the old man's voice, no matter what her aunt said. Maybelle sighed. She'd better hurry or Aunt Esther would be scolding her for taking too long to see about the cottages. At least this one was empty and all it took was a lick and a promise. Maybelle opened the door, then stood still. Vanessa Taylor was going inside her cottage. A man stood on her porch, staring after her. When Vanessa closed her door, fury turned his features into a mask of hatred. He stared at the shut door, his face ugly as sin, then turned on his heel, hurried down the steps.

Maybelle didn't stir. She couldn't move for the life of her. The memory of those glaring eyes and twisted lips were seared into her mind. She'd never thought white folks had the power, but sure as the tides rose and fell, she knew what she'd seen. She'd seen the Evil Eye.

City Hall on Broward's Rock was a modest one-story building south of the police station. Justine Prior, the mayor's secretary, was the last person out of the office. She pulled the door shut, waggled the knob to be sure the lock caught. Not that they had to worry too much about crime. After all, the police were right next door. Justine glanced toward the station. Billy Cameron, the acting chief, and his wife, Mavis, who served as secretary, dispatcher, and all-around helper, were hurrying down the front steps of the station. Seemed like Billy and Mavis were always in a hurry, on their way to a ball game, a meeting, a church group, or dinner with friends. They were laughing.

Justine almost called out, then clamped her lips tight. Much as she loved Billy and Mavis, it would be worth her job if she tipped them off. What good would it do? *Que sera sera.*

Max Darling ambled along the boardwalk. The gentle breeze off the harbor ruffled his thick blond hair. His blue eyes held a reflection of laughter. He looked toward Annie, winked.

Annie Darling shot her husband an affectionate and just slightly impatient glance. Okay, okay. There really wasn't any hurry this gorgeous August afternoon. There was the easy hum of activity from the harbor where yachts and sailboats rode in the pea green water. A sail was unfurled on a ketch rig, an outboard choked and sputtered, sunburned guests lined the rails of a boat returning from a morning of deep-sea fishing. Along the boardwalk, customers thronged the shops, buying everything necessary for a happy holiday: beachwear, Low Country baskets, jewelry, trinkets, and, of course, books. God was in his heaven and all was right with the world on the little South Carolina sea island of Broward's Rock.

The island was at its busiest during the dog days of August, teeming with tourists who needed beach books. The temperature was in the mid-nineties and the air squishy as melting asphalt. What was more cooling than relaxing in a beach chair beneath an umbrella with a wonderful mystery and a jug of iced tea? As proprietor of Death on Demand, the best mystery bookstore north of Miami, Annie was happy to oblige both with books and with tea or coffee to go.

Annie was in a hurry to get back to the store. In fact, she'd been reluctant to take time for lunch, though Max would certainly have been startled had she turned down an invitation to Parotti's Bar and Grill, her favorite restaurant in all the world. There were, of course, books to unpack and customers to welcome. Deliberately, she shied away from the real reason for her rush. This was no time for Max to pick up on her thoughts. She slowed to a saunter. Surely she could pretend to be as relaxed as Max. Sure she could. *No problema.* She'd play it cool and no way would Max realize she was in an itching, tearing, urgent hurry to get back to the store. She walked even slower.

Max slipped his arm around her shoulders, gave a squeeze. "Okay, what's the deal?"

Annie felt a moment of panic. Was all her hard work for naught? Had Max found out? During the last week, she'd noticed that he'd occasionally shot her a quizzical, almost uneasy glance. Sometimes he'd looked ready to speak, his eyes alight with excitement, then he'd turn away. Yet when she'd asked, he'd shrugged away her inquiries. Had he tumbled to the secret?

He lifted his hand, brushed her cheek gently with his knuckles. "Come on, Annie. If you were a microwave, you'd be pinging. A greyhound at the post couldn't be more ready to race. What gives? Is it the boxes you need to unpack? New books by Ridley Pearson, Lindsey Davis, Joanne Pence, Rochelle Krich, right?"

She felt such a rush of tenderness she almost cried. Damn. How perfect could a husband be? So, okay, Max could be dilatory and too laid-back and he and the notion of hard work had never meshed, but he was so attuned to her moods that her best effort to be casual didn't fool him for a minute. Of course, he assumed she was eager to get to Death on Demand because of the slew of boxes that had arrived Saturday. And he cared enough about her and her world that he'd taken time to note the names of the authors on the unopened boxes.

"Hey, I'll give you a hand." He jerked his head toward the dark windows of his office. "My place is slower than a funeral dirge. I told Barb to take the week off. She's gone shopping in Atlanta. And we can talk about stuff." There was a note of eagerness in his voice.

Annie stopped, planted her heels on the boardwalk. Talk about stuff! That was the last thing she had time for. Oh no. Not today of all days. "Max—" She gazed out at the bustling harbor, seeking inspiration. Almost all the slips were taken. Yachts plied the Inland Waterway in August and Broward's Rock was a favorite stop. Slip 13 was empty. That was where island mystery author Emma Clyde moored *Marigold's Pleasure,* named in honor of her spinster detective, Marigold Rembrandt. Emma was due home today from a cruise to Merida. Empty. No one there ... "—Honey"—she beamed at him—"that would be great but you really shouldn't leave your office empty. Why, all kinds of people may need help."

She swept her hand at the front window where gold letters announced CONFIDENTIAL COMMISSIONS. Max was quick to insist that he wasn't a private detective. The sovereign state of South Carolina had specific and demanding requirements for private detective agencies. Max, however, was eager to solve problems, whatever they might be. No law against that.

Max's expression was quizzical.

Before he could pursue his suspicion, surely still nebulous, that Annie was trying to ditch him, she reached back to her acting days— and yes, she'd been off-Broadway once with an improvisation troupe that, to put it kindly, never quite jelled—and launched a diversion. "Max, I was talking to your mom just the other day"—all right, it was two years ago but in Laurel Darling Roethke's madcap world, a year was a moment, a day simply a breath—"and she said she'd had the strongest sense that you were fated to save someone"—Annie almost said *from a fate worse than,* then decided Max would believe many things about his mother but triteness wasn't one of them—"from the most unexpected circumstances. What if today's the day!"

He intoned in a resonant voice reminiscent of The Shadow. "Who knows what fate holds in store for us?" Laurel had given him a collection of the radio serial for Christmas. "Okay, I'll be at my duty station."

Max was still smiling as he stepped into the long, narrow—and deadly quiet—front office. Barb's computer was shrouded with a plastic cover and there were no delicious smells. Truth to tell, Confidential Commissions was rarely overwhelmed with assignments despite the tasteful ad that ran every day in the personals column of the *Island Gazette:* Troubled, puzzled, curious? Contact Confidential Commissions. 321-HELP.

Max squinted thoughtfully. Maybe they needed to jazz up the ad. Something like "You got troubles? Call Max. He's The Man."

It was awfully quiet without Barb. Barb wore her bouffant hair Texas-style, kept up a running chatter, and, to while away the time, cooked up a variety of delectable messes, as she called them. He missed the chatter and the food. Last week Barb had baked brown sugar icebox cookies that sent Annie into transports of joy, recalling them as a special treat from her childhood.

Anyway, for the moment, he had nothing on his agenda. Not even a lost dog. But, and his grin was Halloween-pumpkin big, there was the Franklin house. His step quickened. He'd not been this excited in years. He'd almost told Annie a dozen times but he wanted the moment to be perfect. They were going to have a blast.

He flipped on the lights, hurried across the room, didn't even take time to slide into the huge red leather chair behind the massive Italian Renaissance table that served as his desk. He pulled out a folder, flipped it open, feasted his eyes on the real estate circular. Some of his elation seeped away. Of course, the house was a mess right now, hadn't been painted in years, windows boarded up, shutters dangled, part of the roof sagged in. But it was freestanding on almost an acre of land, and the basic structure was sound, a classic plantation house on a sturdy foundation of stucco over tabby, a two-story piazza with Ionic capitals on the first-level columns and Corinthian on the second. The main core of the house was T-shaped. There were central hallways on both floors and a handsome Palladian window—not marred at all—on the landing of the stairway.

Max closed the folder, leaned back in his chair, smiling as he day-dreamed. He couldn't wait to tell Annie, but she'd been very distracted lately. When the time was right . . . Until then it was too bad he didn't have a case. It always pleased Annie when he was busy. Well, maybe something would happen this afternoon. He would hope for the best. Maybe a good-looking girl would rush to him for help, waving a treasure map she'd found in Grandma's trunk. Blackbeard's gold . . . That would be fun. . . .

The bell jangled at the front door.

Annie paused at the front window of Death on Demand. Should she change the display? Instead of new releases, the books on view were collectibles that caught the essence of past days as memorably as long-ago photographs by Arthur Telfer or Charles J. Belden or Chansonetta Emmons. The books lay face up, some scuffed and faded, but treasures still: *The Scarlet Pimpernel* by Baroness Emma Orczy, *The Mystery of Dr. Fu-Manchu* by Sax Rohmer, *The Moonstone* by Wilkie Collins, *Suicide Excepted* by Cyril Hare, and *Blue Fire* by Phyllis A. Whitney. Oh hey, she loved these books; let them enjoy another moment in the sun. The baroness's famous book was published in 1905. It was fun to wonder whether a book published in 2005 by Janet Evanovich or Faye Kellerman might grace a bookstore window in 2105.

Besides, she didn't have time to think about a new display. Not this week or next. She opened the door and plunged inside. She didn't stop to admire her domain as was her usual custom: the table featuring New Arrivals; Edgar, the stuffed black raven on his pedestal; bookshelves slanting away from the central corridor; hundreds of wonderful titles by authors ranging from Susan Wittig Albert to Margaret Yorke; and the sofas and armchairs waiting to cosset readers. Agatha, the elegant black cat who ruled the store, curled atop a red cushion. She languidly lifted her head, watched Annie with somnolent golden eyes. Hmm, Ingrid must have fed her a succulent lunch.

Annie detoured a few steps, stroked a sleepy Agatha, then bolted to the central cash desk, flung out her hands. "Ingrid, any word on the jazz band?"

Ingrid's iron gray hair frizzed even without humidity. Bright blue ink smudged her green smock near the bookstore logo, a silver dagger with a red tip. She gestured with her pen. "It's a no-go. The band's van crashed into a seawall down in the Keys and they can't get here, not even by Saturday a week. Leader said probably they wouldn't get out of the Keys until some Saturday next year. He said they'll be playing in Key West until they are old men with long beards. But"—she spoke above Annie's wail—"not to worry. I've already talked to Ben"—Ben Parotti, owner of Parotti's Bar and Grill as well as the ferry and a good deal of island real estate—"and he said his wife's nephew who's a deejay in Savannah had a cancellation by the Jaycees for that Saturday and he's got a thousand—well, maybe a hundred—CDs with songs from the twenties and he'll handle everything."

Annie leaned against the counter in relief. "Oh, golly, Ingrid, that's great. I mean, I'd rather have a band. They had bands in the twenties, not CDs, but with only twelve days to go I guess I'd better settle for—"

The telephone rang. Ingrid scooped up the receiver. "Death on Demand, the finest mystery bookstore north of— Oh, hi, Laurel. Annie?" Ingrid shot a questioning look at her boss.

Annie hesitated. But Max's mother had antennae that rivaled a praying mantis's, and she probably knew—Annie determinedly refused to ponder her mother-in-law's uncanny gift for ascertaining Annie's thoughts, whereabouts, and attitudes—that Annie was standing within a foot of the phone. Annie took the receiver. "Laurel, hi." Her tone was so effusive Laurel would know she'd debated not answering. Oh, well . . .

"My dear, I felt compelled to call." The husky voice gamboled. Those who doubt that voices gambol have never listened to Laurel Darling Roethke. Laurel delivered every utterance with such élan that a listener could not be blamed for expecting, at the very least, a pronouncement of cosmic importance.

"Yes?" Annie said expectantly, then she shook her head, her sandy hair—newly cut in an old-fashioned bob—quivering, chagrined that she'd once again bought into Laurel's effervescence. When would she learn? The truth was, Laurel could dazzle with a grocery list. Annie's glance moved to the shelf with classic mysteries and Phoebe Atwood Taylor's *Out of Order,* in which Cape Cod sleuth Asey Mayo struggles with Aunt Eugenia's grocery order. Order . . . Oh Lord, had she ordered enough white wine? Wine wasn't on the menu at Parotti's.

Laurel's throaty murmur rivaled Bacall's. "I am agog with delight . . ."

Annie considered the state of being agog. Agogment? Agogged?

". . . and I know you will agree. Here is the question: What Ohio newspaper publisher became president on his fifty-fifthth birthday?"

Annie was not agogged. "President of what?"

The pause was brief. Then a kindly sigh. "I see. Well, perhaps I shall continue in my quest although one would think that Warren Harding might immediately come to mind."

Annie was silent.

"But then again, perhaps not." Laurel's tone was forgiving. "We do want our partygoers to feel clever, don't we?" Laurel was brisk. "Ah well, I shall persevere. You may count on me, my dear. I will have a question prepared for each table and midway through the evening, we shall ask the guests to canvass their table, agree on an answer and"—a trill of delight—"a spokesperson from each table shall come to the microphone and announce the answer and then we shall vote on the best question and answer and the prize"—her voice rang clear as a Sunday morning bell—"will be a drive with Max in the Stutz Bearcat. I've announced it on the Web site."

"Web site?" Annie experienced a sudden sense of strangling, a not unfamiliar sensation when dealing with her always unpredictable, madcap mother-in-law. "What Web site?"

A burst of cheery laughter. "The party Web site. Of course, everyone is sworn not to reveal its existence to Max. We want his surprise party to be a surprise, don't we? Ta-ta."

The connection ended as Annie gaped at the phone.

Ingrid's lips quivered. "I gather she's been busy."

"Web site. Stuzt Bearcat. Oh, good grief!" Annie leaned across the counter and fumbled for a folder. She spilled out the contents and picked up a computer-generated invitation. Around the border of the thick white cardboard, a tiny couple in twenties garb danced the Charleston. Foil bright blue letters announced:

MAX DOESN'T HAVE A CLUE
COME ALL FRIENDS TRUE BLUE
CELEBRATE HIS BIRTHDAY
AND DANCE THE CHARLESTON, TOO!

PAROTTI'S BAR & GRILL 7 P.M. UNTIL ???? SATURDAY, AUGUST 28
DANCE THE NIGHT AWAY IN A REPRISE OF THE ROARING '20S
PRIZES FOR BEST COSTUME, BEST DANCERS

Annie flipped the invitation over. On the back was a magnificent picture of Max in, admittedly, a bright yellow Stutz Bearcat. "Ingrid"—Annie's tone was desperate—"what am I going to do? That car doesn't exist." She'd taken a picture of Max in his new red Jag and transposed him via the magic of a computer into a photograph of a vintage car. "If Laurel's promised the grand winner a ride with Max in a Stutz Bearcat, what am I going to do? I don't have time to deal with this."

Ingrid was kindly but firm. "If she's promised a Stutz Bearcat on the party Web site . . ."

"Okay, okay, but Stutz Bearcats don't grow on trees. I'll try to find one, but first"—Annie waggled the invitation—"I need to see about the table prizes and make sure everything's all set. Let's see"—she reached for a notebook, flipped it open—"the deep-sea fishing trip is a go. Edith Cummings will give a private class at the library in how to search the Web." Annie grinned. The island's canny research librarian was quite capable of teaching even a rank beginner how to find out obscure facts, such as the best wildlife viewing season in the Bering Sea (summer), urgent advice to a snakebite victim (remain still), and the four presidents who won the electoral college but not the popular vote (John Quincy Adams, Rutherford B. Hayes, Benjamin Harrison, and George W. Bush's first term). "I've ordered a signed Sammy Sosa baseball card from a store in Savannah. It should arrive tomorrow. There are a few things I haven't pinned down." She glanced down the list. Still to be gathered up were a bushel of Vidalia onions and a certificate from the photography studio. Emma Clyde had promised an outing on her yacht. Other confirmed prizes included a spa day, a lawn design consultation, a Gullah dictionary, a basket-weaving lesson, a ghost walk in Charleston, a hot-air balloon ride, a New Year's Day oyster roast for twenty-five, and an autographed copy of *South Carolina: A History* by Dr. Walter Edgar, the Palmetto State's premier historian.

The bell jangled at the front door. The door opened to a chattering horde of middle-aged women. Annie slid her papers back into the folder. Customers took precedence. "I'll man the coffee bar."

Max studied two snapshots lying next to his legal pad. Both were beach scenes. A tanned, muscular young man in baggy blue swim trunks, face twisting in effort, butted a volleyball in the first photo. His shock of short blond hair was bleached almost white from the sun. A tattoo of an anchor bulged on his right bicep. Sand streaked his stocky legs. In the second photo he stood with one hand resting atop a boogie board. His other hand shaded his eyes from the sun. He stared into the distance. The second photo included a portion of a weathered sign: . . . EARD BEACH. A beach towel was draped over a piece of driftwood.

Max recognized the scene. Blackbeard Beach was the busiest beach on the island. He pointed at the photos. "It doesn't look as though he was aware he was being photographed."

His client—prospective client—gave him a startled look. "I hadn't thought of that. It was such a shock to get the pictures. Danny's been missing for over a year." She edged forward on her chair. Her dark hair was glossy and hung long and soft onto her shoulders. She was attractive—perhaps some might consider her beautiful—but to Max's taste her makeup was too vivid and her sidelong glances too inviting. He had the sense that she saw every man as a possible lover. "When I got the pictures"—she fumbled in her purse, lifted out a long white envelope—"I saw the postmark and that's why I'm here. There's a note. . . ." She lifted out a sheet, handed it to Max. Her fingers brushed against his.

Max was aware of her touch, knew it was deliberate. He didn't meet her gaze. He glanced at the address in Savannah—Miss Bridget Walker—then quickly read the two short sentences:

Want to find him? Check out Dooley's Mine most evenings.

Dooley's Mine was a beer joint on a winding lane at the north tip of the island. Max had heard about it on a rowdy fishing trip for groomsmen at a wedding last summer. It was not a place he would take Annie. His frown was quick. "He's officially a missing person, right?"

She brushed back a glossy curl. "I told you. He walked out of his apartment in Atlanta over a year ago, on July 18. Nobody's seen him since." She nodded toward the pictures. "Until now. The police hunted. We put up posters, contacted all of his friends. Nothing."

Max leaned back in his chair. "Miss Walker, you don't need me. Take the pictures to the police. Chief Cameron will find him for you. The station's up at the harbor, a half block from the ferry."

She twined a length of hair around one finger. "I can't." Abruptly, her face was shadowed. She pressed her lips together. "I'm afraid . . ."

There was a sense of darkness, distinct as a cloud enveloping the sun. One moment she had been flirtatious. Now her features sharpened, her eyes were wide and strained.

Max glanced at the pictures. If ever there was a scene of summer fun . . . "Afraid of what?"

She gripped the handles of her straw bag. "Danny may have run away because he was involved in . . ." She glanced around Max's office as if there might be listeners, then scooted forward in her chair, her voice faint but rapid. "What I tell you is confidential, isn't it? That's what your sign says, Confidential Commissions. I have to be careful."

Max was wary. "I'm not a lawyer"—he had a law degree but he didn't practice law—"or a private detective. If you have knowledge of criminal activity, you should inform the police."

"I don't know that Danny's done anything wrong. He got in

with a bad crowd and then he disappeared. He's a good guy. The best brother in the world. We've been crazy with fear for more than a year. Now somebody sends me these pictures." Her voice wobbled. "I don't want to go to the police. What if they went out and found him and maybe some guys were trying to be sure who he was and if the police went up to him and called out his name, maybe they'd shoot him."

Max didn't have any difficulty sorting out the tangled pronouns, though he doubted such a horrific outcome. But the world was a dangerous place and crossing drug traffickers didn't lead to longevity. His glance at the pictures was regretful. The young man looked healthy and exuberant and ordinary, a far remove from shady dealings and packets of cocaine.

"Look"—she scooted to the edge of the chair—"all I'm asking is for you to come with me. We'll act like we're on a date." She glanced at his hand. "Maybe you could take off your wedding ring. Anyway, we'll be together and nobody'll know I'm looking for him. I can watch for him and if he's there, I'll point him out to you. Then you can find out where he lives and . . ."

The last member of the mystery book club from Beaufort straggled out the door in search of their bus. Slow thumps marked Ingrid's weary progress down the central aisle. She climbed onto one of the coffee bar stools, and propped her elbows on the counter. "Can I help it if publishers don't keep the early books of a series in print?"

Annie flicked levers, watched as the espresso machine whirred and bubbled. She poured dollops of the dark brew into small cups, placed one in front of Ingrid, added enough whipped cream in her cup to drop the temperature, downed it in a swallow. She took a deep breath. "They say the customer is always right."

Ingrid wrinkled her nose, sniffed the espresso. "They"—she invested the pronoun with loathing—"forgot to explain to the customer that the retailer is not responsible for the vagaries of publishing."

After a moment of quiet and consumption of espresso, Ingrid returned to the cash desk. She sounded more cheerful when she called back, "We just sold two hundred and forty-six dollars' worth of books."

"Super." But Annie's thoughts were already on Max's party and all the details to be planned. She settled at a table near the coffee bar with her list and the portable phone. Forty-five minutes and fourteen calls later, she was on hold. It would not be ladylike to voice her hatred of voice mail. She took refuge, the phone cradled at her neck, in looking at the watercolors hanging on the back wall. Every month she put up a new selection. The first customer to identify the paintings by title and author received free coffee for a month and a new mystery. She'd especially enjoyed picking out these titles.

In the first painting, a glass-walled verandah room was filled with books and museum display cases. Two men stared at each other. Standing was a roughly dressed man who had the appearance of a tramp, though his browned face was civilized and intelligent. A benevolent-appearing old gentleman seated at a kneehole desk looked up at his visitor, his gray eyes intent.

In the second painting, a squat, flat-bottomed boat rode a swift current in the muddy brown water. The engine and boiler were amidships. A stumpy funnel rose just higher than the tattered awning that roofed six feet of stern. Wisps of steam leaked from the engine. A lean-cheeked, wiry man with a cigarette dangling from his lips shoved wood into the furnace. At the stern, a sunburned woman in a soiled, tattered frock shifted the tiller and looked ahead to white water boiling over and around jagged black rocks.

In the third painting, steam curled above a copper teakettle on a stove made of mud bricks. Rumpled bedding covered a raised plat-form near the stove's flue. A crude wooden dresser and a wooden cupboard completed the furnishings of the single room. The walls were of mud bricks, the floor of tamped earth. The tall Caucasian man in flying gear and the reddish-blond woman in a coat and flying helmet looked alien in that barren room. They stared at each other, each holding a torn half of a sheet of paper.

In the fourth painting, a stocky dark-haired man dressed in black stood at the edge of a precipice. He held a Luger aimed at an un-armed man perhaps twenty feet away. Behind the gunman, a slim young woman, her face twisting in desperation, used every ounce of strength to fling a heavy stone at him.

In the fifth painting, a gray four-door Lincoln Continental was parked between two cars in a chain-link-fenced parking area near a taxi stand. The driver's door and both back doors were open. A paunchy middle-aged blondish man in a crumpled suit was slipping behind the wheel, his face desperate and panicked. A man with a crew cut turned a screwdriver on the interior panel of the right back door.

Annie nodded in satisfaction. Wonderful books, each and every one.

The phone clicked. There was a buzz.

"Damn." Annie slammed one hand on the table. "I got cut off. I wonder," she called out to Ingrid, "if anyone's ever done a study of how many hours everybody in this country spends on hold!" She punched the number again. This time she got through. "Mr. Frasier?"

"Can you speak a little louder." The shout was almost over-whelmed by the high whine of machinery. "I'm in my garage."

Annie's hand tightened on the receiver. So far as she'd been able to determine, Mr. Frasier was the only person within a three-state radius who owned a Stutz Bearcat. "I understand you have a Stutz Bearcat—"

"What's . . ." A clack drowned out the words. "Can't hear you."

Annie shouted. "Your Stutz Bearcat—can I rent it for the week-end of the twenty-eighth?"

"Don't have to yell at me, lady." The negotiations, all but over-whelmed by noise, were finally resolved.

". . . and you'll bring it over on the ferry that Saturday?" When she clicked off the phone, Annie downed another espresso. So she was going to be wired. Some days required a little extra zing. All right. The car was arranged for. And one Laurel Darling Roethke was damn well going to meet Mr. Frasier at the ferry landing on Saturday, August 28, and get the damn car.

She glanced at the clock. Oh hey, she needed to shove all the party stuff back into the storeroom. Max would be here in a minute and they'd go home and she and Max would have a wonderful dinner and it would take all of her control not to tell him what a grand party she was planning—

The phone rang.

She clicked it on. "Death on Demand, the finest—"

"Annie." Max's voice was rushed and clipped. "I have to miss din-ner tonight. I've got a case. I've promised not to say anything about it to anyone—"

Annie recognized his tone. If Max made a promise, he kept it.

"—but if all goes well, I can fill you in when I get home. I'll call if it runs late." The line went dead.

Annie put down the phone. She felt oddly deflated. Well, that was childish. Sometimes she got really busy. Max never complained. She certainly couldn't be unhappy about Max taking his work seriously. She was always encouraging him to work. She'd insisted he go to his office this afternoon, and obviously a client had hired him. Okay. She'd go on home, though the house would be dim and silent. She and Max both had missed her young stepsister's effervescence since

Rachel had moved in with Annie's dad, Pudge, and his new wife, Sylvia, and her son Cole. Not only was Rachel gone, the entire family was high in the Andes on a backpacking trip, so Annie couldn't invite them over for pizza. They'd be home next week in time for Max's splendiferous birthday party.

A few minutes later, as Annie nosed her car into the garage, she lifted her chin in determination. She'd fix a fried flounder sandwich heavy on Thousand Island dressing and a big glass of iced tea, unsweetened. She stepped into the kitchen, flicked on the lights, and knew, deep inside, that home without Max was like a dance with no music.

Smoke coiled from a crackling fire. A half dozen teenagers, boom boxes blaring, held skewers over the flames. The smell of roasting hot dogs mingled with the sweet scent of the sea. The sun still rode on the horizon, a hot red ball. Max leaned against the fence on the boardwalk. His gaze drifted up and down the beach. Lifeguards were beginning to fold umbrellas, stack beach chairs. The beach crowd was thinning, though joggers pounded past every few minutes and sunburned children still squealed and ran. Max saw the sign: BLACK-BEARD BEACH. A volleyball game was in progress. The photographer had likely stood just about here to get his picture. Today there was no stocky player in baggy blue trunks. Max wished he had the pictures with him, but Bridget had grabbed them up, refused to leave them. She'd seen his irritation, promised she'd have copies made, give them to him tomorrow. "They're all I have of Danny."

Max waved away a swarm of gnats. If he had the pictures with him, he could inquire of the two lifeguards on duty, a redheaded giant slathered with zinc oxide and wearing an Australian bush hat, floppy T-shirt and knee-length trunks, and a petite brunette scanning the water with binoculars. As far as Max could tell, and he'd looked carefully, Bridget's brother wasn't on the beach this afternoon. That would have been too easy.

He heard the faraway peal of church bells. Six o'clock. He should have been busy stirring a pot at home. He wiped a trickle of sweat from his face. He could almost taste a Bud Light and fish chowder. Instead, he had a dinner date at a cheap beer joint. Slowly, he twisted his wedding ring, pulled it loose. He held it for a minute then shoved it in his pocket.

Dust roiled beneath the Jag's wheels as Max turned into the parking lot. The encroaching maritime forest was dense with undergrowth. Tangled ferns poked out into the clearing. Pickups predominated in the parking lot. At the far end, an old school bus was splashed with psychedelic colors. Faded lettering proclaimed MAMA'S HOT. A purple neon sign flickered on a tall pole. Three letters were dark: DOO EY'S NE. A central wooden porch with a peaked roof projected from a long, windowless cement-block building. White paint hung in strips from the porch. Crossed miners' picks hung on the porch posts. An old-fashioned lantern dangled from the lintel.

Max enjoyed the bullet-swift power of his Jaguar and its shiny red finish. It wasn't the car for a man seeking anonymity. Maybe Bridget's fears had some basis. This was a place where anything could happen, most of it bad. He pulled into a space next to a mud-streaked pickup with oversize wheels. He glanced at the bumper sticker: GOTCHA IN MY SIGHTS. He didn't need to see the gun racks to know what sights.

Max frowned. Bridget had said she planned to check into the Buccaneer. He'd offered to come by and get her but she'd insisted that she'd meet him. He glanced at his watch. It was a quarter past six. He'd run into more traffic than expected. If she'd gone inside without him . . .

He swung out of the car, slammed the door, clicked the lock. Usually he didn't bother to lock his car. After all, it was hard to get a stolen car off an island. But this was a sorry place. He hadn't taken a half dozen steps before he felt hot and irritated. He'd never grown accustomed to the shock of August heat. At the beach, there had been a sea breeze and an illusion of coolness from the shade of the canopy above the boardwalk. In the blaze of late afternoon sun in the dusty parking lot, he felt like he'd stepped into the Sahara. He strode toward the front porch, the shade as beckoning as an oasis. His throat felt parched as brown grass. Sweat beaded his face, oozed down his back and legs. His shirt and slacks clung to him.

The front door banged open. A weedy man in his twenties tumbled outside.

Max stopped, watched warily. It looked like the young man had been given the heave-ho.

Before the screen door closed, a short, stocky, bald-headed man stalked onto the porch. He stopped, hands loose at his side, rocking on the balls of his feet, and watched as his victim picked himself up, backed toward the steps.

He glared at the older man. "Jesus, it's a crime to make a man go out in this heat. Kill a damn dog, that's what it could do." He brushed back a tangle of shoulder-length blond hair. "You got no call to shove me around."

"The lady said no." The stocky man's voice was soft as a snake's slither.

"Lady?" Thin lips curled in a sneer. "Hell, she—"

"Time to leave, buddy." The bald-headed man moved forward, hands curling into fists.

The skinny young man shot him a truculent look but moved quickly to stamp down the wooden steps.

The doorkeeper/bouncer/manager remained on the porch, watching.

Max started forward, hoping the lady in question wasn't his client. Surely she hadn't been damn fool enough to go inside by herself.

A glad cry sounded behind him.

"Max!" Her voice rose in a joyful lilt.

He felt a frisson of anger as he swung to face her. It was a lover's cry. He stopped and stood stone still. It was his client but gone was the demure shirtwaist dress she'd worn earlier. She was strikingly noticeable in a short orange and ivory sarong with a deep V-neck.

She ran toward him, hands outstretched, a smile wreathing her face. Dust puffed beneath her feet. She reached him, flung her arms up to draw his head down for a kiss.

He pulled back. "Hey . . ." His voice was a growl.

"Please." It was a desperate cry. "Don't pull away. They may be watching. Maybe the man on the porch is part of it. We don't know. Please . . ." She pressed her cheek to his.

At a distance, it could be nothing but a lover's embrace.

She kissed him, then laughed and reached up to wipe gently at his cheek. "A spot of lipstick." She pulled his arm close to hers and they were moving toward the building. Her face was bright with a smile. She looked up at him adoringly, and all the while she talked fast and low. "No one will pay any attention to us now. They'll be watching for a woman alone. Oh, please, look like you're happy to see me."

Max forced a smile. Bridget Walker better ease up. He wasn't a lapdog. He'd agreed to help search for her brother, but he didn't like the way this was starting. Not by a damn long shot.

The stocky man on the porch frowned as Max and Bridget came up the steps. "Yeah?" He didn't ask who they were or what they wanted. He didn't have to. The implication was clear to Max. This wasn't the right place to be. They didn't fit in.

"Oh, I can hear the music. It sounds wonderful." Bridget looked eager. "We've heard Dooley's Mine is so much fun." She moved fast, plunging into the darkness.

The round-faced man watched with an impassive face and cold eyes.

Jaw set, Max strode past him. Once inside, Max blinked, trying to adjust to the darkness and the noise. Slowly the room took shape. Papier-mâché boulders arched above booths, turning each into a dark cave. Red lanterns swung from posts by each booth. Tables with red lanterns as the centerpieces bracketed a small dance floor. Drinkers jammed the bar along the far wall. A whiny tenor sang of a gold-digging woman and the man whose life she ruined.

Bridget tugged at his arm. "There's an empty booth right there." She pointed to her right.

Max bent down, no longer trying to smile. "This doesn't make sense. For one thing, how are we going to see Danny if he's here?" Dooley's Mine reminded Max of a painting of hell, faceless figures milling in darkness broken by occasional flashes of light from head-lamps worn by waitresses in skimpy miners' togs.

"It will work out." She sounded feverish. She didn't wait, hurry-ing toward the booth.

Max stared after her. He was angry with his client, angrier with himself. He'd lost control of the evening. He wanted to turn his back, stride away, churn dust as he sped out of the dusty lot. That's what he wanted to do. But that wasn't an option. He couldn't leave a woman alone in Dooley's Mine. She wasn't equipped to handle the kind of attention she would receive if she were unescorted. At the same time, he knew he was being manipulated. He didn't doubt that Bridget un-derstood the position in which she had placed him. That's why she'd left him at the door, headed straight to a booth. She was counting on his reluctance to abandon her in what could be a dangerous situation. He took a breath and, head down, strode to the booth. He stood by the flickering red light of the lantern, looked at her with steely eyes.

She held out a hand in a silent plea. Her face was dimly visible in the pulsing red light. "Max"—she lifted her voice to be heard above the pounding bass—"give it a chance. Come on, let's have a beer and hamburgers. Give it that long. Come on," she repeated. "That's fair enough, isn't it?"

A beer and hamburgers. That was reasonable enough. He was too angry to be hungry, but he was damn thirsty. He would almost have traded his car for a cold beer. He slid into the booth.

The light from a waitress's headlamp speared into the booth. She was a dark shape behind the glare. "Yeah?"

Bridget didn't give him a chance. "Beer for both of us. Dos Equis. Chilled glasses. And we'll have hamburgers. Honey, do you want fries or onion rings?"

The endearment jarred. Once again his face hardened into a tight frown. And he preferred Bud Light. But it didn't matter. Any beer would be welcome at this point.

She didn't wait for an answer, burbling to the waitress. "Make it fries and rings both. I'm starving."

The waitress's hand hovered above her pad. "What do you want on your burgers?"

When she had the order and moved away, Max rested a hand on the Formica tabletop, then quickly removed it from the sticky surface. Maybe a hamburger here wasn't such a great idea. "Look, Miss Walker—"

"Bridget. Please." Her gaze was entreating. "I understand. You don't think we can find him. I know it's dark as it can be. But maybe that can work for us. Why don't you take a circuit of the room? If anybody notices, you can say you're looking for a friend. You can check out the booths, look at the bar. I'll keep an eye on the front door. By the time you get back, we'll have our beer and some food."

Max surveyed the long, dimly lit room. The headlamps of the waitresses bobbed, splashing narrow beams of light into booths and across tables. It was by no means certain he'd be able to distinguish the features of every man in the room, but he could certainly make a pretty complete canvass. It also made it possible for him to remove himself and his anger from the booth and proximity to a soon-to-be-former client. Once he got Bridget Walker safely out of Dooley's Mine, she would no longer be his responsibility and she could seek help elsewhere.

"I'll give it a try." He was relieved to be free of the booth and Bridget. It wasn't hard, given the darkness and the general disorderly movement of customers, to drift around the perimeter of the long room. The music was raucous, voices loud and blurred by alcohol. He bent near most booths. If anyone noticed him, he began to speak, "Jack? Oh, sorry. Thought I saw an old friend . . ." When he'd finished the circuit, he dropped into the booth. Before he spoke, he reached for the tall glass, beaded by cold. The beer was exquisite, icy, fresh, perfect. Max drank down half the glass. He'd been achingly dry. The beer was a lifesaver. He felt more kindly toward Bridget. She was looking at him with huge, hopeful eyes. Slowly he shook his head.

"No luck." He wished he could have found Danny, been able to lift the fear and sorrow from her eyes. "I'm almost sure he's not here. I guess—" He bent his head toward the door.

"No." She pressed her lips together, bent her head.

A tray resting on her hip, the waitress delivered their burgers, fries, and onion rings. The light from her headlamp swept over Max's glass. "Another beer?"

"Sure. We're celebrating." Once again it was Bridget who spoke, though her glass was almost full.

The waitress turned away.

Max called after her. "And the check." He wouldn't have ordered another beer, but he was thirsty enough to drink it. He lifted his glass and drained it.

Bridget was frowning. "Can't we stay for a while? Danny might come later."

Max added a dash of hot sauce to his hamburger. He picked it up, didn't like the greasy feel of the bun, but took a bite. The message that had accompanied the photographs of Danny had been vague: *Check out Dooley's Mine most evenings.*

Max had no intention of returning here on a regular basis. There was more than one way to discover if the missing man ever visited Dooley's Mine. Max took another bite, chewed slowly. He blinked, put the hamburger back on his plate. He didn't think he'd eat any more. Something was making him feel sick . . . food poisoning wasn't that quick . . . couldn't expect the food here to be very good . . . he swallowed . . . his throat felt thick . . . everything looked funny . . . muzzy . . . out of focus . . . Bridget moved closer and away . . . her voice came from a long distance . . . arms so heavy . . .

2

Annie turned on the faucets full force. Bubbles coalesced into glistening mounds as water thundered into the bathtub. The sweet scent of roses was enticing. The water would be warm and silky, help her relax. She was ready to climb the two broad steps into the oversize bath. Yet she stood unmoving, her tense body reflected in a wall of mirrors. She was scarcely aware of the mirrors, her eyes locked instead on the tiled counter. She'd placed the portable phone next to her cell phone.

Surely the cell would ring any minute now. It was her link to the world. A link to Max . . .

She turned off the water. The only sound was the slap of her bare feet as she hurried across the bathroom, grabbed the clothes she'd dropped in the hamper. She pulled them on, the pale blue silk tee and cream-colored shorts. She grabbed up the phones, slipped into huaraches, and left the water to grow cold, the bubbles to dissolve.

When she reached the main hallway downstairs, she skidded to a stop. It was silent, frightfully silent. No bang or clang in the kitchen, no Max deciding to whip up a batch of double chocolate brownies, no salsa swelling from the CD player.

"Oh, Max." She spoke aloud, her voice lifting as if in a question. She looked at the grandfather clock. All right. He'd said he might be late. It was just a little past eleven. Certainly, that was still a reasonable time of night. But where was he, what was he doing that she'd had no word? He'd said he would call. It was unlike him to not be in touch. Unlike him? It was completely contrary to his nature. He was always thoughtful.

Max. She massaged the tight muscles in his throat. He would have called if he had been able. Therefore, something unexpected had happened, something that prevented him from contacting her.

She took a deep breath. *Steady.* It was as if he were here. That's what he would say. *Steady, honey.* Okay, she'd figure it out. He'd taken on an assignment. When he phoned, he said he didn't know when he'd get home. Wherever he was, he was still on the job. Perhaps he was on a stakeout and couldn't call because he must make no sound. Perhaps he'd lost his cell and there was no available phone.

Annie walked into the terrace room, flipped on all the lights. Dorothy L., their plump white cat, lifted a startled head. Dorothy L. had a tendency to nap until very late at night. Her favorite time to ease outside was around three o'clock in the morning. Annie put the phones on the coffee table. She flung herself on the rattan sofa, picked up a small cushion, rubbed her fingers across the tasseled fringe. For some reason that she truly couldn't fathom, Max couldn't get in touch with her.

Max was in danger.

She gripped the cushion so hard her hands ached. She might have been carved from ice. Deep inside, she felt sick. The sensation was beyond thought. The dreadful burgeoning horror within her was instinct.

Max was in danger.

The only sounds in the room were her quick breaths and the thump as Dorothy L. dropped to the parquet floor and padded toward her.

Annie stared at the phones, willing one to ring.

She jumped to her feet. She had to find Max. She grabbed her cell and ran toward the kitchen. Quickly, she scribbled a note—*Out looking for you. Call my cell if*—she scratched out the word, wrote—*when you get home.* She propped the note in the middle of the kitchen table, grabbed her car keys and purse.

She turned left on Laughing Gull Road. They always laughed about their commute, three minutes total from their house to the harbor and her bookstore and Max's office. Why hadn't she gone to his office earlier? Why had she waited, stewing and fretting? She'd find out about his job. He always created a file. She'd find out who hired him and why and what his objective had been tonight. She drove too fast, knew she should slow down. Deer were often abroad at night. Coming around a curve too fast, a driver could end up with a dead buck or doe and a smashed car. She flew through the stop sign at Sand Dollar Road, screeched left. Tall pines blocked the moonlight. Her headlights speared into the gloom. There were no other cars. She came around a curve. Usually lights sparkled at the country club, but it was closed on Mondays, contributing to the lack of traffic. Even though it was August and the height of the tourist season, this portion of the island was quiet. The shops on the boardwalk overlooking the marina closed at ten. Broward's Rock nightlife was confined to the north end of the island, primarily Parotti's Bar and Grill, a jazz club, and a couple of beer joints.

Annie welcomed the lights of the marina. It was a relief to be free of the pressing weight of darkness on the tree-shrouded road. There were only three cars in the lot, so she was able to park next to the path to the boardwalk. She grabbed the cell phone, flung herself out of the car, broke into a jog. Everything was suddenly familiar and reassuring, the cheery splashes of light from yachts in the harbor, the crackle of oyster shells underfoot, a distant strain of music, the scent of a cigar from a solitary stroller on the pier, the slap of water on the pilings. She'd check Max's computer, find out who'd hired him. There would be a paper file, too. Although she often chided Max for appearing slothful, actually he was orderly and precise. It was more that he rarely was called upon to exercise those talents. She'd find something to reassure her, convince her that Max's silence was necessary, understandable. Who knew? Maybe he'd tried to call and he'd been in one of those pockets on the island where cells didn't function. She slowed for an instant. Why hadn't she thought about that possibility earlier? She felt buoyed by hope. Everything was going to be all right.

Annie's shoes clattered on the boardwalk. The shops faced the marina in a crescent. Death on Demand was the first unit. Annie was almost to the door of Max's office when she saw a flash of light. It was a single quick bright gleam but she knew it came from Confidential Commissions.

She broke into a pulse-pounding run. Max, oh, Max . . . No light glimmered when she skidded to a stop at the door to Confidential Commissions. All was darkness beyond the plate glass. She grabbed the knob. Locked. She fumbled in her pocket for her keys, pulled them out, flicked through to Max's office key. She poked the key in the lock, turned, flung open the door. It banged against the wall.

"Max?" Annie looked into darkness. Though she couldn't now see the contents of the room, she knew the outer office of Confidential Commissions, white wicker chairs with sea green cushions, a sisal mat on the heart-pine floor. During winter downtime, Barb had insisted on repainting the walls aquamarine and replacing the Modigliani prints with seascape watercolors in white frames. Barb's white-pine desk was perhaps twenty feet ahead. Filing cabinets stood against the wall behind her desk. A door led to a storeroom-cum-kitchen where Barb enjoyed creating delectable treats when business was slow, as business often was.

Max's office door was to the left, midway between the front door and Barb's desk.

Annie stared with such intensity her eyes ached. Her ears thrummed. It was as if she stood beneath a huge breaker, knowing tons of water would crash down, envelop her. The darkness felt malignant, menacing. A sound broke the silence. Was it the whispery shuffle of a footstep?

Framed in the doorway, she knew she was silhouetted in the faint wash of light from the marina. The glow behind her emphasized the utter lack of light she faced. It took every ounce of her will to move forward. She reached for the light switches on the wall to her left.

The silence exploded in a rush of footsteps. A momentary stab of light near Barb's desk illuminated the floor. A dark form plunged toward the storeroom door.

Annie's hand swept across the wall. Damn, the switches were here. Or here . . . Light flooded the anteroom as the door to the storeroom slammed shut.

Throat tight, heart thudding, Annie raced across the room. She twisted the doorknob even as her mind warned: *Danger, danger, danger.* The door was locked. She didn't have interior keys. Whirling, Annie ran back through the anteroom and the open front door to the board-walk. She heard a car engine. She pelted to the end of the boardwalk and down the wooden steps. As she reached the alleyway, red taillights disappeared around a stand of pines.

She turned, heading toward her car, then slowed, catching her breath. It was too late. The car was long gone and could turn a half dozen ways. Moreover, she didn't have a description of the car or the driver. She had a vague sense from the taillights that it was a sedan. More than that, she couldn't say. All she knew with certainty was that danger had been near when she and a faceless, formless figure stood in darkness. Despite the heat of the August night, she felt cold and clammy.

Once again she ran, heart pounding, lungs aching, legs straining.

Billy Cameron, acting chief of police, frowned as the telephone shrilled. He glanced at the clock. Midnight. No good news comes during the midnight hour. He grabbed the phone, answering on the extension out in the garage. He held a paintbrush in one hand. He was almost finished with the toy chest he was making for Lily's birthday, pink with blue forget-me-nots. Lily was almost two and Billy still considered her the miracle of his life. That's how they all felt about the tiny little girl who'd come as a late-life surprise to Mavis, and an adored little sister to Kevin. Billy hoped he'd caught the phone before it woke Mavis. As he listened to the high, frightened voice of Annie Darling, he waited for the kitchen door to open.

Billy tried to sort out Annie's breathless report. Billy wasn't sure what had Annie so riled up, somebody sneaking around Max's office or Max's failure to call her, but he knew her well enough to decide without further consideration that she needed him at Confidential Commissions. Pronto.

He cut her off. "Got it. On my way. Stay there." He hung up. He was a big man, but he could move quickly. There was no time to change from his T-shirt and paint-spattered jeans to his uniform, but he retrieved his gun from the locked safe. He snapped the holster to his belt next to his beeper. On his way out, he scrawled a message on the chalkboard by the phone in the kitchen. There was no one stirring in the house. Mavis and Kevin and Lily were still asleep. Billy grabbed his cell and was out the back door and into the patrol car in three minutes. Four minutes and forty seconds later, he strode toward Confidential Commissions, one hand resting on his holster, heavy-duty flashlight in the other. Light spilled from the open front door, glaringly noticeable in contrast to the darkened windows in the rest of the shops.

He frowned as he stepped inside. The anteroom was empty. "Annie?"

"In here, Billy." Her voice was high and strained.

Billy Cameron stopped in the doorway to Max's office. Desk drawers gaped open. The computer monitor glowed green. Annie clicked the mouse; the monitor emitted electronic burbles and the screen darkened. Annie pushed up from Max's big red chair, gazed frantically around the office. "I can't find a file anywhere. There should be a file."

Billy swallowed hard. When he'd first met Mavis, she'd been a battered wife, escaping with her toddler son. Mavis had looked like that, her eyes like dark pits, her face tight and fearful. "Hey, Annie. What's going on?"

Annie clasped her hands. "Max got a case late this afternoon." Her voice was jagged and uneven. "He called and said he couldn't tell me what he was doing or when he'd be home, but he'd be late. I haven't heard a word since then. Something's happened to him—"

Billy felt the tightness in his chest ease. He maintained his stolid expression, a look that had served him well over the years. It didn't do for a cop to signal his assessment of a situation. As far as he was concerned, a good cop took it all in, didn't let anything out. He would have thought Annie Darling had a better handle on reality than to go to pieces because her husband got busy and didn't give her a call or maybe had car trouble. He hoped she and Max weren't having trouble. He would have thought they had a great marriage, but only the people inside a house know the truth about that marriage.

Annie glared at him. "Listen to me, Billy. You think I'm being silly. I'm not. He'd know I'd be worried if it got late—" She choked back a sob. "So he would have called me. Something's happened to him and—"

Billy nodded slowly. Something had happened. Best-case scenario: Lost his cell phone. Ran out of gas. Had a wreck, pinned in his car. Worst case: He met a gal and . . . Billy hoped not. He liked Annie and he liked Max.

"—now I know it's something bad." She shivered. "I came to try and find out where he might be tonight and there was somebody here and they ran away."

Billy rubbed a sticky hand against his jeans. He needed some turpentine. "Okay." This was more like it. Breaking and entering he could deal with. Maybe Max had gotten involved in something dangerous. Broward's Rock was an idyllic sea island, but there were drug deals and drunks and fights. "What happened?" Billy reached for his notepad, shook his head. He'd left the house without a notebook or pen. He pointed toward the desk. "Can I borrow some paper, a pen?"

Annie found some index cards, brought the cards and a pen to him. She talked, fast.

Billy listened, making notes. When Annie concluded, he pointed at the desk, the open drawers. "This the way you found it?"

Annie looked startled. "No. I was trying to find the file."

Billy frowned. "What file?"

Annie dragged fingers impatiently through sun-streaked hair. "When he gets a new case, he always makes a file. Name, address, phone and cell numbers, e-mail address of the client, objective, relevant information, contacts, fee. I've checked the computer and the filing cabinet and his desk. I didn't find a thing about a new case. The only funny thing is a folder that was tucked beneath the desk pad." She pointed to an orange folder on the desk. She took two quick steps, held it up. "Maybe it has something to do with the case. It's a real estate circular about an old wreck of a house for sale near downtown. Some of the information is highlighted. There's a name and number written on it."

Billy was glad to have something concrete but the circular didn't tell him much. He knew the old Franklin place. It had been on the market for a long time. He had patrols keep a check on it. It was a fire hazard and the kind of place that might attract kids and they could get hurt playing inside it. He glanced at the sheet, saw the name, Darrough, and a phone number. He tucked the folder under his arm. Then he jerked his head toward the desk. "You made this mess?"

Annie waved away the handful of letters she'd plucked from the out box. "Those are just bills and a letter to his sister, stuff like that. Nothing about a new case. Anyway, none of this matters. What matters is Max. We've got to find him. Can you call Lou? Maybe Mavis could take a car and look, too."

Ever since he became acting chief when Pete Garrett was called up for duty after 9/11, Billy had worked long hours. Billy had hired the island's first woman officer, Hyla Harrison, when Joe Tyndall's reserve unit was sent to Iraq. Now three did the work of four, alternating night duty. Lou Pirelli was at the station now. The station was the place to start. Billy slipped the real estate circular from the folder, folded it and tucked it along with the cards into his pocket. He punched automatic dial on his cell.

"Police." If Lou had slipped into a catnap, his voice gave no hint.

"Yeah, Lou. Billy here. Had a break-in—" Billy's eyes narrowed. Was it a break-in? "—or unidentified—" Again he hesitated. Annie had made the mess. "—person at Confidential Commissions, plus Max Darling's out of pocket. You got any report of a car wreck, problems anywhere?" He knew the answer. His beeper would have buzzed if anything had broken the nighttime quiet of the island. Billy's orders were strict. He wanted to know everything that happened on his island. That's how he thought of Broward's Rock, his island, and everybody on it his responsibility to protect.

"Nada. Need me to come over?" Lou sounded eager. The cot in the break room at the station was comfortable enough, but Lou liked people and fun and excitement. He wasn't a TV fan except for baseball, and his beloved Braves had played a day game.

"You stick there. Check the hospital. Ditto on the mainland. Check the highway patrol for an accident involving—" He glanced toward Annie.

She swallowed. Max had gotten a new car for his birthday. "Red Jaguar coupe. Plate number ConCom1." He'd been pleased with his choice for the license plate.

"—a red Jag coupe. Personalized tag: ConCom1. Beep me if any call comes in about anything out of the way." Billy knew that didn't make a lot of sense, but nothing about this night was making sense. He clicked off the cell.

Annie was shaky but determined. She moved toward him. "I'm going out. I'll look for him by myself."

Billy held up a big hand. "Hold up. Give me a chance to see what we've got here."

With Annie at his elbow, they checked the anteroom. Barb's desk was clear, her computer covered, no disarray. The filing cabinets were closed and appeared not to have been touched.

Billy rattled the knob to the storeroom. "I should have checked out the alleyway first. You stay here."

Annie didn't. She was right behind him as he strode through the front door and down the steps to hustle into the alley, the big swath of light from his flash swinging to and fro. He swung the beam over the loading dock behind Confidential Commissions. The door stood open.

"Billy, look." She gestured toward the door and ran ahead to the stairs leading up to Confidential Commissions' back entrance.

He caught up with her and took the stairs two at time. The door was open to darkness within. He was inside, the light on by the time she joined him.

The storeroom was in perfect order, the kitchenette sparkling clean and boxes of supplies in orderly rows on shelves. Billy dropped the beam to the grainy cement floor. The light stopped a few inches from the interior door, making a bright circle around a smudge of mud with a distinct mark. "Going in, probably." He thought aloud. "Somebody came in with a muddy shoe, left that mark. I'll get a picture, then take it up." He clicked off the flashlight, hung it from his belt. He skirted the mud streak, studied the door into the anteroom. The lock was depressed in the knob. "I'll check for prints before I open it. Now, I want to get things straight. Does Max check to be sure the back and front doors are locked before he leaves for the day?"

Annie twined her fingers together. "I think so. I can't imagine he wouldn't. Billy, we don't have time to waste. We've got to find Max." She moved toward the back door, her eyes twin pools of misery in a bloodless face.

He wished Mavis were here or another friend, someone to grab Annie's hand, pull her close, try to give her comfort. And he wished Annie could understand that he was doing his best. There had been no sign of trouble anywhere on the island. No calls to the Broward's Rock Police. Where was he supposed to look for Max? Here was the place to begin. Understand what had happened here and they would know where Max was. "This break-in—" Once again he felt like he'd slammed into a wall. So far as he could tell, there had been no break-in. "You opened the front door with a key?"

"Oh my God, what difference does it make?" She was frantic with impatience. "Yes, I used my key."

He thought it through. No break-in at the front then. Frowning, he looked toward the back door, which still stood open. He moved toward it, muttering to himself. "Doesn't look like there's any damage here."

Annie burst past him without a word, clattered down the wooden stairs.

Billy lifted a hand, called out, "Annie." By the time he reached the railing on the back porch, she was at the end of the alley, turning the corner. Gone.

Billy felt the hot rush of blood to his face. Where did she think she was going? What good would it do? He drew in an exasperated breath. He felt jumpy and uneasy. As far as he could see, Annie had overreacted big-time. Sure, Max hadn't been in touch since he'd called her at the bookstore. Billy checked his watch. Twelve twenty-two. Yeah, it was late, but maybe Max thought Annie would have gone on to bed and he didn't want to call and wake her up. It was probably going to turn out he'd had car trouble and his cell wouldn't work. He wasn't going to be happy about Annie racing around the island in the middle of the night hunting for him.

Billy yanked his cell from his pocket. Lou answered on the first ring. "Get on the horn to Hyla. Tell her Max Darling's unaccounted for, Annie's beside herself and she's driving around the island looking for him. I don't know where she's gone, but have Hyla make a circuit, keep her eyes open. You dig up anything?"

"Nada." Lou was regretful. "No wrecks. No fights. No calls. Quiet as a graveyard."

Quiet as a graveyard . . . Billy dropped the cell in his pocket, turned back to the storeroom of Confidential Commissions. Quiet as a graveyard here too. There was nothing to show anyone had been here except for that single smear of mud. And no proof it hadn't been there awhile. Might turn out Max had made that track himself. In any event, he'd dust the interior knob for prints first thing in the morning. Hell, he'd dust all the knobs. He would attend to that smear of dirt. Just in case it meant anything. But for sure there was no evidence of a break-in. Which meant . . .

He pulled out the index cards, wrote swiftly:

Arrived Confidential Commissions 12:06 A.M. in response to call from Annie Darling at 12:01 A.M. She said she found front door locked, opened it with a key, surprised an intruder. She said someone turned on flashlight to find way out through the back. No description. Intruder could have been male or female. Exited through storeroom door. Mrs. Darling gave chase. Storeroom door locked. Subsequent investigation in alley behind the office revealed loading-dock door open. No evidence of break-in.

   Conclusion: *Intruder gained access with a key.*
   To be determined: *Who has keys?*

Billy thought that list would be short. Max. Annie. Max's secretary. The agent for the leasing office. They could scratch the leasing agent. The building that housed the harbor-front shops was owned by an Atlanta outfit. As for Barb, she'd invited Mavis to join her on a shopping trip, but Mavis couldn't afford the time off. Barb had left yesterday. Annie had used her key on the front door. That left Max's key.

Billy wrinkled his nose. He didn't like the way this was shaping up. If it was Max's key, who had it and how did they get it? He underlined *Who has keys?* And added:

Smear of dirt found in storeroom near anteroom door, possibly indicative of intruder. Investigating officer observed no apparent search or theft of the premises. Disarray observed by investigating officer resulted from search made by Mrs. Darling while hunting for information on new case file. Possibly extraneous but Mrs. Darling found a real estate circular in a folder beneath the desk pad.

Conclusion: *Reason for entry unclear.*

Billy clicked off the storeroom light, shut the back door. It had an automatic lock. Once again he used his flashlight, lighting his path to the end of the alley and along the side of the building to the front boardwalk. It only took a moment to turn off the lights in Max's office and the anteroom and pull the front door shut.

He felt uneasy as he walked to the cruiser. He didn't see what else he could do. Lou would call him if there was anything to report, good or bad. He might as well go home. But his face creased in a worried frown and he felt dissatisfied and uneasy. Annie must have seen someone. She wouldn't have made up that dark figure. But nothing jibed with breaking and entering.

Annie hesitated when she reached Laughing Gull Road. If Max had returned home, he would have seen her note, called her at once. She took a deep breath, pressed on the gas, shot ahead, the only car on Sand Dollar Road. She should have kept that real estate circular. That was the only odd thing she'd found. The circular must have something to do with his new case, because Max certainly wouldn't have any interest in an old boarded-up wreck of a house.

Triggered by the pass mounted on her windshield, the exit barrier from the gated community lifted. It was a scant mile more to Broward Rock's waterfront, harbor, and main street. She turned two blocks short of Main onto Bay Street, passed Sea Side Inn, where lights gleamed softly. Next came an island restaurant in yet another incarnation. When it had carried the famous name of Raffles, its owner had found the name more inspiring than wise. Now it was known as Rick's and the theme, of course, was Moroccan. The current owner's name was actually Rick, and the influence of *Casablanca* was evident.

Annie turned the wheel, curved around another stand of pines. There were no lights here, the road rutted, rarely traveled. Another half mile and she turned into what had once been a stately drive. Huge live oaks interlocked branches above her, but the road was eroded and the car bounced over bone-jolting potholes. The only hint of light in the black tunnel came from the beam of her headlights.

She drew her breath in sharply when she reached the house. After the darkness of the tunnel, the house looked ghostly in the creamy moonlight. Annie slammed out of the car. "Max?" Her cry was hopeless, forlorn. There was no one here, no one and nothing but the remains of great beauty made desolate by time. She would find no answers here. Yet, Max had that circular. . . .

Annie took a flashlight from the car pocket. Its stalwart beam seemed puny against the unrelieved darkness. She flashed the light over the front of the house. Once it had been beautiful, but now shutters hung askew, windows were boarded over, paint peeled from elegant columns. A thrumming noise set her heart racing. She whirled, lifting the beam to catch a brief glimpse of a Mississippi Kite. When the hawk was out of sight, she turned back to face the forbidding house. Jaw set, she made a circuit around the house, thorns of wild roses scratching her legs, and almost tumbled into a stagnant fish pond. If anyone had been there, there was no trace. Every door was locked, the boarded windows firmly blocked. When she reached the broad front steps, she turned back to her car, shoulders slumping. If only she'd kept that circular. She tried desperately to remember the name written—in Max's handwriting—at the bottom of the sheet, but she couldn't. She'd have to ask Billy.

All the way home, she willed the cell phone to ring, but it lay silent on the seat. When she reached their house, the only light shining from the front window was the one she'd left on. She punched the automatic door opener. Slowly the door lifted and the lights came on. The garage was empty. She jumped from her car, ran through the garage, shoes clattering on cement, banged into the house. The note was lying untouched on the kitchen table. Her eyes went directly to the phone. No red blink signaled a message. She held the cell phone tight in her hand.

The kitchen was just as it had always been, a long, inviting, homey room with a central work station, a white wooden table, bright yellow walls. A brilliant toucan cocked an inquiring head on each of the pale blue place mats that sat at either end of the table, awaiting their breakfast dishes. Everything was as it had always been and nothing was as it should be. The very normalcy and familiarity of the kitchen was a wrenching contrast to the frantic scrabbling of her thoughts and the terror that made her feel old and stiff.

She walked to the refrigerator, poured a glass of orange juice, drank without tasting it. She ate a handful of peanuts and forced her racing mind to slow. Her instinct was to scour the island even though she had no idea where to start. If she had help . . . She glanced at the phone, then at the clock.

One o'clock in the morning was a shocking time to call anyone. But there were friends she could rouse, friends she could count on. Was she at that point? Was Max's failure to call or come home an emergency?

Fear twisted inside her. Yes. He would never—not if he had a choice—leave her to worry and wonder about him. Worry? She was beyond worry. She was an organism devoured by fear. But she had to push past that agony, try to find answers to an impossible riddle.

Annie hurried across the kitchen, grabbed up the phone from the counter. She made the calls and heard familiar voices dulled by sleep sharpen and respond.

Henny Brawley was confident. "We'll find him," she said. Henny had ferried bombers across the country during World War II, married a fellow pilot who was lost in a bombing raid over Berlin. A retired teacher, she'd served twice in the Peace Corps. She was a world-class mystery reader and Annie's best customer and best friend.

Annie almost managed a smile when she heard Emma Clyde's gruff instruction. "Brew coffee. Get out the island maps." If anyone could take on the denizens of evil and prevail, it was smart, tough, imperious Emma Clyde. Creator of famous sleuth Marigold Rembrandt, she was the author of almost a hundred mysteries. The author's cold intelligence and intractable will were reflected in her piercing blue eyes, square face, and blunt chin.

Ingrid Webb drew in a sharp breath. "Oh, Annie. We'll be right there." Ingrid was the best clerk anyone ever had. She herself had once gone missing. Ingrid and her husband, Duane, would understand Annie's fear. Duane had an old newspaper editor's disdain for the obvious. He always looked for the reason behind the story.

Annie blinked back tears when Pamela Potts's soft, sweet voice made a mournful coo. "I'll say a prayer as I come." Pamela, earnest, serious, and literal, was the island's most active volunteer. Annie didn't expect Pamela to offer cogent insights, but having her near would be a reminder that the world can be good.

Edith Cummings didn't hesitate. "I'll be right there. I'll check out the police scanner, see if there's anything that's come in." Edith rode a computer like a smart jockey; she was a research librarian who could answer any question. Now the question was the most important Annie would ever ask: *Where is Max?*

Vince Ellis tried to be encouraging. "Max is like a cat, Annie. He'll land on his feet." Vince owned the *Island Gazette*. He was a first-rate newsman and a former lightweight boxing champion. If they got any leads on Max's whereabouts, Vince would fight for facts with the same intensity he'd shown in the ring.

She wished Frank Saulter were in town. He was her oldest friend on the island and the former chief of police, but Frank was on a hiking trip with his grandson.

When she'd finished the calls, Annie felt a hot burn of tears, blinked them back. Her friends and Max's friends were coming. It was like holding out chilled fingers to a warming fire. For the first moment since fear caught her up, made her a prisoner, turned her insides to ice, she felt a flicker of hope. If smart minds and good hearts could make a difference, they would.

Annie still stood by the counter. They were coming. Knowing that, seeing them in her mind, gave her strength to pick up the phone again. There was one more call she had to make.

Laurel Darling Roethke came awake in an instant. She looked at the luminous dial. One-forty. She turned on the light, picked up the phone on the second ring. "Hello." She kept her voice even though her heart thudded. From the caller ID, she knew the origin of the call. Neither Annie nor Max would call at this hour unless there was an emergency. Was Annie ill? Had Max been in an accident? Had Max received bad news about one of his sisters?

"Laurel . . ."

Laurel barely recognized Annie's voice, it was so thin and strained.

Laurel felt a twist of anguish deep within. Was that how a heart broke? Please, God . . . "Annie, what's happened?"

Emma Clyde was the first to arrive, her Rolls-Royce squealing to a stop in the drive. She swept in, candy-striped caftan swirling, and took charge. The island mystery writer, imperious and intense, outlined the search efforts to begin at daybreak. She dispatched Vince Ellis to the *Gazette* office to run off hundreds of pictures of Max. She instructed Henny Brawley and Pamela Potts to begin the phone canvass for volunteers at six A.M. sharp. "Start with the Altar Guild. They should be early risers." She sent Ingrid and Duane Webb to Confidential Commissions. "Wear gloves but make an inch-by-inch search." She pulled Laurel Darling Roethke into a bear hug embrace and, at three A.M., ordered Annie to bed.

There was no word from Max.

Annie thrashed awake, swept by panic and a devastating sense of desperate needs unmet. Her mind was a jumble of voices and faces and odd disconnected memories: darkness filled with menace, stolid Billy Cameron in T-shirt and paint-spattered jeans, the thrum of hawk wings, the strangeness of their kitchen when she came home from Confidential Commissions, the uncharacteristic gentleness in Emma Clyde's raspy voice, the sweetness and desperation of Laurel's embrace.

Annie pulled herself up, gazed around the bedroom. Her eyes felt grainy. Her head hurt, a dull persistent ache. The blinds were closed but, even so, the brightness of an August day seeped around the edges, spelling a morning half spent.

The bedroom door opened. Pamela Potts stepped inside, carrying a tray. A sheaf of papers was tucked under one arm. She eased the door shut. "You were moving around, calling out. I knew you were waking up, so I hurried down to get you some breakfast."

"Pamela." Annie's throat was dry and scratchy.

Pamela placed the tray and the sheets of paper on the round table near the French doors to the balcony. Her blond hair swept back in a businesslike bun, Pamela looked crisp in a white blouse and blue slacks. But when she turned to face Annie, the hollows beneath her eyes spoke of sleepless hours sitting at the bedside.

Annie tumbled from the bed, stared wildly around. "I shouldn't have slept so long."

Pamela hurried to reassure her. "You needed the rest. Everything's under control."

Annie struggled to be calm. If Max had called or come home or been found, she would have been awakened for the happy news. Under control . . .

Pamela was firm. "Come and eat now." It was vintage Pamela, soothing voice, genuine concern, nursery school firmness. She was at Annie's side, shepherding her toward the table. "I've brought up the latest reports." She pointed at the pile of papers.

Annie stopped, jerked to face her. "What?"

Pamela's big blue eyes were encouraging. "There's a huge search under way. Everyone's looking for him. Here's what's happening . . ." She waited for Annie to sit down at the table, then took the opposite chair.

Annie ate fast, the sooner to be done. She knew the Belgian waffle was excellent, but didn't care. Max always put powdered sugar and fresh strawberries on Belgian waffles. She swallowed hard, kept on eating. She had to get outside. She had to hunt. Maybe she'd find something. There had to be something to find. She listened to Pamela.

Pamela peered nearsightedly at the top sheet. ". . . at last count

Henny was directing one hundred and fifty volunteers in an island-wide search. There are about thirty kids from the Haven. Henny said they were falling all over themselves to get out and help . . ."

Max was on the board of the community recreation center, which offered games and crafts and a meeting place for island kids who didn't live on the posh side of the island. Annie looked across the room at an amateurish but vigorous charcoal sketch of Max playing volleyball with the bigger kids. Max had made sure there were plenty of supplies for the artist.

". . . two Boy Scout troops, the Red Lion softball team . . ."

Annie finished the orange juice, took too large a gulp of coffee, scalded her tongue.

". . . Emma's drawn up a list of questions that need to be answered." Pamela tapped the legal pad. "Ingrid's gone to grocery shop. Duane's cleaning up one of their cabins—"

Annie was sure she had misunderstood. "Grocery shop?"

Pamela nodded energetically. "Getting things ready. Billy sent out a missing-person bulletin this morning about two A.M.—"

Annie was glad and terrified at the same time. For Billy to officially deem Max a missing person meant Billy believed something had happened to Max. He was a victim. . . . Annie pushed away unbearable images. Max was alive. He had to be alive. If he weren't, she would know. Oh God, she would know . . .

"—and they started coming on the first ferry. Some of them hired boats. Anyway, Duane's cleaning up one of the cabins for you and—"

Annie finished the coffee, tried to make her mind work. Ingrid and Duane managed Nightingale Courts in addition to Ingrid working at the bookstore. Why would Duane clean up a vacant cabin for her? What was Pamela talking about?

"—Ingrid thinks we can smuggle you across the lagoon to—"

"Wait a minute." Annie pushed back the plate. She'd managed half the waffle, one piece of bacon. "Why smuggle me out? Where?"

Pamela's tone was patient. "—to one of their cabins. It would be dreadful if you went out the front door. There are cameras everywhere with cables and sound trucks—whatever a live feed is, they're doing it—and they're so pushy and they've got microphones and the flashes from the cameras make you blink. They smile but their eyes are colder than ice chips. They even tried to get me to talk to them and I just said I thought they were rude and I didn't have a thing to say. One of them yelled, 'So the family refuses to say where he might be? Is he a drunk? Gambler? Has he got a—'" Pamela broke off, her face flushing.

Annie wrapped her arms around herself. She didn't need a prompter to finish Pamela's sentence. *Has he got a girlfriend?* "Media." Of course. Once Billy sent out the missing-persons alarm and the wire services picked up the police report, reporters would be in full cry. These were the dog days of summer. There was no hurricane brewing in the tropics, no celebrated murder case in court, no Washington scandal dominating the headlines. Television was reduced to reruns. A missing person, especially an athletic, handsome, rich man in his late twenties, was a gift from news heaven, sure to spice up the five o'clock, offer fodder for titillating speculation on talk shows, plump up the headlines in the morning papers. *Missing Person: Maxwell Darling, 29, 6 feet 2 inches tall, blond hair, blue eyes, 182 pounds, no visible scars . . .*

Annie's eyes were suddenly alive and eager. "Did Emma"—she knew without asking that Emma was in charge—"hand out pictures of Max?"

Pamela spread out her hands in a helpless gesture. "Emma insisted Vince make copies of a picture he had on file and pass them out." She wasn't a private who would challenge the general, but disapproval flashed in her eyes.

Annie clapped her hands. "That's great. They'll be everywhere. On TV and in the papers, on the Internet. Someone will see a picture and recognize him. It's our best chance to find him."

Pamela's lips rounded in an O. Her face brightened. "I hadn't thought of that. Why, Emma did the right thing. And Edith rushed out with a picture and said she was going to make flyers, put them all over town. Laurel told her to offer a ten-thousand-dollar reward for any information on his whereabouts. Laurel went with Edith to help distribute the flyers."

Laurel. Last night Annie had seen the echo of her own anguish in Laurel's lake blue eyes. As they'd clasped hands, Laurel had smiled her insouciant, unforgettable, brilliant smile. "We will find him." There had been only the tiniest of quavers in her husky voice.

"That's wonderful." Annie felt a surge of affection and respect for her mother-in-law. Laurel was unpredictable, madcap, and original. Now she'd proved that she was practical as well. Why hadn't Annie thought about a reward? In fact, it was time she thought, and thought hard. It was like stepping out of shadow into sunlight. Maybe sleep had lifted her out of that first frozen state of shock. Maybe she was buoyed by the friends who came to help. Maybe it was that tiny flame of certainty burning in her soul that Max was alive.

Annie bounced up. She'd take a quick shower, hurry down to help. She'd check with Billy, get the name that had been on the real estate circular. And maybe, before that, someone somewhere would have seen Max. There would be a call and they would find him.

Lights for various lines flickered like fireflies on his desk phone. Billy ignored them. He turned his chair, leaned back wearily, and stared out the window at the harbor. The onshore breeze was unusually stiff, fluttering the flags along the walk, bristling the pea green water with whitecaps. The ferry was pulling out on its run to the mainland. Two motorboats whopped over the waves. Far out in the Sound a catamaran tilted, slicing through the water on a slant like a carnival ride. Only a few hundred feet up in the air, a Piper Cub turned and headed back over the island. Vince Ellis had called and told Billy he was taking his plane up to survey the island. If enough of it were visible, a red Jag might be spotted. But there were miles of dense forest and deep lagoons where a car, no matter how bright its paint, would remain unseen.

Billy rubbed the back of his neck. His eyes were bloodshot and achy. He'd slept for a few hours, then hurried to the office to join Lou. He'd swung by the Franklin house on his way to the station, checked the doors, found the house inaccessible. He'd given a shout or two, but any hope that Max might be there withered in the hot early-morning silence. So far, he'd had no response from the message he'd left for the real estate agent whose name was scrawled on the circular Annie had found. It didn't seem a promising lead, but at this point he was ready to grasp at any possibility. He made call after call. The sum total of all his effort was, as Lou liked to say, nada. No one matching Max's description had been injured or arrested on the mainland. Moreover, ferry owner and captain Ben Parotti was sure that Max's red Jag had not been on any ferry leaving the island after six P.M. Max and Annie's speedboat was in its slip at the marina. No boats had been reported stolen. Billy lifted his arms, stretched, trying to relieve the tight muscles in his shoulders. Short of water wings or a helicopter, Max Darling was on the island. Hyla Harrison was in a patrol car, cruising the back roads. She'd alerted Billy to the citizen search parties dispatched by Henny Brawley. Billy wished he had an officer to coordinate the search. It was too bad Frank Saulter, the retired chief, was out of town and not due back for another week. Billy might have to deputize some volunteers. He had a feeling of events spinning out of control. He glanced at the bright orange flyer Mavis had brought in a while ago. Under Max's picture, a headline blared:

$10,000 for Information Leading to Whereabouts of Max Darling

Billy had scanned Max's description, clear and distinct in twelve-point type. Maybe it would help, but ever since he'd sent out the missing person alert early that morning, he'd felt beleaguered. Calls were coming in so fast, Mavis could scarcely answer, many of them media demands for information.

Billy knew the pressure was going to get worse. There would be a demand, especially by the mayor, to break this case open. What case? Billy didn't have enough information to spit on. Disregarding the fact that he knew Max and Annie, these were the facts:

1. *Subject calls wife, indicates business appointment, tells her he'll call if the job runs him late.*
2. *Wife insists subject would notify her if delayed.*
3. *Wife goes to subject's office, glimpses intruder.*
4. *No evidence of break-in at office, indicating intruder gained access with a key.*
5. *Disarray in office result of wife's search.*

Billy swung his chair back toward his desk. Actually, there hadn't been sufficient evidence to justify sending out the missing-persons call at two A.M. but he'd done it anyway. Protocol required a twenty-four-hour period for a disappearance. Billy folded his lips in a tight line. Yeah. There was protocol, which the mayor liked to talk about, and then there was instinct. Okay, add knowledge to instinct. After all, he was a small-town cop and he knew his people. Sure, there could be something going on between Annie and Max that he didn't know about. Barring that, the fact that Max hadn't been heard from since he talked to Annie late yesterday afternoon spelled trouble. As far as Billy had been able to discover, Max had disappeared without a trace after his call to Annie. Well, not quite. There was one sighting after she spoke with him. Billy pawed through the slew of papers on his desktop. Here it was:

Statement of Jiggs Holt, twenty-four, green card from Brisbane, Australia, senior lifeguard at Blackbeard Beach:

"We keep a little telly on the table tuned to Fox News. I saw a flash about the gent who disappeared right here on the island. I thought to myself, coo, that's the fellow who was here last night, about six o'clock. Tall blond guy. Late twenties, maybe. Looked like he could handle himself. He was on the boardwalk but he wasn't dressed for the beach, dark blue polo, tan khakis, loafers. No hat. No sunglasses. I noticed him because he had the gimlet eye on the volleyball. Rough game. He was giving those dudes the once-over like he was looking for somebody. Maybe he and some guy were on the outs over a dame. You never know, so I kept him in sight. See, I'm in charge and I pay attention to anything out of the way. I head off a lot of trouble that way. But I decided he was okay. He didn't look mad or crazy, just like there was somebody he wanted to find. About five minutes later he turned and walked away."

Billy remembered the earnest expression of the big redheaded lifeguard. Despite splotches of zinc oxide on his pink face, Holt had been serious and believable. Once again Billy went with instinct. News flashes brought all kinds of tips, some silly, some honestly mistaken, some rock solid. Unless Max had a twin—Billy flipped to another sheet, yeah, Annie said Max was wearing a navy polo, khakis, loafers—then Max had been at Blackbeard Beach around six P.M.

That was the last time anyone had seen him.

Blackbeard Beach.

Billy leaned back in his chair, folded his hands behind his head, stared unseeingly at the ceiling. Was Max meeting a client there? Doing surveillance on a case? But Annie hadn't found any trace of a file for a new client, only that house circular.

He moved forward, grabbed his cell, punched a number.

"Officer Harrison." Hyla Harrison's voice was pleasant, precise, and remote. She always reminded Billy of his high school chemistry teacher. The kids thought she was a nerd until the day she ran back into a burning building to save a child.

"Hyla, got a tip that Max was seen at Blackbeard Beach at six o'clock last night. Take his mug shot and . . ."

Annie heard the chatter on cell phones in the terrace room. She looked up from her place on the sofa in the den and watched as Emma marked search information on the gridded map of the island spread out on the Ping-Pong table. Outside, the muted rumble of car engines and an occasional honk of a horn indicated the continued presence of the media.

Annie put down the sheaf of papers organized by Emma. She'd read every last word as she finished the lunch fixed by Pamela. Everything had been done and nothing had been learned. Max hadn't been seen here and there and everywhere. He hadn't left on the ferry. He wasn't in the hospital or in jail. And Billy hadn't returned her call asking for the name on the real estate circular.

Annie forced herself to remain on the sofa. She wanted to jump to her feet and plunge out to her car and force her way through the gauntlet of reporters. She wanted to do something, anything to find Max. She didn't have to look at the clock. She knew how many hours and how many minutes since she had heard Max's hurried words. With every minute that passed, she felt older and sicker. Despair curled within her, waiting to envelop her, destroy her.

Her cell phone rang. She stopped breathing. She clutched it in a shaking hand, pressed the button, couldn't manage an answer.

"Dear child."

Not Max. Annie slumped against the cushions, faintly heard Laurel's husky voice. "Is there any word?"

"No." The word was as hollow as her heart.

A faint breath. "Henny and I have taken the flyers all over the island, passed them out, posted them. Do you want me to come there?"

A horn blared outside. A car door slammed. Annie thought about reporters with their cameras and shouted questions and poking microphones. "No. I'll call when . . ." Annie couldn't finish.

". . . when he comes home." Laurel's voice was wobbly, but certain. "Annie, he will come home."

The intercom on Billy's desk crackled. Mavis's voice was excited. "Billy, Line 2. This may be the break."

"Roger." Billy clicked on the speaker phone, punched Line 2. "Chief Cameron."

"Yeah. Hey, Chief, what's the deal on the reward?" The whispery voice was hopeful, smarmy, and wary.

Billy glanced at the orange flyer. "The reward is being offered by the family. If you have information that finds him, you qualify. Where is he?"

"I don't have an address." The tone was sarcastic. "I can tell you where he was last night and who he was with. If that information gets you to him, I should get the reward, right? But the thing is, I don't want to get crossways with a tough hombre. Here's the deal, I'll give you my name on the condition you keep quiet about me. Just say you had a tip when you go to out to Doo—uh, go where I tell you. But if this leads you to him, I expect you to put in a good word for me with the family, okay?"

"Sure. Where did you see him?" Billy hunched forward.

"Let's get it in writing." The caller was determined. "I called you at three forty-five. You got that written down?"

Billy marked the time on his tablet. "Yeah. So who are you?"

"Harry Stafford. One-six-five Pigeon Roost Lane. Got that?" He was insistent.

"Yeah. Where did you see him?" Billy listened, face creased in a frown, big hand flying over the tablet. At the bottom of the page, he scrawled DOOLEY'S MINE in capital letters.

3

E mma rattled the knob to make sure the door was locked. She flicked the blinds down, turned off the lights, making the den dusky as a cave. "Now we can have some peace and quiet. All right, take a deep breath. Close your eyes." Emma's usually brusque tone was muted.

Annie blinked at her. It was on the order of a rhinoceros attempting a lullaby.

The author frowned, her square face impatient. "Close your eyes." This was a bark, gentleness forgotten. She loomed over Annie, iron gray hair spiky as a porcupine, blue eyes compelling. Emma was as commanding as a field-grade officer despite the candy stripes of her summery caftan. Only the smudges beneath her eyes hinted at fatigue, though Annie knew she'd snatched only a few hours sleep on the sofa in the terrace room.

Annie squeezed her eyes shut, but tangles of thought burgeoned in her mind, undisciplined as weeds in an overgrown lawn.

"Relax. Pretend you are standing in the doorway to Confidential Commissions." Emma's gravelly voice was encouraging. "You are there. It is dark. You hear a sound. Relaaaax . . ." No stage hypnotist could have been more soporific. "What do you see?"

The image was there. A quick—oh so quick—light. A tiny narrow beam that flashed illumination thin as a laser, there for an instant, then gone. Annie held to that glimpse, tried to recall. She'd seen a portion of the floor. The beam must have been turned down. Then nothing. Whoever held the flashlight turned past Barb's desk and the light clicked off. She had no picture of the fleeing figure. It might have been a man. It could have been a woman. "I didn't see him. Or her. God, I don't know. It could have been anyone." Hot tears seeped beneath her closed lids.

Kleenex was thrust into her hand. "You were there. That's what matters. If you hadn't gone to the office, we wouldn't know someone had been there."

Annie opened her eyes, swiped at her face. "What difference does it make if I can't give a description?"

"It's proof someone knows where Max is." Emma's voice was bleak. "Proof . . ." She broke off, her face heavy, her gaze somber.

Annie's head throbbed. Emma always made sense, but not this time. "Proof of what?"

Emma walked to the mantel, picked up a framed snapshot of Annie and Max deep-sea fishing. Her back was to Annie. She didn't answer directly. "You didn't get a look at the person. But you know it wasn't Max."

"Of course." Annie sat up straight, eyes flashing. "There was something dreadful there in the dark."

"I believe you. You sensed danger, evil. Someone was there and it wasn't Max." Emma replaced the picture, put it precisely between two other snapshots. "There had to be a purpose in that visit. When we know the reason, we may know everything. For now we can be sure of this: Someone used a key to get into Confidential Commissions. It is clear to me"—she slowly turned, faced Annie, her face sad—"that someone has Max's keys."

Annie looked deep into Emma's primrose blue eyes and wished she hadn't. Unwillingly, she understood. Emma believed someone had Max's keys. There was no good way those keys could have been taken.

Billy heard quiet ease over the long room like fog rolling to shore. He stood in the foyer of Dooley's Mine, his face at its most stolid. He smelled beer on tap, old sweat, must and mold as he surveyed the booths turned into caves by the papier-mâché boulders and the red lanterns that cast a sickly glow. He liked a beer as well as any man, but he wanted a beer and a hot dog at a ball game or a cold can of Bud while he watched his lure bob in the water or a frosted glass at Parotti's while Kevin played the jukebox and Mavis offered bits of apple to Lily as they waited for their burgers and fries. Out of cop's habit, he scanned the faces, knew them without having ever seen them before. He knew the stories of the lost and lonely or the stridently convivial who drink beer or whisky in a dimly lit bar on an August afternoon. Some of them, the ones watching him carefully, their voices falling silent, didn't want any truck with a cop. Now or ever.

Neither did the stocky man moving soft-footed toward him, round face wary. Despite his bulk—Billy estimated he was just under six feet, maybe 250 pounds—he wasn't fat. Muscles bunched beneath his red tee, bulked up legs in tight jeans. He stopped in front of Billy. "Ted Dooley. You looking for me?"

Billy had done some checking before he arrived. Ted Dooley owned and ran Dooley's Mine. He had been a person of interest in a couple of drug cases, nothing ever proved. He'd lived on the island for five years in a nearby cabin. No disturbance calls had ever been logged in from Dooley's Mine. Billy looked into his pale green eyes and cement-slab face and wasn't surprised. "Got some questions, Mr. Dooley, about one of your customers last night."

Dooley's gaze dropped to Billy's badge. He double-checked the ID beneath the plastic cover, then his eyes skated to the shoulder patch. The owner's expression never changed. "I doubt I can help. I don't keep tabs on people unless they get out of line." He folded his arms. Purplish tattoos made the skin hard to see.

"I expect you can help." There was a warning in Billy's voice. "I understand there was a problem. I have an eyewitness." Even though the light was poor, Billy caught the narrowing of Dooley's eyes.

Dooley's challenge was quick. "You already know about this guy, so what can I add?"

"That's what I intend to find out." Billy pulled a notebook from his pocket, flipped it open. "Now, if you'd rather come down to the station . . ."

A humorless smile gashed the slab face. "No need, Chief. Let's step outside."

When the door closed behind them, Dooley walked to the end of the porch, leaned against a post in shadow. The spot opposite him was in bright, full sunshine. Bill stepped into the blazing sun, squinting to see, heat ladling over him. Dooley waited.

Billy brought out the picture of Max. "This man was here last night."

Dooley stared down at the photograph. His heavy face twisted in a glare. "Sorry bastard. I don't know what kind of pills he was popping in his beer, but I want to make it damn clear we don't serve drunks. If a man can't handle his drinks, he's out of here. Nobody will ever sue Dooley's Mine saying we let some jerk get drunk and drive off. Hell of it is, I would have sworn he was sober when he got here. I should've known something was screwy. He came across the parking lot by himself and then his girlfriend—"

Billy didn't change expression. Here was confirmation of the informant's story—"came racing after him. Seemed funny at the time. Why'd he come ahead of her? Anyway, he got a hug and a kiss from his hottie out in the parking lot. I was leaving and I got an eyeful. She ran up, grabbed him, looked like she wanted to climb all over him. He wasn't having any. He looked irritated as hell, like he wanted to get the hell out. I'd say he was trying to break up with her. But he was sober. She hung onto him and insisted—"

Billy held up a hand. "Can you describe her?"

Dooley shrugged. "Mid-twenties. Black hair. Expensive clothes. Not the kind we have here usually." Another lift of those heavy shoulders. "Except sometimes over spring break. College kids living it up." The green eyes looked like pond scum.

Billy made a mental note. Next spring break he'd have officers out here, checking IDs.

"You ever seen either of them before?" Was this the first time Max had been here with a woman?

Dooley jammed his hands in the pockets of his jeans. "Nope." His head jerked toward the picture of Max. "I'd never seen him or the dame either. They came in as I was showing a guy out. Like I said, I don't put up with any crap." He gestured toward Max's picture. "She was all over him but he looked mad. I kept an eye on them. I don't like scenes. People come here to get happy. Anyway, she pulled on him and they came inside. After they ordered, he got up and moseyed around the room, like he was hunting for somebody—"

Billy underlined *hunting*. It was an echo of the lifeguard's report.

"—then came back to the booth. I went by a couple of times, decided it was okay. He didn't look happy but they'd settled in. Maybe fifteen minutes later Roxanne, their waitress, came and got me, said the gal was trying to get him up and he was swaying on his feet. I went over there. He was woozy, blinking. His words were slurred. I couldn't make them out. Anyway, she said sometimes he drank too much and she'd take him home. I told her nobody walked out of my bar and drove a car in that condition. She said she'd drive. She shoved her hand into his pants pocket, got the keys. He struggled at that. I got on one side and she was on the other. He was ambulatory. We got him to the car. A red Jag. I put him in the passenger seat. He kind of pawed at the air, kept trying to talk. She went around, got in the driver's seat. She drove out of here."

Billy looked across the lot. "Which way did she turn?" Dooley's Mine faced north on River Otter Road, which ran east-west. River Otter dead-ended at the marsh to the west. As Billy vaguely recalled, there was an old rental cabin there and other inexpensive rentals down off-shoot lanes. Running east, River Otter led to Sassafras Lane, which wound south and west toward Main Street and the harbor.

"To the left." Dooley turned over his hand, thumb pointing west.

Left. West. The dead end. Billy felt like a hound with a sniff of fox. He'd expected Dooley to say the Jag had turned right toward Sassafras en route to Main Street or a residential area. "West?" Billy felt puzzled, sounded skeptical. He forgot the blazing heat, the suffocating air. He focused on the cold-eyed man glaring at him.

"Listen, Chief, I don't know why the hell she turned left. Maybe she was a stranger in town. Maybe he pulled himself together, raised hell. Maybe she was going to find a turnaround, let him drive. That was her lookout." Dooley's face was hard and determined, "I want to be real clear. If she let him drive, it didn't happen here. If there was a wreck last night and he was behind the wheel, I don't have any liability. You got that? I came up on the porch, but I stayed here"—he jerked a stubby hand around the porch—"and watched the Jag leave. I watched it turn left."

Billy itched to get to the patrol car, drive west on River Otter Road. Henny's search parties had started at the south because, as far as they knew, Max was last heard from when he called Annie from Confidential Commissions. More than likely, the scruffy, less inhabited north end of the island was yet to be explored. Billy was hot, thirsty, and sweaty. The air-conditioned patrol car would be as cooling as an ice floe. He almost grunted a perfunctory thanks and turned to hurry down the steps. But Billy remained standing on the porch. He'd learned a long time ago that uncorroborated evidence was suspect. People would tell you anything they thought they could get away with. He needed to try to come up with some confirmation of Dooley's claim before he turned left on River Otter Road. And there might be more productive avenues to explore. For starters, he wanted to get a precise description of the woman—he wouldn't call her Max's girlfriend, not until he had to—and maybe get a drawing they could circulate.

Billy gestured toward the road. "Got any proof? Anybody else in the lot when they drove off?"

"Oh, sure. People were everywhere. You know, hanging out in the goddam heat instead of coming in for a cold drink. Look, Chief, I—" He broke off with a look of startled surprise. "Oh, yeah, yeah. I didn't remember until you asked. No reason I should have. There was another car. I only got a glimpse of it. I was turning to go in when I saw it. A silver sedan. Big car. It turned left too."

Billy had watched a lot of faces since his rookie days. He'd learned to discount half of what he was told, was suspicious of the rest. There were many ways to lie. Some liars had a steady gaze and a bright look. Some had shifty eyes and shaking hands. Some were truculent, others benign. For all he knew, Ted Dooley had done summer stock in another life. But there had been an instant there—a swift flash of time—when Dooley's face had appeared unguarded with an expression of remembrance.

"What kind of car?" Billy leaned forward, pen poised above his pad.

Dooley's face crinkled as he thought. "I wasn't looking at it. I saw it but I didn't pay a lot of attention. All I know is, it was silver and expensive. Maybe a Lexus. Maybe a Mercedes. I just barely saw it."

Billy thought a Lexus or a Mercedes should have stood out in this parking lot. He stared at Dooley, waiting, face skeptical.

Dooley glowered. "Hell, man, I'm not a parking lot attendant."

"Any thoughts on the driver?" Billy didn't expect much.

Dooley turned his stubby hands palms up. "Tinted windows. Besides, I knew it wasn't one of my regulars. Not in that kind of car. So why should I care? Probably somebody got lost and was using the lot to turn around. Like I say, I keep an eye on my place. I'm not saying I knew everybody who was here last night. But nobody stood out except"—he glanced again at the picture—"him and his lady friend. Anyway, I didn't get a clear look at the second car. So I guess that doesn't help. Unless the Jag and a silver sedan smashed into each other." He looked hopeful.

That's when Billy decided Dooley was telling the truth. There had been a silver car and it had turned to the left on River Otter Road behind the Jag, two cars heading toward a dead end.

The white laundry van pulled into the drive, coasted to a stop beneath a porte cochere. Drapes were drawn in the windows of the two-story house, which had an unmistakable air of desertion. The Millers spent the summer on Cape Cod, returning to the island after Labor Day. Duane Webb swung down from the driver's seat. His eyes scanned the front garden as he opened the back door of the van.

Annie slipped from the shadows of a honeysuckle-covered arbor.

She hurried across the drive, tossed in a duffel, and climbed into the back of the van.

Duane gave a thumbs-up. "Not the fanciest conveyance but the owner's in my poker group." He slammed the door, twisted the key in the lock. Once in the driver's seat, he spoke over his shoulder. "I locked it in case anybody gets nosy. When we reach the gate, stay down." The van began to move, picked up speed.

Annie wedged herself between the duffel and thick canvas bags of laundry piled almost to the roof. If there was air-conditioning, it didn't reach her. She sat with her knees bunched almost to her chin. In her mind, she knew their route. She'd rowed across the lagoon to the Miller dock. It was a short row, a long way to drive. She pictured the houses on the curving road, the Jessops, the Daniels, the Chavezes, the Kinkaids, the Darlings . . . Annie swallowed. Their house, hers and Max's, their happy wonderful house that shimmered with glass, shining windows that let in the sunshine.

The van slowed, stopped. Duane's voice was grumpy. "Look, buddy, I'm picking up laundry. If you people will let me through . . ."

Voices clamored. "Do you know the Darlings? Do you stop at their house?"

"Never been on this route before. Hey . . . back that car out of the way for me."

The handle on the back door moved, but the door stayed shut. It had been smart of Duane to lock the door. He'd been a city editor for a long time. Duane knew the lengths reporters go to for news.

Annie was covered with sweat by the time the van lurched forward. It was disorienting to travel with no view of the outside. She knew they were at Sand Dollar Road when they slowed for a stop. Duane turned right. It wasn't until the van picked up speed that he yelled, "You okay?"

"Sure." She forced the answer. It was a lie. She wasn't okay. Her head throbbed. Nausea bubbled in her throat. Her hands shook. Sweat beaded her face and back and chest and legs. But at least she was free for the moment of the house that had turned into a prison. She couldn't go in and out without shouted questions, the flicker of flashbulbs. She was determined to hunt for Max. Once she got to the cabin at Nightingale Courts, she could . . .

Annie kneaded one cheek with a clenched fist. What could she do? Join a search party? She would be outside, moving, looking, caught up in an effort, no longer feeling useless. The prospect was tempting. Maybe one of the groups would find Max. She refused to accept what that thought meant. She wasn't going to envision Max in a state where he could be *found*.

Annie shifted uncomfortably on the hard metal floor of the van. If a search was successful . . . She pushed unbearable images away. Max was somewhere. He was alive and he needed her. She held to that belief. He was alive. If he weren't, she would know. There would be an emptiness that could never be filled. She had to think and plan and figure, find out what had happened and who had kept Max from her. Last night someone had been in Confidential Commissions. Emma was convinced the intruder had used Max's keys.

Annie grabbed her duffel, loosened the cord, pulled out a notebook. Emma had insisted there were four questions that must be answered. Though it was dim in the interior of the van, she had no trouble reading the questions even though she knew them now by heart:

Emma's Questions

1. *Who hired Max?*
2. *Where did Max go when he left his office?*
3. *Who was in Confidential Commissions when Annie arrived?*
4. *Where is the file on the new client?*

Annie remembered Emma's decisive tone: "When we know the answers to these questions, we will know everything."

Those were the questions. How could she find answers? There was an itinerant artist who often set up his easel and camp stool at that end of the boardwalk. He sketched with fine color pencils. He had an eye for faces. Perhaps he'd noticed someone entering Confidential Commissions.

Annie flipped to a fresh page, wrote rapidly.

1. *Check with artist.*

Max's car was distinctive. How many people would it take to canvass the island, ask if a red Jag had been seen shortly after five o'clock yesterday? Annie fought away a sense of futility. The search had been under way for that very Jag throughout this long day. If anyone had contacted the police, she didn't know about it. Surely Billy would have let her know—

She heard the ring of the cell phone despite the muffling mound of laundry bags. Annie stiffened, scarcely breathed.

"Hello?" Duane's voice lifted in inquiry.

Annie bent her head, straining to hear.

"Hey, Vince. Yeah? River Otter Road? I don't think I—Yeah. Got it." The van hurtled ahead. "Annie, that's Vince. He picked it up on the police scanner at the *Gazette*. They've found Max's car."

Brakes squealed. The van rocked to a stop. "Oh, Jesus." Duane's voice was stricken.

Annie clambered over laundry bags, scrambled into the front seat. She looked through the streaked windshield at the Broward's Rock Police cruiser turned sideways to block the dusty dirt road.

Yellow crime scene tape dangled across the road, strung between two live oaks.

Annie wrenched open the door, jumped to the ground. She heard Duane's shout behind her. She ran and ducked beneath the tape, pounded around a curve in the narrow rutted road. She skidded to a stop, a hand at her throat.

The steaming salt marsh, spartina grass undulating in the onshore breeze, stretched toward the Sound. The distinctive gassy odor, a smell she had always loved, now seemed alien, threatening. A breeze stirred the palmetto fronds, but did nothing to dispel the choking summer heat. The blazing late-afternoon sun turned the chrome on Max's car a blinding silver. The red Jag, trunk lid raised, was parked on a slant in front of a wooden cabin on stilts. The island's newest police officer, a stringy redhead with a long pale face, stood by the Jag, hand resting on the butt of the .38 Special in her holster. The dull gray Broward's Rock Forensics van was a few feet away, the back door open. Another cruiser was parked near the cabin.

Most ominous to Annie was the dingy black Dodge sedan nosed next to the cabin steps. Annie struggled to breathe. She knew that sedan, knew its owner. Dr. Horace Burford was the island's medical examiner as well as chief of staff at the hospital. His presence spelled death.

Crime scene tape . . . Max's car . . . Dr. Burford . . . Annie's vision blurred. She wavered on her feet.

Duane's hand gripped her elbow. "Stay here." His voice was hoarse, stricken.

Duane's command pierced the numbness that threatened to overwhelm her. She made no answer. She couldn't answer. Instead, she shook free of Duane, plodded one heavy step after another toward the car, a hand outstretched.

"Annie." Duane was beside her, imploring her.

The police officer jerked around to face them. "No access. Crime scene." Her voice was high and sharp.

Annie walked on. She didn't look at the officer. Her eyes could not move away from the dark opening of the trunk.

"Halt. No entry. This is a crime scene." She moved to block Annie.

Annie stopped a scant foot away.

Lank red curls poked from beneath a visored cap. Dark glasses hid her gaze. The pale face twisted in a scowl. The police officer loomed in front of Annie, upheld hands palm out. "Halt."

Annie couldn't see past the officer. Annie's head throbbed. Her heart thudded. Abruptly, she jerked to one side, darted past the officer, and stared into the open trunk, a roaring in her ears. Empty, oh God, it was empty except for a tire tool that looked as if it had been flung there, one end resting on the back wall of the trunk. ". . . move away. I'll have to arrest you . . ."

Annie didn't budge, though she felt the harsh grip at her elbow. The tire tool was smeared with a darkish substance and there were clumps of hair. Dark hair. Not blond. If a tire tool had been used as a weapon, who had been hurt? Where was Dr. Burford? Where was Billy? Annie's head jerked toward the cabin. She yanked free of the officer, broke into a run, clattered up the wooden steps.

"Halt. Halt!" The shrill shout rose behind Annie.

Suddenly Billy was in the doorway. "Annie, you can't come in."

She looked past him, saw Mavis with a camcorder and Dr. Burford kneeling on the floor. Dr. Burford's stocky body blocked her view.

"Max." Her voice was dull, dead as death itself.

"Not Max." Billy was grim. "There's a dead woman in here. His car's outside and there's a bloody tire tool in the trunk of his car. Max is nowhere to be found. That's all we know."

A dead woman. Annie felt frozen in place, her body rigid. A dead woman but no Max. Max had accepted a case, expected to be late coming home. The victim had to be his client. She was dead. And Max . . .

Dr. Burford pushed himself up from the floor, his craggy face creased in a glower. Dr. Burford hated death. He especially hated violent death. "Okay, Billy." He didn't look toward the doorway, moved to give Mavis a clearer shot of the body. "I'll do some tests. Looks like the tire tool's the murder weapon. Multiple trauma, crushed brain stem. Been dead"—he gave a heavy sigh—"roughly twenty to twenty-five hours."

Annie stared at the body, the battered head, blood crusted against dark hair. The woman lay facedown. Had she been struck from behind? Blood spattered the floor and the orange and ivory sarong. The low-cut sarong revealed smooth shoulders, pallid in death.

Annie's hands clenched.

Billy was watching her. "All right. You're here. Do you know her?"

Annie felt a surge of anger. How would she know? How would anyone know? "I can't see her face. But Max would have told me if his client was someone we knew." She jerked her eyes away from the body, saw two crystal champagne flutes and a bottle of champagne tilted in a bucket. Water lapped near the rim of the bucket. When ice melts, the volume increases. It made no sense, a woman dead in a seductive sarong and unopened champagne and Max's car and no Max. He would have tried to protect his client. Annie was certain of that and equally certain the dead woman wasn't wearing a sarong because she was with Max. Though why in the world . . . Annie shook her head back and forth, pushed away unanswerable questions. If someone had killed a woman and someone had Max's car keys—the thoughts jumbled in her mind—that meant Max was . . . hurt? Worse than hurt?

Annie clutched Billy's arm, felt rigid muscles. "Have you looked for Max? Oh God, Billy, you have to look for him." She gestured toward the marsh, simmering in the August sunlight.

"We're looking for him." Billy's voice was grim. "I've got an APB out. Everybody in the state's looking for him."

Annie heard the roughness in his tone. Billy sounded like a cop, a cop seeking a criminal. Didn't he understand? Max had taken a case. He'd gone out, planning to be home late that evening. Annie swallowed hard. "If this is his client, where is he?"

Billy's face, the face she had thought belonged to a friend, was closed and hard, unyielding. "Client?" Billy turned over his hand as if pushing away the word. "Client . . ." Now the tone was weary. "Look, Annie, I'm sorry. Sorry for you. Sorrier for a dead woman. I've got to deal with the facts. Max and a woman—probably the one who's lying on the floor of this cabin—were at Dooley's Mine last night. Max had too much to drink and—"

Annie stared at him. She heard Billy speak, but his words made no sense. Max never drank too much. Two beers or one scotch or a glass of wine. That was all he ever drank.

"—he and the woman left. She was driving the Jag. We'll match prints. See if the victim's are on the steering wheel. If that's the case . . . Anyway, that's all we know except Max isn't here. There's no sign of him. None. Yeah, we're looking for Max. God, Annie, I'm sorry."

Annie willed her hands not to shake. She huddled in the passenger seat of the laundry van and punched the familiar number into her cell as Duane scowled at the long line of cars on Main Street. He blew the horn, bulled his way into the bumper-to-bumper traffic. "It's freaking hot. Why don't they go to the beach?" he snarled.

The call was answered on the first ring. "Yes, Annie." Emma Clyde's in-your-face voice was muted, gentle. "It's already on the news. CNN broke in with a flash. Unidentified woman found dead near his abandoned car."

"Max." Annie wiped away a hot rush of tears. "Is there any word?"

"I would have called you." She tried to sound matter-of-fact. "I've alerted the search parties. They're en route to the north end of the island. I understand there are some dogs on the way but they won't get here until tonight. Everything possible's being done to find Max. So"—now she was the decisive Emma of old—"we need to start at the other end."

Annie stared. Other end?

Emma's tone was brisk. "The victim. We have to find out who the victim is. So far, if Billy knows, he's staying mum. I don't suppose you know?"

Annie would have shuddered if she'd had the energy. She was too weary, too sick at heart to push away the immediate image that popped into her mind, the bloodied battered head, the inert body in the dramatic sarong. "I didn't see her face. But I'm sure it's not anyone we knew. Max would have told me when he called if his client was someone we knew."

"All right. I'll keep after it." Emma always expected success. "As soon as we know, I'll come out to—well, in case we are being over-heard—"

Annie understood. Cell phone conversations were subject to interception.

"—I'll meet you where you are going. For now, rest, eat, get ready to fight."

Billy Cameron took a deep gulp from the icy cold can of Dr Pepper, courtesy of the cooler Mavis always carried in the crime van, and waited for the air-conditioning to cool the cruiser. Although the sky was brassy and cloudless, he felt as he did when a hurricane was churning north toward the island—apprehensive, pressed on all sides, much to do, little time in which to do it. Since he was a kid, he'd had a trick to help when he was overwhelmed. He said the mantra aloud. "One thing at a time. One thing at a time." He punched the windows, heard the whirr as they lifted. It was maybe a little cooler now inside than out, though sweat rolled from his face, trickled down his chest and back and legs.

"Rock Around the Clock" pealed from the cell phone. Billy picked it up, checked the caller ID. The mayor. This wasn't a call Billy intended to answer. Not now. Not until he knew more. He pictured portly Mayor Cosgrove, plump as a pig, green eyes glistening with irritation. The Broward's Rock Police Department had been on the mayor's blacklist ever since Pete Garrett refused to hire the mayor's nephew. As far as the mayor was concerned, Pete's call-up to his National Guard unit was reason to celebrate. Billy had been acting chief ever since and now was in line to become chief, since Pete had sent word he wouldn't be returning. But Billy had also turned down the nephew's application, instead had hired Hyla Harrison, an experienced cop from Atlanta who'd returned to the island to live with her ailing mother. Now the mayor's ire was aimed at Billy. The mayor could wait.

Billy waited until the call ended, ignored the ping indicating messages, punched the number of the *Gazette*. "Yeah, Vince. Need some help. We got an ID on the victim, one Vanessa Taylor. That's off the record for now. I'm not releasing anything until I've notified next of kin. Here's the address on her driver's license: 211 Tree Swallow Lane. Ran a check. House belongs to—" Billy found the notes, "a Lillian Whitman Dodd. Do you know anything about Taylor or Dodd?" Billy could navigate the island in a dense fog, but he didn't know every resident, especially not those who lived in the island's posh gated community, which definitely included 211 Tree Swallow Lane. Vince Ellis moved in those circles.

Vince's reply was quick. "I know a little about both of them. Vanessa Taylor. Damn. She was young."

Billy lifted the can of Dr Pepper, welcomed the biting tang. Even though a mountain of tasks loomed over him, he could enjoy this moment's respite and be grateful for any help Vince could offer.

Vince took a breath, then talked fast. "I met Vanessa at a party there last Christmas. She's—she was Mrs. Dodd's secretary. Lillian Dodd's from Chicago originally. She and her first husband, Howard Whitman, retired here about twenty years ago. He was a lot older than she and he died about ten years ago. About four years ago, she married Jon Dodd. He has an advertising agency. She's very active in island charities. Nice woman."

"Vanessa Taylor lived there?" Billy knew there was a world in which rich women had secretaries, but it wasn't a world he inhabited. What did some rich woman without a job need a secretary for?

"Oh, sure. That's part of the attraction, getting to live the life of Riley until something better comes along. The secretaries are never long term. Lillian hires a young woman, gives her a luxurious home, good salary, lots of fancy trips, and an expensive gift when she moves on. I'd guess it's a fun job. Seems to me Vanessa had been there a couple of years."

"How about her family?" Billy shifted into drive and the cruiser swung away from the cabin.

"I don't think she was local. Lillian will know. Hey, Billy, I'll get a story ready but I'll hold it until I hear from you." There was a pause. "The island's swarming with media. You ready for it?"

Billy didn't have to ask what Vince meant. Was he ready for the incessant clink of flashes, the shouted questions, the mikes poked toward his face? "I'll manage." He wasn't sure that he would but he would try. Most of all, he was determined not to let the news hysteria interfere with his investigation. "Thanks, Vince."

As he came around the curve, Hyla Harrison gave a sharp salute, pulled aside the crime scene tape. Billy nodded and edged past the sideways cruiser. Bars of "Rock Around the Clock" continued to boom, the mayor again, CNN, the *Atlanta Journal-Constitution*. . . . There were more calls than he could possibly answer. Billy turned off his cell. He needed to concentrate. He had to remember he was a cop and a good one. He would follow evidence where it led. But Max . . . No, make it *Suspect*. Think about the Suspect he was seeking and the old checklist: Means, motive, opportunity.

Means: Tire tool. Tests would soon prove whether the stains and hair and skin matched the victim's wounds and what fingerprints were on the tool.

Motive: It looked a lot like an illicit relationship gone wrong.

Opportunity: If the victim was the woman observed with Suspect at Dooley's Mine, Suspect was in the company of the victim shortly before her death.

Means, motive, opportunity.

If Max turned out to be a murderer, Billy knew he would never again look into a friend's face with confidence. Billy pushed away the swirl of discomfiting facts interlaced with memories: Max drunk according to a bar owner who should know, Max looking toward Annie with his heart in his face, an angry Max at a cheap bar with a woman who wasn't his wife, Max laughing as he picked up Lily. . . . Instead, Billy marshaled his thoughts. He needed to monitor the search for Max, file reports on the status of the investigation to date, coordinate with other state investigators, prepare a release for the press, seek information about the victim.

The victim was his first responsibility after securing the crime scene. He'd considered calling the Dodd house and asking about Vanessa Taylor, then decided he'd go in person. In the best of all possible worlds, he would have another officer with him as he made this call, but the office was too short on personnel. Every hand was occupied, Mavis completing the transfer of evidence to the crime van, Hyla Harrison arranging for Max's car to be hauled to the station, Lou Pirelli manning the station. So it was up to him to find out everything possible about the dead woman. Would he get confirmation of the Suspect as her boyfriend?

Cicadas rasped. Frogs rumbled. Birds chirruped as they settled into the trees for the night. The final crimson streaks of the setting sun streaked the marsh. The spartina grass rippled in the offshore breeze. Annie huddled at the end of the pier. Nightingale Courts stretched behind her, all the cabins brightly lit. This was high season. Many of the cabins were monthly rentals, only a few available for tourists. It was a stroke of luck that there had been a cancellation that made a cabin available for Annie.

She'd tried to gulp down the sandwich Ingrid had brought her. It was as if her throat had congealed. She'd managed a portion, pushed away the rest, drank the Coke. Normally she didn't like soda, disliking the sweetness. Normally . . .

She rested her head against her bent knees, wrapped her arms around her legs. The search for Max continued, but it had been so long now. More than twenty-four hours since she'd heard his voice. How could she hope?

Because . . . She lifted her head. Tears streamed down her cheeks. Because he was the light of her life. Because if he were dead, the world would be cold and barren forevermore. Because . . .

Agonizing pain pulsed in Max's head. Nothing existed but pain. Pain encompassed him, enveloped him. He lay still, unable to move. If he moved, his head might swell and explode. Nothing could ever hurt more. . . . As consciousness returned, Max felt the bubble of nausea in his throat. His eyes burned. His arm stung. He swallowed, opened his eyes, opened them to darkness and suffocating heat. Abruptly, despite the brutal rocking in his head, he struggled over onto his side and was wretchedly sick. Weak and shaking, he crawled away from the vomit, slumped facedown on the floor.

Dark. He grappled with the darkness. He couldn't see anything. He was on a floor. He felt grit against his skin. It was dark and silent and hot. The silence was oppressive. No people, no voices, nothing but him. The musty air was suffocatingly hot and stale. His clothes were damp with sweat. His arm stung. His throat ached with dryness. With enormous effort, he lifted his head and slowly looked around. Moonlight spilled through a window.

Inside. It took his mind a moment to make the connection. It was night and he was in a room. Somehow he knew he was alone. There was no sense of any other human presence. It was not so much thought as instinct that got him to his hands and knees. His breaths were shallow. Laboriously he crawled toward the window. Windows were in walls. Walls had light switches. He found the wall, eased himself, trembling, to his feet. One hand swept the wall.

Lights blazed. He squinted and surveyed the room—a lumpy brown sofa, fake leather recliner, double bed with a brown chenille spread, kitchenette, wooden table with three chairs. He didn't know where he was. Or why.

Dizziness forced him to lean against the wall. He fought another wave of nausea. As it subsided, he became aware again of the discomfort on his right arm. He looked down. Ants swarmed on his skin, stinging. He brushed the ants away, felt something sticky on his arm. Something nasty.

What had happened to him? Where was he? Annie . . . Alarm

flared in his mind, made his aching head worse. Annie . . . This room held no echo of Annie. He didn't know this dirty, ill-furnished room. He was certain he'd never been here in his life. How had he gotten here? Why was he here? Why was he sick? He grasped after tendrils of memory, but there was darkness in his mind and uncertainty and something dreadful, something he didn't want to remember.

He leaned against the wall, sick and shaken. He had to get help. He didn't know where he was or what had happened to him or what he was going to do, but he had to find help. He was weak and sick. Maybe if he got a drink of water . . . Water. God, yes. He needed water.

He took two steps, used the back of a sofa for support. He waited several minutes, then started across the room, his steps unsteady. He stopped to brace himself on the top of the recliner, rested for a moment, made it to a kitchen chair, held to the back.

He reached the small bathroom, turned on the light. He planted his hands on the sides of the sink, closed his eyes until dizziness passed. When he opened them, he looked into the dingy mirror. Bloodshot eyes stared out of a pale face grimed with dirt. Uncombed hair bunched in tangles. He needed a shave. The bristle on his cheeks was odd. He'd shaved when he got up. When was that? He couldn't pull a picture of his day. He couldn't remember . . . Thirsty. God, he was thirsty. His throat was parched.

A sudden sharp recollection bloomed. He was standing in a dusty parking lot, walking with the blaze of the sun on him, sweating, irritated, desperate for something to drink. The image faded.

Water . . .

He turned on the cold tap. The water came in uneven spurts, a rusty orange. When it ran clear, he cupped his hands, lifted water to his dry lips, fuzz-coated mouth, parched throat. The water wasn't cold and it tasted metallic, but he didn't care. He drank, fought a wave of queasiness, drank again. His pounding head felt better. He lifted another handful of water to splash against his burning eyes and dirty face. With his right arm close to his face, his nose wrinkled at a fetid odor. He looked at his skin. Water ran down his forearm toward his elbow, water stained a faint coppery color.

The smell of blood.

He traced a finger on his skin, held it up, saw unmistakable pinkness. He turned his hands up, stared at them, tried to understand. Had he bled? His hands were dirty but he didn't find a cut or scratch. His arms were unmarked. He was shaky and confused, his head hurt and he was disoriented, but he didn't have the pain of an injury. Where had blood come from?

Panic swept over him. He ran his hands, fingers spread wide, down his shirt and felt a crusty patch near his belt. He yanked the shirt loose, held it and his T-shirt away, stared down at his chest. Not a mark. But the heel of his hand grazed that sticky substance. He didn't think. He didn't reason. In a rough twist he pulled and the polo shirt came over his head. He turned it in his hands. Navy blue didn't show stains, but he saw the irregular darkness on the front of the shirt.

Water splashed into the basin, still running full force. Max thrust the shirt beneath the faucet. He squeezed the sodden cloth. Pinkish water rose in the bowl.

Max's heart thudded. Blood. A lot of blood. On his shirt. But he wasn't hurt. Where had the blood come from? He hated the smell that swirled around him, clogged his nose. He flung the shirt onto the floor, washed and washed and washed his hands until finally they felt clean.

The shock of the stained shirt pierced the dull fog in his mind. He had to remember what had happened to him. Why was he here? Why was there blood on his shirt?

He stared into the mirror, saw the gauntness of his tired face. He lifted a shaking hand, ran his fingers over the bristle on his cheeks, tried to remember. . . . A happy morning. That was how his day started. With happiness. With Annie's quick words and cheerful smile and eager plans. An ordinary, everyday kind of morning. Memories came then, walking hand in hand with Annie along the boardwalk, Barb out of town so his office was unnaturally quiet, lunch with Annie at Parotti's, her obvious distress when he'd offered to come help unpack books, the quiet in his office and savoring once again the circular about the Franklin house, and then a new client. Dark haired. A missing brother. Blackbeard Beach.

That's where his memory stopped. He could feel the warmth of the sun on the boardwalk, hear the grunts and thuds of the volleyball game, see the lifeguards. Beyond that moment there was nothing but blackness. He felt as if he were teetering on the edge of a chasm and knew he was going to fall into inconceivable emptiness. He'd gone to the beach looking for his client's brother. Funny. He remembered the brother's name. Danny. He couldn't recall her name, the attractive, seductive woman who'd hired him. He scowled and his image in the mirror was suddenly angry. She'd done something he didn't like. What was it? Once again he had the sensation of helplessness. Then relief swept him. He'd made a file. Her name would be there and whatever else she'd told him. He needed to get to his office, get in touch with her. Maybe he'd fallen down, banged his head. Maybe that's why he couldn't remember anything. He smoothed back his tangled hair, didn't find a lump, no trace of sticky dried blood. Something had happened. He had to find her. The sense of urgency built inside. He had to find her. That would solve everything. Or at least begin an effort to corral the time he'd lost. How much time? Once again he swiped at his face, felt the bristle of beard.

He turned, walked unsteadily toward the front door. He patted his pocket for his car keys. No keys . . .

Another brief memory flared, a hand sliding into his pocket and his sense of helpless fury. He squeezed his eyes shut, tried to think past that instant. Someone took his keys. Why? When? But the black curtain wouldn't lift. He opened his eyes. Maybe in time he would remember.

He stumbled to the front door, turned the knob. At least the door wasn't locked. Thoughts caromed like billiard balls. Dumb. Of course he could open the front door. The lock was on the inside. Maybe he was crazy. This was all crazy. . . .

He came out on a rickety front porch. The cabin overlooked the marsh. Moonlight silvered the water, bathed the clearing in cream. There was a pier but no boat. Maybe it was just a fishing dock. A rutted dirt lane snaked out of sight into the woods. Even though he'd not expected to find his car, he struggled against disappointment. If his car had been there, he could have called Annie on his cell and asked her to bring extra keys. He was assailed by sudden worry. He needed to call Annie. ASAP. She'd be wondering where he was.

He'd told Annie—he remembered that clearly—that he was going to be late. Why was he going to be late? Something about the case. But it wasn't late. The moon was just starting its climb into the sky. Again bleary puzzlement fogged his mind, made it hard to think. The moon was just up . . . why did he need a shave . . . the case . . . a kid named Danny . . . blood . . . He held to the railing, climbed down the steps, took one step, another, forced himself to keep going.

The road had to lead somewhere.

4

The lights flicked on. Annie shaded her eyes. She didn't move from her defeated huddle on the sofa of the Nightingale Courts cabin. She'd not bothered to turn on the lights as night fell. More than twenty-four hours with no word of Max.

"Annie"—Emma was stern and determined—"look at me."

Emma's voice seemed far away. Annie sat stiffly, frozen and numb. That was her only defense against the deep and pervasive pain threatening to destroy her. If she permitted herself to think and feel and know, she would disintegrate into pieces, so many pieces she'd never be whole again. It was as if she observed herself sitting at the end of the white wicker divan, wan and pinched, hunched and disheveled, in the incongruously cheerful room with pink-and-white-striped walls and white wicker furniture and gaily patterned cushions. The room wasn't meant for misery. She closed her eyes, blotting out the present, wished she could blot out knowledge and memory and fear. Now

Emma had come to Nightingale Courts. Annie wasn't up to coping with Emma. Maybe she would go away if Annie kept her eyes shut.

Heavy footsteps clumped over the matting. Annie felt an iron grip on her arm.

Emma's deep-as-a-cavern voice barked, "This isn't doing Max any good."

Slowly Annie opened her eyes, looked up into Emma's scowling square face, corrugated as ill-set cement. Do Max good? What could possibly make any difference now? He'd been missing for more than twenty-four hours. . . .

Emma loosed her grip on Annie. "I've got information." Emma patted the huge woven purse hanging over her shoulder. "There's enough here to convince me they'll find Max and find him alive. More about that in a minute. Now, here's what I've done. For starters, I've called that good-looking young trial lawyer over in Chastain, the one who's won all those malpractice suits. He takes high-profile criminal cases, too. He's becoming a legend in his own time and richer than a courtroom of CEOs. Butter won't melt, but he's tougher than rawhide. Handler Jones, that's his name. He's on his way. Max is going to need him. And I have some photos of the victim."

"Alive? You think Max is alive?" Annie came to her feet. "Emma, what have you got?"

Emma nodded approval. "That's better. Get your dander up. All right, here's how I see it. We know Max didn't kill that girl. Right?" She was Emma at her most assured.

Annie sat bolt upright, eyes now wide and determined. "Of course we know that."

Emma's smile was satisfied. "Exactly. Since he's innocent, he had no reason to run away. If he was going to be killed, there would be no point in taking him somewhere else. Say it was supposed to look like murder-suicide—"

Annie's insides lurched.

"—he'd be dead in that cabin. So, he wasn't killed. What happened to him? The fact that he disappeared means the murderer took him somewhere. Why?" Her heavy shoulders lifted and fell. "Obviously, the intent is to make Max the scapegoat. Therefore, Max will be found. He has to turn up for that plan to work."

Emma's bald pronouncement was like a jolt of pure oxygen, whistling through Annie's mind with electrifying speed and effect. Max was alive. Of course he was alive. If his death had been planned, his body would have been found in his car or in that cabin. Max didn't commit murder, so he hadn't run away. That meant he'd been taken away. But how could . . . Annie's eyes widened. "Billy said Max was drunk when he and that girl left Dooley's Mine. I knew that was crazy. But now I see. He must have been drugged."

"Yesss!" The word cracked like a dragon smacking his tail. "That fits right in. Maybe he had a beer and someone dropped Ecstasy or one of those other street drugs in it. That would make him appear drunk. If he passed out, he could be hauled away. And"—Emma glowed with self-approval—"I've got more proof. Gilt-edged. Incontrovertible." She rustled in her bag, found a notepad, flipped over several pages. "I talked to Mavis. Bloodhounds searched the vicinity of the crime scene tonight after smelling one of Max's T-shirts." Emma's blue eyes glinted with satisfaction. "I scrounged around your house and found a T-shirt in the laundry hamper. I gave it to Mavis. I knew it was the thing to do. Here's the payoff. The dogs found no trace of a trail from Max's car to the cabin and no trail leaving the clearing. That means Max was never in the cabin and he left in a car. Whose car?" The last was almost a purr.

Annie reached out, clutched a strong, stubby hand. "Emma, you're wonderful."

Emma was never modest. She nodded in agreement, gave Annie's hand a squeeze, pulled free. "I simply thought it through just as Marigold would have. Now—"

Annie had always been irritated by Emma's habit of referring to her mystery sleuth Marigold Rembrandt as if she were alive. At this moment, Annie didn't care. All she cared about was the path that Emma had chopped through the impossible thicket of facts: Max and a woman, the woman dead, Max gone, Max's tire tool the probable murder weapon.

"—we have to get to work. There are going to be dark days ahead. So, when did you eat?"

Annie was startled by the unexpected demand. "A while ago."

"Not recently enough obviously." Once again Emma delved into her bag, brought out a sack, handed it to Annie. "Sit at the table." It was an order.

Annie found herself at the kitchen table. The sack was warm in her hand. In a moment, she was unfolding the wrapper from a fried flounder sandwich heavy on tartar sauce, one of the specials at Parotti's Bar and Grill. It was a feast, the sandwich on crusty French bread, sides of cole slaw, baked beans, and corn pudding. Annie realized she was ravenous. Max alive . . . She took a huge bite and nothing had ever tasted better than the succulent white fish in just the right amount of crispy batter.

Emma bustled to the refrigerator. "I'll bet Ingrid stocked the fridge. Ah, here we are." Emma brought two cans of Pepsi to the table, settled opposite Annie.

Annie picked up a napkin to wipe away a dollop of tartar sauce and saw a scrawl in pencil: *Annie, We're looking everywhere. Ben and Jolene.*

She felt a quick sheen of tears, happy tears. As she ate, she felt strength returning, born of food and hope and friendship.

Emma pulled several folders from her oversize purse. "I went by the *Gazette*." She reached into her purse, brought out her cell phone, placed it on the table. "Vince will call us when they find Max. Vince got the victim ID from Billy. Here are some printouts of the pix and story." She pushed the computer sheets toward Annie. "Her name's Vanessa Taylor. Twenty-three years old. Secretary to—"

Annie looked at the photographs as Emma talked. The first was a studio portrait, dark sultry eyes and high cheekbones and richly red lips in an oval face framed by shoulder-length hair dark and shiny as crow feathers. *Thinks she's a hottie.* Annie's judgment was swift and cold. The thought was followed by a sickening twist of remorse. Vanessa was dead. The promise of passion so evident in that photograph was forever lost. Annie shouldn't be judgmental. The retort in her mind was swift. *Oh yes she should.* She had to know everything about Vanessa Taylor: what she'd wanted from life, what she'd taken, what she'd given. Somewhere in Vanessa's past lay the answer to Vanessa's murder and Max's disappearance.

"—Lillian Dodd. You may know her. She's been president of the Iris Society and she's on the board of—"

Annie looked at more pictures. A snapshot on a tennis court caught Vanessa as she raised her racquet for an overhead smash. She looked intent, strong and athletic. Her tennis dress fit a little too snugly, emphasizing a voluptuous body. In a photograph of a garden, Vanessa stood next to a distinguished-looking older woman. Vanessa wore a lovely yellow linen sleeveless dress with a scalloped neck. Annie checked the caption. . . . *philanthropist Lillian Dodd and her secretary Vanessa Taylor at the ribbon-cutting ceremony* . . . Lillian Dodd's long, elegant face had a look of pleasant command. Her violet silk dress had the aura of style and wealth.

"—of several charities."

Annie shook her head. "I've heard of Lillian Dodd. I don't know her."

"How about Vanessa?" Emma's gaze was intent.

"No. We didn't know her." We. She and Max. The two of them. Billy Cameron thought Max was on a date. How could Billy believe that? Max had gone out to help a client. *Max, where are you? What happened to you?* Annie's mind teetered on the edge of the black abyss of despair that had claimed her until Emma had come, insistent that Max was alive. *Oh God, please let him be alive. . . .*

Every step was an effort. Max strained to see. He was on the road but it was dark as a closet. Only an occasional shaft of moonlight found a break in the canopy of the trees. His legs were wobbly and occasionally he stopped to shake. Sick. He still felt sick. Mosquitoes whined. He swatted no-see-ums, heard rustling in the undergrowth. There might be a fox or cougar. One foot after another . . .

The darkness and his wretched awakening in the strange cabin, the blood on his shirt and the hot night—it was all a nightmare that didn't end. He didn't know where he was or what had happened to him, but he was caught up in something dreadful. He had to find Annie. When he found Annie, everything would be all right. If he kept on going, surely there would be some habitation. He could ask for help.

Suddenly he stopped to listen and realized dully that he'd been hearing a yelp of dogs for some time, and muffled shouts. The sounds came nearer and louder. The baying of hounds reached a crescendo.

Running feet thudded. Flashlight beams stabbed through the night, pointing high and low, swinging back and forth, coming together in a blaze of light to converge on him. Before, there had been darkness. Now a brilliant circle surrounded him.

Blinded by the stark beams, Max squinted, shielded his eyes with one hand, took a step back before the onslaught. Hounds yelped and snuffled around him. Shouts rose. "That's him . . . Max Darling . . . that's him."

"Hands up," came a shrill cry. "Police officer. You are wanted on suspicion of murder."

Billy Cameron's face crinkled in surprise and relief. "You got him?" He listened. "No shirt, just a tee? . . . Where'd you find him? . . . Yeah. Straight here." He clicked off the phone. Strange as hell. None of it made sense. First thing would be to talk to Max, get his story. The lights flickered on his phone like fireflies. He didn't have to check caller ID to identify the callers. The mayor. The media. First things first. Maybe Max could come up with an explanation. But the tire tool and the girl hanging onto him . . . Billy sighed. He stood, squared his shoulders.

". . . by tomorrow we'll have dossiers on Vanessa and all the people she knew. From what I've discovered at this point—"

"Beer Barrel Polka" blared from Emma's shapeless purse. She reached inside, pulled out her cell phone. She glanced at the caller ID number.

Somehow Annie knew. She felt as if there were nothing any-where but the blue-eyed woman holding a cell phone, taking a call that might spell the end to happiness and love and dreams.

Emma held the phone for a frozen instant, long enough for an-other bar of raucous music to sound, long enough for Annie to put out a hand as if to catch herself from tumbling into emptiness.

Emma clicked on the cell.

Annie waited without breath, without movement, her world hanging in the balance.

Emma's face split in a triumphant smile. She covered the mouthpiece, "Max is alive! Vince just got word from one of the search parties." She listened, nodded. "Where are they taking him?"

Annie felt as if she'd stepped from the depths of darkness to a pinnacle of light. Her heart sang. She jumped to her feet, grabbed her cell, punched automatic dial for Laurel, and started for the door.

Wrists manacled, Max jolted in the back of the police car as it sped, lurching around curves, siren blaring. Murder? He'd thought the nightmare couldn't worsen. And there'd been no answer when he demanded to know what had happened. Whose murder? Where? Nausea swelled in his throat as he remembered pink staining his fingers and the sticky patch on his shirt and the smell of blood. Oh God, what had happened during the dark hours he couldn't remember?

"The street's jammed." Not even Emma's Rolls-Royce could make headway in the gridlock near the harbor. "I'd say the word's out and every news outlet from here to L.A. is on hand. We'll never get through."

"I'll get through." Nothing was going to stand in Annie's way. Not now. Max was safe. She didn't give a thought to Vince's report that Max was being taken to the police station for questioning. It only mattered that Max was alive. To see him, she'd fight her way through any crowd, brave the hordes of media, bang against the door of the police station, do what she had to do.

". . . the back way. You don't want them to get pictures of you."

Annie reached for the handle. "I don't care."

Emma reached out and grabbed Annie. "Yes you do. The media will come up with pix of you, one way or another. That can't be

avoided. But we don't want video that will make you easy to identify. Since you and Max didn't know the victim, there's a chance the
murderer's never met you or heard you speak. That could be an advantage for us."

Annie wanted to tear herself away and find Max, but Emma's
crisp, cool pronouncement kept her in the car. . . . *an advantage for us.*
Annie stared into Emma's blue eyes, eyes that gleamed with a cold
intelligence. Annie sank back into the seat and Emma released her
grip. Annie wanted to bang out of the Rolls, run like the wind to the
station, find Max, but she understood on a gut level that she had to
listen to Emma.

"Max is in custody. I don't know if he's been arrested yet, but the
evidence against him is staggering." Emma was calm but emphatic.

Annie wanted to shout that an accusation against Max was absurd.
He'd taken on an assignment, been caught up in something not of
his making, but she remembered Billy's grim gaze and the abandoned
Jag with the bloodied tire tool in the open trunk. "Once he tells us
what happened—"

Emma flapped a stubby hand in dismissal. "Perps always have a
story. Cops look at evidence. That's why he'll likely be taken before
a circuit court judge and charged with murder. I'm afraid it may be
up to us to prove he's innocent. Find out what Max knows. Call me
on your cell when you leave the station. Here's how you can get inside. . . ."

Blinding lights from the television crews illuminated the front steps
of the Broward's Rock Police Station. Despite Lou Pirelli's shouts
through a bullhorn, a crowd of media and tourists attracted by the
excitement jammed the sidewalk, overflowed onto the front lawn.

"Keep the walk clear. Back off." Despite Lou's roar, his voice was scarcely heard above the din of shouted questions, the shuffle of shoes on the street, and car horns. "Clear the walk."

Annie was at the far edge of the crowd near a line of palmettos that screened the fenced area behind the station. Beyond the glare of the television, the crowd was a dark mass in the shadows. The only other illumination came from streetlamps spaced along the harbor-front and light spilling across the water from boat cabins. Annie edged behind the palms, intending to slip through the darkness to the back door. A rising murmur of expectation from the crowd kept her in place. A patrol car, red light whirling, turned the corner. The siren shrilled in short bursts and cars moved out of the way.

Annie watched, her heart thudding. The car stopped, lights still flashing. Someone in the crowd shouted, "He's in the back seat."

"Make way," Lou's voice boomed. Lou moved down the walk, gesturing for the onlookers to move back. At the curb, he opened the back door, reached inside.

Max came out of the seat, Lou's hand firmly on his elbow. Flashlights flared. Max's hair was tangled, his face unshaven. He looked exhausted and bewildered. His T-shirt and khakis were wrinkled and dirty. His hands were manacled in front.

Reporters surged forward, pressed around Lou and his prisoner. Harsh quick questions came from every side: "Did you kill her, Darling?" "What happened? Lovers' quarrel?" "Who is she?" "How did you meet her?" "Were you drunk?"

"Max . . ." Annie mouthed his name. She balled her hands into tight fists. His pallor and the slight unsteadiness as he walked frightened her. His face was sunken. What had they done to him? She tried to move into the crowd, found the way barred by bulky stubborn bodies. She had to reach him.

"Out of the way," Lou roared. "Get back or be arrested for interfering with officers in discharge of their duty."

Max stared out at the crowd, eyes squinting against the harsh lights. The thin redheaded policewoman was at one side, Lou at the other.

Annie felt sick and furious. Damn them. Damn them all.

The reporters' shouted questions were louder. "Why'd you kill her? Was she trying to blackmail you?" "Was she trying to break up with you?" "Where'd you hide?"

Annie felt crushed by sweaty bodies pressing toward the sidewalk. She shouldn't have tried to get through. Emma had told her what to do. Annie struggled to turn around. She jabbed and poked, ignoring startled cries, and reached the outskirts of the crowd. She darted across the uneven ground to the palmettos and ducked behind them. No one paid attention to her. Every eye looked toward the front steps of the station. Annie ran, sweating in the hot August night. She fell once, tumbling over a palm frond lying on the ground.

She stayed in the shadow of the palms when she reached the rear of the building. A huge light illuminated the back door and the narrow concrete porch. She looked toward the Sound. Once she neared the steps, she would be as visible as a moth impaled on a pin. Anyone on a boat would be able to see her. But it was her only chance.

Emma's instructions had been precise. "Go in the back entrance. Act like you belong."

Annie took a deep breath, squared her shoulders. She walked briskly up the sidewalk as if she were staff and on her way to work. She felt neon conspicuous in the apple green cotton sweater and white capri pants she'd put on without thought this morning. She hardly looked official. But who would care about someone entering the back with a captive Max on view to the world on the front steps? The circus always drew the crowd, and the circus was in front of the station. Fragments of thought roiled in her mind. . . . *Max looked awful . . . How had Emma gotten the code to the keypad on the back door? Did she get the right code? Would it work? If it worked and Annie got inside, what was she going to do? Oh, Max, Max . . .*

Annie climbed the steps, punched the numbers: one-three-five-seven. She grabbed the metal handle, pulled. The door swung out. Annie slipped inside, shut it behind her. She rested against the cold metal panel, drawing in deep gulps of air. She stood in a cement-floored corridor between two empty cells. Dim lights burned high in each cell. Each unoccupied windowless cell contained a metal bunk with a thin mattress, a toilet, and a washbasin. No sound penetrated the thick walls. Silence surrounded her, an oppressive silence compounded by the dim lighting, stale air, and waiting cells. Ahead was another steel door like the one behind her. Both doors were controlled by keypads.

Beyond that door . . . Annie tried to remember the layout of the station. Billy had finally moved into the chief's office, since Pete Garrett wasn't coming back. That was the biggest office of three on the north side of the building. One office was shared by the patrol officers. Across the hall were an interrogation room, a conference hall, and a break room with adjoining restrooms.

Annie pushed away from the back door, walked swiftly up the corridor. She raised her hand to the interior door's keypad, then hesitated. If she opened the door to the main hallway, she might be immediately discovered. She was under no illusions. Billy Cameron might be her friend, but friendship stopped at the front door of the station. He would demand to know how she'd gained access to the station. She had no intention of telling him. Emma was not without resources, including Joe Ray Lucas, a local high school computer wizard who kept Emma's computers up and running. Emma said Joe Ray could crack any system. Annie intended to stay mum about Emma. She'd simply claim the doors were open. Who could prove differently? Annie whirled, hurried back to the exit. She punched the keypad, opened the door, covered her finger with the hem of her blouse and depressed the lock. One door open. She turned, raced to the door to the main hall. Quickly she punched the pad and eased the door open. Once again, finger covered, she depressed the lock. If they found her, if Billy asked, she'd say, *I knocked and when no one came, I opened the door. Locked? Why, it opened right up. . . .*

Annie held the interior door ajar, pressed her ear against the crack.

"... what the hell's going on?" Max's voice was rough and angry and underneath Annie heard a thread of fear. "Who's dead? Why am I being held? Your new cop wouldn't tell me anything, wouldn't let me call Annie. Billy, I've got to talk to Annie. She'll be scared as hell. I've got to tell her this is some kind of mistake."

Billy was brusque. "You're claiming you don't know the woman who was killed last night? Or how she died?"

"Last night?" There was a wondering tone in Max's voice.

"The victim was last seen with you Monday night at Dooley's Mine." Billy sounded irritated. "Her body was found this afternoon. You've been missing since Monday night and—"

Max interrupted. "What day is it?"

"Tuesday. Tuesday night."

"Oh my God. Tuesday ..." Max's voice was hollow, stricken. "You've got to call Annie, let her know where I am."

Annie pushed against the door until she could see a slice of the hallway. Billy and Max stood only a few feet away. Past them, watching with a frown, was the new policewoman.

"He was walking up Goose Creek Road. In the dark." Her tone was accusatory. "The dogs found him and—"

"I'll talk to him, Hyla. Check with Mavis. See what you can do in front with that mob."

Max took a step closer to Billy. "You've got to call Annie—"

Billy held up his hand. "I expect she knows. Everybody's been looking for you and Emma Clyde's organized everything. I just had a call from her, so I'm sure Annie knows, but I'll have Mavis call her. Max, I need to warn you. Everything you say may be . . ."

Annie listened to the Miranda warning, saw the look of dogged determination on Billy's face.

Max stared at his old friend. Shock and disbelief flattened the muscles of his worn face. "Billy, I don't know what's happened. Tell me."

Billy shook his head. "We'll get to that. Emma called to say that Handler Jones, that criminal lawyer from Chastain, is on the way. We'll wait until he gets here and then—"

There was a flurry of sound from the front of the hallway. Mayor Cosgrove's high-pitched voice was shrill with excitement. "Chief, the media is waiting. We'll make a joint appearance to announce the arrest." The mayor's portly figure came into view. He was nattily dressed in a gray pinstripe suit, blue shirt, and red tie. Annie knew this wasn't the mayor's customary attire on a Tuesday night in August. Usually he could be seen strolling the boardwalk in a flamboyant Hawaiian shirt, khaki shorts, and espadrilles, greeting residents and tourists with smiles.

Billy stood like a rock in the hallway, his big face drawn in a frown. "There's been no arrest."

"No arrest?" The mayor's pale green eyes bulged. "What do you mean? I told the media we'd have an announcement pronto. They're out there waiting, Fox, CNN, NBC, CBS, MSNBC, ABC, TBS. The nation's watching. This will put Broward's Rock on the tourist map. We'll outdraw Kiawah and Pawleys Island. Everybody will see that this town stands for something. We don't care how rich a man is—if he's a murderer, we grab him." Cosgrove's glare at Max was equal parts venom, triumph, and pleasure.

Annie had never liked Mayor Cosgrove. When last year's town budget was drawn up, he'd tried to cut the share allocated to the Haven from the local community chest funds. Max volunteered at the Haven, the recreation center for low-income kids. Max had challenged the mayor at a vociferous meeting of the town council and won the day to the cheers of the audience. The mayor had yielded with apparent good humor—"I am here to serve my constituents"—but his green eyes had glittered with fury.

"We've picked up a suspect." Billy's tone was dogged. "That's as far as it goes. He's got a right to a lawyer. When the lawyer gets here, we'll have a formal interrogation. When I've gathered that information, I'll decide whether there is sufficient evidence to make an arrest."

The mayor's face turned blotchy. "I told the media we'd have an announcement. You be out there in five minutes and you better have a statement ready." He turned and stalked toward the front of the station.

When the door slammed, Billy turned to Max. He pulled a key from his pocket. "I'll take off those handcuffs."

A clink and rattle and the cuffs were loose in Billy's hand.

Max rubbed at one wrist. "So I'm not under arrest?"

"No." Billy was gruff. "I learned how to investigate from a good chief. I do it the way Frank did."

Frank Saulter had been the chief of police when Annie first came to Broward's Rock. She wished Frank were here now, but Billy would do his best to follow his old chief's example.

"We'll have a formal interrogation as soon as your lawyer arrives. If you can explain what happened . . ." Billy broke off, his face weary and sad. "Until then, you'll have to wait. I have to put you in a cell. If I had enough staff, I'd let you wait in the interrogation room, but everybody's busy and I'm shorthanded." Billy gestured toward the end of the hall.

Max lifted a shaky hand to his face. He swayed.

"Hey, Max." Billy frowned. "You okay?"

"My head hurts like hell. I was sick when I woke up. I threw up. I'm thirsty. God, I'm thirsty." Max's face squeezed in thought. "I can remember that I was hot and sweaty and wanted a beer and then I don't remember anything."

Billy's look was thoughtful. "How about food? When did you last eat?"

"Food?" Max sounded vague. "I had lunch with Annie."

"Monday?" The question was swift.

"Monday." Max rubbed at his face. "Yeah, it was Monday and you say . . ." His voice trailed off.

"We'll get you some food and water. As soon as I get you settled in the cell, I'll bring you a bottle of water and a Pepsi from the break room." Billy jerked his head toward the end of the hall. "Come on."

Annie eased the door shut, sprang the lock. She looked frantically up and down the corridor between the cells. No place to hide. She raced to the exit door, pushed it open, swept her hand down to re-lease the lock, closed the door behind her. She walked down the steps as if this were a customary departure. Not too fast. Not too slow. She forced herself to stay on the crushed-shell path until she was at the edge of the lighted area, then took three swift steps into darkness and the shelter of a live oak.

She tried to gauge the time it would take for Billy to lock Max in a cell, go to the break room for water and a soda, and return. She had to wait long enough, but not too long. Billy would likely send Lou on foot to Parotti's for food. That would be quicker than getting a cruiser through the crush of traffic outside the station. Annie had to get inside after Billy departed and before Lou arrived.

She waited seven minutes. She stared at the luminous dial of her watch. Never had time passed this slowly. Finally, knowing this was her one chance, afraid to try, afraid not to, she moved out from the shadows of the live oak, once again walked briskly toward the back door. As she punched the code into the keypad, eased open the door, she strained to hear within, blocking out the distant rumble of the crowd.

No sound. Nothing. Not a voice. Not a footstep. Annie pushed the door open, slipped inside. Once again she depressed the lock before pulling the door shut behind her. Her first glance was toward the interior door. It was closed.

Max sat on the bunk, head back, Pepsi can tilted high. He drank in a long gurgle as if desperate for liquid. The hand holding the can quivered.

Annie dashed up the corridor. "Max." Her voice was low and anguished, loving and frantic.

He jerked toward the bars, stared in disbelief, then scrambled to his feet, the soda can tumbling from his hand. "Annie." His drawn, beard-stubbled face lighted with joy.

They came together at the bars, reached out to each other. Annie felt his lips against her cheek. ". . . don't know what happened . . . don't remember . . . woke up and it was dark . . . thought it was yesterday . . ."

Annie smoothed back a tangle of lank hair from his forehead. "I was so afraid. Oh, Max"—tears ran down her cheeks—"I was so afraid. I thought you were dead." Her voice broke.

"Hey, I'm all right." He held her arm, his hand warm and reassuring and precious against her skin.

But he wasn't. He was in terrible trouble. The pressure of passing time, minute after minute clicking past, pushed against her. She wanted to kiss him, caress him, welcome him back to life and love, and there was no time. She bent nearer, felt the hard, unyielding pressure of steel against her shoulder. She talked fast. "I have to leave before they come with food. Do you remember—"

"Wait." His voice was urgent. "Annie, tell me what's happened. Those reporters yelled at me, asking me if I killed her. Who do they think I killed?"

She told him about Dooley's Mine and Vanessa Taylor and how it looked like he was on a date and had too much to drink.

Bewildered, he shook his head, then grimaced at the pain. "No. No way. I was trying to help her find her brother. And her name wasn't Vanessa. Her name . . ." He looked helpless and frightened. "Oh, God, I don't remember."

Annie held tight to his hand. "She must have given you a fake name. But she was Vanessa Taylor and she lived here on the island. She drove your car away with you in the passenger seat. That's the last time she was seen alive. They found the car this afternoon at a fishing cabin. She was dead in the cabin and the tire tool in the trunk had blood on it. And you were gone."

"Oh my God." He breathed the words, his eyes dark with shock. His hands fell slack at his side. "Blood—" If possible, his wan face went even paler. "My shirt had blood on it. I woke up in some cabin. I don't even know where it was. I was sick. I went in the bathroom and washed my face and I smelled blood—"

She heard the frisson of horror in his voice.

"—and my shirt felt sticky." He licked his lips. "I don't remember much at all. I was mad. I know that. Something she did, the girl who hired me. But that wasn't her name." His voice was shaky. "I don't remember her damn name. What did this Vanessa Taylor look like?"

Annie described dark hair and sultry eyes and vivid red lips.

Max was nodding. "Yeah. That sounds like her. She came to the office. She wanted me to look for her brother. I don't know what she did that made me mad." Fear roughened his voice. "I don't know how blood got on me. They think she was killed with my tire tool?"

"Stop it." She pressed her fingers against his cheek, turned his face toward her. She saw uncertainty and unreasoning fear in his gaze. "You never hurt anyone. Never. We'll find out what happened. There must have been something in your drink. Max, you must have been drugged."

The rigidity eased from his body. He took a deep breath. "Drugged." He clawed at his bristly face. His body sagged in relief. "That's why I got sick. That's why I don't remember." He blinked, worrying it in his mind. "You said I was at that tavern with her? Why?"

Annie wished Billy could see Max's blank stare. He not only didn't know Vanessa Taylor, he didn't remember being at Dooley's Mine. She knew his lack of response to Vanessa's name meant that she had been a stranger to him. But only she knew Max's every expression, gradations of humor or interest or knowledge or disgust or happiness. Max's face at this moment was proof of his innocence, but it wasn't proof the world would accept.

He frowned. "Was anybody with us?"

Annie remembered Billy's grim report. "No. Just the two of you."

Max jammed a hand through his hair. "Then she must have doped me. Why would she do that? I was helping her. We were going to look for her brother."

"I found a real estate circular under your desk pad. Did it have something to do with her brother? It's an old, broken-down house." The kind of house where bad things could happen. She looked at him hopefully. Maybe the house would help Max remember.

"Real estate . . ." A look of inexpressible sadness touched his face. "Oh yeah. The Franklin house. No. That doesn't have anything to do with her. Whoever she was." He shook his head. "The Franklin house doesn't matter now. Oh God, I don't understand why I was at Dooley's Mine. I don't remember going there but it must have had something to do with her brother. If," he spelled it out, his voice puzzled, "it was just the two of us, she drugged me. Why?"

Annie knew his reasoning was sound and yet it made no sense. It was Vanessa who had died. What had prompted her to decoy Max to the tavern then drug him so that he appeared to be drunk? Certainly she wouldn't have connived her own death.

Annie felt sick and terrified. No one would believe that Vanessa had drugged Max. And there was the further horror of blood on Max's shirt. Each new fact was worse than the one before. She hadn't believed anything could be more incriminating than the tire tool, but a bloodied shirt . . . By now the dogs would have led the way to the cabin where Max had been. The police would have found the shirt. Max was caught in a devilish trap. She'd hoped he would be able to explain, tell them what had happened to him on Monday night. Now she knew better. Max couldn't help.

And the minutes clicked by. She looked at her watch, tried to figure how much time had passed. Billy would have called in an order. Ben Parotti would hurry to get it ready. Lou was likely even now walking back to the station, sack in hand.

"We'll find out." She hoped Max didn't hear the hollow sound of her voice. How could they get past the dreadful facts, discover meaning and reason behind the circumstances that made it look as though Max was a philandering husband and a murderer? She fought anguish as she looked at him. "You're here. You're safe. We'll find out what happened. The lawyer will be here soon. Tell him to call me as soon as you've spoken to him. Tell him to report everything to us. Emma and I and everyone who's helping, we'll find out what happened. Here's what we know now. . . ."

When she finished, he rubbed knuckles against a grimy cheek.

"So somebody got in the office using my keys and deleted the file. I was helping her look for her brother—"

"We'll sort that out later." Annie knew it was time to go.

"Later—" He looked around the cell, took a deep breath. "This is a hell of thing. I don't see any way out."

"Somebody planned this." She felt a quiver of horror at the thought.

They embraced, the bars hard between them, shared one last kiss.

Billy Cameron stepped through the front door of the station into the glare of the television lights. He had no difficulty looking solemn. He felt like a man walking out toward a twenty-foot wave, knowing that at the slightest misstep he would be crushed. If he'd been a betting man looking on from the outside, he'd have said the suspect was guilty, ten to one. Billy was on the inside and the suspect was a friend he'd known for years. If the mayor hadn't shown up, lusting for Max's arrest like a shark scenting blood, Billy would have limited his statement to the fact that the investigation was continuing and a news conference would be held the next morning at ten. Now the mayor stood at his elbow, jiggling with impatience, and Billy had to face reporters as hungry for news as starved dogs.

Billy clutched a sheet of paper in his hand. He looked out at the throng of reporters and behind them a close-packed crowd. "The investigation into the murder of Miss Vanessa Taylor is continuing. Miss Taylor's body was found at four-eighteen this afternoon in a rental cabin on River Otter Road. The victim had been dead for approximately twenty to twenty-four hours. Cause of death was blunt trauma, including a crushed brain stem. Miss Taylor was last seen alive on Monday evening at Dooley's Mine, a local restaurant, in the company of Mr. Maxwell Darling. Mr. Darling is presently cooperating with the police in their investigation." He heard the mayor draw in an exasperated breath. Billy continued in a brisk monotone. "In line with the policy of the Broward's Rock Police Department as established by the town council, witnesses are afforded an opportunity to confer with counsel before interrogation. As the investigation is ongoing, no further information can be released at this time. Mayor Cosgrove is giving his personal attention—" Billy looked toward the mayor.

Cosgrove gave a dignified nod, his face avuncular for the cameras, but his swift stare at Billy was cold and hard.

"—to the investigation. The mayor has pledged that every resource of the community will be devoted to solving this crime. Thank you for your attention."

Billy turned, ignoring the shouts behind him. "The mayor said an arrest had occurred. What's the deal? Is an arrest imminent?" "Are there any other suspects?" "What's Darling's story? Where's he been?" "Was she married?" "Was she pregnant?" "What does 'blunt trauma' mean? Was she beaten?" "How about the weapon? Was it found? Any fingerprints?"

The mayor was right behind Billy when the door closed. "I've been on the phone to the circuit solicitor. I told him what you had and he said that's plenty for an arrest. He'll be here in the morning. We can set up a ten o'clock news conference at City Hall." Cosgrove smoothed back a thin strand of pale hair. His stare challenged Billy. "I'll see you then."

Annie reached the parking lot of the Sea Side Inn, three blocks from the police station. She'd walked fast after calling Emma, arranging to meet her in the shadows at the back of the hotel parking lot. The lights of Emma's Rolls pierced the gloom beneath the overhanging branches of the live oaks. Annie ran the last few steps, opened the door, slid into the passenger seat.

A glad cry came from the back. "Annie, my sweet. Did you see our dear boy?"

Annie felt lifted by her mother-in-law's memorable, husky voice. It was almost as if a cloud of joy flowed toward Annie, surrounding her, banishing the pain of Max's haggard face, the uncertainty in his eyes. Max was alive, oh glory be. Annie found herself speaking with energy. "He's fine, but he doesn't know what happened to him last night." Quickly Annie shared the little she knew. "He'll have the lawyer call us."

Laurel leaned forward, patted Annie's shoulder. "Be of good cheer. We can accomplish what we must."

Food helped. Water helped even more. The memory of Annie's face—the faith in her eyes, the comfort of her touch, the determination in her voice—helped most of all. Max jammed a hand through his tangled hair, started to shake his head impatiently, winced. Despite the water and two Advil, his head still ached. Instead he spoke gingerly. "I don't remember anything after the volleyball game. I went to the beach to look for her brother. She thought he was hiding out here on the island, that maybe he'd got into trouble over drugs."

Handler Jones took off his horn-rim glasses. With them, he looked close to forty. Without, he might have been twenty-five. Lean and lanky in a summer seersucker suit, he had a shock of chestnut hair, bright blue eyes, and a cheerful expression. He didn't look like one of the South's most successful trial lawyers. He looked like a scout-master or a lifeguard or a long-distance runner. He had continued to smile despite Max's halting, incomplete, uneven recollections. Now he tapped the glasses against the legal pad filled with quick, neat printing. "Here's what we'll do. First thing, we'll demand a blood test. That will prove you were drugged. I'll arrange for an expert to search your computer's hard drive for that missing file. I'll get an inquiry started tonight into the woman's background."

Max felt as if a heavy weight had been lifted. Once that file was found, it would prove he'd been hired.

The glasses slid back into place. "You can make a statement. I'll announce to the press that you are cooperating fully, that you were engaged by a woman to search for a missing relative, that you did not know Vanessa Taylor and have no knowledge pertaining to her murder or to any events of the evening of Monday, August 16, moreover that you suffer from amnesia resulting from a drug administered to you without your knowledge. But"—for the first time he didn't smile—"it's obvious you are going to be arrested for her murder."

Billy Cameron's eyes burned with fatigue. He picked up the Dr Pepper can, drank, wrinkled his nose when he realized the soda was tepid and flat. What was it, his fifth or sixth today? He had trouble remembering when Tuesday had started. He glanced at the wall clock. Just short of midnight. He's sent everyone home, Mavis looking weary and forlorn, Lou Pirelli uncharacteristically somber, Hyla Harrison excited at her involvement in a cause célèbre. Now Billy was all alone in the station. Except for the prisoner, of course. Was Max asleep? He was fed and shaved and showered, dressed in an orange jail jumpsuit. He'd been afforded counsel, made a statement, signed it, been booked and charged with murder. Tomorrow morning Mayor Cosgrove would bustle out onto the front steps and announce the arrest to the waiting media.

Billy looked at his desk. Folders were skewed across the surface. The nearest, a bright blue, held Max's statement. Billy stared at the folder. He'd had no choice but to arrest Max. Billy leaned back in his chair, folded his hands behind his head, stared at the ceiling. He didn't need to refresh his memory of Max's answers. And lack of answers.

Max claimed a woman, not calling herself Vanessa Taylor, came to Confidential Commissions Monday afternoon, hired him to look for her missing brother. He denied knowing Vanessa Taylor and insisted he wasn't involved romantically with her. "... this woman was a client. She walked in the door Monday afternoon and I'd never seen her before in my life."

Max had no memory of going to Dooley's Mine. "... she talked about it. That's where her brother was supposed to be ... she had a snapshot of him, check her purse ... playing volleyball ... blue swimsuit ... that's why I went to Blackbeard Beach ..."

Max insisted he didn't know where she'd died. When told of the cabin's location, he maintained he had never seen it. "... never been to any fishing cabin on River Otter Road."

Max said he hadn't touched his tire tool since he'd had a flat last spring. "... you can check with the Gas 'N' Go. I brought a tire in early April."

Max swore he wasn't the figure Annie glimpsed Monday night in Confidential Commissions. "That's crazy. Why would I delete that file? Don't you see, that proves somebody set me up."

Max described the cabin where he'd awakened. "... don't know how I got there. You'll find where I was sick. I figured it out. She must have drugged me at Dooley's Mine. Something knocked me out. That explains why I don't remember anything after going to the beach. When I made it to the bathroom, I was washing up and I smelled blood ..."

Billy lifted his arms, stretched, trying to ease a cramp in his shoulders. He'd promised Mavis he'd settle on the cot in the break room as soon as possible. But not yet. Not quite yet.

Billy drew the chair closer to the desk made for him by his stepson. Billy was as proud of the desk as if it had been specially ordered from a fine furniture store. He shifted the desk pad to protect his arm from the sticky varnish. The varnish hadn't dried properly and the desk had an uneven cant from a short leg. Kevin had made the desk for him in a woodworking class at the Haven. Without Max, there wouldn't have been enough money to open the pool this summer. . . .

Billy glanced at the slew of folders. He had to make sense of everything he'd discovered this afternoon as well as the information Lou and Mavis had gathered. But first, before time dulled his recollections, he wanted to record his visit to the home of Vanessa Taylor's employer, wealthy Lillian Whitman Dodd.

Billy remembered one of Frank Saulter's dictums: When it's murder, start at home. Vanessa Taylor may have died in a fishing shack, but that wasn't where she began her last day. When he'd jotted down his observations, he realized he'd been bugged by Mrs. Dodd's response. Sure, the news of Vanessa's murder shocked her, but there was something more. He frowned, trying to evaluate Mrs. Dodd's response. Had there been a glimmer of fear? Billy shook his head impatiently. Time enough to wonder about Mrs. Dodd and the household where Vanessa lived. Now he needed to face the facts as he'd found them, without favor or detriment to Max.

Billy knew the mayor would dismiss this exercise as a waste of time, but after midnight Billy considered he was on his own time. He shifted folders, checked information, searched out disparate facts, made quick notes. When he was done, he studied the sheets:

Evidence of Accused's Guilt
   1. *Observed with victim at bar, appeared on intimate terms with her.*
      His demeanor suggested a disagreement or quarrel with victim.

2. *Victim last seen alive in company of accused. Victim's fingerprints found on steering wheel of accused's Jaguar. Victim's car found in parking lot near marina shops, suggesting she and accused left area together.*

3. *Accused's Jaguar found in proximity to body. Tire tool found in trunk confirmed as murder weapon. Accused's fingerprints (smudged) on tire tool.*

4. *Accused's bloodstained shirt found in cabin less than half mile from murder site. Attempt had been made to wash out bloodstains. Awaiting laboratory confirmation confirming stains from victim's blood.*

5. *Entry into accused's place of business accomplished without break-in, suggesting use of keys. No computer file found to prove accused's claim he was hired by victim.*

6. *Preliminary report of victim's family lists as survivor one sister. The contents of her purse did not include snapshots of a young man in blue trunks playing volleyball.*

Evidence of Accused's Innocence

1. *No trace of accused's fingerprints found at cabin where death occurred. Particular attention was paid to door panels, champagne bottle, table. Several surfaces did not reveal prints, indicating the area had been polished.*

2. *Bloodhounds did not trace accused from car containing murder weapon to murder cabin or from murder cabin to cabin where accused apparently stayed on Monday night. Since the Jaguar was parked at the crime scene and the dogs found no trail indicating the accused walked to the second cabin, it appears the accused must have been transported in a second car. What car and who drove it?*

3. *The victim's fingerprints found only on driver's door, driver's seat, and steering wheel in accused's Jaguar, which precludes her having been a passenger in the car and makes the location of her car irrelevant.*

4. *Results of blood test indicate accused had imbibed gamma-hydroxybutyrate, known on the street as Liquid Ecstasy, Goop, Scoop, or Georgia Homeboy. In combination with alcohol, the drug can cause amnesia and incoherence. Accused claims he was administered the drug without his knowledge, did not take it voluntarily.*

5. *Silver car left Dooley's Mine shortly after the Jaguar departed.*

6. *Island realtor Cynthia Darrough—*

Billy drew a line through number 6. As the circuit solicitor would emphasize, the realtor's report concerning Max and the boarded-up Franklin house was hearsay and clearly irrelevant to the crime. But to Billy, her poignant recital was the last bit of information he needed to convince him that Max was not the unfaithful husband he'd been set up to appear.

Billy studied the list. Number 5 might turn out to be the most important fact he'd learned. Frank Saulter always said, "Look for the anomaly." Billy hadn't known the word when he first heard it. He'd listened and nodded and later he'd gone to the library and looked up *anomaly*. The definition stuck. Abnormality. That's what Frank meant. Look for something odd, something that doesn't make sense, something not in the natural order of events. Monday night the Jag turned left on River Otter Road, heading toward a dead end. Seconds later a silver car also left the bar's parking lot and it too turned left. If that wasn't damned odd, Billy didn't know what would be. Two cars turned toward a dead end within seconds of each other. Two drivers who didn't know their way? Or one car following the other? Or two cars with a common destination, the fishing shack on the marsh? A second car—Billy frowned, shuffled through papers. Yeah. here it was. Ted Dooley said Vanessa came running after Max in the parking lot at Dooley's Mine. That was another anomaly for sure. If they'd arrived in the same car, they would have walked together. Even if they'd been fighting and he'd walked on ahead of her—and what would be the sense of that?—they should have been within a few steps of each other. If Vanessa came hurrying across the lot to catch up with Max, maybe she came separately. Billy had the same quick surge of excitement he felt when a bass tugged on his line. He'd bet the station that Vanessa Taylor reached Dooley's Mine in the silver car that later followed Max's Jaguar onto River Otter Road.

The cell phone in his pocket played its rollicking tune. Billy plucked it from his shirt pocket, looked at caller ID. He punched on. "Yeah."

"Honey, you have to get some sleep." Mavis's voice gentle.

Funny how he felt better knowing she was at home and thinking of him. "Right. Pretty soon. You okay?"

"Lily's got an earache. I've been rocking her." A slow drawn breath. "And watching the news without sound. Saw the mayor. He made a big deal about Max being in custody. The news brief ran under his picture and some pictures of Max being brought into the station: 'Broward's Rock Mayor Cosgrove said apprehension of society suspect exemplified the American ideal of equal justice.'"

Billy grunted. His fingers closed on the empty Dr Pepper can, crushed it.

"The mayor—" Mavis stopped.

"Yeah?" Billy tossed the soda can into the wastebasket.

"On his way out, he said you should be in his office at nine. The circuit solicitor is coming. He said there'd be plenty of time to get all the ducks in a row before the news conference."

Billy waited. He knew his wife, knew there was more that had to be said, something she didn't want to say.

Reluctantly, she spoke. "He said they'd get everything wrapped up in time for you to get off to that conference in Columbia. He said the circuit solicitor can handle everything from here on. He said it's very fortunate for you that the murder is solved and your presence on the island isn't required."

Billy looked at the wall calendar. The annual state law officer's seminar in Columbia was set for Wednesday through Friday. He always looked forward to attending. If he were involved in a major investigation, he would cancel.

"He said it was essential for you to attend, that he couldn't recommend you to the council to replace Pete Garrett until you complete that advanced course in antiterrorism."

Billy gripped the phone. There was silence but between them ran that current of perfect understanding that a good marriage enjoys.

Finally, gruffly, he spoke. "I got to think."

"I know. Do what you have to do. Love you." The connection ended.

It was nearing one in the morning when Billy walked down the hallway to the break room. He washed his face, settled on the cot in a curtained alcove. He stared into darkness. Tomorrow morning when he met with the mayor and the circuit solicitor, he could insist on investigating further or he could agree the case was solved and out of his hands and leave for Columbia. If he insisted on investigating further, the odds were good the mayor would put him on unpaid leave. That would effectively shut down the investigation.

Either he played ball or he'd be out of the game. That was the black and white of it. But Frank Saulter had another dictum: Don't show your hand.

Frank played his cards close to his vest. Maybe Billy could do the same. Maybe he could play the high-stakes game of his life. In the morning, he'd agree the case was closed. He'd go to Columbia. It would be up to Mavis and Lou and Hyla to keep on looking. If the mayor found out the search was still on, Billy's career would be finished, kaput, done, smashed.

Billy stared into darkness.

5

Summer sunlight streamed through the ceiling-high windows of Emma Clyde's garden room. In the blaze of sunshine, the boyish face of Handler Jones looked every one of its forty-six years. The glare revealed crow's-feet edging sapphire blue eyes, highlighted streaks of silver in chestnut hair, emphasized blondish fuzz on unshaven cheeks. His blue seersucker suit, though expensive and well fitted, was wrinkled and creased.

He stood in the center of the room. Horn-rim glasses in one hand, Jones looked at each of them in turn, Annie and Emma sharing the white sofa, Laurel perched on a sea blue ottoman, Henny with a pad and pencil at the Queen Anne desk. He drawled, "Ladies, forgive my disreputable appearance." His words flowed thick as honey. "I worked late last night—"

Annie knew that was true. She'd spoken with him on the phone for almost an hour after he left Max at the jail. From Billy's questions, he'd gleaned the facts of the prosecution's case. From Annie, he learned about Max's call just before five on Monday and her frightening encounter at Confidential Commissions that night. He'd listened, asked quick, perceptive questions, bid her good night with a cheerful assurance that Max was in good hands.

"—getting materials together. Now here's our situation—"

Annie had looked him up in Martindale-Hubbell. Before they gathered at Emma's for an early lunch and council of war, she knew Jones's age, education (the Citadel, Vanderbilt law), firm (Jones and Associates), major clients, dramatic successes.

"—the arraignment is set for two o'clock this afternoon at the courthouse in Beaufort. We'll try to get him out on bail, but in a high-profile case such as this, it's unlikely the judge will agree. He's already been transferred to the county detention center."

Annie pushed away the image of Max being taken in handcuffs from the station. The last time they'd taken the ferry to the mainland, they'd been on their way to the waterfront in Savannah to watch the Fourth of July fireworks.

"Even if we can't get bail set"—Jones was cheerful—"there are definitely points in this case that I can use to argue if we get to trial." He shot Emma Clyde an admiring glance. "Ms. Clyde did us a great service by hiring the bloodhounds, making that search. Our strongest support for the defense is the fact the hounds didn't find any trace of Max between his car and the murder cabin. I'll press the prosecution for proof he was in the cabin. If they can't come up with fingerprints or any trace of his presence in the murder cabin, we'll have another strong argument for the defense."

Annie remembered the down-at-heels cabin with its weathered wooden steps. Murder cabin. That's how she would always think of it.

"We have other support for Max's story. My expert found the missing file on the hard drive of Max's office computer. I've printed it out."

Annie felt a surge of hope. Here was confirmation. Billy Cameron would have to listen to this.

Emma clapped her stubby hands together. "That's excellent." Henny smiled as she made notes. Laurel's admiring beam enveloped the lawyer.

Jones paused, looked at Max's mother, elegant and patrician as always, her white-blond hair shining in the shaft of sun, her deep blue eyes aglow with approval. She was slim and appealing in a cornflower blue V-neck blouse and a shimmering shadow-dot blue silk skirt and soft blue lattice slide patent-leather heels.

Annie smiled too. Yes, Max was in terrible trouble and their world had been turned on its ear, but Laurel was always amazing and delightful. Her attraction the opposite sex never failed, from boys of ten to men of ninety. Handler Jones was no exception.

The lawyer stood a little straighter, had the age-old look of man in presence of woman. "Ma'am." He drew out the word like a caress. With a gallant nod toward Laurel, he cleared his throat.

Emma prompted him, her tone dry. "You printed out the file?"

"Ah, the file." His smile was sunny-side up. "It confirms Max's story absolutely, including the time the file was created. It was deleted at 11:56 P.M., which correlates with Annie's call to the police at 12:01 A.M. reporting an intruder. Further, the blood test reveals Max ingested GHB, commonly known as Liquid Ecstasy, Goop, Scoop, or Georgia Homeboy. GHB is one of several drugs often found at raves, the all-night dance parties attended by teens and young adults. These are the date-rape drugs. GHB is a white powder. It easily dissolves in water or alcohol. It causes a variety of effects but when combined with alcohol can make the recipient appear drunk. Further, there were traces of Valium in his blood. This combination could easily affect his speech and gait and put him into a deep sleep."

Annie leaned forward, eager and relieved. "This proves Max

is innocent. They'll have to let him go, start looking for the real murderer."

Handler Jones slowly shook his head. His look at Annie was kindly. "I wish that were so. But the prosecution won't have any trouble with these facts. They'll say he came back to his office after killing her and erased the file to hide his contact with her and then took the drug to try and create an alibi. Here's how the circuit solicitor will make his closing argument if we get to trial." Jones's bent forward, eyes steely, jaw jutting. "Ladies and gentlemen of the jury"—his voice was quick and hard as a sword thrust—"the defendant was desperate to erase evidence of his link to the dead woman. He claims Vanessa Taylor came to him to launch a search for her missing brother, using the name of Bridget Walker. Ladies and gentlemen of the jury, the dead woman *had* no brother. Are we to believe the victim lied? I think not." A sarcastic drawl. "Clearly the defendant created a file to cover his evening out with a woman other than his wife. He made up a search and a brother. Not only did the victim not have a brother, there were no pictures of a young man in blue swim trunks found in her purse. This story, ladies and gentlemen of the jury, was made up out of whole cloth. The fake name was created by the defendant to provide a cover for his illicit relationship. We won't assume the defendant had murder in his heart when he planned an evening out with a beautiful young woman who was not his wife. But sometime that night, passions turned ugly and murder occurred. The defendant is in a quandary. How can he hide the fact that he was in the company of the dead woman? He knows he must erase that computer file because he cannot produce a Bridget Walker to support his claim." Jones's voice rose, filled the garden room. "The testimony of the defendant's wife underscores that it was Maxwell Darling who came to his office in the dark of that deadly night. Ladies and gentlemen of the jury, that office was not broken into." A pause for emphasis. "That office was entered"—he spaced the words dramatically—"with . . . a . . . key. The claim of the defense"—the lawyer's tone was scoffing, dismissive—"that the defendant's drugged state was the result of an amazing conspiracy can be dismissed out of hand. We have testimony that he and the victim were by themselves at Dooley's Mine. No one joined them. No one was seen with them. Are we to believe that the *victim* drugged the defendant? Ladies and gentleman, would you have the victim conniving her own death? No, the answer is clear. The defendant was in an inebriated state when he and his victim departed Dooley's Mine. We know that the two of them drove in his red Jaguar" —heavy emphasis on the make of the car—"to a remote cabin. There she died from the blows of the tire tool from the Jaguar"—heavy emphasis—"and then what did the defendant do? Perhaps he was re-gaining sobriety. He knows he has committed a heinous crime. How can he escape justice? First he hurries to his office, removes the file linking him to the victim. Did he consider surrendering himself? We do not know and the defendant will not say. We do know that he fled to a nearby cabin—"

"The dogs," Emma cut in sharply. "They found no trace of Max between the Jaguar and the murder scene."

Jones waved a dismissive hand. "The defense has put on testi-mony that dogs that investigated the scene found no trace of the defendant between his rich man's Jaguar and the murder cabin. Dogs are not perfect, ladies and gentleman of the jury, but the evidence of blood can be proven without doubt. We know the defendant fled to a nearby cabin and in that cabin we found his shirt—there is no ques-tion about the ownership—his shirt massively stained with the blood of the helpless victim. He tried to wash the blood from the shirt. That must have been a difficult moment for him. Perhaps he felt remorse. We do not know his thoughts, but we know he imbibed drugs and alcohol and sank into unconsciousness."

Jones broke off, looked around the room.

"It's a lie!" Annie's cry was passionate.

Emma reached over, patted her arm. Henny murmured, "Charles Laughton in *Witness for the Prosecution.*" Laurel's radiant look dimmed.

The lawyer was once again affable and charming. "We have a tall mountain to climb, ladies. But that's why I'm here."

Annie was never a fan of braggarts. She didn't like show-offs. Yet there was something enormously appealing and reassuring and comforting in Handler Jones's confidence. Call it chutzpah, arrogance, or audacity, the result was a current of energy that lifted their spirits. Emma's corrugated face was set in determination. Henny said, "Good show," her voice as clipped as Bulldog Drummond. Henny loved role-playing, calling to mind famous mystery sleuths of past and present. Her evocation of H. C. McNeile's stiff-upper-lip sleuth was clearly inspired by Handler Jones's optimism. Laurel blew him a kiss.

Emma's demand was abrupt. "What can we do?"

The lawyer's gaze swept his audience, firm, friendly, energetic. "Our best hope is to discover everything possible about the deceased and see if we can come up with some alternate suspects. With that in mind, I had my team of investigators pull an all-nighter and bring together a dossier on Vanessa Taylor." He bent to his briefcase, pulled out a folder. "I have a copy for each of you." He put on his horn-rims. He looked older, abruptly less cheerful. "We tried to get in touch with her surviving sister. No luck there. She's older than Vanessa, lives in Chicago. Her husband is ill and she takes care of him, works two jobs. The home telephone answering machine has a message saying she declines to speak with any member of the press. I suppose they started pestering her immediately. At her jobs, no one will transfer a call to her. I'll have an operative in Chicago attempt to make contact, but I don't think we'll get any help there. Vanessa's body will be shipped to Chicago when it is released after the autopsy. A funeral is tentatively scheduled for a week from this Wednesday. However, Vanessa and her sister apparently weren't particularly close. Vanessa hadn't been back to Illinois since moving here several years ago. I think it's more important to focus on her life here on the island. Let's think for a moment why anyone might have wanted Vanessa Taylor dead."

Annie again pictured him before a jury, hair artfully tousled, handsome face expressive, making point after point.

"The usual motives for murder"—he might have been a professor explaining the structure of an atom—"are hatred, jealousy, greed, fear, and revenge. Hatred? According to my sources, Vanessa was attractive, lively, charming, a good companion. She did not appear to have a relationship with anyone that was intense enough to cause hatred. Jealousy? There are possibilities here. If she was involved with a man, was she trying to end the affair? Greed? This doesn't seem likely. She had no money aside from her salary and no one profits from her death. Fear? Did she threaten someone in some way? We don't know. Revenge seems unlikely. But we do know"—his voice rose with confidence—"that her death was the result of a carefully laid plan created specifically to shield the murderer. And I believe"—he leaned forward—"that her murderer is a man. Max was set up to look like a philandering husband—"

Annie wanted to flail at the world. This was the picture of Max being flashed on television screens everywhere. It was a lie and cruel and bitter to endure.

"—taking a woman to a seedy bar. The plan was to incapacitate Max. The murderer had to be strong enough to handle Max when he lost consciousness. That argues Vanessa's co-conspirator was a man. Moreover, Vanessa was bludgeoned to death. I'm not saying a woman could not have done it, but in my experience that method of murder is unlikely for a woman."

Emma was emphatic. *"Cherchez l'homme."*

"We have to find him." The lawyer gave a quick frown. "But as far as my team was able to discover, Vanessa wasn't involved publicly with any man. This is a roadblock." It wasn't Jones's nature to admit discouragement, but his usual smile slid away. "Obviously we will continue to search. The long and short of it is that she lived very quietly in the home of her employer. She took her meals with the family. Mrs. Dodd has declined to make a public statement. We traced Vanessa back to her arrival on the island a few years ago. She came here with a college friend, waited tables at Parotti's Bar and Grill. She answered an ad in the *Gazette* and got the job as Mrs. Dodd's secretary a year and a half ago. Her ex-roommate married and now lives in Des Moines. Name's Judy Denton. One of my operatives contacted her. Judy said she and Vanessa e-mailed and Vanessa's e-mails revolved around the family. Vanessa didn't mention any friends from their time of working at Parotti's or any new friends. Judy was wry about that, said it didn't surprise her, that Vanessa loved the life of the rich and that waitstaff wouldn't fit into that background. Judy said Vanessa would probably have dropped her except their contact was through e-mails and it gave Vanessa a chance to brag about drinking fine wine every night at dinner and parties on yachts and trips to Cape Cod. Judy said Vanessa acted like she was a member of the family, not just an employee. Vanessa helped Mrs. Dodd's daughter shop and was helping her with the wedding plans. Vanessa never mentioned dating. Judy kidded Vanessa about that, asked her if she'd taken a vow of chastity. Vanessa's answer was cryptic. She said she was biding her time. Judy took that to mean Vanessa had her eye on a man but for some reason wasn't able to say anything about him and didn't want to describe him in e-mails. Judy said she frankly couldn't imagine Vanessa without a man in tow, preferably two. She brought up *Gone with the Wind* and Scarlett flirting with the Tarleton twins." He flipped through several sheets, quoted.

"'That's Vanessa. Men buzz around her like flies to a honeypot, just like Scarlett. Vanessa enjoyed sex. There has to be a man in the background somewhere. I don't know why she didn't e-mail about him, but I expect there's a blow-by-blow in her diary.'"

Emma folded stubby fingers into a fist, punched her right hand high. "A man in the background." Her crusty tone exuded satisfaction. "That's how it has to be, of course."

Henny looked at the author inquiringly. Laurel's blue eyes narrowed in thought. The lawyer cocked his head to one side, listening.

Annie had a glimmer of understanding. A man in the background . . .

Emma's gaze was cool and definite. "Vanessa's murder was carefully planned so the blame would fall on Max. Why? Either to destroy Max or to protect the murderer. Does Max have an enemy who would go the length of another person's murder to entrap him?" She looked at Annie.

Annie was emphatic. "No. I'm not saying everybody loves Max"— she thought of Mayor Cosgrove's malicious smirk—"but he certainly doesn't have that kind of enemy."

Emma's spiky iron gray hair quivered as she nodded in agreement. "If the scheme was not a plot against Max, then the circumstances of the murder were arranged to avoid detection of the murderer. Clearly there is an unseen figure at work. Vanessa isn't a woman who cares much about other women. From everything her friend said, Vanessa was all about men and sex. So, yes, somewhere there is a man in the background. He persuaded Vanessa to approach Max, suggested she hire him to search for an imaginary brother. That was a clever touch." There was the novelist's admiring tone in her voice. "It was one more brick of guilt piled on Max. Vanessa had no brother. The pictures she showed Max weren't found in her purse. The file was erased from Max's computer. Think what this tells us." There was a compelling glint in her primrose blue eyes. "Someone programmed all of this. Someone spoke with Vanessa, someone she trusted, someone with whom she was on intimate terms. I suspect very intimate terms. She was persuaded to approach Max—"

Jones broke in, shaking his head. "That's tough to understand." The lawyer was clearly troubled. "That's the weak link in our argument. What conceivable excuse could the murderer give?"

Emma's blue eyes were startled. "Oh, that's easy. He told Vanessa Max had some kind of incriminating information about him and he had to get Max's keys and get into his office. Or he claimed Max was blackmailing him and he wanted to set up a situation where he could get pictures of Max in a compromising situation, maybe snuggled next to Vanessa in a shot that didn't show her face. Or he told Vanessa Max had some kind of plot against the family and if he were under the influence of drugs they could question him, the old truth-serum ploy. Or he—"

Annie intervened, knowing the novelist's inventive mind was quite capable of spinning innumerable variations on her theme. "It doesn't matter how he managed it. We know that's what happened."

"Abominably clever." Henny's dark eyes were somber.

Jones frowned. "That's too complicated for a jury to understand. Or believe."

Annie looked at him sharply. Was there doubt in his voice? But he gave her a quick thumbs-up.

Emma was decisive. "We've got to find the murderer, bring him out of the shadows, get some proof. We have to find out more about Vanessa."

Annie looked out of the window at the battered cream Toyota parked in front of the cabin. It was Duane Webb's fishing car and he'd offered it to Annie to use as long as she stayed at Nightingale Courts. While Ingrid held the fort at Death on Demand, refusing all comment about Annie and Max, and Annie slipped across the island to Emma's house, Duane had once again borrowed his friend's laundry truck and returned to the house on the lagoon where he'd picked up Annie yesterday. Then Duane rowed across the lagoon and slipped inside the back door. "Good thing I went in your house the back way," he told her when he met her back at Nightingale Courts. "I took a look out of the blinds in the living room and there's still two sound trucks and a bunch of reporters. Thought there would be. But I got you a bunch of clothes." He'd placed a suitcase near the bedroom door. And he'd plopped down Dorothy L.'s carrier as well and a sack of her food. He'd smiled when Annie gathered up the plump white cat and held her close. "Thought you could use some company. Give us a ring, anything you need," and he was gone.

Annie glanced at the TV set. She'd turned it off after seeing innumerable shots of a bedraggled, handcuffed Max in soiled T-shirt and chinos and pans of their home, variously described as "Multimillionaire Suspect's Home," "Murder Suspect's Wife Remains Secluded," "No One Answers Door at Suspect's Palatial Residence."

And now . . . Annie paced back and forth in the small living room. Dorothy L. looked up, giving a sharp mew. Annie paused to smooth her thick white fur. Dorothy L. was Max's cat really. She adored Max, followed him from room to room. Annie picked her up, buried her face in sweet-smelling fur. Dorothy L. was patient for a moment, then wriggled free.

Annie resumed pacing. The arraignment would begin in only a few minutes. It was too late for her to reach the mainland and the county courthouse in time. Emma had insisted Annie remain on the island. Handler Jones had spoken with Max, who had specifically ordered Annie not to come. "It will be a circus. I don't want you and Laurel there."

Annie ached inside. She should be there, dreadful as it would be to see Max in an orange jail jumpsuit, hands and ankles manacled. What would the press make of her absence? Would there be snide innuendos: *Members of the murder suspect's family were not in court today to offer support. . . . Annie Darling, wife of the accused, has avoided the press and released statements supportive of her husband only through intermediaries. . . . Repeated calls to the Darling home have gone unanswered. . . . Although unwilling to speak on the record, an island resident said there were rumors of marital discord involving the Darlings. . . .* Annie knew the press would be able to find someone eager to say something negative. None of that mattered. Freeing Max was the only thing that mattered. Emma had been forceful. "We've got to find out everything we can about Vanessa. We don't have any time to waste. You could spend the rest of the day getting from here to the courthouse and back. You won't accomplish a thing going to the arraignment. The upshot would be your picture plastered all over the papers and shown on the nightly news. I've got a hunch"—her blue eyes had glittered like polished steel—"we need to keep you under wraps. I never ignore a hunch. So you keep out of sight and study the dossier."

Annie paced to a wicker chair, forced herself to sit. She reached for the dossier. Maybe this time when she read it, she'd see something she'd missed. Vanessa Taylor had lived for a year and a half at the Whitman house. What did she do for fun? She was a woman who liked men. And they were looking for a man. How could they find out? It was maddening to think that Handler Jones was with Max at this moment, defending him, and she was here, feeling helpless and useless. Emma and Henny were working the telephones, calling every friend and acquaintance in hopes of learning more about the Dodd family. Laurel had murmured vaguely that one of her oldest friends, such a dear man and always so understanding, was just the person to call when wanting to broker something a bit on the unusual side, and with a sweet smile she'd drifted from the room. Annie was glad her mother-in-law felt that someone could help. Of course, a manly presence always bolstered Laurel. Annie wished she had a plan, someplace to go, something to do. Instead she was reduced to rereading the report on Vanessa Taylor.

Her cell phone rang. Quickly she jumped to her feet, found her purse, pulled out the cell. Her hands were hot and sweaty, her heart thumped. Would she ever hear the ring of a cell phone without dread and fear bubbling within? She glanced at caller ID. Unknown caller. It could be a reporter. But it could be something about Max. She punched on.

"Hello." Her throat felt stiff.

"The Chapel of Saint Mary." Billy Cameron spoke softly as if afraid he might be overheard. "Sometimes I stop there in the afternoon to say a prayer."

The connection ended.

The chapel door opened to a cloister. In the courtyard between the chapel and the church, canna lilies, crape myrtle, and hibiscus flowered. A glossy-leaved magnolia drooped over the reflecting pond.

Annie pulled open the heavy red door, stepped into the narthex. Ahead were the double doors into the chapel. To the left was the votive chapel and the stand with votive candles. The draft from the door stirred the flames of a half-dozen lit candles. Annie hesitated, then veered left. She picked up a packet of matches, lit one, held it to a wick, saw the small flame blaze, shining and golden. She knelt and said the familiar prayer with which she began every day: *God be in my head and in my understanding; God be in mine eyes and in my looking; God be in my mouth and in my speaking; God be in my heart and in my thinking; God be at mine end and at my departing.*

When she rose and walked into the nave, she had a sense of peace. She was alone in the chapel. She slipped into one of the back pews, lowered the kneeler, again knelt, closed her eyes in prayer.

In a few minutes, the breeze stirred at her back as the door opened. It sighed to a close and steps sounded on the stone floor, then the kneeler sagged beneath a heavy weight.

She opened her eyes. Billy knelt beside her, head bowed, hands clasped. Annie lifted her gaze to the nearest stained-glass window. Saint George, magnificent in armor touched with gold, rode triumphantly astride a great white horse. He held aloft a mighty lance, poised to slay the fire-breathing dragon lunging toward him. The white of the horse, the gold of the saint's plumed helmet and sword, and the crimson of his saddle glittered bright as jewels.

The kneeler creaked as Billy straightened. "Slaying dragons." Billy's voice was soft in the hushed quiet of the chapel. "That's what I'm supposed to do. Keep the beast away from the people in the city." He shifted on the kneeler and it creaked again.

Still wrapped in peace, Annie looked at her old friend, at a face grooved by weariness, eyes dark with discouragement but gaze steady and determined. He had summoned her here. She waited, knowing he would speak.

"I'm on my way to Columbia. Terrorism course for law enforcement. As far as the mayor's concerned, this case is over. There's some stuff I can do. I've set up a special number for people to call with information about Vanessa Taylor, particularly sightings of her in the last week or so. Vince is going to run a piece in the *Gazette,* asking people to report, anonymously if they wish, any places she was spotted along with a description of her companions. See"—his smile was wry—"I slid that right past the mayor. He thinks I'm looking for confirmation Max was fooling around with her. I figure some man was involved with her and set up an elaborate frame by having her hire Max. I didn't say anything about this to Posey. He would have laughed me out of the room. As far as the circuit solicitor's concerned, the evidence against Max is overwhelming. I met with the circuit solicitor at the mayor's office this morning." Billy rested his forearms on the back of the next pew. "He already knew the facts. He's going to oppose bail, says there's plenty of evidence to justify a first-degree murder charge. I'd worked up a list of facts that don't jibe with Max as the murderer. Circuit Solicitor Brice Willard Posey—"

Annie had tangled with Posey on other occasions, remembered him as overbearing, impatient, and arrogant. On any occasion, public or private, he introduced himself with all three names.

"—had an answer for everything. Posey says Max must have worn gloves in the cabin and that's why there aren't any of his prints there—"

Annie was quiet even though she could have erupted in a cheer. This was big. This was what Handler Jones had hoped to elicit from the police witness.

"—but that means he took the gloves off to swing the tire tool. Funny thing to do, but hell, I'm just a cop. I guess I don't understand how a murderer can be kind of crazy." It was as though the words were quoted. "I sure don't understand why he'd have gloves with him in August or where the gloves could be right now. Posey says that's just another indication that the crime was premeditated. Posey says the bloodhounds got it wrong when they didn't pick up Max's scent between the Jag and the cabin steps. As for the blood test, Posey said all it does is prove Max was high and of course he's claiming he didn't take the stuff himself. And the silver car—"

Billy looked sharply at Annie, his eyes intent.

Annie scarcely breathed. This was important. This was why Billy had met her at the chapel. He wanted her to know there had been a silver car and it mattered.

"—was a coincidence. Now Posey can argue all he wants to that Ted Dooley—he's the guy who owns Dooley's Mine—made up that car. I don't buy it." Billy's tone was ruminative, as if he were thinking out loud. "I'm sure the silver car existed. Dooley doesn't want anybody believing a drunk leaves Dooley's Mine driving a car. Dooley made sure Max was in the passenger seat and he watched the Jag go out of the lot. When Dooley was turning to go back inside, he saw a silver car turn out of the lot. That car turned left, just like the Jag, and that's the way to the dead end and the cabin where Vanessa Taylor was killed. As God is my witness"—Billy glanced up at Saint George—"Dooley was telling the truth. Now, sure, maybe that silver car turning left after the Jag doesn't mean anything. Coincidences happen. Yeah"—Billy's jaw jutted out—"one coincidence I can swallow. Two makes me gag."

Billy pushed up from the kneeler, slid back onto the pew.

Annie slipped onto the seat, turned toward him. Her eyes never left his face.

"Like I told Posey, everything about Vanessa Taylor, no matter where you start, ends up at the same place, the Whitman house on Tree Swallow Lane." He saw the question in Annie's face. "Yeah, it's still called the Whitman house even though she's married again. Husband now is Jon Dodd. First husband kicked off—natural causes—nine years ago. Anyway, living at the house are Mrs. Dodd, her husband, her daughter Heather from the first marriage, her secretary Vanessa Taylor. Frequent visitor is daughter's fiancé, Kyle Curtis. Kind of a clubby atmosphere at that end of the island. The place has a pool, of course, and a cabana and some guest cabins. Pretty ritzy. Lots of people in and out, especially their next-door neighbors—"

Annie felt a rising excitement. Billy's exhaustive survey of the Whitman house and its occupants obviously meant he believed someone connected to the house was involved in Vanessa's death.

This confirmed Handler Jones's research indicating Vanessa Taylor had no obvious social existence outside the Dodds and their circle. Emma's instinct, as always, had been right on. They needed to know everything possible about Vanessa. Annie's hands tightened. Somehow, some way, she must help find out the truth about Vanessa.

"—the Goldens, Sam and Martha. Course, like Posey said, there wasn't time to follow up every lead about where Vanessa went and who she knew and where she hung out. Posey said it didn't matter. Max was with her the night she died, no doubt about it. His tire tool killed her. His fingerprints were on the weapon. Now, he claims somebody slipped him a mickey, but the only candidate is the dead girl. That doesn't compute. Posey said the case is wrapped up solid." Billy's nose wrinkled. "Maybe I would have agreed—except for the silver car. Then when I went out to see Mrs. Dodd, she acted as spooked as Lily when she sees a clown—"

Annie had been carrying a platter with cups of Kool-Aid when a clown came into Lily's class at Vacation Bible School. Lily panicked and ran full tilt into Annie, dousing them both in sticky purple punch.

"—and sure, it's a shock when someone you know is murdered, but Mrs. Dodd stood like a stone. She asked who'd done it and it was like she was waiting for the shoe to drop. Posey says that sounds like a soap opera but I know what I saw. I told her we were searching for the owner of the car found near the murder cabin. She asked whose car. I told her. That's when she started to breathe again and a little color came back in her face. That's when I got curious, asked her who Vanessa spent time with and damn if it didn't come back to that house. Mrs. Dodd couldn't come up with another name. Either Mrs. Dodd didn't know much about Vanessa or there wasn't anybody in Vanessa's life but the people at that house and people who came to that house. Pretty soon Mrs. Dodd's husband came in, slick guy, you know the kind, looks like he ought to be in a golf club ad. He was all over her, upset for her. Seemed to me he might have been a little upset for Vanessa, but quick as possible, he shooed her off to her room, said he'd take care of everything. He was efficient, got me the name of Vanessa's sister so I could call, told me he'd have the family lawyer get in touch with her, see what arrangements she'd want made. Sounded to me like he intended to get him and his wife removed from any involvement. You'd think she could have called the sister, not a lawyer. It was the husband who took me out to the cottage where Vanessa lived, one of four in a stand of pines between the beach and the main house. He unlocked the door. I took a look around, didn't see anything helpful."

Annie wished she'd been with him. "One of her friends said she kept a diary. Billy, if she was having a love affair, that's sure to be in there. Did you notice a diary?"

He shook his head. "I looked over her desk. There was a computer. That's probably where she did her work for Mrs. Dodd. I saw some letters to charities, that sort of thing. When I'd finished, Dodd asked if they could do anything more for me. He walked out to the cruiser with me, then went inside. I almost left but I decided to take a stroll around. If anybody asked . . ." He gave a lopsided grin. "I don't know. Maybe I could have said I was trying to get a feel for Vanessa's background. But nobody asked. I'd already seen the cottages, so I went around the back of the house to the other side. I found the garage. It wasn't locked. I went in a side door. That would have been a little harder to explain but nobody asked. There were three cars—a silver Lexus, a red PT Cruiser, and a black Porsche." His heavy shoulders lifted in a shrug. "Sure. The island crawls with silver cars. Favorite color of the rich. But what are the odds Dooley sees a silver car follow the Jag and in the garage of the house where the murdered woman lived there's a silver car? Not only that, the garage is open and the keys to the cars are hanging on some nails by the door. Anybody who knew the family could use one of those cars. I know it's not much. Nothing to take to a judge or jury. But it sticks in my craw. That and the call I got from Jon Dodd this morning. Congratulated me on solving the crime, said how disturbing it had been for them, fine girl, almost like one of the family, hoped they could be helpful to Vanessa's sister, had instructed their lawyer to make arrangements for the shipment of the body, intended to make a substantial contribution in Vanessa's memory to her college, and if any further assistance was needed we should feel free to stay in contact with their lawyer since they were leaving this weekend to drive up to Cape Cod."

"Leaving . . ." Annie felt the blood rush from her face. If the Dodds left, they would take with them all the intimate knowledge about Vanessa.

"Yeah. Getting the hell out of Dodge, I'd say. It doesn't leave us much time."

Somehow. Some way. Before Saturday . . .

Billy slid out of the pew. He was turning to go when he gave Annie a sweet, lopsided smile. He pulled a folded paper from his pocket, held it out to her. "Here's that real estate circular you found in Max's office."

Annie's fingers closed around it. "Max—" She broke off. She'd almost said that Max had told her it had nothing to do with the woman who hired him. But Billy must never know she'd talked to Max in the jail last night.

"When I gave the circuit solicitor my list of reasons why Max is innocent, I almost told him about this. I didn't bother because he wouldn't care." Billy's eyes glinted. "And sure, that silver car Dooley saw is real evidence. But after I talked to Cynthia Darrough, I knew Max never ran around on you. Give her a call, Annie. You'll be glad you did."

Annie watched the cruiser pull out of the church lot, Billy on his way to Columbia. Although she counted Mavis a friend and liked Lou Pirelli, there would be no help for her at the police station without Billy. She was on her own. If Max were to be freed, it was up to her and their friends. Annie walked swiftly toward her Volvo, though the late afternoon heat pressed against her, steamy and soggy as wet towels at a spa. She slid behind the wheel, turned the air conditioner on high, waited until there was a faint hint of cool before raising the windows. She was bursting to share the information she'd received from Billy. But first . . .

She yanked her cell phone from her purse, turned it on. The quick beep indicated messages, but she had a call to make first.

"Cynthia Darrough?" Annie knew her voice was high and strained. "This is Annie Darling."

"Max Darling's Annie?"

"Yes. Billy Cameron—"

The light sweet voice broke in. "Oh, Mrs. Darling, I'm so sorry about everything that's happened, but Chief Cameron said it was all a mistake and everything would be ironed out—"

Annie held tight to the cell, wondered how Billy could be so optimistic. If the Dodds left on Saturday . . .

"—and I surely hope so because your young man—"

Annie's eyes were wet. How sweet and how Southern, calling Max her young man. And he was, oh, God, yes, he was.

"—is just the nicest boy. Oh, I know Mr. Darling isn't a boy, but he's the age of my oldest grandson, who turns thirty next month, and I wish my Edward was as thoughtful for his wife. Mr. Darling told me all about how he wanted to keep it a secret and surprise you if he was able to buy the Franklin house—"

Annie's eyes widened. Buy the Franklin house? That ramshackle, down-at-heels, boarded-up wreck of a house?

"—and you and he could fix it all up. He said you have a nice house—"

Nice house? Annie loved her house, the first permanent place she'd had to call her own since her mother died. She loved the banks of windows and their cozy den and the terrace room and library and Max's kingly kitchen.

"—but he wanted to have a place that was big and rambly with plenty of room someday for kids. And he liked the idea of being close to town. He said he grew up in a big family and he loved having people in and out and lots going on and he knew you'd be thrilled. You'd have room for lots of visitors and someday when you had kids, there would be enough for a bunch. He laughed and said, 'Not the Brady bunch, but maybe three or four.' He was so excited, thinking about making the Franklin house a beautiful home for you and him and someday for your family." A soft sigh. "When he talked about you, there was so much love in his voice. Now, you tell him Mrs. Darrough knows right enough he didn't do that awful thing."

Annie held tight to the cell. She couldn't break down now. She had to keep on, fight for Max. "I'll tell him, Mrs. Darrough."

When the connection ended, Annie held the circular to her face, pressed her lips to the now creased and wrinkled sheet. Finally she gently refolded the piece of paper and slipped it into her pocket, a talisman for Max. Her lips still curved in a smile as she called up the messages on her cell:

1. "Annie, you won't be able to keep your schedule for altar duty. I've already spoken to Father Cooley." Pamela Potts's sweet, high voice was breathless and determinedly matter-of-fact. "Ingrid said Duane got Dorothy L. for you, so that's all right. I dropped by the store a couple of times today to hold Agatha, since I know Ingrid's so busy—"

Annie's eyebrows rose. Agatha was a notorious biter. Only an innocent such as Pamela would even think of picking her up and holding her.

"—and I'm going to where—"

Pamela's careful subtlety was obviously to prevent an eavesdropper from knowing Annie was at Nightingale Courts.

"—Dorothy L. is staying, to give her some attention. Since you won't be at your house, I'll run by every so often to keep an eye on it. You and Max are in my thoughts and prayers. Everything will come right. It simply has to." The last was an anguished bleat.

2. "I just saw the news on TV and I'm on my way back to the island." Max's secretary sizzled. "I'll get in tonight and go straight to the office. Leave me instructions on what to do."

3. "Handler Jones calling at ten minutes after three. If you ring my cell phone before three-thirty, I'll be with Max and you can talk to him." He gave the number, spacing each digit so that it was clear and easy to understand. "The arraignment . . ."

Annie's heart lurched. She looked at the dashboard clock: three twenty-six.

She saved the messages and with fingers that trembled punched the number of the lawyer's cell.

"Handler Jones." He might have been announcing an Oscar.

"Annie Darling. Is Max there?" Max in jail. Max in an orange jumpsuit. Oh God, Max . . .

There was a moment when background noise crackled and there was a distant thump or bump. Then Max's voice, strong and clear and warm.

"Annie?"

"I'm here." Too far away. Not able to reach out and touch him. Concrete and bars and horror stood between them. "Max, are you all right?" The question was small and paltry, a tiny stone against a boulder of trouble.

"Fine. Handler's got things under control. Listen, Annie, I only have a few minutes and they're coming for me. Don't worry. Handler has people looking through her background—"

He didn't have to say whose background. Vanessa Taylor dead dominated their life.

"—and he's on top of things. Obviously, I was set up from beginning to end. We have to find out who put her up to hiring me. Don't worry about a thing. Handler's got a bunch of people on the case and he'll keep you informed. You stay out of it. Somebody's dangerous as hell and—oh, here they are—"

A door banged. A deep voice muttered in the background. There was a shuffle and sound of steps and another door.

Handler Jones's mellifluous voice poured over the cell. "Max is in good spirits. As he said, we're giving it our full attention. Now, I know you want to come over here and see him. Visiting hours are from seven to ten every evening, so that would be all right, but he's adamant he doesn't want you or his mother over here. He's confident we'll figure everything out and he'll be out of here pretty quickly."

Annie understood more than Jones imagined. She knew that Max didn't want her to see him in the squalor and sadness of a detention facility on the mainland. If she insisted, if she went, Max would know that she didn't think he would soon be free. He needed to believe that he would soon be free.

She felt the hot burn of tears. She kept her voice steady. She too had to believe. "Tell him that's fine. We'll get this behind us as quickly as possible. We may have a new lead. The owner of that bar—Dooley's Mine—saw a silver car turn out of the parking lot Monday night, following Max's Jag. When Billy Cameron went to tell Mrs. Dodd about the murder, he looked in their garage and saw a silver car." How many silver cars were on the island? She pushed the question away.

"Another pointer to the Whitman house." The lawyer sounded pleased. "I wish we could get somebody inside, but the staff has been there for years."

"There's probably not time for that. The Dodds are leaving the island Saturday, going to Cape Cod." She said it flatly, angry with people she didn't even know.

Handler gave a low whistle. "That's very interesting. I'd like to know who made that decision and why. We'll see what else we can find out. I'll be in touch."

Annie called up the saved messages, clicked to the third, listened to the remainder of Handler Jones's:

". . . didn't have any surprises. The judge has taken the request for bail under advisement, will rule next week. I don't think there's any chance he'll grant bail, not in a high-profile case like this. The circuit solicitor's emphasizing the brutal nature of the crime. On the plus side, Max feels much better physically, still a minor headache. He's comfortable. In a cell by himself—"

Annie knew Jones intended to reassure her, but every word was a blow. Max in a cell. Max unable to walk where he pleased or call when he wished. Max in terrible danger of facing trial for the murder of a woman he'd thought he was helping.

"—and I've given him a legal pad, pen. He hasn't been able to remember any more and can't provide any substantial aid to the investigation, since he had no prior knowledge of the victim. I've explained that I think it will be better if he isn't privy to the investigation reports. I want to be able to assert that he is utterly unfamiliar with the victim and her background. I've faxed more information to Mrs. Clyde and will be in touch soon."

4. "Annie, Father Cooley here. I understand from Emma that

Max's difficulties will soon be cleared up and the perpetrator of this terrible crime unmasked. You know that I stand ready to be of any assistance possible. You and Max and the poor lost girl are in my prayers. And know that 'God is our refuge and strength, a very present help in trouble.'"

5. "My sweet, I doubt Max will agree but I thought he looked quite dashing in that odd shade of orange." Laurel was upbeat. "His appearance was encouraging. We can feel confident that our dear boy is recovering from the physical trials of his ordeal and will meet this challenge with grace and courage while we bend every effort to gain his release. I have a friend, a most accomplished leasing agent, who thinks he can help. He is such a charmer—the handsomeness of a young Valentino, the savoir faire of Fred Astaire, and the appeal of Brad Pitt."

Brad Pitt? Was Laurel's male admirer a bit on the young side? That wasn't any business of Annie's. She made it a point not to dwell upon her mother-in-law's several marriages and liaisons. The ways of love are mysterious and Laurel's intentions, Annie was sure of it, were always of the best. Annie frowned, trying to decipher the breath of sound that reached her. Was it a silken sigh or a ripple of merriment?

"That and a substantial bonus for immediate occupancy may work wonders. He is a fine fellow—"

Definitely on the young side.

"—and I'm counting on him for his assistance. I will let you know what happens. I've taken Terence's good advice to heart, 'Nothing is so difficult but that it may be found out by seeking.' Fortunately, I have never met Lillian Dodd. More anon."

Annie punched Pause. . . . *I have never met Lillian Dodd.* What was Laurel doing? Where was she? Annie would not, unfortunately, be surprised by any eventuality: Laurel parachuting into the garden of the Whitman house, claiming a slight mistake in navigation. Laurel pretending to be a vet making a house call. Laurel arriving in pest-control garb to fumigate. Damn. Whatever happened, Annie had to keep Laurel away from the Whitman house, both for her safety and for the ultimate success of their investigation, though Handler Jones had bemoaned his inability to get an agent into the house as part of the domestic staff. Someone in the house . . . Laurel . . . someone in the house . . .

Annie saved the messages again. First things first. She pressed Laurel's numbers, home and cell. No answer at either. Quickly, Annie called Emma's numbers. Again, no answers. If Emma were engaged in her phone canvass, she would ignore incoming calls. How about Henny? The result was the same.

All right. If she couldn't contact them, she could leave a message for each. She decided to dial their cells:

"Laurel, Annie." Of course she would know it was Annie. This was not starting out on the right basis. Annie knew she dare not sound chiding. What was the proper tone? But Laurel, who prided herself upon insight, wasn't likely to be fooled. Annie decided on directness. "Laurel, keep away from the Whitman house. Please get in touch with me as soon as possible."

"Emma, I have a plan. Come to the place I'm staying as soon as possible. Bring everything you've learned about Vanessa." Annie left the same message for Henny, then called Ingrid's cell, knowing the Death on Demand number was probably flooded with calls. "Annie." Ingrid's voice was high and thin.

Although the air-conditioning was finally cooling down the car, Annie turned the fan higher. "Bad?"

"Bad? Now I understand Lizzie Borden. If I had an axe—"

"Take a deep breath." Annie put the car in drive, headed out of the church lot. She needed to get back to her cabin at Nightingale Courts. There was much to be done.

"They aren't even buying books." Ingrid's voice quivered with outrage. "People everywhere and all they want to do is get a souvenir. We ran out of bookmarks by noon. They're taking pictures of everything, and somebody stole Edgar."

The stuffed black raven perched above the entrance to the children's section was in honor of Edgar Allan Poe, the founding father of mystery.

"He looked molty." Annie was dismissive. "We'll put a tea set there, something elegant Miss Marple would have enjoyed."

"Annie, has anything—" Ingrid broke off.

Annie understood. Had anything happened, anything good? Was Max still in jail? Ingrid didn't want to ask.

"He's fine." As she said it, she suddenly felt it was true. Max was fine. He was alive and safe and somehow she was going to prove his innocence. "I'm fine. We're making progress. Listen, Ingrid, I want you to close the store and here's what I want you to get for me. . . ." She talked fast and she drove fast.

6

Annie paced on the porch overlooking the lagoon, looking for flaws in her plan to plunge into Vanessa Taylor's world. Her gaze swept the water. She paused, moved to the porch railing and watched an alligator swim past. The triangular black snout slid through the dark water. The ridges of his back looked like indentations in the water. His tail swept back and forth, propelling him forward. If she hadn't seen him, she would never have known of his presence, he moved so silently. That's what she needed to do, glide easily through the next few days, unheeded, unheralded, unknown, but dangerous and deadly for her prey.

If Annie could submerge herself in Vanessa's life, she might discover the reason for her murder. Vanessa hadn't died as a result of passion. She'd died as the result of a carefully devised plan that could only have been engineered by someone she knew well. Vanessa wouldn't have cooperated in deceiving Max for a casual acquaintance. Vanessa must have agreed to the scheme against Max either to please someone or because she had no choice. Had she been in some desperate situation? Or had she been a willing conspirator? Whatever her motive, something in Vanessa's life had caused her death, and there was no question that for the last year and a half Vanessa's life had centered around the Whitman house.

There might be a way to gain access to the house. Annie's plan might be crazy. It certainly was daring. Could she do it? Could she assume a new identity, meld into the background as the alligator merged with the lagoon? She would have to be brave and skillful and clever.

She turned, went back into the cabin. She'd lost count of how many times she'd read the dossier on Vanessa. To succeed in her venture, she must absorb every fact within these pages as instinctively as she recalled her own past. She must forget the way purple-black clouds bank high in a May sky in Amarillo, forget her days at Southern Methodist University and the elegant campus with its Georgian architecture, forget her sojourn in New York and coffeehouses in Soho. She must think of the flat plains of Illinois and the majestic skyline of Chicago and Sears Tower and choppy waves on Lake Michigan. Annie settled once again on the sofa and picked up the dossier:

Vanessa Taylor: Twenty-three years old. Born in Peoria, Illinois, youngest daughter of Charlotte and Henry Taylor. One sister, Genevieve, nine years older. Father an insurance adjuster, mother an elementary school teacher. Family moved to Wilmette when Vanessa was six. Attended public schools, graduating from New Trier High School. Cheerleader, choir, lead in West Side Story, *waited tables for spending money, two years in junior college, came to the Carolina coast three summers ago, waited tables at Parotti's Bar and Grill, hired as Lillian Dodd's secretary a year and a half ago.*

Brownie leader Arlene Hubbard: "Sassy. There was always a current of antagonism between Vanessa and women. Maybe that puts it too strongly. It was more that she thought other girls and women unimportant. But when a man came into the room! Then she was brighter than a new penny. And did she strut her stuff. Even when she was a little girl there was something provocative about her."

Middle school music teacher Harold Childers: "An enchanting girl. Lovely voice. I always felt the other girls were jealous of her. It didn't seem to bother Vanessa. Once she sang 'Bali H'ai' in a variety show. You would never have thought she was seventeen."

High school English teacher and yearbook adviser Emily Howie: "When Vanessa entered a room, everyone noticed. She had the sparkle of a diamond even though her background was rhinestones. She always had inexpensive versions of the latest fashions. She made an excellent appearance. No grunge for Vanessa. She managed to be part of the preppy crowd even though she didn't have the money or background. I always felt Vanessa would come out a winner. I'm sorry to know that didn't happen."

High school best friend Gina Lambertino: "We had so much fun. We'd go into town for Cubs games, a bunch of us. I'll always remember Vanessa singing 'Take Me Out to the Ball Game.' She was special. Everything was more fun when she was along, like there was a spark of electricity. If she wasn't there, everything seemed ordinary. I thought she'd be a model or an actress. She could charm anybody. Everybody—especially guys—always looked at her. She had some magic signal that brought guys from every direction. I guess she attracted the wrong guy."

Junior college admissions office secretary: "I wouldn't tell you this if she was alive but maybe it might help. It's all gossip, of course, but this is a small campus. Everybody blamed her and I didn't think that was right. She shouldn't have led him on, but he was in his forties, old enough to know better. I don't know why she was attracted to him. Maybe she wasn't. Maybe she just wanted to see if she could *attract an older man. Anyway, she did. He moved out and his wife sued for divorce. Then Vanessa dumped him. He shot himself in the rose garden near Old Central. Of course, he made that decision. She left at the end of that semester."*

Former roommate on Broward's Rock, Judy Denton: "I was the one who found us jobs on the island. I'd worked there for a couple of summers. I broke up with my boyfriend and Vanessa was ready to do something different. She'd had a bad experience, a professor who came on to her hot and heavy. When she told him to cool it, he committed suicide. It was a fresh start for both of us. We had a great time. She played the field, one good-looking guy after another. Then I met Stan and pretty soon I didn't see her so often. Stan and I got married and came here. Vanessa and I kept up by e-mail. It was pretty much the same old same old from her—lots of parties and beach time and football weekends in Atlanta—until she got the job with Mrs. Dodd. . . .

Annie skimmed the material described earlier by Handler Jones, picking up toward the end.

". . . I'm sure there was a guy. Of course, she loved to brag but I guess she didn't think it was politic to talk about him in her e-mails. I think the family all used the same system and maybe it would have been embarrassing if someone else saw it. Anyway, I'll bet dear old diary's X-rated."

Annie stared at the page. This was the second time Judy had mentioned a diary. Billy hadn't seen one when he looked at her cottage, but that was a cursory once-over. Annie continued reading:

"Vanessa was always cagey about her diary. I wouldn't have known she kept one but I found it tucked in a bunch of magazines. I didn't

*know what it was. It was just this floral cloth book and I opened it
and she walked in and you would have thought I was stealing the
crown jewels. She yelled something about I was a snoop, just like her
sister. I ended up throwing it at her and we didn't speak for a couple
of days. I didn't see it again but whenever she curled up in her own
room, saying she was going to read for a while, I think she was writing in her diary. So nobody may ever find it. She moved it around
a bunch of places when we roomed together. Of course, I don't know
why anybody would be looking at her stuff in that cottage, but I'd
guess she wouldn't want the maids to see it. Anyway, on Monday
she dashed off an e-mail to me at 3:07 P.M.—that would be 4:07
P.M. her time—and she wrote, 'Dear Judy, Got to run. You know
what a good secretary does. She makes herself indispensable. Well,
I'm trumping that. No more secretary days for me. When tonight
is over, there are going to be some changes made. Let the good times
roll . . . V'"*

Annie let out an exultant whoop. Surely Handler Jones understood the importance of this report. *No more secretary days . . .* When
he told Billy . . . Annie sagged back against the sofa. She didn't need
the savvy lawyer to puncture her brief euphoria. Vanessa's declaration
that she expected a big gain from her evening's activities could be
used to build the case against Max. The prosecution could claim that
the changes to be made depended upon Max. The prosecution could
claim . . . Annie didn't need to continue.

Annie knew the truth. Vanessa had connived to lure Max to Dooley's Mine, drugged his drink, then taken him in the Jag to the cabin
where she died. Vanessa expected a payoff. Instead, she was murdered.
The only link to the murderer was Dooley's brief glimpse of a silver
car. Who drove that car? That's what Annie had to find out and find
out soon.

———

Emma chose a Pepsi. Henny and Ingrid opted for iced tea. Annie wished for a jolt of espresso, settled for a double-bagged cup of instant coffee, black as asphalt. She was the last to slip into a chair around the white wooden kitchen table in the Nightingale Courts cabin. One chair was empty. Laurel hadn't responded to Annie's messages. Annie felt a tug of worry, but she'd hope for the best. There wasn't time to divert energy or effort to discovering her mother-in-law's whereabouts. She'd ask Ingrid to find Laurel. Annie glanced at the cardboard box on the floor next to Ingrid. Good. Ingrid had done as Annie had requested, though she could have had no inkling of how Annie intended to use her purchase. For now, Annie had to focus on the concerted effort necessary to make her venture possible. She needed help in large ways and small, and the moment to ask was here.

She looked at each friend in turn. Emma had the commanding aura of a Marine brigadier despite her spiky hair, a newly dyed, striking azure today, and the casual drape of her blue-and-pink-striped caftan. The mystery writer's costume might be casual, but her mind absorbed facts, nuances, and suppositions with the ease of a CEO. Henny was as alert as a bridge player with eight spades, dark eyes glowing behind the half-rim glasses perched on her nose. She gave Annie a thumbs-up with the effervescence of Diane Keaton at a cocktail party. Ingrid brushed back a wisp of graying hair, tried for a smile, was unsuccessful.

"Thank you for coming." Annie willed tears away. She'd thought she had herself firmly under control. There had been too much emotion in too short a time, the icy horror of Max's disappearance and the hours that crawled past, each one more frightening than the last. She'd thought he was dead, beloved Max lost to her forever. She pushed away the memory. That was time she didn't want to think about, never wanted to relive. The blinding relief when he was found had been succeeded by anger over his arrest, an impotent fury at the unseen forces that had placed Max in jeopardy. Now was the moment for calm. She needed every ounce of concentration she could summon.

"Of course we came." Emma's matter-of-fact tone was as good a tonic as a sea breeze on a muggy day. "I've been looking at several options, but you said you had a plan." There was only the slightest hint of surprise. After all, it was Emma who plotted. Annie merely sold books.

"I intend to get into the Whitman house." Annie spoke confidently, then stopped. Was it fair to ask her friends, her best friends in all the world, to connive in committing crimes, including conspiracy, theft, and misrepresentation?

Henny clapped her hands together. "Way to go."

Emma raised an inquiring eyebrow. "Do you have a friend on good terms with the family?" Her blue eyes narrowed as if scanning a mental Rolodex.

Annie's head shake was definite. "That wouldn't be much help anyway. I want to stay there."

Ingrid twined a strand of frizzy hair around one finger, a gesture she made when nervous or uncertain. "I don't know if that's wise. If the murderer is someone at the house, you'll be in danger."

Henny removed her glasses, frowned in thought. "It does look as though the murderer has to be an intimate of the household. From everything we've gathered, Vanessa had no social life beyond that house. It's equally clear there was a carefully calibrated plan to ensnare Max. The effect has been to remove any scrutiny from her everyday life. So far as we've been able to determine, the men she saw most often included Jon Dodd; the daughter's fiancé Kyle Curtis; and the next-door neighbor, Sam Golden. If we're right and one of those men was involved with her, that house would be very dangerous to a snooper."

Emma waved a stubby hand in dismissal. "Annie, I'd already thought about gaining access to the house. It isn't possible. The staff has been there for years. Mrs. Dodd doesn't use an outside cleaning service. More private that way. The lawn care is done on a weekly basis and I doubt that would provide any opportunity for meaningful contact. I'm afraid we'll have to depend upon the information we can glean elsewhere. But"—her smile was bright—"we have gathered a great many interesting facts. And some fascinating minutiae. For example, Lillian Dodd lived in Brazil for several years and speaks Portuguese. Jon Dodd collects letters written by famous Americans, including Ulysses S. Grant and Amelia Earhart. Heather Whitman's favorite game is Parcheesi. She's dated Kyle Curtis since ninth grade. Kyle's dad dumped his mother for another man. Sam and Martha Golden, the next-door neighbors, don't bother to knock when they come over. Sam cheats at cards. Martha carries vodka in a perfume bottle in her purse." Emma patted a several-inches-high stack of legal pads. "And more. Much more. So even if we can't get into the house, we're making progress."

"I'll get in." Annie knew there was a certain bravado in her statement, but she wasn't going to back off. If everything broke her way . . . "Handler Jones's investigators found out a lot about Vanessa. According to her former roommate here on the island, Vanessa kept a diary—"

Emma nodded. "Yes. I remember that."

"—and I intend to find it. Handler Jones also told us about Vanessa's sister."

Henny slipped on the half-glasses, flipped open a notebook. "Genevieve Willet. Husband on SS disability, back injury from working as a longshoreman. Recently diagnosed with pancreatic cancer. Two children: Doug in junior high, Susie in second grade. Works in a medical records office and on weekends as a nurse's aide." Henny's dark eyes softened. "A hard life."

Annie pointed at the folder in front of her. "Jones said she's avoiding contact with everybody." The out-of-touch sister. Annie's plan depended upon that. "Jones told us the Dodds had their lawyer contact her, arrange for the shipment of the body when it's released by the medical examiner."

Emma poured Pepsi over ice, watched the soda fizz and bubble. "He's right in all particulars. Firm of Jackson, Montrose, Ruley and Ruley in Charleston. Young Jason Ruley's handling the details."

Annie planted her elbows on the table. "That's right. No one from the family is in direct contact with Genevieve Willet. They have no knowledge of what she's doing or thinking. So here's my plan. Genevieve hadn't kept in close contact with her younger sister and now she's distraught over missing so much of her life in recent years. She wants to gather up all of Vanessa's belongings, bring them home. She especially hopes to find Vanessa's diary. Her family situation is such that she can't travel to Broward's Rock herself. One of Vanessa's oldest friends from high school was at the house last night. She's between jobs and she volunteered to drive down here and pick up everything. She's promised Genevieve that she'll talk to everyone Vanessa saw on a regular basis, bring home a scrapbook of memories and recollections. It's a two-day drive from Chicago. Vanessa's friend left early this morning. She'll arrive late tomorrow afternoon."

Henny grinned at Annie. "You'll be tired from the drive, I expect. Who contacts Lillian Dodd? I'll be happy to call."

Emma was judicious. "The plan has merit. But there are obstacles. You'll need Illinois license plates for your car—"

Henny chimed in. "And an Illinois driver's license—"

Emma pulled her stack of legal pads nearer. "I have some ideas about the license plates and the license as well. Actually, consider that statement struck. Never say aloud or put in writing or e-mail anything you wouldn't want running on the news ticker at Times Square." Her voice was a purr. "I know I have Lillian Dodd's cell number in here."

Ingrid glared around the table. "Stop it. All of you. This is insane. Fifty years ago, sure, anybody could show up anywhere and claim anything. But this is the twenty-first century. You'll never get away with it."

Annie looked into Ingrid's worried brown eyes and knew Ingrid was frightened at the prospect of Annie trying to step into Vanessa's life. If Annie found out too much, she would be in terrible danger.

Henny frowned. "Ingrid's right to object." She waved her hand at the materials piled atop the kitchen table. "We've discovered a great deal. Maybe we should concentrate on winnowing through the reports. Surely we can narrow the list of suspects. Right now we're looking at men Vanessa saw regularly at the Whitman house. Jon Dodd. The daughter's fiancé. The next-door neighbor." Her face brightened. "There may be a simple way to find our quarry. Vince is running a notice in the *Gazette* asking for information about Vanessa's activities the last few days, with special note of her companions. I'm going to make up a flyer with Vanessa's picture and flood the town with it."

Annie reached over, squeezed Henny's hand. "That's a great plan. I'll add a reward. Offer ten thousand." Ten thousand. A lot of money to someone. A pittance for Max's life.

Henny looked upbeat. "If Vanessa was involved with a man, some-body has to have seen her with him. If we keep looking, we'll find some trace somewhere. All it takes is patience."

"We can't be patient." Annie looked bleak. "The Dodds are clos-ing the house, going to Cape Cod this weekend."

Emma's blue eyes glittered. "Smart as hell. Somebody is. Frame Max and get out of town. So if you're going to get the lowdown on these people, it has to be now."

Henny pushed up from the table. "Okay, Emma, find that phone number for Lillian Dodd. Your cell registers Unknown Caller when you call someone with caller ID, doesn't it?" She answered her own question. "I know it does. Funny. Chicanery is so much harder in many ways with all the modern inventions. Like Ingrid said, fifty years ago you could show up anywhere, say you were anyone, and it would be hard to disprove. Now there are electronic barriers ev-erywhere." She gave Annie an admiring glance. "That's why Vanessa's friend is driving, right? You can't get a plane ticket as—what's your name?"

Annie knew the decision had been made to support her without a word being said or a poll being taken. Emma and Henny had signed on. And Ingrid was picking up the box from the floor. Annie had a quick memory of the chapel, Billy's tired voice, and the glorious reds and blues of the stained-glass window. "Georgia. Georgia Lance." Saint George defeated his dragon. Now she must defeat hers.

Emma scribbled on a sheet. "Two Illinois license plates. One Il-linois driver's license, name of Georgia Lance. We'll pick a street near where the Taylors lived." She glanced at Annie. "Five feet five. One hundred and fifteen pounds. Gray eyes. Blonde—"

Annie reached over, took the lid from Ingrid's box. She lifted out a glossy wig, dark as a lagoon at midnight. She slipped it on and was surprised at its lightness. Over her short bobbed hair, the wig felt natural.

Henny bent forward, eyes intent. "I'll get my makeup kit. I can change the shape of your eyebrows, use a base that will make you look darker skinned. We'll add some gold-rim glasses. With the makeup, glasses, and wig, you could walk into church and nobody would recognize you. But first things first. All of these details can be managed by tomorrow. Now we need to get in touch with Lillian Dodd."

Emma ripped a sheet from a notebook. "Here's the number."

Henny took the slip of paper and Emma's cell. She stepped away from the table, her eyes half closed. Sun slanted through the porch window, highlighting the strand of silver in her black hair.

They all were silent, waiting. Henny Brawley had played many roles as a starring member of the Broward's Rock Players, including Mame in *Auntie Mame,* Abby Brewster in *Arsenic and Old Lace,* and Miss Jane Marple in *Murder at the Vicarage.* Annie watched as Henny, a consummate actress, became a bereaved sister, worn down by fatigue, sorrow, and worry. The muscles in her face sagged, her lips turned down, her shoulders bowed. She looked defeated, emotionally vulnerable, yet hopeful.

There wasn't a breath of sound as she punched the number.

Annie's nails dug into her palms. What if the number rang and there was no answer? Henny couldn't leave a message and ask for a return call. The area code would be wrong. They hadn't thought about that, prepared for that eventuality. There were so many possible pitfalls and snags. This call had to go through and go through now. If there weren't an immediate answer, Henny should end the call. Annie opened her mouth to call out—

"Hello? Mrs. Dodd? This is Genevieve Willet, Vanessa's sister." Henny's voice was husky with a breathless quaver. "I'm glad I caught you. I wanted to thank you for the help from Mr. Ruley—"

Annie knew Henny was smart, but every word reinforced that conviction. The implication was that Genevieve Willet had obtained Lillian Dodd's cell number from the lawyer. Even if Mrs. Dodd called Ruley, the lawyer would be quick to confirm that he'd spoken with the older sister, made all the necessary arrangements. The question of the cell phone number was unlikely to arise.

"—and he's been very nice, made everything easy for us. The police chief has been in touch too. Of course, we're shocked by everything that's happened and I'm at a loss to understand. Vanessa never mentioned the man they've arrested. Mostly she talked about your family and friends . . ." Henny's voice caught, as if suppressing a sob.

Emma made a circle with thumb and forefinger, raised it high. Ingrid gazed admiringly at Henny. Annie felt her hands begin to relax. Henny was on top of her game.

Henny cleared her throat. "I'm sorry. It's so hard. But knowing more about Vanessa's life helps. Her oldest friend was here last night— Georgia Lance—they were in high school together—and we got to talking and I told Georgia how sad it was that I didn't even have a picture of anyone there or know what Vanessa's room looked like— she loved the cabin and your house and always said working there was so much fun—and Georgia said maybe she could help. She's between jobs and she said she'd be glad to drive down and get Vanessa's things and talk to all of you and bring back Vanessa's belongings. I wanted to let you know that Georgia left real early this morning. I just had a call from her and she's hoping to get to Asheville tonight. She thinks she'll arrive on the island by two or three tomorrow afternoon. Vanessa always told me how kind and generous you are, Mrs. Dodd"—Henny's voice was hesitant, embarrassed, hopeful—"and how you had some guest cabins there and were always putting people up. I hope it isn't too much to ask but by the time I came up with gas money for Georgia, well, I'm on a tight budget and she's out of work right now and it would sure be a help if she could stay a day or two and get Vanessa's things all packed up for me."

Now Henny looked at Emma and made a circle with her thumb and forefinger. "Mrs. Dodd, you're just as nice as Vanessa said you were. Georgia won't be any trouble and I know you'll like her. She's a sweet girl. You'll find her easy to talk to. I hope you and everyone there will help us out, tell us all about Vanessa's friends and work. She was awfully happy with you and that's how I want to remember her. And—oh, I have another call, I think it may be the funeral home—I'll let you go but thank you again for all your help and your kindness." Henny clicked off the cell.

"Brava!" Emma clapped her stubby hands together in admiration. "There was no time for her to ask for your number. Henny, well done."

Ingrid's eyes were rounded in amazement. "Henny, you were perfect."

Annie jumped up, took two quick steps, and hugged her old friend. "You did it. Henny, you did it!"

Light glowed from ceiling fixtures down the long hallway. The overhead lights in the cells were off. A deep cough rattled in the nighttime quiet. In the next cell a man snored, the gulping, heaving, strangled snore of sleep apnea. A shoe gritted on the concrete hallway. A toilet flushed.

Max turned restlessly on the narrow bunk. He'd never felt so helpless. He'd always approached life with casual ease, not arrogantly sure everything would always work out but confident of his abilities. He could reason. He was disciplined when he needed to be. He was fortunate to be healthy mentally and physically, and he appreciated that good fortune. He loved and was loved, and there was no greater richness in all the world. He knew that ultimately no one can control a car that careens out of control to smash into yours, or the vulnerability of the body to infections poised to attack when defenses are low, or the mindless dangers everywhere in a world gone mad with terrorism. But he'd never envisioned himself accused of a crime with no way to prove his innocence and every new fact discovered more damning than the last.

Max stared at the high window, far out of reach, a pale oblong illuminated by moonlight. This time last week he and Annie had lain in their hammock on the terrace and watched the golden globe of the moon high in a cloudless sky and listened to the chorus of frogs, Annie nestled in the crook of his arm, her body close to his. Annie's hair smelled sweet. Her skin was soft as magnolia petals. Her lips . . .

Max clenched his hands into fists. Lost. Everything lost. His life had been taken from him and there was nothing he could do to save himself. He didn't know the girl, had never seen her before she came into Confidential Commissions. So it did no good to pummel his mind for facts. He knew nothing that could help. He had no memory after his visit to Blackbeard Beach until his painful awakening in the fishing cabin.

Handler Jones had tried to be reassuring, insisting that Max's lack of knowledge was an asset. The lawyer had further insisted that Max should be content to leave the investigating up to Jones and his staff, although he'd promised to keep Annie apprised of whatever he learned.

Max pushed up, swung his legs over to the floor. He knew Annie. She would climb a mountain, brave a torrent, face down a serpent, do whatever she had to do. He had to talk to her, tell her to keep away, leave everything to Handler Jones. Somewhere out there, hidden behind a face that smiled, was a murderer who was quick to kill and left no trace.

Annie knew she should be in bed. Tomorrow she was going to need every ounce of energy and intelligence she possessed. But sleep wouldn't come, not even when Dorothy L. snuggled next to her, her soft throat rattling with a joyous purr. When the luminous dial of the travel alarm showed a quarter after two, Annie got up, leaving the fluffy cat a contented mound beneath the sheet. She fixed a club soda with a squeeze of lime. Dear Ingrid. The small kitchen was well stocked. Annie saw the box of chocolates, wasn't tempted. Chocolate was for happy days when the world was bright and shining and horror didn't curl beneath the surface of her mind, implacable and unremitting. She wandered irresolutely around the small living room, the sisal matting scratchy against her bare feet. She'd forgotten her house shoes. But she had enough clothes for a few days, all she would need. She'd taken big trips before, she and Max, a three-week Kenyan safari, a caravan in Egypt, a Baltic cruise. This time she was going alone. She loved guide books with their maps and nuggets of information and starred itineraries. What would be a good title for the materials that had been gathered for her? She turned toward the kitchen table, slipped into the nearest chair. She yanked a legal pad near, scrawled, *One Woman's Guide to Murder.* She crossed it out, wrote, *A Primer for Death.* She shook her head, tried again: *Dragon's Lair.* She scored jagged peaks all the way around the words. That's where she was going, into the den of the dragon, where the scaly beast, eyes glittering with hatred, fiery tongue flickering, awaited her. Georgia Lance on her quest for justice.

Annie sipped the fizzy club soda, welcomed the burst of carbonation against her tongue. The den of the dragon . . . She riffled through the information they'd gathered on the Whitman house, found an article from a house-and-garden magazine. She studied the main photograph. The two-story pale lemon stucco house on high stucco foundations rose behind the beach dunes as gracefully as a dolphin arching above a wave. Pine trees formed the backdrop, the vivid green emphasizing the faint coloration of the stucco. Huge windows overlooked piazzas on each level. The Whitman house exuded light and airy space.

Annie read the caption beneath the photograph: *Lillian Whitman Dodd gleefully describes her home as a meeting of East and West, Florida Mediterranean merging with California Spanish.*

Annie scanned an excerpt from an accompanying article:

The eclectic decor and furnishings of the Whitman house reflect Dodd's wide-ranging interests and well-traveled background. "I pick things I like. I love the old Spanish influence in California and I once lived in Boca Raton. I don't care about design purity. I'm looking for comfort and beauty." The home is planned for entertaining, and Dodd's New Year's Day oyster roast is an island tradition. The grounds are extensive and include four guest cabins. Dodd's extensive charitable endeavors often bring overnight guests, and she enjoys being able to share Low Country hospitality. "There's always fresh pineapple in the guest quarters as well as carved pineapples on the newel posts of the porch."

Annie chased after a tag of memory. There was a quotation, something about every sweet thing having a sour side. . . . She blinked, her eyes grainy with fatigue. She couldn't quite remember. In any event, it was likely Lillian Dodd's propensity for hospitality that was making it possible for Annie to invade her home. That was an ugly recompense for generosity. What if Annie told her the truth? Oh yes, she could imagine it now. *Mrs. Dodd, I know you'll understand. My husband's the one who's been arrested for Vanessa's murder but he's innocent. Someone close to you, an intimate of this house, connived with Vanessa to lure my husband to a cheap bar and drug him and then that person killed Vanessa and I'm here to find out the truth.*

The truth . . . the truth . . . the truth . . . Annie's head jerked.

She'd nodded off and now her neck ached. She came awake, put the picture to one side. There was more about the Whitman house. Oh yes, Duane Webb had gathered this information. A retired city editor, Duane was always accurate and he had an old newsman's knack for discovering the unexpected. She read Duane's report with interest:

The two-story house contains 3,800 square feet. The front entrance is on the west. The east facade faces the ocean with a terrace and pool. Between the house and the beach is a stand of pines. Four cabins curve in a semicircle around a lagoon. A huge pittosporum hedge screens the cabins from the house. The three-car garage and a mainte-nance shed are to the south beyond another stand of pines.

It's quite a spread. House was built to order by Lillian Whitman and her first husband. Cost over a million then. Conservatively ap-praised now at two and a half million. Main house has living, dining, library, office, kitchen, solarium, family room with a billiards table and home theater television. Living room walls are Chinese-style watercolor on silk wallpaper. Floral fabrics include Coraggio, Kravet, and Scalamandre. Furniture a mix. Spanish Mission in the living and dining rooms, Low Country plantation in the library, including cypress paneling and an Adam mantel, Danish modern in the family room. Upstairs there are five bedrooms in addition to the master suite. Two bathrooms downstairs, five upstairs.

The staff includes the cook, Esther Riggs, and her husband Wil-liam, who doubles as chauffeur and general handyman. The maids are Esther's nieces Maybelle and Cora. Esther ends every conversation with a Bible verse. William's known to drink a little too much bour-bon when he gets the chance. Maybelle believes in black magic. Cora goes to school at night, working on a degree in computer science. Had a confidential talk with Luther Kinnon—

Annie knew Luther well. He ran a successful landscaping and yard business. His youngest son Samuel had been accused of murder one July Fourth that none of them would ever forget and it was thanks to Annie and Max that Samuel's innocence had been proved.

—and when he knew I was trying to help you and Max, he got busy and found out a lot. Luther says he talked to all of them and nobody in the back of the house had any use for Vanessa. Esther pursed her lips and said, "Boast not thyself of tomorrow; for thou knowest not what a day may bring forth." William muttered that Vanessa had a spiteful tongue. Maybelle tossed her head and said she'd told Vanessa that the Evil Eye was on her and Vanessa had laughed. Cora wondered if anybody had claim on Vanessa's clothes.

Annie felt chilled. Surely someone grieved for Vanessa. Annie resented how Vanessa had deceived Max, but she had already paid a bitter price. She too had been deceived. It was the shadowy figure behind Vanessa who deserved scorn. That shadowy figure . . . Annie replaced Duane's report and the magazine printout in the house folder, picked up a folder entitled "Dossiers" and began to read:

Lillian Jennings Whitman Dodd—b. April 2, 1954, in Fort Worth, Texas. Father Mitchell Jennings, oilman, mother Agnes Hale, homemaker. Educated private schools, BFA University of Texas 1975, m. Howard Whitman in June 1980. He was a good deal older than Lillian. They met on a cruise to the Galapagos. He had been married twice before, no children. Whitman was a mining engineer who moved into management. They spent several years in Bolivia and later Brazil. After his retirement, they moved to Broward's Rock. One daughter, Heather. Whitman died nine years ago. Lillian met Jon Dodd at a local bridge tournament and they married four years ago. Lillian has always been active in art circles wherever they lived. She collects works by American Impressionist painters, including William Merritt Chase, Childe Hassam, and Guy C. Wiggins. She is active in charities and serves on several boards. She is renowned for elegant dinner parties. Guests receive a memento of the evening, sometimes a silver charm or piece of engraved crystal or miniature painting.

Annie finished the club soda, felt impatient. Lillian Dodd appreciated vivid splashes of oil on canvas, knew how to make guests feel cosseted, and was generous to her community. What made her laugh or cry? Who did she admire or loathe? Did she have friends or hangers-on? Annie skimmed down several paragraphs, then nodded in approval. Emma and Henny were as gifted at snagging tasty personal morsels as terns diving for menhaden.

Longtime Art League director Maurice McKenna: "Lillian goes out of her way to encourage young artists, everything from anonymously paying a month's rent to replenishing art supplies to picking up a hospital bill. She isn't judgmental, dismisses iconoclasm as youthful spirits even when it's a surly artist in his sixties. Once she said, 'Everyone's different but artists are even more different. They see things the rest of us don't see and they're not easy to understand. I find them fascinating. It would be wonderful to be outside looking in.' She sounded wistful. I think she's always felt constrained to be who she is because of who she is. If that makes any sense."

Hairdresser Sheila Becker: "I wish she'd let me frost her hair but she says she wouldn't feel comfortable. She's never had a face-lift. I can always tell. The scars are there."

Art dealer Louis Adler: "Shrewd. Not a trusting woman. I don't know if she was bilked at one time but something in her past has made her very cautious."

Social acquaintance Missy Moffat: "Oh, she's charming. But I've always thought there's something a little icy about her. A friend of hers once told me that Lillian holds a grudge, that she's not nearly as nice as most people think she is."

The Reverend Robert Cooley: "As with most people, the outward perception of Lillian often doesn't always match the reality of her being. I think she often feels lost and anxious."

Golf pro Hal Kelly: "A powerful swing. Can easily play from the men's tee. Nerveless putter."

Annie looked at the photos printed on a sheet. On a dance floor—a nightclub? charity ball? country club?—Lillian's silver chiffon dress swirled as her partner pulled her near. She was laughing. He smiled in return. Annie checked the caption: *Lillian and Jon Dodd*. They were a handsome couple. She was slender and graceful, with a thin, attractive, intelligent face framed by smooth straight brown hair. He looked comfortable and expansive, ruddy cheeked with straight black brows, a shock of black hair that looked as though it defied comb or gel, light green eyes and olive-toned skin. Annie realized that Lillian was taller than average, almost as tall as her companion. Annie looked at the text beneath the photo: *Lillian and Jon Dodd lead off the dancing at the annual Gala Ball at the Island Hills Country Club*. The next photograph caught Lillian, face intent, body lightly balanced, as she swung the sailboat tiller to windward. The wind lifted her hair, fluttered the loose-fitting red-and-white-striped tee. In the final photograph, she studied a chessboard, chin on her hand, expression alert, determined, and analytical.

Lillian Whitman Dodd would be a formidable opponent. At chess. Or any other endeavor.

Annie felt an instant of breathlessness. Tomorrow Georgia Lance had to be formidable too. Tomorrow . . . She glanced at the clock. Two twenty-five A.M. Tomorrow was here. She must finish quickly, snatch what sleep she could. There would be time to reread the dossiers before she arrived at the Whitman house, but she'd learned as a student that facts absorbed at night had a way of lodging deep in her mind, ready to be utilized when needed. She flipped to the next page:

Jon Buchanan Dodd—b. January 12, 1951, in Birmingham, AL. Father Calvin, an attorney. Mother Alice, a homemaker. BBA University of Alabama 1972, several years as a congressional aide in D.C., ten years with Atlanta PR agency, twelve years as assistant to Chamber of Commerce director in Jacksonville, opened a public relations agency on Broward's Rock seven years ago. A brief marriage to Helen Porter ended in divorce. No children. Master bridge player. On the Men's A ladder in tennis. Collects national political campaign buttons and letters written by famous Americans. Most recent acquisition: a letter written by Abraham Lincoln to his first vice president, Hannibal Hamlin, on June 16, 1864.

Bridge opponent Tom Gorman: "Don't play bridge for money with Jon Dodd. Somehow he always wins. Smiles a lot. Reminds me of a barracuda."

Client Harry Rodriguez: "Best money I ever spent. He put my store on the map. Business doubled the first month after his campaign started."

Doubles partner Sidney Schwartz: "Jon has a hell of an overhead smash. He's quick at the net. Good sport. He doesn't lose too often."

Secretary of the Jacksonville Chamber of Commerce, Janet Goodrich: "You can always count on Jon. He delivers. He's friendly, pleasant, responsible, and he never met a woman he couldn't charm."

Annie blinked tired eyes. Had he charmed the secretary and she hoped for more? It would have been interesting to have heard the tone of voice when Janet Goodrich spoke of him. Admiring? Sarcastic? Factual?

Annie studied the photographs of Jon Dodd. The most recent was from the island's Fourth of July parade. He held aloft a white straw boater with a red, white, and blue band. A flag T-shirt was in bright contrast to white shorts. He looked like a younger version of Jack Nicholson, with the same swagger and self-confidence. His cheeks flamed. Sunburn? High blood pressure? Bourbon? In a formal studio portrait, he was grave with a slight smile. There was no touch of gray in his curly black hair. In an informal snapshot, he sprawled on a picnic blanket, completely at ease, his head thrown back as he roared with laughter.

Annie tipped her glass, finished the soda, crunched a piece of ice, and turned to the next page:

Heather Whitman—b. January 15, 1982, in La Paz, Bolivia. She was six when her parents moved to Broward's Rock. Graduated from Broward's Rock High School. Played tennis, soccer, and field hockey. On the swim team, state record in the 200 backstroke. Editor high school yearbook. BA in English from Clemson. Junior year at sea. Tennis intramurals singles champion. Became engaged in her senior year to Kyle Curtis. They had been dating since junior high school. Returned to island after graduation to plan December wedding.

High school best friend Ellen Massad: "Loyal to a fault. Once she decides you're on her team, that's it. I've tried to tell her Kyle's bad news and she never would listen. She thinks everybody gives him a hard time. I guess he's always been swell to her, but I think he's like a train without brakes and there's sure to be a smashup."

College roommate Gina Fitzwilliam: "I hoped she'd go to New York with me. I mean, you're only young once. But all she wants is

Kyle. What a bore. If you're married at twenty-two, well, I mean, what's the fun in that?"

English professor Roland Cardew: "Heather has an original turn of mind. She doesn't care if a writer's out of fashion. She wrote her senior thesis on Kipling's 'When Earth's Last Picture Is Painted.' I liked that."

So did Annie. The rousing poem had color and cadence. Annie smiled. The poem was a favorite of Emma's and she was only too willing to recite it. Often. Annie loved the second verse, relishing the image of brushes of comets' hair splashing paint on a ten-league canvas. Emma's favorite was the third verse with its paean to the glory of work for sheer pleasure.

Annie wished that she could meet Heather Whitman as a friend, not enter her world ready to destroy it. But Vanessa and her murderer had made the Whitman house and all who frequented it fair game as far as Annie was concerned. Her eyes dropped to the page:

Bridal consultant Nora Delmonte: "As far as I'm concerned, if she breaks one more appointment she can find a new consultant. Nice enough girl but I'm not a damn therapist. If she wants an outdoor wedding, it's time to make some decisions."

Longtime friend Jimmy Frazier: "Maybe I'm a last-century kind of guy. Do or die for a lady who doesn't give a damn. I passed up a chance to go with a national law firm in Chicago because I knew she was coming back to the island. You know that old George Jones song. But I don't think I'll stop loving her even when I'm dead."

Annie studied Heather's pictures with interest. Eyes merry, lips curved in laughter, Heather caught a bridal bouquet with an athlete's sure grasp. The shocking-pink short-length bridesmaid's dress made the other bridesmaids look gawky and frumpy. Heather was slim and appealing, the pink a nice foil for her dark hair. In a studio portrait there was a hint of rebelliousness in the direct, challenging stare of vivid blue eyes. She wasn't conventionally pretty, her nose a shade long, her chin pointed, her cheekbones sharp, but the combination was striking and intriguing. In a snapshot, she strolled hand in hand on the beach with a tall, lanky young man. She looked up at him, her expression quizzical. He was gazing not at her but at the horizon.

Annie flipped to the photographs of Kyle Curtis. He was Heather's companion on the beach.

Kyle Curtis—b. June 4, 1982, on Broward's Rock. Father Wilton a dentist, mother Teresa a realtor. One older sister, Margaret. Marriage ended in divorce when Kyle was twelve. Wilton now lives in Atlanta with his partner Mike Thayer. After his father's departure, Kyle twice ran away from home. He had been an excellent student. His grades slipped. He was considered a disciplinary problem in high school. Two DUIs. Kicked off the football team for fighting with the quarterback. He graduated from high school at the bottom of his class, didn't go to college, got a job as a seaman on a yacht that berths on Broward's Rock. Two years ago he used his savings plus a loan from his mother to buy a small oceangoing catamaran. He now runs his own business: Cat with Curtis.

Best friend in high school Julius Cray: "Man, did he know how to party. And creative! He got into the school computer system and sent a message to the faculty: 'Good morning. All classes dismissed for student holiday as a result of unused extra snow days.' He signed the principal's name and about half the teachers fell for it. We spent the day at the beach. But the best was when he got into the assistant principal's desk where she kept an extra pair of underwear. I mean, what kind of emergency was she expecting? Anyway, he got the panties —

they were slinky black—and ran them up the flagpole upside down. And Mrs. Coburn is a massive lady. That one got him suspended for two weeks. It's a miracle he ever graduated."

High school coach Roy Dollarhide: "A fine athlete. Tight end. Faster than a fox and just about as deceptive. Kicking him off the team probably cost us the state championship, but I had to do it. I don't think he and his dad have ever straightened things out. I wish Kyle could understand that people do the best they can. Anyway, Kyle never missed a chance to screw any girl who was willing. One of them was the quarterback's girlfriend. When he found out, he started taunting Kyle about his dad and they had a hell of a fight in the locker room before I got in there to break it up. Kyle threw the first punch, so he was the one that had to go. I can't help what had been said. You got to learn you can't always bust somebody when they make you mad. No matter what was said."

Skipper of Daisy's Delight Chester Maguire: "Good sailor. Guts. A passenger went overboard trying to reel in a blue marlin. Kyle went right in after him and there were sharks out there. I hated to lose him as a hand but I had to let him go when the owner's daughter got a little too friendly."

Annie understood Heather's passion for Kyle when she looked at his photographs. In a beach photo, a wide-brimmed hat shaded his face, providing only a glimpse of a cocky smile. His muscular body—broad shoulders, slim waist, powerful legs—gleamed with suntan oil. Boxy red trunks sagged from his hips. Sunlight glistened on the dark mat of hair on his chest. Everything about the way he stood—head tilted back, arms akimbo, legs widespread—proclaimed king-of-the-hill insouciance. Annie felt a smile tug at her lips. He wasn't the answer to any mother's prayer, but he was definitely an adventurous girl's easy choice. A snapshot pictured Kyle rappelling up a cliff. The close-up showed an unshaven face drawn in a tight frown of concentration. Muscles bulged in his arm as he pulled himself higher. A party pic caught Kyle and Heather unaware. She looked at him, eyes wide in dismay, a hand lifted in appeal. He lounged back against his chair, face stubborn, arms folded.

Annie wondered what had caused the disagreement. Did he want to leave? He didn't look comfortable. There was resistance in every line of his body. Was she insisting they stay? Was it a wedding reception? Whatever, Annie wondered if there would be a lifetime of miscommunication awaiting them.

Kyle would often be at the Whitman house, so he knew Vanessa. How well did he know her?

Annie pushed back her chair, stretched, stood. She opened another club soda, poured it over fresh ice, and carried the glass back to the table. She turned to the final dossiers:

Sam Golden—b. March 1, 1951, Monroe, Wisconsin. Father Stanton a dairy farmer, mother Betty homemaker. Four brothers, Aaron, Richard, Theodore, and Michael. Active in 4-H. In high school, excellent grades, lettered in three sports. Received appointment to West Point. Graduated ninth in his class. Infantry officer, assigned to Ft. Benning. Met Martha Whelan at a classmate's wedding. They were married in 1982. No children. They were stationed at Ft. Bliss, then he was deployed to Korea. Next duty station was Ft. Hauchuca. After his commitment had been served, he resigned his commission. They spent time in Paris, Acapulco, and San Francisco, moving to Broward's Rock ten years ago.

West Point classmate Lt. Col. Henry Harrison: "Sam was a good officer, but Martha hated the life. She didn't want to be a gypsy. Looks to me like they travel a lot. Of course, Ritz-Carltons are fancier than army posts. She inherited millions when her folks died, so they don't have to work. He'd be happier if he had some-thing to do."

Sam's oldest brother, Aaron: "Haven't seen much of Sam in re-cent years. People's lives take different paths. If he'd stayed in the Army . . . We'd hoped he and Martha would come home for our daughter's wedding. But they were in Nice."

Rare-book collector Joshua Rhodes: "He'll buy anything about the Peloponnesian War. Nice gentleman. Soft-spoken, courteous. A pleasure to deal with."

Annie saw more than a difference in age between his picture as a senior cadet and a recent studio portrait. The young West Pointer stood ramrod straight, blue eyes confident and eager, black hair cut short, face stern and resolved, the epitome of spit and polish. Now his dark hair was streaked with silver, his gaze remote, his expression vaguely sardonic. In a snapshot, he stood beside his wife, hand firmly on her elbow. She looked up at him, mouth twisted in anger. His face was sad.

Martha Whelan Golden—b. June 15, 1954, in Peoria, Illinois. Fa-ther Charles real estate investment, mother Serena homemaker. One sister, Melissa, who died in a car accident in high school. Martha had excellent grades in high school. At Northwestern, she majored in his-tory. Roomed for two years with Lillian Jennings. Lillian is her closest friend. Martha's parents were killed in a small plane crash two years after she finished college. Married 2nd Lt. Sam Golden in 1982. Lived at various army posts until he resigned his commission. Lived abroad, traveled widely, settled on Broward's Rock ten years ago and bought the house next to Lillian Whitman.

Family cook for the Whelans in Peoria, Hilda Morrissey: "Poor little Miss Martha. First Missy died. She took that so hard. Tried to be perfect. Martha didn't care much about school but all of a sudden she had to make all A's. Missy had planned to go to Northwestern, so that's where Miss Martha went. Then when Mr. and Mrs. Whelan died, she was like a waif. I was so glad when she met Mr. Sam and got married. If they'd had a family . . . But they didn't. Sometimes, you know, it's harder to be left alive. Poor little Miss Martha."

Bridge player Madge Burton: "Martha's partner is sick and tired of putting up with her. Martha doesn't fool anybody with that little bottle of 'perfume' in her purse. A few sips in the ladies' room and she thinks she can bid any way she wants to. And she's not any too damn sweet when she's high."

Body shop repairman Luke Cheval: "Mr. Golden doesn't even think about calling the insurance company. I don't know how many times she's bashed in one of their cars. He hides the keys but then she goes next door and takes one of Mrs. Dodd's cars. Everybody knows they keep the keys hanging on the wall. Mrs. Dodd was real nice about it the time Mrs. Golden clipped the fountain in the front drive.

In the family Christmas card photograph, Charles Whelan looked prosperous and proud. Serena Whelan had a gentle smile. Their two daughters, both in red velvet dresses, stood between them, Melissa holding a huge gray tabby, Martha with one hand lifted to stroke the cat. Martha was slender and ethereal, red-gold hair swirling in soft curls, green eyes eager and excited.

Annie lifted the glass, drank deeply, but the buzz of the soda did nothing to diminish the sadness of a photograph taken before happiness and safety were swept away.

Martha was still ethereal in her wedding picture, but the shadows were there, eyes that held sadness, the faint droop of lips no longer quick to smile. In a snapshot taken at a bridge tournament, she stared at her hand. Her face was lined, her eyes bleak, her mouth hard. She looked impatient, pouty, and dissatisfied.

Annie closed the folder. Now she had a picture in her mind of the Whitman house. Within hours she would meet Lillian Dodd, her husband, Jon, her daughter, Heather, and possibly Heather's fiancé, Kyle. The next-door neighbors, Sam and Martha Golden, would be present at some point. The images in her mind would become people with hopes and fears, dreams and disappointments. One of them hid a terrible secret if Annie's instinct was right. If Georgia Lance ferreted out that secret, Max would be free. He would come home to love and life.

If Georgia Lance failed . . .

7

W here is she?" Max struggled to keep his voice low. If he made a disturbance, the guard would haul him back to his cell. He wanted to smash a chair through the screen, grab his lawyer by the shoulders. The guard sat on a straight chair near the door of the conference room, face impassive, arms folded. Three panels in the overhead fluorescent light were dim, making the dingy room even darker.

Handler Jones's boyish face was troubled. "I don't know. Your secretary called this morning and asked me to tell you that Annie will be occupied for the next few days, that she's left the island. Barb said you weren't to worry—"

"Not worry!" Max's voice was hoarse. "She's trying to find the murderer. I know she is. We've got to stop her."

The lawyer turned his hands palms up. "I've got calls in to Emma Clyde, Ingrid Webb, and Henny Brawley. No one has responded."

———

Emma's tone was demanding. "What was her boyfriend's name when you were juniors?"

Annie's skin felt itchy beneath the wig. She poked up a finger and scratched. "Frank. Frank Jacobs. Six foot three. Center on the basketball team. He and Vanessa dated for two years." Annie had studied Frank's "O" Club picture. He was lean but muscular, with a beaked nose and a mop of curly red hair.

Makeup brush in hand, Henny tilted her head to look critically at Annie's face. "Mix a little of the peach powder with the base. That will make you look sallow. And no fingers under your wig, you've tilted it." She held a hand mirror in front of Annie.

Annie gazed at her reflection. The line of her eyebrows was changed. They were black as hot asphalt and arched as a startled cat's back. The faintly pink tint of the wire-rim glasses made her gray eyes less distinct and striking. The makeup transformed her fair complexion into a muddy tan, hiding the spatter of freckles on her nose. Vivid coral lipstick was far brighter than any she ever chose. She reached up, straightened the wig. "Henny, you're a marvel."

"Not bad. Not bad. It's almost as much fun as stage makeup." Henny wiped her fingers on a tissue. "You're definitely okay with your appearance. But more important than the way you look"—Henny's tone was suddenly grave—"is the way you feel. You're Georgia Lance. You don't know Annie Darling. You know nothing about her or the island or the Dodds or the Whitman house. Everything's new to you. But you know a lot about Vanessa."

"Lots of slumber parties." Emma riffled through some sheets. "Where's her birthmark?"

"A strawberry mark an inch below her right elbow."

"Favorite band?"

"Backstreet Boys."

"Favorite baseball team?"

"Cubs."

"Favorite player?"

"Carlos Zambrano."

"What was she scared of?"

"Thunderstorms."

"What was her cat's name?"

"Pretty Miss."

"What did she call her big sister?"

"Ginny."

Emma straightened the sheets. "You'll do." A frown corrugated her face. "I hope to God. Look, Annie, don't take any chances. If you get scared, get the hell out of there."

The front door banged open. Face flushed from exertion, Ingrid bustled inside. Her arms were full with several FedEx packages, a sack, and a shopping bag. She used her foot to push the door shut. She looked at the clock. "Whew. I made it. As long as we get you to the noon ferry, the timing will work out. It's been hectic. I've been busy every minute, but"—her faded eyes were worried—"I can't find Laurel. Obviously, she doesn't want to be found. I got a call from Barb a few minutes ago. Laurel sent a message to you." Ingrid reached the table, unloaded the packages. "Barb insists that Laurel said, 'If we don't see anything from the outside in, well then, we must look from the inside out. And, of course, there are only six degrees of separation. More anon.' That was it. Do you have any idea what she meant?"

Annie long ago had ceased trying to understand the convoluted patterns of her mother-in-law's mind. "God knows."

Emma looked skeptical. "Possibly. But wherever she is, whatever she's doing, we don't have time to worry about it right now." She looked at the packages on the table. "The Illinois license plates?"

Ingrid pointed at a FedEx box with the pleasure of a conjuror producing a fat rabbit. "It arrived on the early ferry. Emma, how did you do it?"

"Oh"—the author's tone was vague, but her eyes were amused— "I thought what I'd do if I needed an object for a scavenger hunt, rather an elaborate hunt. Say someone wanted a California license plate. Well, if you had a friend who often went shopping, say to the Beverly Center, what would be easier than taking along a screwdriver and in a remote area of the parking garage, lifting the plates? Another possibility would be finding one of those pull-apart junkyards. In any event, I suppose someone seeking something like that might make a couple of phone calls and presto"—she waved a stubby hand at the box—"the next morning the needed items would arrive. Now, it's time to load the car. Duane can drive it over to Beaufort. He'll change the plates and leave the car at the lot at Saint Helena's. Georgia's suitcases will already be in the trunk. I'll take my houseguest sightseeing"—she looked at Annie, an unrecognizable Annie with dark hair and olive-toned skin and wire-rim glasses perched on her nose—"and of course we will visit historic Beaufort."

Emma's Rolls-Royce slid to a stop in the shade of a live oak at the far end of the church parking lot. She parked next to the shabby cream Toyota with Illinois license plates. The car was dusty with a few artistic mud splashes. It looked as if it had been driven a long way.

As Annie opened the door, Emma said gruffly, "Maybe you better not take your cell. If anyone got hold of it, it would be easy to trace it to you."

"No one's going to get hold of it." If necessary, she'd tuck it under her pillow at night, keep it in a pocket during the day. She pushed away the uneasiness that threatened to engulf her. She was going to be fine. After all, her quarry had no idea the fox was sniffing near. The murderer at this point should be relaxed, confident his scheme had succeeded. "I'll be careful with the phone. And Emma"—Annie reached out to touch her old friend's arm—"thank you."

Emma was brusque. "No thanks needed. Just find the bastard."

Annie found the keys tucked beneath the backseat floor mat. By the time she stood up, the Rolls-Royce was gone. Annie slipped behind the wheel, started the motor, turned on the air-conditioning. As she waited for the car to cool, she glanced down at the passenger seat. She picked up a printout of the MapQuest route from Wilmette to Broward's Rock: *Total estimated time: 16 hours, 6 minutes.* The route was marked with a bright red pencil. On the floor was a crumpled food sack. She opened it, found a receipt from a McDonald's in Spartanburg. She wondered who Emma had called there with her story of a scavenger hunt. But if anyone was curious about Georgia Lance and her car, they were welcome to look. In her purse, which she would leave unguarded in the guest quarters, her billfold contained an Illinois driver's license as well as assorted credit cards, all belonging to Georgia Lance. Annie hadn't inquired of Emma as to the origin of these items. Quite likely Emma's young computer guru had myriad talents in the creation of computer-generated materials, talents which were better left undisclosed. There was even an Illinois Power and Light bill, a little crumpled, and a couple of cash receipts from Marshall Field's.

As she turned the car, a Carlos Zambrano bobblehead wobbled from its perch on the dash. Georgia and Vanessa had sat in the bleachers at many a Cubs game. Annie looked at her watch. Her timing was perfect. She would catch the two o'clock ferry to the island and arrive at the Whitman house just before three. Three o'clock on Thursday afternoon. The Dodds were leaving on Saturday for Cape Cod. Annie's face—she glanced at the unfamiliar visage in the mirror—set in resolve. Between now and then . . .

————

Henny Brawley slammed the trunk lid of her old black Dodge. Three boxes held a thousand copies each of the flyer she'd created. She carried a folder with two hundred. That was enough for a start. Somewhere on this island someone must have seen Vanessa Taylor in the company of her murderer. Even if Vanessa's usual contact had been at the Whitman house, a love affair surely brought them into public view somewhere. If not . . . Henny pushed that thought away.

She would be methodical and visit every island business, ask if she could leave twenty-five copies. She climbed the steps to the boardwalk that fronted the harbor. Her first stop was a dental office. She stepped inside, glad she wasn't a patient. She never entered a dentist's office without remembering the unfortunate Greek businessman in Agatha Christie's *One, Two, Buckle My Shoe*. As she waited behind a sunburned woman in halter and shorts with one hand pressed to her cheek, Henny scanned her flyer: A bold headline in red topped the sheet: BE A DETECTIVE AND EARN TEN THOUSAND DOLLARS. Beneath the headline was a picture of a smiling Vanessa on the left and a square box with a huge question mark on the right. Next came a boldface paragraph:

Efforts are under way to trace recent activities of murder victim Vanessa Taylor. If you have seen Vanessa and can describe her companions, please call Barb at 321-HELP. If the information provided leads to the arrest and conviction of her murderer, a ten-thousand-dollar reward will be yours.

The woman in front of her moved toward a seat. Henny reached the counter, put down a sheaf of flyers, smiled. "I'm Henny Brawley and . . ."

The fountain in the paved courtyard reminded Annie of a hacienda she and Max had once visited in San Miguel de Allende. Water splashed from a stone porpoise into a blue-tiled basin, providing an illusion of coolness. The drive curved around the fountain. Annie parked near the front door of the two-story pale lemon stucco house. Of course, one branch of the drive led to the south and the garage, the other to the north and the lane to the guest cottages. But she had never been here, didn't know that fact, would wait until she was told and then she'd drive the car there. By the time she'd mounted the broad shallow steps, she was hot and sweaty. She would certainly look the part of the weary traveler.

An art-glass door glittered in the midafternoon sun. Annie pushed the bell. She was Georgia Lance, Vanessa's old friend. She'd driven nine hours from Asheville and she was tired and sad about Vanessa but excited to see a place she'd never been to. . . .

The door opened. A petite young black woman in a neat gray uniform looked at her politely.

"I'm Georgia Lance. Mrs. Dodd is expecting me." Annie looked into an entry hall bright with flowers in a tall jade vase on a glass table.

"Yes, Miss Lance. Please come in." The maid held the door.

Annie was aware of dark intelligent eyes and a swift, covert, curious glance.

"Mrs. Dodd is in the living room. If you'll come this way." The maid turned toward an archway.

Annie heard a murmur of voices. She reached the archway to a long room with dark Monterey furniture. Instead of the expected leather cushions, there were bright splashes of orange and red fabrics. Instead of the expected cream of stucco, silk-covered walls were cool and elegant with stylized storks among green rushes. The mixture of styles was odd but came together to create a sense of both comfort and challenge.

"Mrs. Dodd"—the girl's voice was soft—"Miss Lance is here."

Annie swept the room with a quick glance. Lillian Dodd looked regal in a high-backed chair that might have come from a castle in Seville. Her dark hair was brushed back in a bun. A double chain of lapis lazuli looked bright against her white V-neck blouse. The delft blue linen skirt was perfectly matched in color by her ankle-strap sandals. Sitting opposite Lillian was a dramatic figure in a red and gold turban and cream sheath dress. Oversize red-framed glasses almost obscured the elegance of a beautiful woman's bone structure. Almost, but not quite.

Annie paused in the archway. It was good that hesitation might be expected, because she could not have managed another step. She stared at the turbaned woman, who was still talking.

"... thrilled that the contessa asked me to see you. Actually, she required it of me and you know how imperious she can be." A trill of laughter. "I promised faithfully to bring her note of introduction immediately and that explains my rush to see you the moment I arrived on your glorious island. Although I am always hesitant to look up a friend of a friend—my dear, that can sometimes be simply excruciatingly difficult—I can tell that we are simpatico. I will certainly be able to fulfil my promise to return laden with pictures of you and your family and full to the brim"—a graceful hand swept toward the ceiling, a huge aquamarine stone sparkling in a shaft of light from a west window—"of the most intimate details of your lives these past few years since you and Joyce parted. And I—" The oversize glasses were lifted, Nordic blue eyes widened in surprise as they surveyed the archway. "Ah, we have a guest." The husky voice evinced anticipation and delight.

Annie knew that face, knew that voice, knew that gesture, knew those wide blue eyes. She was torn between panic and fury. Laurel *here*. Laurel's talent for outrageous behavior had often afforded Max and Annie amusement, sometimes compounded by fear. This time she was risking the careful plan Annie had devised. But Annie understood her mother-in-law's decision. Annie had made the same decision. Vanessa Taylor's life had been circumscribed by the Whitman house. The seeds of her death would either be discovered here or not at all. Annie felt frozen until her gaze locked with Laurel's and in her dark blue eyes she saw warning and encouragement and a mother's desperate determination to rescue her child.

Using all the guile at her command, Annie contrived to look bewildered as though uncertain who might be her hostess.

Lillian Dodd rose, came across the terra-cotta floor. She smiled at the maid, said, "Thank you, Cora," and turned to Annie. "Hello, Georgia. I'm Lillian Dodd. You've had a long drive. Did you have any trouble finding us?"

Annie looked earnest. "I got directions at a Gas 'N' Go right after I got off the ferry. I wrote them down"—indeed she had and they were lying in the front seat of the Toyota next to the MapQuest printout—"and they were perfect. I didn't know it was all going to be so beautiful. And your house—Vanessa said everything was gorgeous but she didn't tell me how tall the trees are. I don't think I've ever seen such tall trees."

"This house is truly a gem in an ornate setting." Laurel's husky voice lifted in enthusiasm.

Lillian looked toward her turbaned guest. There was intelligence and cool appraisal in Lillian's dark brown eyes. "How gracious of you, Lady Hamilton—"

Lady Hamilton? Annie was no authority on mistresses but she had a vague memory that Lady Hamilton knew Lord Nelson better than well.

Lady Hamilton rose with a quick smile. "Oh, please. I am Maisie to everyone from the scullery maid to the Prime Minister. After all, I am American born and that, of course, is what drew the contessa to me, since she grew up"—a lilting smile at Lillian—"as Joyce Bainbridge in Fort Worth. When she knew I was coming to the island, she was ecstatic to be able to direct me to her dear childhood friend Lillian Jennings. What great good fortune that the lovely home next door was available to be leased! I scarcely expected to be so near. We've made a good start this afternoon on catching up with all the wonderful adventures of the years since you and Joyce were together. But now I must leave you to your guest." She looked kindly at Annie. "Lillian has been telling me of the great sadness that brings you here. I have commended her for her generosity in inviting you."

Lillian made an impatient gesture. "We are very glad to have Vanessa's old friend stay here. If there is anything we can do to help Georgia bring comfort to Vanessa's sister, of course we are happy to do so."

Laurel was fluttering toward the archway. She paused to look back. "I know this invitation comes at short notice." A beaming smile. "But time is of the essence, since you plan to leave on Saturday—"

Annie looked at her mother-in-law with respect. She'd obviously both ingratiated herself as Lady Hamilton and gleaned information.

"—I hope you and your husband and daughter and her young man and Miss Lance will come to my house for dinner. Shall we say seven?"

Annie knew Laurel was capable, but leasing a house, moving in, and planning a dinner party all in the same day was amazing even for her.

"Lady Hamilton, that is very gracious of you, but I'm sure Miss Lance is weary from her drive. We'll have a quiet evening here. Another time perhaps." Lillian's voice was pleasant but her expression distant.

"Oh, of course I understand. It would have been such a pleasure to have everyone. I'd already spoken to your dear friends the Goldens." Laurel's smile was bright. "Joyce enjoyed meeting them here on her last visit. I had a lovely conversation over the phone with Martha just before I came over to see you. She and Sam accepted my invitation. I'm afraid I told them I was sure your family would come if you didn't have a previous engagement. I had hoped this evening would make it possible for me to bring Joyce up to date on everyone."

Lillian was a moment in responding, then she turned both hands over, an oddly endearing gesture. "Please, Lady Hamilton, come and join us this evening. You will be most welcome. I'll call Martha and invite them."

"That is simply dear of you." Laurel reached the archway, looked toward Annie. "Miss Lance, I wish you the greatest of success in gathering memories of your friend. I'll look forward to seeing you this evening."

Lillian moved to open the front door.

As it closed behind Laurel, Annie took a step toward her hostess. "Mrs. Dodd, I didn't realize you were leaving town this weekend. I hope I'm not being a bother."

"Not at all." The response was quick and warm. "We're glad to be able to help Vanessa's sister and I'll be happy to have you stay in the cottage as long as necessary. The staff will be here to help." Lillian's face was somber. "It's all so terrible. I still find it hard to believe that Vanessa is dead."

"That's another reason I came." Annie's voice was uneven. "We can't believe it either. Vanessa never mentioned that man to us, the one who was arrested. We don't think it makes any sense."

Lillian's brows drew down in a frown. "There doesn't seem to be any question about his guilt. Anyway"—she forced a smile—"let me show you to your guest cottage. When you're ready, I'll introduce you to everyone." She took a deep breath. "And take you to Vanessa's cottage."

"That would be perfect." Annie could scarcely contain her eagerness. Her first goal was to gain access to Vanessa's cottage and make a search for her diary. Judy Denton thought the diary might be hidden. If only Judy were right, if only a diary existed. Annie knew she mustn't hope for too much. Whether she found a diary or not, she was in the Whitman house and soon would meet those whom Vanessa had known. Annie smiled at Lillian Dodd and followed her down the hallway.

Billy Cameron glanced at his watch. In ten minutes he had to be downstairs for the second session of the afternoon: Protection for Harbors. He felt a curl of ice in his gut. How many miles of unprotected harbors existed in the United States? Too many. The possibilities of terrorism— a boat loaded with explosives, a kamikaze plane, mines—were infinite. Intelligence was the only answer and that was beyond the scope of a country cop. Of course, he had plenty of friends among the charter boat captains and the fishing-boat captains. He made it a point to check with them, asking them to keep an eye peeled for anything odd, an unfamiliar boat in an unexpected place. That was all he could do.

His cell rang. He smiled, clicked it on. "Hi, honey. Anything new?"

Over the crackle of a poor connection, Mavis talked fast. "There have been a couple of calls to Crime Stoppers, but nothing that looks helpful. The circuit solicitor held a news conference and you'd think he caught Max singlehandedly. Most of the media's left town. Lou went back to Blackbeard Beach. He found a couple of people who saw Max there late Monday afternoon and he was by himself. I guess that doesn't help."

"Shows he was telling the truth about going there. And"—Billy's face pulled in a frown—"if he was alone there, if we could prove he drove to Dooley's Mine by himself, that would be a help. That would mean she got there some other way." Billy felt a tingle of excitement. "Her car was found nearby the marina parking lot. Have Lou keep nosing around. Tell him to try and find someone who saw Max in his car at Blackbeard Beach. Ditto, if he can find someone who saw him arrive at Dooley's Mine. If Lou can trace Vanessa to a silver car, that would be a hell of a link."

"Will do. The conference good?"

"It's okay. I'm having trouble concentrating. I keep thinking about that damn silver car. The kids okay?"

"Kevin woke up with a sore throat. A summer cold. Lily brought her favorite Pooh to kiss him and make him well."

Billy smiled. He never thought about Lily without a catch in his heart. His little girl, so kind, so beautiful. "Hug 'em for me. See you tomorrow night."

He clicked off the cell and straightened his uniform shirt and turned off the light of the hotel room. He picked up the conference packet, but instead of harbors he thought of a silver car. If Lou connected Vanessa to that car . . .

The long hallway was cool. Ceiling fans whirred. When they reached a cross hall, Lillian gestured to her left. "This hallway leads to the kitchen on one side and the dining room on the other. The exit at the kitchen end of the hall is nearest to the cottages. I know it's confusing at first but think of it this way, this hall goes to the cottages, the hall straight ahead leads to the terrace and pool and the boardwalk to the beach. The Golden house is beyond the cottages, the Spruill house is beyond the garages. Lady Hamilton is staying at the Spruill house. We'll go by the kitchen on our way out."

The cross hall was equally wide and shadowy and cool. Lillian walked swiftly, Annie at her side.

Archways opened on their left to a long room with a dining room table and china cabinets. Lillian stopped midway up the hall and pushed open a white swinging door. They stepped into a huge, well-kept kitchen. Annie saw two ranges, a freezer, a massive refrigerator. A central island served as a preparation area. Gleaming pans hung from hooks above the island. The marble countertops were immaculate. There was a smell of baking.

A wiry black woman, head covered with a triangular calico kerchief, looked up. She was pouring a mixture into a blue bowl and beating it with a whisk. Across the room a plump young woman was unloading a dishwasher.

"Mmm." Lillian looked toward the bowl. "Something smells wonderful."

The whisk continued to beat. "Tonight we'll be having pear fritters with pear custard sauce."

Lillian smiled. "One of my favorite desserts. Georgia, I want you to meet Esther, the world's greatest cook—"

The calico kerchief quivered as Esther nodded. Bright dark eyes swept Annie.

"—and Maybelle, who keeps everything sparkling."

The plump young woman at the dishwasher smiled shyly.

"This is Vanessa's friend, Georgia Lance. She's come to take Vanessa's things home to her sister. Georgia's staying in Cottage three."

The cook looked gravely at Annie. "'For we must needs die, and are as water spilt on the ground, which cannot be gathered up again.'"

In the silence that followed, Lillian sighed. "Nothing can bring Vanessa back to us." Her face was tired and drawn. "Georgia, you are certainly welcome to take all of your meals with the family, although the kitchen in the cottage is stocked. Is there anything you would like to have Maybelle bring you?"

"Oh, that's thoughtful of you." Annie frantically tried to think of something to ask for that would likely not be included in the usual guest provisions. It would be a heaven-sent opportunity to talk to one of the staff. "Why, yes, I'd really appreciate . . . some celery and carrots." Almost any kitchen would have celery and carrots. "That's my favorite snack." Of the many lies she'd told this day, this surely would have amused Max the most. *Oh Max, are you scared? Do you know we're trying? Someday I will tell you about this and you'll laugh.*

Esther had resumed whisking. "Maybelle will bring them out in a few minutes."

As they left the kitchen, Esther's voice intoned: "'There is no peace saith the Lord unto the wicked.'"

As the door sighed shut, Lillian smiled. "Esther is not only a great cook, she is a good woman. Every conversation is peppered with biblical quotations, but there is nothing sanctimonious about Esther. She's a good tether to reality when I get too immersed in the here and now and forget that life isn't a series of committee meetings. This morning at breakfast she placed the last casserole on the sideboard, then turned and announced: '"Whoso diggeth a pit shall fall therein."' I suppose she was referring to the man who killed Vanessa. He definitely is caught in a trap of his own making—"

Annie forced herself to look inquiring and pleasant.

"—but I know I don't want to dwell on him or what happened to Vanessa." Her voice was somber.

They reached the end of the hall. Lillian held open the door. As they walked down the steps, heat rolled over them like a heavy wave. A path of crushed oyster shells wound past a long lagoon into a grove of pines.

"It isn't as far as it looks." Lillian walked briskly despite the heat. The shells crackled underfoot. Crows cawed. Wasps buzzed near sweet-scented Japanese honeysuckle. Lillian ducked to avoid a wasp. "The cottages are nestled in the pines on the far side of the lagoon. There's a lane through the pines. I'll ask William—he's Esther's husband—to bring your car around. He can help with your luggage."

They reached the lagoon and followed the path to the far side. They passed two cottages. Annie looked back across the dark water at the house. It was another fifty yards to the third cottage. When they reached it, Lillian pointed to the south. "The garage is on the other side of the house. You can't see it from here but you are welcome to park there. There is also a place to park here beside the cottage. Vanessa always parked by her cottage. She was in Cottage two."

Lillian unlocked the door. She stepped inside, turned on the light, and held the door for Annie.

Though the decor was as impersonal as a hotel, the living room was cheerful. Bright red and blue cushions were in dramatic contrast to the shining white of the wicker furniture. Seascapes of catamarans and sailboats decorated bamboo walls. A conch shell was centered on a glass coffee table. A light oak coffee bar separated the living room from a small kitchen dining area.

Annie looked admiringly around the room. "Thank you for letting me stay. The cottage is lovely and being here will make it easy to box up Vanessa's belongings." At the last, Annie looked suddenly forlorn. "I still can't believe she's gone. It had been so long since I'd talked to her. And now—" She struggled for composure.

Lillian hesitantly touched Annie's arm. "I'm sorry."

Annie managed a smile. "I'm sorry for you too. After all, she'd been living here for more than a year. Just like one of the family."

There was a curious expression on Lillian's expressive face, a mixture of dismay and chagrin. "Vanessa—" She broke off, shook her head.

Annie was eager. "Please, won't you tell me? That's what I'm hoping for. Memories to take back to Ginny."

Lillian once again turned her hands over. Annie saw the gesture as an unconscious revelation of reluctant acquiescence. "I wish I could be more helpful. I never felt I knew Vanessa well. She was cheerful and pleasant. She did a good job for me. She enjoyed shopping and knew quite a bit about fashion. She was always willing to be an extra at a party where there would be single men. She loved to dance and play tennis. But I always felt there was a person beyond the smile that I never knew. And—" abruptly Lillian's face was grave—"I'm afraid her death is proof of that. She had never mentioned that man to me, the one who was arrested, and yet she was the kind of woman who attracts men. She—" Lillian broke off.

Annie wondered if the sudden hardening of Lillian's face indicated anger. There was some emotion that she quickly hid.

"Oh well, whatever her faults—"

Faults? Annie wanted to interrupt, but Georgia's job was to be pleasant.

"—she was very young. I always hoped she'd find a young man to date, but she never seemed to have an outside social life but—"

Annie interrupted. Even if it might seem rude, this was information she must have. "No social life at all?" Her voice rose in disbelief. "But Vanessa loved parties and being with people."

"Oh, she certainly had all of that." Lillian rushed to explain. "She was always part of our activities and that seemed to satisfy her. I wondered why she didn't date. Now the answer seems clear. She was involved with a married man and had to keep him a secret. But I know this isn't what you want to tell her sister. I'm sorry."

Annie wondered how Lillian would respond if Annie pointed out there were two other married men who knew Vanessa quite well, Lillian's husband and Sam Golden. Instead, Annie said quietly, "I don't think Ginny would be surprised. She wants to know the truth. I'm going to try and find out what I can. I guess you can tell me what she was like that last day?"

"Last day?" Lillian looked puzzled.

"On Monday. Was she just as usual?" Vanessa had e-mailed Judy Denton that everything was going to be different. Annie watched Lillian carefully.

Lillian gave no inkling the question mattered to her. Instead, she looked apologetic. "I didn't see Vanessa Monday. Heather and I spent the weekend in Atlanta and we didn't drive back until Tuesday. I'd only been home a little while before the policeman came to tell me. I don't know if it would have made any difference if I'd been here. Jon didn't realize Vanessa hadn't come home Monday night. But there's no reason why he should have checked. When I'm out of town Vanessa's free—" A deep breath. "She was free to do as she wished."

Annie felt a tingle of excitement. Yes, Vanessa had been free to do as she wished that Monday. The same was true, since Lillian and Heather had been gone, for Lillian's husband and Heather's fiancé. "I doubt that it mattered." Annie spoke slowly. Deep inside, she wondered if the time of Vanessa's death had been chosen because Lillian and Heather were out of town.

"I hope not." Lillian sighed. She tried to smile. "I'm sure you want to rest a bit. Come up to the house whenever you wish. Dinner is at seven. We'll be in the family room before dinner. I'll give your car keys to William. And here"—Lillian pulled a key on a plastic ring from the pocket of her skirt—"is the key to Vanessa's cottage."

Annie wanted to hurry straight to Vanessa's cottage, but she forced herself to wait. This was a well-run household. Surely the maid would soon arrive with the requested celery and carrots.

She had time to use her cell phone to check messages on her home number. There were a half dozen she deleted as soon as she recognized them as calls for media interviews. Most of the other calls she saved for later consideration. Three were important:

1. "I've distributed almost a thousand flyers." Henny was upbeat. "I may have a lead. At Seaside Realty, a girl at the front desk said one of the agents thought she'd seen the murdered woman Saturday night at that new restaurant where Raffles used to be. I've got the agent's name and I'm trying to track her down."

2. "Dear child." Laurel's husky voice gave no hint she had been surprised to encounter Annie at the Whitman house. "Such an instructive meeting with Lillian Dodd. Of course it was natural that I should want to hear all about Heather for my report to Joyce. Lillian was obviously very concerned about her daughter and tried to avoid any discussion of the wedding plans. I was quite obtuse and persistent. I warbled on about dear young people and how stressful it is to marry and that the best tack to take when there are last-minute hesitations is making sure they have every chance to talk. She seemed to pounce on that. Sometimes it's easier to say things to a stranger. She looked utterly weary and said everything can get very confused and upsetting. Then she looked at me with this rueful smile and said, 'I hope you're right. I may have made a huge mistake. Heather hasn't been answering her phone when Kyle calls. She makes us say she isn't here. But she's miserable. I called Kyle, persuaded him to come to dinner. I don't know why I did it. I've opposed their getting married right from the beginning, but I've never seen her so unhappy. Maybe if he comes, it will make a difference. But please, if you see Heather, don't tell her what I've done.' I promised utmost discretion."

Annie gave a mental thumbs-up to her mother-in-law. Her visit with Lillian Dodd had been instructive indeed. What was wrong between Heather and Kyle? Annie had a quick memory of Kyle Curtis's photograph, a bold gaze and dangerously attractive face, a man who would be attractive to many women. Vanessa certainly would have been very careful not to let her employer know if she became involved with Heather's fiancé. That would explain why her e-mails to Judy Denton made no reference to a man.

Annie looked impatiently toward the door. She'd wait a few more minutes, then go on to Vanessa's cottage. If she could find Vanessa's diary . . .

3. "Some encouraging news." Handler Jones's smooth drawl was light as Tennessee whisky. "I have a friend at the state crime lab. The preliminary report on Max's clothes showed traces of the dead woman's blood but no spatter pattern consistent with his wielding the weapon. The expert thinks blood and tissue were swiped against Max's pants and likely his shirt as well. There's no way to gauge the shirt, since he tried to wash out the blood. The prosecution will use that against him but we can come back with the lack of a pattern on his trousers. I'll be seeing Max in the morning and I'll bring you—"

A knock sounded on the front door.

Annie punched Save, clicked off the cell, slipped it in the pocket of her skirt. She hurried to the door, opened it, pulled the screen door wide. "Come in."

The plump maid stepped inside. She gazed at Annie with avid curiosity as she handed her a bowl covered with plastic wrap.

Annie shut the screen, left the front door open. "Thank you." She smiled. "You're Maybelle?"

"Yes'm." She smiled in return. "Is there anything else I can do for you?"

"Yes." Annie kept her voice light. "I'd like to visit with you about Vanessa."

Maybelle's eyes became round. Her face was suddenly solemn.

Annie pointed toward the sofa. "Mrs. Dodd said I could speak with everyone. Please come and sit down and let's talk for a moment."

Perhaps the mention of her employer was reassuring. After a hesitant moment, Maybelle edged toward the sofa, sat stiffly on the edge of a cushion, looking as though she'd like to jump to her feet and run away.

Annie placed the bowl on a side table, sat opposite Maybelle. "I promised Vanessa's sister I would find out everything I could about the day Vanessa died. Did you see her Monday?"

A jerky nod. "In Mrs. Dodd's study. I was looking for her. I went to the study—that's where Mrs. Dodd has her computer—because I knew Vanessa was there and I felt like I had to tell her what I knew." The diffident mask of a servant fell away. "Vanessa didn't pay me no never mind." Maybelle's plump face was a study in conflicting emotions. She looked resentful, yet smug. "She was high and mighty even though I warned her. See, people don't believe me when I tell them."

Annie leaned forward. "When you tell them . . ."

Maybelle's eyes glittered. "I know about the magic. I told her what I saw. I saw the Evil Eye. She laughed and laughed, well, I guess she didn't have the last laugh. The Evil Eye means Death and Death always comes. I saw the Evil Eye, sure as the sun goes down. The Evil Eye looked at her and—"

"Maybelle, you get back to the house." The gruff voice sounded through the screen door. "Got your luggage here, miss."

Maybelle gave a little gasp and came to her feet. She rushed to the door. As she pushed through the screen, head down, shoulders tucked, a lanky man with grizzled hair swung Annie's suitcase inside. "Don't you give her the time of day, miss. Esther don't want that kind of talk. Esther says, 'Resist the Devil, and he will flee from you.' Maybelle don't have the sense God gave a rabbit in springtime. I'll see she don't bother you again."

———

Annie stepped into Vanessa's cottage and felt a shiver ripple through her mind and body. She wasn't prepared for this moment. She'd not thought beyond gaining entrance and searching for Vanessa's diary. Yet now she stood, stricken. She smelled a faint scent of lilies, saw a book spread open on the coffee table, a pale blue cardigan draped carelessly over the back of a chair, a Belk shopping bag yet to be emptied, flowers drooping in a pale green vase for want of fresh water, a room left with every intention of return.

Although the furnishings were similar to those in Annie's guest cottage, this room reflected Vanessa. She had chosen the matted prints, the Chicago skyline in a swirl of snow, a heron perched on one leg in the dark water of a lagoon, a ribbon of train track in a misty rain. She had curled comfortably, creating a slight depression in the soft cushion of a chintz-covered chair. She had held the book. . . . Annie walked nearer, saw photographs of French chateaus in the Loire valley, a world far from Vanessa. Had she wanted to visit there, see grand buildings in faraway countries?

Annie felt ashamed. She was here under false pretenses, claiming to be Vanessa's friend. That was far from true. If Vanessa were here, Annie would confront her angrily. Vanessa had lied to Max. Max had thought he was helping her and it was all a lie.

Annie's fingers lightly touched the blue sweater, a beautiful cashmere sweater. Its owner had been only a few years younger than Annie. Abruptly, Annie's anger fled. Vanessa had been tricked too. Vanessa had left this room on Monday, gone out with a devious plan to execute. She'd played a role, not knowing that she was a victim too.

The room no longer resisted Annie. She wasn't quite sure why. Was it because she'd made room for understanding as well as anger in her heart? Or was it because she now felt that she was in league with Vanessa? If Annie succeeded in her quest, not only would Max be freed, Vanessa would be avenged.

Annie checked the obvious places first—bookcases, desk, chest of drawers, and vanity in the bedroom. She scanned the bathroom, looked in the cabinets. Then it was a matter of pulling out cushions, running a hand beneath furniture, lifting the mattress, peering at the shelving in the closets.

It was almost six when she gave up. Tomorrow when she packed Vanessa's belongings in boxes, she would shake out everything, make a final thorough search. As she walked back to her cabin, she was already focusing on what was to come, dinner at the Whitman house and her introduction to the men Vanessa had known.

Billy Cameron stood behind a potted palm in the hotel lobby. Conference attendees were streaming toward the banquet hall. He'd get there in a minute. He punched the cell, was pleased when Lou Pirelli answered.

"Lou, Billy. Anything?" He didn't have to explain what he meant. Lou knew that Billy was frustrated to be 170 miles away and blocked from directing a search for that damnable, elusive silver car.

"Yeah. Sometimes you find out the old-fashioned way. You know how hard we've tried to find anything at all on that silver car, the one Dooley saw leaving the parking lot right after Max's Jag? I decided to walk River Otter Road between Dooley's Mine and the murder cabin. I wasn't looking for anything special, but I thought maybe I'd get an idea. I spotted a shack about halfway and I saw a guy sitting on his front porch. I—"

Billy covered one ear, strained to hear over the din of conversations around him. Lou was always low key, but tonight his voice sounded excited.

"—went up to see him. Old man, bib overalls, drinking a beer, had a shepherd on a chain. Damn dog lunged like he wanted to sink his teeth in my throat. There was tar paper over the front window. One of the porch steps was missing. I had to stay a couple of feet from the stairs because of the dog. The guy looked at me like I was pond scum. I told him I was police and we were trying to find anybody who'd seen cars on River Otter Road about sundown Monday. He folded his face up in a frown, said he didn't hold with people coming where they weren't wanted. Cars and trucks and whatnot up and down the road all week and he was damn tired of it. Wished that girl had picked herself someplace else to get killed. Got so he didn't even bother to look, there'd been so many. I almost gave it up right then but something about the way he'd said he'd stopped looking made me wonder how much he'd seen earlier. So I tried again. I told him it was real important if he remembered any cars on Monday evening before all the traffic started. Since River Otter Road was a dead end and there were only fishing shacks down the way. He'd wondered what was up Monday night because those shacks sure weren't fancy like the cars he'd seen. I'll tell you, Billy, I almost stopped breathing when he said that. Then he got this cagey look on his face, looked like a weasel near the henhouse. He wanted to know about the reward that he'd seen written up in the paper. Well, hell, I thought he was getting ready to play me like a fish, make up something and try to get some money. But I told him the truth. The family would pay ten thousand dollars for any information that helped convict the murderer. He wrinkled his nose and said any fool knew it took years to get a murder case to court and he'd probably be dead before any money got ponied up. I said he didn't have anything to lose by trying. He didn't say anything for a minute, guzzled some beer and leaned back in his rocker and all the while that damn dog kept lunging toward me, not making any sound but his lips curled back. The old man finished his beer and tossed the bottle over the bushes and it landed with a clink. There were probably a hundred beer bottles behind those bushes. He rubbed his nose and asked if I could take what he told me and get the reward. I told him no way and if he had any information, I'd write it down—I got my notebook out—and he could sign it and I'd sign it and date it and he could keep it to prove what he'd told me."

Billy moved out of the way of a bellman with a filled luggage cart. "Smart, Lou."

"About seven Monday evening, he saw two cars pass, a red Jag and right behind it a silver Lexus."

"A Lexus. For sure he said it was a Lexus?"

"For sure."

Billy's smile was grimly pleased. One of the cars in the garage at the Whitman house was a silver Lexus. Oh damn, Lou had done good work.

"He said Buck Finney who owns the cabins rented them out some but not to big-dollar people. It's pretty clear he and Finney don't like each other. The guy—his name's Lester Lyle—went on and on about Finney trying to shoot his dog once. Lyle said he wondered why the cars hadn't come back. He decided to take a look-see. He went down his road and walked about a hundred yards and then, he said, 'That silver car had pulled off the road onto an old track that used to lead to the marsh. I went up and looked at it—' "

"License number?" Billy hoped against hope.

"No. Said he didn't think of it, no reason for him to notice. Said he went up to the car and looked it over but nobody was in it. And then he said he was damn hot and tired and if some fool didn't know the old track was overgrown, he sure wasn't going to slog after them to tell them something they'd figure out pretty soon anyway, so he turned and went back to his place, said he was hot and thirsty and wanted another beer. I wrote it up just the way he'd told me and we both signed it and I gave it to him, then I had him show me where he'd seen the car. By this time the sun was heading down and this patch was in deep shadow. But the ground looked sandy. I put up crime scene tape, marked off the area. I'm going back tomorrow, go over it inch by inch. It hasn't rained since Monday. If we're lucky, there may be some tread prints."

"Sweet Jesus." Billy's smile stretched wide as a hallelujah. If Lou found prints, he'd make molds, and if the tire treads matched the silver car at the Whitman house, there would be a link that couldn't be denied.

Annie pushed in the kitchen door. Esther bent near a pot, eyes intent, poking inside with a fork. William murmured to himself, ". . . five . . . six . . ." as he placed dessert dishes on a tray. Hands in plastic gloves, Cora dipped chicken breasts in a flour mixture. William turned toward the opening door.

Annie held up a disposable camera. "If you don't mind, I'll take a few pictures. Vanessa often wrote home about how wonderful the staff was"—she smiled but there were no corresponding smiles—"and how much she enjoyed the delicious dinners. I promised her sister I'd get a picture of each of you. I won't be a minute. Please go on with what you are doing."

As the door closed behind her, Annie held up the camera, snapped Esther, who ignored her. Cora offered a bright smile. William stood straight and gazed at her with grave dignity. When she'd taken two pictures of each, she looked hopefully around. "Where is Maybelle?"

Cora once again was dipping the breasts, first in milk mixture, then into a flour mixture. "Her night off. We alternate serving. This is one of Maybelle's nights when she goes to one of her meetings."

Esther slapped the fork onto the range top. " 'Be sober; be vigilant; because your adversary, the Devil, as a roaring lion, walketh about, seeking whom he may devour.' That girl won't listen and I've told her and told her."

Cora's voice was gentle. "Don't worry so, Auntie. It's all nonsense."

Annie remembered Maybelle's staring gaze and her halting words. *I saw the Evil Eye.*

"God tells us not to delve in darkness." A timer buzzed. "Here now, I've got to get that casserole out."

"Please tell Maybelle I'd like to get her picture tomorrow." Annie was pleased. It was a piece of luck that Maybelle was off tonight. Now Annie had a good reason to seek her out tomorrow and discover what she meant when she spoke of seeing an evil eye. Annie's search for a diary was a bust so far, but maybe her luck was going to turn. "Thanks very much."

It was a few minutes before seven when Annie reached the main hallway. She heard a murmur of voices to her left. Lillian had said they gathered in the family room before dinner. As she neared the end of the hall, she heard the clink of glasses and a gurgle of laughter. With a glance behind to be sure she wasn't observed, she moved lightly and eased next to the archway.

A woman's voice was strident. "You are much too easily put upon, Lillian. Why should that girl be staying here? It would have been much easier for you to have William box up Vanessa's things, send them off. If this girl is as much of a tramp as Vanessa—"

"Martha, let me show you something." The man's voice boomed. "Come here, honey. Look what Jon's bought for Lillian's birthday. Now, isn't that something!"

There was a squeal of excitement. "Lillian, you didn't even mention it. Why, that's the prettiest bracelet I've ever seen. Oh, look at that diamond butterfly. And those rubies on both sides . . ."

Annie stepped into the archway. She had a moment to observe the dramatic room and its occupants. Pale lime cushions dotted overstuffed white sofas. The paved floor was alternating bands of obsidian and cream. The coffee tables and side tables were made of glass. A huge oil painting almost filled an interior wall, its swirl of colors—orange, green, a brilliant crimson—bright as a kaleidoscope.

Lillian Dodd was again in blue, a scalloped-hem dress with a V-neck and graceful sash and matching loop sandals. Her face looked tired as she held out her arm to the woman admiring the bracelet. Unkempt red-gold hair straggled unevenly to frame a ravaged face with bleary green eyes. Martha Golden was shockingly aged from the photographs Annie had studied. Her pleated low-cut silk dress hung from bony shoulders, sagged low against her hips. She wasn't fashionably thin. She was emaciated, her arms thin to the point of caricature. Perhaps she looked more worn than usual in contrast to Lady Hamilton, who was lovely in a mauve eyelet dress. Lady Hamilton's brilliant blue eyes studied Lillian, not her new jewelry. Heather Whitman stood near the mantel, her dark hair a nice contrast to her terra-cotta dress. She too looked sharply different from the photographs. In the pictures, she'd been happy. Now her face was remote and sad. She stood by herself. Across the room, Kyle Curtis lounged with one elbow propped on a grand piano. His eyes were Heathcliff brooding, his mobile mouth twisted in a bitter frown. The only man smiling was Jon Dodd. Jon gazed at his wife, eyes warm, lips curved in a soft smile, beaming pride and satisfaction as she displayed the lovely bracelet. Sam Golden looked somber. He was only an arm's length from his wife, his face wary and tense.

Vanessa had spent the last year of her life in the company of these three men. The most careful scrutiny had not revealed contact with any other men. Kyle Curtis. Jon Dodd. Sam Golden. The murderer had to be one of them.

Annie stepped into the family room.

8

ere's Georgia." Lillian's smile was kind, her tone positive.
Lady Hamilton flashed an encouraging smile. Annie felt buoyed and was glad her mother-in-law was there. Now there were two of them to hunt and scratch and dig for information.

Lillian looked around the room. "I know everyone will be pleased to welcome Vanessa's friend Georgia Lance. Georgia, this is my husband, Jon . . ."

In the flurry of introductions, Annie picked up a mélange of impressions:

Lillian Dodd was anxious that she be received politely and uncertain whether that would happen.

Jon Dodd's cheery smile mixed oddly with a murmur of condolence.

Heather Whitman's stare was cold and hostile.

Kyle Curtis had no interest in Annie's presence. He never moved his brooding gaze from Heather.

Martha Golden lifted her wineglass, drank greedily. Her eyes burned in her ravaged face. She said not a word of greeting.

Sam Golden's deep voice was gentle. "We're sorry you have come on such a sad mission."

There was an awkward silence.

Martha jerked toward him, her face twisting. "Sorry? You're sorry? I'm not sorry. She was a slut. Bad things happen to—"

Lillian and Jon and Sam all spoke at once.

"Martha, won't you try on my new bracelet?" Lillian was slipping it from her arm.

Red cheeks flushing, Jon strode toward Annie. "What would you like? Wine? Red or white? Or whisky? We run to a little of everything. Gin and tonic. Rum and coke. Bourbon? Scotch?"

Annie gave him a grateful smile as if thankful he was ending a painful scene. "White wine, please."

Sam gripped his wife's bony arm. "Sugar—"

"Don't you 'sugar' me. I—" Her tone was as sharp as a slap.

Lillian slipped an arm around Martha's thin shoulders, held up the bracelet. "I was so surprised when Jon gave it to me."

Like a child diverted by a plaything, Martha took the bracelet, turned it around and around. The diamonds flashed and the rubies glowed.

Jon brought Annie a glass of white wine, handed it to her with an almost courtly bow. "As Sam said, we're awfully sorry about Vanessa." His face was suddenly sad. "Damn nice girl. She was fun to have around and a real help to Lillian."

Cora stepped inside the family room, nodded to Lillian. Immediately, Lillian gestured toward the French windows. "We're having a buffet on the terrace tonight. Esther's fixed her famous buttermilk pecan chicken."

Despite the heat of the day, the terrace was cool and pleasant as a result of the lengthening shadows and the sea breeze and a fine mist from nozzles on posts beneath a thatched roof. The breeze rustled the sea oats on the dunes. A vee of pelicans skimmed toward the darkening water.

Blue-and-white-checked cloths covered two tables. Blue pottery plates were at one end of a buffet table. Annie hung back, hoping to sit with Kyle and Heather, but Lillian arranged the seating. Annie was at a table with Sam Golden, Heather Whitman, and Jon Dodd. At Lillian's table were Martha Golden, Lady Hamilton, and Kyle Curtis.

"Lady Hamilton, if you'll lead the way." Lillian was the encouraging hostess. "And Georgia . . ." Serving dishes held stir-fried carrots and bananas, eggplant soufflé, and black-eyed peas. The chicken was arranged on a blue platter. There was an instant when Annie and Laurel stood side by side and Annie heard a swift whisper. "Beach. Midnight." Laurel leaned forward to spoon tomato relish over black-eyed peas.

Jon and Sam remained standing until Annie and Heather were seated. As they began to eat, Annie said shyly to Heather, "Vanessa was excited about helping you with the wedding plans."

"Was she?" Heather cut a piece of chicken and it seemed to Annie that the jab of her fork was savage.

Jon gave his stepdaughter a swift glance, then turned to Annie. "So you and Vanessa grew up together. I'll bet you have some great memories." His smile was almost fatuous.

"Oh, I do. Vanessa was special." Annie pushed the wire-rim glasses higher on her nose and looked from Jon to Sam. "When Vanessa walked into a room, everyone noticed."

Sam's craggy face softened. "I remember the first time I saw her. She was over there by the pool"—he waved a hand toward the sparkling pool—"and she had on one of those things that kind of wrap around and she was laughing. Her hair was shining in the sunlight and her skin was smooth and tanned. Her laugh . . ." He broke off, put down his fork.

"Vintage Vanessa." Heather's look was sardonic. "She always knew when a man was near. It was a performance especially for you, Sam."

"Not for me." His voice was wistful.

Annie saw pain in his eyes.

Jon lifted a hand and Cora stepped near to refill their wineglasses. As they ate, he kept up a constant chatter, trying, Annie felt, to mask Heather's silence and Sam's abstraction. Lillian's husband was a pleasant dinner companion, discussing the most recent films, the latest bestsellers, the watercolor exhibit at the Island Art Center, players on the DL for the Braves. Annie could see the other table. Lillian orchestrated an adroit and determined social chatter, with Lady Hamilton as a cheerful participant. Martha occasionally moved food about on her plate, but she ate little and steadily drank wine. Kyle sat in sullen quiet but Annie saw anguish in his eyes when he glanced toward Heather.

Annie felt surrounded by dark emotions held in check by social conventions. "More wine?" "The secret to the recipe is adding sesame seeds to the ground pecans." "I wouldn't discount the Braves." "The harbor definitely needs to be dredged again." Several times Annie tried to talk about Vanessa but Jon steered the conversation another way.

When they finished dessert, Annie made her decision. Time was speeding past and she could no more stay its flight than stop the tide as it ran out. Soon the Dodd family would be gone to Cape Cod. Annie's connection to the people who had known Vanessa was limited to this evening and tomorrow. Before Saturday morning she had to break through the social patina, bring the hidden emotions to the surface. She pushed back her chair, walked to the other table. She spoke loudly enough that everyone could hear. "Mrs. Dodd, I really appreciate being here. Thank you for a wonderful dinner. But I need to get back to the cottage. Ginny's going to call me"—Annie looked at her watch. It was a few minutes before eight P.M.—"at seven o'clock her time. She may have more news about the investigation." Annie stopped, lifted a hand to her lips. "Oh, I don't know if I was supposed to mention it. But"—she brightened—"I don't see why not. I'm sure the police will be back in touch with everyone who knew Vanessa and"—she looked toward Lillian—"you may already know about it. Anyway, thank you for being so kind to me. I'm really glad to have met everyone. Oh, before I go, let me get some pictures. Ginny will be pleased to see Vanessa's friends." She pulled the camera from her pocket, pressed the flash button. In an instant, she was snapping shots: Jon, Heather, and Sam. Then she turned to the other table: Lillian, Kyle, and—

Martha held up both hands in front of her face. "Not me." The command was abrupt and harsh.

Annie murmured, "Oh, I'm sorry. That's fine. I know some people don't like to have their pictures taken. Well, I'd better hurry—"

It was Lillian Dodd who spoke sharply. "Know about what?" Her face looked strained and fearful.

"The investigation." Annie looked at her directly. "It just goes to show the police are really careful. I talked to Ginny before dinner and she told me it looks like the man they arrested isn't the right one. She said the police think there was another man and they're looking for him. Something about a silver car."

Annie sagged onto the sofa in the cottage. She was weak and shaky as if she'd crossed a canyon on a high wire. She'd tried to look at all of them in the instant when she'd loosed a tiger in their midst. Jon's hand paused midway between dessert dish and his lips. Slowly he put down the spoon. His gaze settled on Kyle. Lillian's eyes jerked toward Kyle. Kyle's dark brows drew down in a quick, intense frown. Sam looked shocked and uneasy. Martha muttered, "Silver car. That's funny." Her words were slurred. "Just like yours, Lillian." Heather sat still as stone. She too—reluctantly, unwillingly, hopelessly—looked toward Kyle.

Kyle. Handsome. Dangerous. Different. It was as if Annie was playing a game with an arrow in the center and when she spun the arrow, it stopped and pointed to him. But she couldn't offer impressions to the police. She couldn't scoop up the fear that swirled around her listeners, hand it to Billy Cameron. She had to find facts. She had to link Kyle to Vanessa, prove he was the shadowy figure behind her death. Police . . .

Annie pulled out her cell. She punched a familiar number. Billy wouldn't be there, of course. Everything depended upon who answered. She held the phone to her ear, resisted the impulse to readjust the wig.

"Broward's Rock Police." It was a woman's voice. Not Mavis. Annie knew she couldn't talk to Hyla Harrison. "May I leave a message for Lou Pirelli?"

"I'll connect you to his extension."

When Lou's recorded voice answered, Annie waited for the message to end, then spoke quickly, "Lou, Annie Darling. I hope you can do me a favor. If Mrs. Dodd calls and asks about a new investigation into Vanessa Taylor's murder, could you say you can't comment on an ongoing investigation?" She paused, took a deep breath. "Please, Lou." She ended the call.

Annie popped to her feet, began to pace. She'd accomplished her goal. No one who heard her artless revelations would doubt that a search was under way for another man. Unless—what if Lillian called Genevieve Willett? Vanessa's sister was out of touch, declining to answer calls, but she wouldn't refuse a call from Lillian Dodd. If Lillian

Dodd reached her, not only would the report of a new investigation be revealed as a sham, Annie would be unmasked as an intruder. Annie felt queasy. If only—

Her cell phone rang. Annie took a deep breath, answered. "Yes?"

The husky whisper was light as spun sugar. "Powder room. Martha and Sam just left. She's reached the lugubrious stage and getting weepy. Why don't you walk that way, see what you can hear."

The sky glowed blood red as the setting sun sank behind a low bank of dark clouds. Henny Brawley rested comfortably in a canvas chair on her porch overlooking the marsh. She sipped her favorite drink, a cooler made with orange-spiced tea, orange juice, lemon juice, and honey. She considered the icy sweet-tart drink a perfect complement to the close of a hot summer day. Usually she was at peace as night fell over the marsh, enjoying the refreshing cooler, basking in the beauty of rippling cordgrass and dark water splashed with crimson and mysterious hummocks. Tonight she was waiting.

How could a woman as striking as Vanessa have carried on a love affair on a small island without someone somewhere seeing her in the company of the man? Of course, and Henny's thought was bleak, the prosecution would claim she had managed just that with Max. So far, the flyers Henny had left at every business on the island had brought forth not a single response except for the hesitant suggestion from a secretary at Seaside Realty: ". . . Rita said something the day after that girl's body was found, about seeing her Saturday night. But I'm not sure and Rita's got a lot on her plate right now. She's out of the office until Monday. Her mom's having some problems." Henny persisted. She obtained a phone number. She placed a call to Rita Powell, faced the aggravation of an answering machine. She made her voice as warm and reassuring and official as possible. ". . . seeking help from citizens in investigating the death of Vanessa Taylor. We understand you saw Miss Taylor on Saturday night. It would be helpful to police to obtain a description of Miss Taylor's companion." She ended, of course, with the bait. ". . . a reward of ten thousand dollars to anyone with information helpful to the investigation." She didn't claim to be official. Certainly it wouldn't be her fault if her status was misconstrued.

Her telephone rang. Henny scooped it up. "Henny Brawley." A brisk tone. An official tone. "Mrs. Powell, we appreciate your call. Yes, this is in regard to the murder of Vanessa Taylor. Now, if you could describe what you saw on Saturday evening . . .

Annie slipped from the shadows of a weeping willow, eased behind an urn next to a flagstone terrace. She'd changed into dark clothing, a T-shirt and slacks. Her sneakers made no sound as she took a cautious step, then another.

"Where are you going?" The call was high and shrill.

Annie lifted a spray of wisteria. Sam Golden stopped midway down a flight of steps. He looked up at his wife, who leaned against a brick pillar. In the red glow of the sunset, he looked big and powerful. His face, touched by copper, was etched by sorrow and weariness.

"Thought I'd take a walk on the beach." His voice was heavy, the voice of a man without hope. "I thought you'd gone upstairs to rest."

"Rest." Her voice quivered. "You'd like for me to rest, wouldn't you?" The words were slurred, but they came fast and furious. "Don't think I didn't know how you chased after her. She won't be on the beach now, will she? Did she make you mad, Sam? You went out to meet her Monday night, didn't you? I saw you go. I looked out my window. You thought I was—" She stopped, pressed trembling fingers against her mouth.

"Go to bed, Martha." He turned and thudded down the steps, strode toward the boardwalk to the beach. His figure was silhouetted against the red sky and then he was out of sight, hidden behind the dune.

Martha sank down to the steps, huddled there. She bent forward, head pressed against her knees. Racking sobs shook her thin body.

Annie took a hesitant step toward the stairs. Martha Golden needed help. She reached the base of the stairs. "Mrs. Golden . . ."

Martha's head slowly lifted. Tears streamed down her face. She struggled for breath, pushed herself unsteadily up. "Get out of here. I don't want to talk to you. Why should I? She was a slut. A slut!" Her voice rose into a scream. She turned and walked unsteadily across the porch, yanked open a door.

Annie turned away, walked back toward the cottages. She reached the dark pines and plunged into thickening gloom. She had left on the porch light to her cottage. She was grateful to see that beacon. The pines loomed like black sentinels against the dark sky. She was hurrying up the steps when a low voice called, "Georgia." Annie stopped and turned, looking into the shadows where a man stood.

Jon Dodd strolled toward her. In the pool of light from the porch, his dark hair was shiny as ebony, the flush in his cheeks more pronounced than at dinner. His expression was uncomfortable, as if he did not relish his errand. "Wondered if we could visit for a minute." He had a pleasant tenor voice. "Maybe take a stroll on the beach. I'd ask you back to the house but Lillian was afraid Heather might see us. If you're too tired to talk, that's fine. I guess you've just had a stroll."

Annie walked down the steps, stood a few feet from him. Her flare of alarm was subsiding. She had no sense of danger emanating from him. He was a stocky middle-aged man in a fine-mesh polo shirt and linen slacks, clearly wishing he were elsewhere.

"Why shouldn't Heather see us?" She looked up into light eyes that blinked as he made a quick grimace.

"She'd think we thought— Damn." His tone was rueful. "I'm no good at this. And like I told Lillian, probably we'll hear from the police if there's anything to this. I mean"—he spread a hand in apology—"I'm not saying you don't have it right. But Lillian's worried." He nodded toward the steps. "We can sit there. I won't keep you long."

They sat on the middle step. Annie smelled cinnamon aftershave, knew he'd shaved before dinner.

Jon straightened the creas in his slacks. "I've made a botch of this. I guess I might as well be honest, but if you can keep this to yourself, we'd appreciate it. It's what you said at dinner, about the police thinking there's another man involved." His discomfort was obvious in his worried gaze and perplexed frown. "Vanessa—well, she was attractive. Very attractive. It was Lillian who noticed first. A few weeks ago she told me she was worried that Kyle was falling for Vanessa. I didn't think much about it. Sure, Vanessa played up to Kyle. She was young and there weren't any other young men around. Then I noticed it too. Oh, he tried to act like Vanessa was bugging him, but that was pretty transparent. Anyway, Heather was furious and she stopped talking about the wedding. Lillian thought she was going to break their engagement. Don't think he didn't try to right the ship. That didn't surprise me. I've always thought he had his eyes on Heather's income. She has some trusts from her father. Kyle can't make much of a living with that catamaran charter business. Heather wouldn't pay any attention when Lillian warned her. I didn't even try." He was rueful. "Heather's not my number one fan. I don't think she'd like anybody her mother married. Anyway, none of that matters. But Heather matters. And if he's . . . well, we've got to find out. You said Vanessa's sister was going to call." He looked at Annie hopefully. "Has she heard anything more from the police?"

"She talked to them, but she didn't find out any more." Annie sounded exasperated. "They told her they couldn't release any information right now. She was aggravated. She said she didn't see why they didn't tell her something. She doesn't see who it could be. She said the only men Vanessa ever mentioned"—Annie watched him carefully—"were the ones she saw in your house."

Jon turned a haggard face toward her. "I was afraid of this. I hate to tell Lillian." He pushed up from the step, stood for a moment with his head bowed. "God, I hate to tell Lillian."

Annie watched as he walked slowly away, shoulders slumped, hands clasped behind him, a man clearly reluctant to return home with news that could not be welcome.

Annie watched an owl swoop toward the dune. She shivered, knowing the owl sought a succulent rat for a midnight feast. She hurried across the boardwalk, reached the thick sand. Moonlight glittered on the water, the breakers ripples of white lace against the darkness of the sea. She drew a deep breath of salty air. The offshore breeze tugged at her loose blouse. The tide was in, leaving a narrow ribbon of soft sand for walking. Annie turned to her right. The house Laurel had leased was perhaps a hundred yards ahead. Annie saw lights gleaming from the second floor.

A fishing pier stretched out into the water. When Annie was perhaps twenty feet from the pilings, she heard a low call from the deep shadows beneath the wooden stairs. Annie hurried forward. She and Laurel came together with a quick embrace.

Laurel pointed in the darkness. "There's a huge log. Driftwood. We can sit there."

When they settled, Annie knew they were safe from observation, deep in the darkness beneath the pier. Quickly, she described the tawdry exchange between Sam and Martha Golden.

Laurel was thoughtful. "Obviously, Vanessa attracted him. But I don't think he's the one. The cook at the house I've rented loves to talk. We had a lovely chat—"

Annie smiled in the darkness. Few could resist Laurel's charm, which was genuine and enchanting.

"—all about the houses up and down the beach and the people who live there. Phyllis is friends with some of the domestic staff at those houses, especially Cora at the Whitman house. Of course, Vanessa's murder was the most exciting thing that has happened in years. Phyllis said Cora told her that Monday afternoon she was dusting in the hall—"

Annie concentrated, trying to sort out the pronouns.

"—and Vanessa was in the library and she must have been talking on the phone and her voice was all sugary and she kind of cooed, 'Why, Kyle, you know I'm mad about you,' and laughed. Cora told Phyllis that Vanessa then said the strangest thing. She said, 'Oh well, you can relax after tonight. Everything will be out in the open.'"

Annie pictured the brooding face of Kyle Curtis, his occasional bitter glance toward Heather. "Kyle and Vanessa. That's what it looks like." She described Jon Dodd's reluctant appearance at her cottage.

Laurel listened without comment until Annie concluded. "So he and Lillian are afraid Kyle's guilty. I think Heather is afraid too. After you left tonight, Kyle waited a minute, then he strode over to Heather. I couldn't hear what he said, but she just looked at him without answering. He gave her a black look and stalked off the terrace without another word to anybody. Heather ran into the house. That left me with the Dodds. I tried to pretend like everything was fine and thanked them for a lovely evening and left. Hmm." Laurel paused, then said quickly, "Kyle could have taken the Dodds' silver car. But why?"

Annie was accustomed to Laurel's quick shift in thoughts. "Because he knew he was going to kill her and he didn't want to be in his own car."

Laurel's whisper was faint. "Diabolic, if so."

Annie shivered. Yes, but it would be in keeping with the entire plan, so artful and cruel. Vanessa dead. Max accused. But perhaps they were beginning to unravel the complex web. What did Vanessa's odd comment to Kyle mean? Perhaps that overheard phone conversation—Vanessa laughing aloud only hours before her death—would prove to be the undoing of her murderer.

"It's time to get in touch with Billy." Laurel shifted as if to rise.

Annie put out a restraining hand. "We can't."

"Oh, my dear." Laurel's whisper lifted in surprise. "Billy will listen to us."

"He might listen"—Annie was grim—"but he's in Columbia. A law enforcement conference. We don't have enough to take to him anyway." Billy had not been on the Dodd terrace this evening. They could tell him about Sam Golden and Kyle Curtis but they had no proof, nothing to tie either man to the cabin where Vanessa died. "Kyle Curtis doesn't know Vanessa was overheard. Tomorrow I'll talk to him."

Laurel drew in a quick breath. "That could be dangerous."

Annie gave her mother-in-law a reassuring pat. "I'll be careful."

Annie turned restlessly in the bed. A strange bed. Comfortable enough but no bed was ever comfortable unless Max was nearby for her to curve against. She needed sleep. Would sleep ever come again with sweetness, carrying her into bright dreams filled with sunshine and laughter? Now if she slept, it would be fitful. Waking or sleeping, she felt the pressure of foreboding. She'd arranged everything. Tomorrow she'd go to the marina, pick up boxes to use in packing Vanessa's belongings. Barb would be waiting near the gift shop. They would pass and when they did, Annie would pocket a small tape recorder. Cats by Curtis was near one of the piers. The box store didn't open until ten but there was plenty to do—breakfast at the Whitman house, perhaps talk to some of the family, perhaps snatch a moment with Maybelle.

Annie twisted, turned, felt the square of paper in the pocket of her shorty pajamas. She lifted her hand, pulled out the folded real estate circular, cupped it in her hand. The Franklin house. Max had a vision for her and for him, a big happy house with open doors for friends and family. She slipped into sleep. Rising in her dream was a restored house, bright with fresh white paint, new glass in its windows, and together, hand in hand, she and Max walked up the broad front steps.

Max pulled the pillow over his face to block out the light. Not to be able to turn a light on or off. Not to be able to walk out if he pleased. Not to be able to make a phone call or drive a car. Not to be able to see Annie. On Monday night, if everything had gone as they'd planned, he and Annie would have walked hand in hand down the boardwalk and felt the softness of the sea breeze, looked at the boats riding in the water, some large enough to sail the Atlantic, some just Sailfish. They would have driven home and fixed dinner. They would have laughed and she would have walked near and he would have pulled her into his arms. . . .

He flung the pillow away, sat up on the narrow bunk, looked toward the high pale square in the wall that was his only link to the outside. All right. He couldn't get out, but he wasn't helpless. He had to do something to fight the fear that bubbled inside him, noxious as poison. Tomorrow he'd insist on seeing Handler Jones, and Handler

Jones was damn well going to do what Max demanded. Handler Jones was going to find Annie and make sure she wasn't getting too close to a killer.

The drumbeat of minutes speeding past began when Annie awoke Friday morning. Twenty-four more hours and the Dodds would be gone and with them Annie's tenuous connection to Kyle Curtis. No matter how slowly and deliberately Annie packed Vanessa's belongings, she couldn't delay her departure for more than a day. Annie jumped out of bed. She'd overslept. It was almost eight o'clock. Damn. She didn't want to miss breakfast with the family. She was in the shower and out in five minutes and dressed and on her way to the house.

The house was quiet when she stepped inside. At the kitchen door, she hesitated, then moved on. Esther would surely frown on Annie asking Maybelle questions that had to do with an evil eye. Hopefully, Annie would track down Maybelle alone at some point during the day. She looked into the dining room but it was dim. She walked on and turned into the main hall. There was a murmur of voices in the family room.

Annie moved swiftly and silently. As a true guest she would never have tried to eavesdrop. Now it was automatic. She stopped at the archway, head cocked to listen.

"... try to get everything packed today. I'll have William bring the suitcases up this afternoon. Oh, Jon, Heather's terribly upset. We were talking about the trip and all of a sudden she threw down her napkin and dashed off. She was trying not to cry." Lillian's voice broke.

"Honey, I know it's tough. But if Kyle's done what we think he's done, if the police turn out to be looking for him, well, it's a damn good thing Heather's dumped him." He was emphatic.

Annie moved down the hall, approached the archway with brisk footsteps. When she stepped into the family room, Jon looked up from his newspaper, Lillian stirred brown sugar into oatmeal.

Annie smiled. "Good morning. Oh, the buffet looks wonderful." She picked up a plate, ladled fresh fruit, spooned up a serving of frittata. "I'm going to work hard on the packing today, I checked and there's a box store on the marina. I called and got directions. . . ."

Lou Pirelli knelt near the last tire print. He aimed a spray of shellac at a sheet of cardboard held at an angle over the print. The cardboard deflected the shellac and a fine mist drifted down onto the print, settling gently into every crevice, topping every ridge. Lou wrinkled his nose at the smell. He pushed up carefully from the ground, walked back to the first print, eyed it critically. Good. Dry as if baked. He smiled. The shellac had hardened quickly despite the wet-rag humidity because the temperature was already nudging ninety. The print had turned brownish yellow, each ridge and crease clear and distinct. There were four prints, all beauties.

He moved quickly to the open door of the crime van, lifted out a sack of plaster of paris. He carried it to the first print. Billy was going to be pleased. Next he brought a big rubber bowl and a container of distilled water, placed them to one side. He measured fifteen ounces of water per pound of plaster of paris. He hummed as he dribbled in dry plaster of paris, moving his plastic ladle back and forth. When he was finished, the bowl brimmed with a thick goop the consistency of pancake batter. No bubbles, no lumps. As he worked, sweat matted his dark curls to his head, ran in rivulets down his face. His shirt and trousers clung to him. He used a clean measuring cup to pour the mixture over the shellacked prints. He kept his hand steady, ignoring the streak of fire that curled around one ankle. He waited until the bowl was empty before he reached back to claw at the ants.

When he finished pouring the plaster of paris into the last print, he retrieved a cold Pepsi from the cooler in the front of the van. He leaned against a fender in the shade as he waited for the molds to dry. He took thirsty gulps of the icy Pepsi and pulled out his cell.

Annie gazed critically at the mirror. She still felt a moment of shock when she saw the unfamiliar image—the glossy dark hair, dramatic eyebrows, and vermilion lips. The prim wire-rim glasses were in sharp contrast to the vivid makeup. Her peach blouse was loose fitting, styled like a smock, unlike anything she ever wore. Ingrid had included it in the last-minute purchases. Annie had smiled when she unpacked, doubting she would wear it. It was an easy choice this morning along with a casual pair of jeans. The oversize patch pockets of the smock were roomy and that was what she needed. She looked a little like a volunteer at a church rummage sale. Max would laugh. She had a sudden sensation of emptiness, almost vertigo. The thought had been so swift. *Max would laugh.* But his laughter would be only a memory if she didn't find out the truth about Vanessa. She frowned as she walked toward the door of the guest cottage. What was the truth of Vanessa? So far, little seemed certain. She had been beautiful. Men were drawn to her. But Annie hadn't found what she'd expected. She'd been sure she would discover a passionate love affair. Instead there was what looked to be an ambiguous relationship with Kyle Curtis and perhaps a hopeful yearning on the part of Sam Golden. There was no indication of any connection to Jon Dodd.

Annie pulled the door shut, started down the front steps. It was certain that Vanessa's death had been carefully planned. The circumstances had required her active though unwitting cooperation. That precluded any possibility she had been killed by a casual acquaintance.

Further, they knew the murderer had to be a man because of the strength required to lift an unconscious Max.

Why would a man want Vanessa dead? Passion. That had been Annie's immediate visceral judgment. But her murder was such a coldly calculated crime. Did that suggest thwarted passion? Jealousy? Perhaps she wasn't murdered because of love or even hate. Perhaps her continued existence posed a threat to the murderer.

Annie was almost to the door of the Toyota when shrubbery rustled behind her. She jerked around.

Sam Golden emerged from the deep shadows of the pines. He walked toward her. His face was shadowed by the brim of a Panama hat. He was a big man, muscular and well built, imposing in a polo shirt and khaki shorts. His running shoes made no sound on the pine straw. He carried a large manila folder under one arm. An expensive Leica hung on a strap around his neck.

Annie stood with one hand gripping the car door. She found it hard to breathe. She was almost sure he'd been waiting for her, standing in the recesses of the pines, watching the cottage. But if he meant her harm, wouldn't he have come to the cottage, knocked, pushed his way inside? Her heart thudded as he loomed nearer.

"Good morning." His deep voice was a pleasant rumble.

The constriction in Annie's chest eased. "Hello."

"I'm glad I caught you, Georgia. I brought some pictures I thought Vanessa's sister might like to have." He held out the manila folder.

She took the folder, managed a smile. "That's very kind of you, Sam." She looked at the camera. "You took pictures of Vanessa?"

He rocked back on his heels. A quick smile tugged at his lips and for an instant his somber face looked cheerful. "You don't know me or you'd know I always take pictures. Some of these"—he nodded toward the folder—"are really good. But I can't keep them. Martha wouldn't like it." A frown pulled down his thick, dark brows.

"I guess you could tell last night. She thought I paid too much attention to Vanessa. But it wasn't anything. Didn't mean anything to Vanessa, certainly."

Annie wondered if the flicker in his eyes meant sadness or bitterness. "Vanessa was beautiful." Her voice was gentle.

"Like a sunset." He looked reflective. "A flame of color but nothing to hold or touch."

"Were you in love with her?" Annie's fingers tightened on the folder.

Sam gave a shrug. "Love? No, I don't think so. Oh, she had a way of looking at you . . . She didn't mean it. I don't think Vanessa knew what love is. Love is—" He took a deep breath. "Caring when there's no reason left to care except you made a promise. Anyway"—his sigh was tired—"I hope her sister will like the pictures." He turned and walked away.

Annie watched him go. Was Sam's visit what it purported to be, simply a kind effort to make recent photographs available to Vanessa's sister? Or was he, in an artful dance of words and emotions, making it clear he wasn't the unknown man in Vanessa's life and death?

Annie almost tossed the folder onto the front seat of the car, then decided to take it inside. The pictures might be very precious to Vanessa's sister. Annie hadn't thought beyond gaining access to the Whitman house. Now she was committed to gathering up all of Vanessa's belongings. Ultimately the boxes must be shipped to Genevieve Willet. The folder of pictures must be sent too. How that would be done or should be done remained in the future, a future that had no reality to her at this moment. The only reality was her determination to find out who was responsible for entrapping Max.

Annie dropped the folder onto the coffee table. The flap opened and photographs slid across the glass surface. Annie bent forward, gathered them up, intending to return them to the folder. Instead, she was caught by the quality and brilliance of the glossy color prints. Sam Golden was a superb photographer. There were a half dozen shots: Vanessa lounging on a low pool chair, one hand dangling in the bright blue water; Vanessa playing the piano, face absorbed, dark hair curling on bare shoulders; Vanessa silhouetted against the darkening sky, lithe and lovely as a dream; Vanessa bending over a croquet mallet, her white blouse and shorts a striking foil for her sultry beauty; Vanessa at a cocktail party on the terrace of the Whitman house, her face utterly triumphant; Vanessa smiling directly into the camera, lips parted in a seductive, enticing, sensual smile.

Slowly Annie dropped onto the sofa, staring at the fifth photograph. That look of Vanessa's . . . Yes, it was definitely triumph. She was staring at someone or something that she felt to be within her power. Annie was sure of it. It was a cat-with-creamy-whiskers look, a football player's spike-in-the-end-zone look, a winning politician's arrogant clenched fist. The picture had been made in early evening, obviously during a party. Japanese lanterns glowed; the women were in swirling summer dresses, the men in blazers and slacks. There was the width of the pool between Vanessa and the men at whom she looked. She was staring, her lips curved in satisfaction, at Kyle Curtis and Jon Dodd.

Billy Cameron tossed his bag into the trunk of his car. He'd driven his own car, a five-year-old green Jeep, to Columbia. Broward's Rock didn't have enough cruisers for him to use one for a trip. He slid into the front seat, started the air-conditioning, put down the windows. His cell rang.

"Billy Cameron."

"Hey, Billy." Lou sounded like he'd won the lottery. "I got four great tire prints. I'm waiting for the casts to dry."

Billy thought fast. "As soon as they're done, get over to that cabin where Max stayed. Go over the road inch by inch."

"There may be a bunch of extraneous prints. We had the van there." Lou was remembering the morning after Max was arrested. "We got his prints and found that bloody shirt. We had a couple of cars there. I don't know if there'll be anything to find."

"Try."

"Sure. But don't get your hopes up, Billy."

Billy drove the precise speed limit, as he always did. It would take him three hours to get home. If Lou found matching tire treads at the second cabin, somebody had a hell of an explanation to make. But who? That was the problem. Say the prints matched the Dodds' silver Lexus. Even if they tied the car to the proximity of murder and to the cabin where Max claimed he was dumped unconscious, they still didn't know who drove it.

Annie rested her elbows on the warm wood of the pier. Often when she and Max came to work, they stopped for a moment to look out over the marina, checking to see what new boats had arrived, noting empty slips for the charter boats. The marina had its August bustle. A huge yacht was moving slowly through the harbor entrance. Weekend sailors who had arrived early were scrubbing down decks, loading provisions, bringing aboard fishing gear. One of her favorites—*J. P. Vanilla*—was maneuvering toward the Sound.

Fury suffused Annie. It was high summer and she and Max should be leaning against the railings, laughing, loving, free.

Footsteps sounded on the boardwalk behind her. Annie didn't look around. A shadow fell across the railing. She felt something brush against her, a weight tugging at her right pocket.

Barb sauntered a few feet to a coin telescope that offered a view of the Sound and a nearby island and close-ups of hummocks in the marsh and sometimes intriguing views of activities on passing boats. She dropped in a coin, bent to look. An almost imperceptible gesture of her left hand beckoned Annie.

Annie scooted until she was only a foot from the telescope. She leaned over the railing as if looking into the luxurious salon of an enormous yacht.

Barb's whisper was just loud enough for Annie to hear. "Thought you'd want to know. Max is raising hell. Wants to know where you are, what you're doing. Wants you to stop it, whatever it is. Says leave everything up to Handler Jones."

Annie didn't turn her head. "Tell him I'm fine and picking up stuff Jones can't find." But not enough and nothing was working out the way she'd thought it would and the Dodds were leaving in the morning and she hadn't found anything that might help free Max. *Oh, Max, I'm trying, I'm doing my best, I love you.* "Tell him not to worry." Annie patted the sagging pocket, felt the outline of the tape recorder. "Thanks, Barb."

"Sure. If you need help, call." Barb pushed the telescope out of the way and moved briskly up the boardwalk.

Annie watched Barb's receding figure. She suddenly felt terribly alone even though vacationers milled back and forth on the boardwalk and weekend sailors moved purposefully on their boats. Annie glanced at her watch. Almost ten. She moved impatiently forward.

Cats by Curtis was housed in a gray wood shack along the far shore. Three big cats were moored to a nearby pier. The massive wooden doors were closed, but a light shone in a ticket window on the left front.

Annie walked to the window. A sweet-faced teenage girl smiled. "May I help you?"

"I'm looking for Kyle." She tried to keep disappointment from her voice. "I thought he would be here when you open."

The girl turned, called out. "Hey, Kyle, somebody to see you."

There was an answering shout.

The girl leaned forward. "He's working out behind the building. There's a path to your left."

"Thanks." Annie turned, moved quickly. As she did, she saw a man fishing on the pier swing around to watch. Despite the floppy bush hat and dark glasses, she recognized Duane Webb. He bent down to his bucket, pulled out a live eel, set to work with his hook. Annie knew he'd been recruited by Barb to watch over her this morning. Annie gave the tiniest of nods, curved around the side of the building. It was lovely to know help was at hand should she need it. She reached into her right pocket, turned on the tape recorder.

She followed the curve of the bank as she walked down the side of the building. Water lapped against another pier. Boats were pulled out of the water and in various stages of maintenance and repair. Kyle Curtis was kneeling by a beached cat. One hand moved rhythmically as he sanded the near hull. Muscles rippled in his tanned back. He wore ragged cutoffs and boat shoes without socks.

When she stopped beside him, he looked up. Dark glasses masked his eyes. He was still for a moment, then came easily to his feet. His dark hair was tousled, his cheeks unshaven. He stood in an easy slouch. He didn't say a word.

Any woman would be aware of his magnetism, his darkly handsome face and full, sensuous lips, the mat of hair on his chest and the rivulets of sweat coursing down his body, the way his shorts hung from his hips, sagging at his midriff. Surely Vanessa had been no exception.

Annie dropped her hand, tugged the pocket to keep it open. "Your conversation with Vanessa Monday afternoon was overheard."

His scowl was quick and ferocious. "What the hell are you talking about?"

"She said she was mad about you—"

"Shit." He crumpled the square of sandpaper in his hand, took a step toward her.

Annie stayed where she was. He was so close now she could see the flecks from his sanding on his chest and arms. "Vanessa said you could relax, that everything would be out in the open. Was she going to tell Heather?"

"There wasn't a bloody thing to tell Heather. I don't know what the hell Vanessa meant. Look"—his truculent face was inches from hers—"I'm tired of all the crap. I wasn't interested in Vanessa. I didn't give a damn about Vanessa. For some crazy reason, Vanessa started after me a couple of months ago. But it was always when Heather was around or her mother or Jon. And yeah, I got sucked into it a little bit. She was a babe. I've always enjoyed babes. I should have told her to cool it, but I kind of got a kick out of it. Especially since Sam was following her around like a lapdog and I like bugging him. He's got that West Point hard-ass attitude. He doesn't like me any more than Jon does. Nobody there likes me. Except Heather. She did until she decided I was running around on her. Hell, I told her there was nothing to it. And that damn Vanessa wouldn't ease up. I figured out she was phony and I told her to lay off. That's why I called her Monday. Heather had told me the wedding was off. Because of Vanessa. I told her she was crazy as a loon and we had a big fight. I called Vanessa and told her I'd had enough, that she had to leave me alone. That's when she said that she was mad about me. She was being a bitch. Anyway, I told her I was going to tell everybody how she'd hounded me. Then she said that bit about everything being out in the open. Like I said, I don't know what she meant but I can tell you it didn't have a damn thing to do with me."

Annie stared at him. What he said didn't make a lot of sense. Why would Vanessa make a play—and a phony one at that—for Heather's fiancé? "Where were you Monday evening?" Would Vanessa's old friend have asked this question? Annie didn't know or care.

He poked his sunglasses higher on his nose. "Out on a cat. By myself."

It could be true. Or false. There was no way to prove his whereabouts. He could have sailed the cat around the island, tied up to the pier, walked to the Whitman garage, taken the silver car.

His mouth folded in an unhappy glower. "Heather didn't believe me. That's a hell of a deal. She ought to know when I'm telling her the truth." His tone was plaintive, like a small boy's anger at injustice. He turned away, walked back to the beached cat, dropped down beside it. But he didn't resume his sanding. He simply sat there in the hot sun, face slack, shoulders slumped.

Lou parked the crime van on River Otter Road. There was no shoulder, simply a steep slant into the ditch. Any car traveling west would be required to swing into the opposite lane, but there was no traffic on the dead-end road. Lou wasn't concerned about road hazards. He'd chosen to walk the fifty or so yards into the woods to the cabin where Max had stayed on Monday night to avoid destroying existing tread prints. A camera dangled from a strap around his left wrist. The drill was the same as earlier. Find a tread print, photograph it, measure it, sketch a drawing for context, shellac the find, mix the plaster of paris, pour.

If he found a print.

He walked on the ridge between rutted tracks. The overhead canopy of trees blocked the sunlight, making it dim and shadowy along the track. Insects swarmed, no-see-ums, mosquitoes, horseflies, chinch bugs. Lou flailed at the bloodsucking whirlwind, all the while scanning the ruts for a half-inch-long tomahawk-shaped impression.

The right rear wheel of the silver car had been repaired. Probably a screw or nail on the road had been picked up, caused a flat or a slow leak, and the patch resulted in that distinctive marker.

Lou kept a steady pace as he made his careful scrutiny. By the time he reached the clearing, saw the ramshackle wooden cabin on stilts, he was covered with welts, perspiring heavily in the humid air, parched for water, and sure of the futility of his quest. He gazed about the sun-blistered patch of dusty ground that fronted the cabin, wished he had a hat. He flapped a hand at a lumbering horsefly. The likelihood of finding what he sought—even if it was there—ranked right up there with the possibility of winning the lottery.

He managed a wry grin. His mother bought a lottery ticket every week. Twice she'd won fifty dollars. She always pointed out that you couldn't win if you didn't have a ticket. He couldn't find a tread if he didn't look. By now the jerk of his arm to ward away biting insects was automatic. As his eyes studied the uneven ground, he tried to picture the movements of the silver car on Monday night. He didn't care about the driver. He was imagining the car. Right next to the steps was the obvious place to stop, especially if a comatose Max was sprawled in the back seat. Okay. The car stops, probably with the back door nearest to the steps. Lou wondered how hard it had been to pull an unconscious Max up the stairs. Maybe the guy used a fireman's lift. Whatever, Lou thought it had to have been a struggle. Max was a solid six feet two, 180 pounds. But somebody got Max into the cabin if he didn't arrive under his own steam. The circuit solicitor would have to listen up if they found treads from the silver car here. That would be too many sightings of the silver car to ignore.

Lou ducked away from a bumblebee, slowly walked toward the steps. When he stood to one side, studying the ground, he saw a crisscross of tracks. Foot by foot, he looked. Tracks, sure. Plenty of them.

The crime van had been here and cruisers and media. No trace of that distinctive marker.

A wasp buzzed near his face. Sweat burned his eyes, slid down his face and back and legs. Lou's face folded in a scowl. Maybe it was only because he'd thought it through that way, but he could see that damn car parked here, knew in his gut it had been here. He hated to be so close and lose out. Okay. The car was parked here but it had to get back to River Otter Road.

Lou squinted against the sun. Okay, the car could have curved in a tight arc. Or the driver could have backed around the side of the cabin, then turned. Lou turned on his heel, bent to stare at the ground, looking, looking. Nope. No car had backed this way recently enough to leave a trail.

Lou moved forward. It would require a tight turn for a big car to make the arc in one try. Maybe if the car backed up here . . . Lou shaded his eyes against the late-morning blaze, felt the squelch of his shirt on his back. God, he was thirsty. He pushed back a straggly clump of a puckerbush and looked down. He wiped the sweat from his eyes, thinking he'd imagined what he wanted to see. He felt a surge of adrenaline, the hunter sighting a buck. There it was. By God, there it was, clear and distinct and unmistakable, the inch-long tomahawk-shaped impression.

Annie plopped the last of the unfolded cardboard boxes in the middle of Vanessa's living room. She hurried outside into the ever-enervating heat, retrieved the small sack with four rolls of easy-tear plastic tape and a package of bubble wrap. She carried the materials with her, dropped them on the coffee table, glanced away from the book Vanessa had left there. A novel by Anne Rivers Siddons. Annie knew she should get right to work, boxing up Vanessa's belongings. That was the ostensible reason for her stay here. Moreover, the sorting out would be Annie's last chance to search for Vanessa's diary. It was beginning to look as though finding that diary might be the only way to learn the truth behind her murder. It had seemed clear-cut last night that Vanessa had engaged in a torrid romance with Kyle Curtis. Annie had felt so confident, she'd arranged to have a tape recorder in her pocket when she talked to him. Yes, she had that angry exchange taped and what did it prove? If he was telling the truth, he'd dallied with Vanessa but never been seriously involved despite the surface appearance of her attraction to him.

Annie paced back and forth in the small living room. Of course, if Kyle had murdered Vanessa, he certainly would have lied this morning. Yet Annie couldn't forget the plaintive sound of his voice when he'd mourned Heather's disbelief. Somehow she didn't believe Kyle was a false lover. Or a murderer.

If Kyle was dismissed as a suspect, that left Sam Golden. This morning she'd felt a swift rush of fear when he'd approached her soft-footed from the shadow of the pines. He'd waited for her, she was sure of it. But when he reached her, there was no threat and she felt no sense of anxiety. He'd brought that folder of pictures. It could have simply been an excuse to see what she was doing as well as a way of distancing himself from Vanessa. Yet he had seemed utterly genuine.

Not Kyle. Not Sam.

Annie felt breathless. Last night Jon Dodd had come down to the cottage. By the time he left, her suspicions of Kyle had hardened into certainty. He'd seemed reluctant to share the misgivings Lillian felt about her prospective son-in-law, worried about the effect of an investigation on Heather, and, of course, for those reasons eager to know if the police had shared more information about their investigation to Vanessa's sister.

Jon Dodd?

Annie felt an instinctive flicker of disbelief. Every hint of connection between Vanessa and a man came down to Kyle or Sam. Heather's anger at Kyle was a flag. Martha's burning hostility to Vanessa was a flag. There was no link to Jon. Nothing.

Annie felt a ripple of coldness deep inside. No link to Jon . . . Was this the careful, clever, cold design that made certain there was no link between Vanessa and her killer? Max had been duped, decoyed, set up to protect her killer. Had the linkage between Vanessa and Sam and Kyle been as cleverly constructed?

If Jon Dodd was the shadowy figure behind Vanessa, surely somewhere there was a trace of their affair. But time was running out. Annie looked frantically around the living room. There were still so many places to look, seeking the diary. Yet the diary might not exist. Vanessa may have left behind the habit of recording her life just as she'd left behind her station as a waitress and before that her growing-up years in modest circumstances. The diary could be the answer Annie sought, yet now wasn't the moment to continue the search. By this time tomorrow morning, the Dodd family would be on its way to Cape Cod, the silver car humming north on I-95. Only a few hours remained to find out the truth about Vanessa and the Dodd family.

Annie whirled, hurried to the door. She clattered down the wooden steps, heading for the Whitman house.

9

Annie's swift pace slowed. The nearer she came to the house, the less confident she felt. Was she desperately trying to fit Jon Dodd into a murderer's mold because she couldn't imagine violence behind Sam Golden's genial manner or Kyle Curtis's surly, self-absorbed anguish? Was she grasping at straws that would crumple in her grip? Or was she scraping away the camouflage created by a clever killer?

Despite her instinctive liking for Kyle, he was most publicly linked to Vanessa. His protestations that he was the innocent victim of Vanessa's pursuit could be a guilty man's attempt to disarm suspicion. If he hadn't responded to Vanessa, why was Heather furious? The broken engagement seemed clear evidence of a romance between Vanessa and Kyle. Why hadn't Heather believed his denials? Because she knew he was lying?

Annie walked slowly up the steps. Heather was hostile to Georgia Lance. Annie was afraid it wouldn't do any good to talk to her, but she had to try. Tomorrow Heather would be gone.

There was one last possible avenue to follow. Maybelle claimed Vanessa died because she'd been struck down by the Evil Eye. Did Maybelle have knowledge or was she simply dramatizing her nearness to murder?

Annie stepped into the cross hall. She heard the distant hum of a vacuum cleaner. Nearer, a faint clatter sounded behind the swing door to the kitchen. She moved past the kitchen. Talking to Maybelle was a priority but she needed to approach the maid alone. Annie reached the main hallway. The hum of the vacuum was louder. Annie gauged the sound to be coming from upstairs. Likely either Maybelle or Cora was vacuuming in the hallway near the stairs. Annie started up the steps, the thick runner underfoot silencing her steps.

The voice behind her was sharp. "Excuse me." The verb was drawled. "Can I help you?" The demand was sardonic, the intent insulting.

Annie forced herself to turn casually, as if relaxed and unembarrassed. She managed a bright smile. "Hello, Heather. I'm looking for Maybelle."

"Oh." Heather's stare was suspicious. "All right. I'll tell her to come down."

Annie still stood in the center of the stairway. "Actually, I wanted to ask her where you were." Let Heather work that out in her mind. Perhaps Annie had inquired in the kitchen and been directed in her search by Esther. "Ginger's asked me to find out more about Vanessa's friends."

Heather's dark hair was swept up in a ponytail. Her blue-and-white-striped T-shirt hung outside boxy navy shorts. Pink-tipped toes peeked from blue woven crisscross slides. She carried a book tucked under one arm. She would have been the picture of summer ease except for the misery in her eyes and the forlorn droop to her mouth. "She wasn't my friend and I don't have a damn thing to say about Vanessa. Now or ever. So, if you'll excuse me." She started up the stairs, ready to brush past Annie.

Annie said quietly, "I saw Kyle this morning."

Heather jerked to a stop like a marionette strung tight, her eyes pools of fear in a stricken face.

Upstairs the sound of the vacuum ceased. There was a murmur of women's voices.

Annie said quickly, "He told me—"

"Shh." The warning was swift. Heather looked past Annie, forced her face into a smile. "Hi, Mother. Georgia and I are going to take a walk on the beach. I want to show her the pier." Heather's fingers closed on Annie's arm.

Lillian was at the top of the stairs. She gave her daughter a look of surprise, but quickly smiled. "It's a lovely day for the beach. When you get back, I hope you'll get started with your packing. Jon's stayed home to help me. He says I always try to take everything I own. When you have time, please check with William and see if he's had the car serviced."

Heather forced a bright smile. "I'll see to it." She gave Annie's arm a tug, then turned and hurried down the stairs. Annie followed. As soon as they were outside, Heather walked swiftly toward the path to the dunes. Annie hurried to keep up. As their steps thudded on the boardwalk to the beach, Heather asked sharply, "Why did you talk to Kyle?"

They stopped just past the dunes. The tide was out. Sandpipers skittered past. Wet sand stretched a hundred yards to a placid sea, green as jade. The gentle waves were shimmering lines of foam. A raft of snowy white herring gulls bobbed beyond the surf. Annie loved the fresh feel of the sea air. The onshore breeze plucked at their clothes, rustled the sea oats behind them.

Annie's voice was measured. "I went to see him because I thought he might be the man the police are hunting for, the man who killed Vanessa."

Heather lifted a hand to her throat. Wide eyes stared at Annie. "Not Kyle. He wouldn't hurt anyone. He wouldn't hurt anyone, ever. It has to be that man they arrested. Or some other man. Who knows how many men she slept with? That's what she was like."

"Kyle claims he didn't kill her or have an affair with her." Everything pointed to Kyle, but Annie was inclined to think he was telling the truth. "He said Vanessa tried to make it look as if they were having an affair and that was a lie. He said he told you he hadn't made love to her. Why don't you believe him?" This was the crux. Why didn't Heather—who knew Kyle better than anyone, who was quick to insist he couldn't be guilty of murder—believe him when he told her there was no affair?

Heather jammed her hands into the pockets of her shorts. She looked away from Annie, her face now as pale as it had been flushed. "There have always been girls for Kyle. Everybody knew it when we were in school. Vanessa was beautiful. He noticed her. I could tell he was flattered when she went after him. She tried to be as sexy as she could around him. She'd wear a low-cut blouse and then the shoulder would slip when she was close to him. She brushed against him in the pool. It was humiliating. After a while"—her tone was grudging—"he acted like he was irritated. He kept telling me he wasn't interested. But"—she was angry and hurt—"he was lying."

Annie moved nearer. "Why do you think so? This morning he swore that Vanessa was just trying to make it look as if he was involved with her."

There was a flash of hope in Heather's eyes, then her mouth twisted bitterly. "That's what he kept saying, but I know better. I heard her talking to him. Last Friday. I was in the hall outside the library. Vanessa was on the phone. I almost went in, then I heard his name. Her voice was—oh, it was sickening. She said, 'Come at midnight, Kyle. I'll be waiting. I want you to—' " Heather broke off. She tried to stifle a sob as she whirled away, ran down the beach.

Annie knew that the words Heather overheard ripped and gouged deep within her, Vanessa describing in a throaty whisper just what she wanted Kyle to do in a lovers' encounter.

As Annie walked back to the house, she balanced Heather's stricken cry with Kyle's sullen fury. This morning Annie had almost succumbed to Kyle's undeniable appeal. More than that, she found it hard to correlate his prickly, defiant, take-me-as-I-am-or-leave-me, screw-you attitude with the meticulous planning that left Vanessa dead in a ramshackle fishing cabin and Max in the Beaufort County detention center. Or was Kyle's apparent openness simply a cover for a devious and twisted personality?

Annie moved swiftly across the terrace, entered the back door. The long hallway was dim and shadowy. The rumble of the vacuum cleaner was louder. As Annie moved toward the front of the house, the roar increased in volume. She caught a flash of movement and stopped just past the archway to the library. She moved back to the opening.

The library was a dramatic room, bookshelves and floor of mahogany, richly red as sunset. Tartan cushions were a cheerful contrast to the white furniture. A hooded computer sat atop a sleek metal desk in one corner. A golden ceramic dragon looked regal on a rustic wooden bench in front of the fireplace. A massive mirror hung above the fireplace. The movement she'd noted had been her image reflected from the mirror as she passed the archway.

Annie pictured Heather walking up the hallway on Friday. When she heard Kyle's name, she stopped to listen. Annie walked into the library. The phone sitting on the desk was portable, of course. Annie walked to the desk, picked up the receiver. As she did so, she looked up at the mirror. Because she was standing at an angle and the mirror reflected yet another mirror in the hallway, the reflection included a narrow portion of the hall. Even if Heather stopped short of the archway, she could have been seen by Vanessa.

If Kyle was telling the truth, Vanessa's pursuit was spurious. If on Friday Vanessa was still intent upon creating this false image and if she saw Heather approaching in the mirror, how easy it would have been to pick up the phone and hold it as Annie was now holding it and talk into it as if addressing her lover. How easy and how cruel.

How impossible to prove.

Annie replaced the receiver, turned toward the hallway, face furrowed in a frown. The conversation overheard by Heather seemed to confirm that Kyle was Vanessa's lover. But wasn't it just as likely Vanessa once again had been a willing conspirator in spinning a web of duplicity, a web that would ultimately trap her as well as Max? If Kyle was innocent, that left Sam Golden or Jon Dodd. If one of them was the unseen killer, how could Annie prove a deadly connection?

The vacuum cleaner's roar was louder now. Annie walked swiftly toward the hall. Maybelle was looping a cord over one hand. She pushed the machine toward the archway.

Annie gestured to Maybelle to come near.

Maybelle clicked off the sweeper. Her round face was wary and she darted quick glances toward the hall to the kitchen.

In the sudden silence, the hallway seemed long and empty and forbidding. Annie moved quickly toward the maid. "Maybelle, we didn't finish our talk yesterday."

Maybelle backed away, glanced nervously around.

Annie wondered why. Had William told Esther about the Evil Eye? Had Esther ordered Maybelle to avoid that kind of talk?

Maybelle's eyes shifted like a horse ready to bolt.

Annie stepped toward her. "Come into the library." It was a direct order given in a pleasant but firm voice. "Mrs. Dodd said you could help me." Indeed she had, but perhaps not in the fashion Annie intended.

Henny maneuvered her old Dodge past the Hummer. The squat monster vehicle was parked between the front steps of the house—Henny gave the structure the benefit of the doubt—and a burbling fountain. Henny continued on past a saucy red Mustang convertible, dwarfed by the Hummer, to a patch of shade beneath a gnarled live oak. She rolled down the windows but in a few minutes stepped out of the car, which was beginning to heat up like a potter's kiln. She moved deeper into the shade, watching the entrance. Rita Powell had promised to look at the pictures—Henny glanced toward the car where a folder lay on the passenger seat—as soon as she finished showing prospective buyers through a house that not only was the talk of the island, but carried a hefty price tag of almost two million. The hope of receiving the reward for information relevant to Vanessa's murder ranked a definite second to Rita's intense desire to sell the house and get the commission.

Henny squinted her eyes, a necessity because the house glittered bright as a nickel in the sunlight. The front door led into a three-story silo-shaped structure that looked like it was made of a silver metal. The remainder of the house, much more sensibly finished in stucco, spread in a batwing design behind the entrance. The house was designed to avoid contamination by materials with toxic components, such as particle board treated with formaldehyde, carpet adhesives that exude chemicals, and oil-based paints containing volatile organic compounds. Henny had read all about it in a feature in the *Gazette*. Presumably the house avoided the need for air-conditioning by using ceiling fans and taking advantage of cooling winds both through open skylights and sill-vent windows. At the moment, Henny would have traded the decidedly hot breeze rustling the nearby palmettos for a large waft of icy air. If she had two million dollars, she could think of better uses than the house with the shiny silo. . . .

The front door opened.

A burly man in a white polo, sagging khaki shorts, and scuffed leather loafers held the elbow of an elegant, model-thin blonde in a crisp white linen dress and matching sling sandals. A thin woman carrying a clipboard followed them outside and turned to lock the door. The trio stood for a moment next to the Hummer.

". . . eager to sell." A vivacious smile was at variance with the realtor's thin, anxious face. "I can give them your best offer—"

"Bucky, it's too damn hot to stand here and talk." The blonde's tone was pettish.

"Okay, okay, Cindy." He helped her up into the Hummer, gave a negligent wave of his hand toward the agent. "We'll be back in touch."

The agent stood slump-shouldered, the vivacious smile gone, as the Hummer roared away.

Henny held her breath to avoid the cloud of dust roiling over her, then moved to the open window of her car, leaned through to pick up the green folder. She walked quickly toward her quarry. "Mrs. Powell?"

The thin face that turned toward Henny was tired and hopeless.

"Henny Brawley. We spoke last night." Henny spoke as she would to a lost child, her voice kind and reassuring.

"Oh, yes." Rita gave a tired sigh. "I've been thinking about it. I mean, I'm pretty sure that girl I saw was the one who got killed, but I can't afford to get mixed up in anything. I'm a single mom and I can't lose my job."

Henny's smile was warm. "You don't need to worry for a minute.

If you can help catch the murderer, you'll not only receive the reward, I'll see to it"—she hoped Vince Ellis would help her out here—"that there's a very positive story in the *Gazette* about how you stepped forward to protect the community."

Despite the heat that rolled against them, intense and suffocating, Rita shivered. "The night that I saw her, I was terribly jealous." She looked embarrassed, defensive. "She was so pretty and she looked like she had everything going for her. She had on a beautiful dress and she was young. I wished I could be young like that and sitting with a man who loved me. There was something about the way she threw back her head and laughed. It was as if she was telling the world she was special." Rita's faded blue eyes were mournful. "I wanted to be her for a night. A few nights later, she's dead. God, that's scary. I'll look at the pictures. I have to, don't I? I have to help if I can. I feel so bad that I was jealous."

Henny patted a bony shoulder, then opened the folder, rested it atop the trunk of the Mustang. The very first photograph was a studio shot of Vanessa, dark hair gleaming, eyes smiling, lips half parted.

"That's her." There was no doubt in Rita's voice. "God, she was pretty."

Henny fanned three photographs on the hot metal: Sam Golden with his craggy good looks, Jon Dodd with gleaming dark hair and red cheeks, Kyle Curtis with his insouciant, rebellious, devil-may-care grin.

Rita pointed, her finger unwavering. "That one. He's the one."

Maybelle's eyes were huge and staring in her plump face. She stood reluctantly in front of the fireplace in the library. "Excuse me, miss, I got to finish sweeping before lunch. Esther will have my hide if I don't get to the kitchen quick as I can."

Annie's face was stern. "You know how the police are looking for the man involved with Vanessa."

Maybelle evinced no surprise. Annie hadn't expected that she would. The staff of a house always knew what was happening within a house. Maybelle simply hunched her shoulders and looked uneasy.

Annie spoke with conviction. "You know who he is." Maybelle would have pushed past her, but Annie blocked the way. Annie reached out a beseeching hand. "Please, Maybelle. You must tell me. Who looked at Vanessa with the Evil Eye?" Annie's world dismissed superstition, but she knew there was another world where a hank of hair could be used to cast a spell and pins poked into a wax figure could spell death.

Maybelle's hands came together. She shuddered. "Esther tells me it's the Devil's work. But there's people that has the power and when they have the power, they can work bad things. In the old days, they'd take a doll and call it by name and poke it with pins and pretty soon that person got sick and shriveled up and died. Sometimes, all it takes is the Evil Eye. I saw it. He looked at her and then she died. She didn't know. She'd gone on into the cottage when he looked at her like that—"

Annie glanced past Maybelle into the mirror. She saw, like a tiny puzzle piece, the curved fronts of a man's shoes. Just that. Nothing more. The front of two unmoving brown loafers. Horror crawled over Annie as if a cottonmouth had dropped from a tree limb to coil around her arm.

"—and she never knew. But I saw—"

Annie broke in. "Mr. Kyle, wasn't it?" She spoke loudly as she reached out, gripped Maybelle's arm, her fingers tight as clamps.

Maybelle looked startled. "Why—"

Annie whispered, "Hall." She felt frozen in fear, those unmoving brown shoes symbols of threat and danger.

Maybelle stared toward the hall, her eyes glazed with panic. Her plump face suddenly looked shrunken. Her lips parted, but no words came.

"You saw Mr. Kyle." Annie's voice rang out. "He was very angry, wasn't he?" Annie watched the mirror and the reflection from the mirror in the hallway. The shoes were no longer there.

Maybelle struggled to speak. She trembled like the top of a pine in a storm.

Annie bent forward to whisper, "He's gone."

Eyes wild with fear, Maybelle stood frozen.

"I'll go see." Annie turned and walked swiftly to the hall. It was empty. She waved a reassuring hand toward Maybelle.

The maid slipped to her side, looked fearfully into the hall. She turned to Annie. "I got to go home. I'm sick." And she broke into a heavy trot, running toward the kitchen.

Annie finished coiling the cord on the sweeper, pushed it along the hallway, left it out of sight behind the stairs. She felt certain the eavesdropper had been Jon Dodd. She had no idea how much he had overheard. She made no effort to go after Maybelle. Home was probably the safest place for her now.

Annie unfolded cardboard boxes, taped them into shape. When several boxes were ready, she carried them into Vanessa's bedroom and started packing, working fast but carefully. She took no chances that she might miss Vanessa's diary. Every piece of clothing was shaken, every shoe box checked, every moderate-sized container opened. When drawers were emptied, she turned them over, looking to see if a diary might be taped to the bottom. As she worked, she struggled against the growing conviction that there was no way to prove that Jon Dodd was the man behind Vanessa's death and Max's involvement.

Who would believe that smiling Jon Dodd had persuaded Vanessa to pretend that Kyle was her lover? Who would believe Jon had coached Vanessa in the story she offered to Max? Who would believe Vanessa had drugged Max at Jon's request? Who would believe Jon's sillver car had followed the red Jaguar to the fishing shack?

Jon would profess amazement at such claims, point out that Vanessa had flirted with Sam and obviously been involved with Kyle. If the car was ever tied to the vicinity of her death, he would shrug and say everyone knew the keys were at hand in the garage. If shown the photograph where Vanessa looked toward him with possessive triumph, he would shake his head, point to Kyle's presence.

What suggested his guilt? Nothing substantive, Annie knew. Every pointer was intangible:

1. *Sam's geniality seemed genuine. Even though Martha was angry because her husband was attracted to Vanessa, there was no indication she intended to leave him, nor did Sam appear devoured by jealousy over Vanessa's focus on Kyle.*

2. *Kyle's up-front, open quarrelsomeness didn't square with the devious planning that had resulted in Vanessa's death. It would have been odd to go to the effort to ensnare Max yet be openly seen as angry with Vanessa.*

3. *Vanessa's pursuit of Kyle was blatant. She could not have expected to hold on to her job. Why hadn't she cared when obviously she cherished the lifestyle that it offered? Why, in fact, had she made her interest in Kyle so obvious? It was the magician's trick, directing attention away from reality.*

4. *Jon was the only man with whom Vanessa had frequent contact who appeared uninterested in her. This would be expected of the shadowy figure who orchestrated her murder.*

5. *In that telling photograph, her face trumpeted triumph. Whatever*

her relationship with Kyle, it could not be called triumphant. He had publicly rebuffed her. He swore to Heather that the pursuit was all on Vanessa's part. If there was triumph, it had to be evoked by Jon.

6. *On her last afternoon, Vanessa taunted Kyle on the telephone, then laughingly told him he could relax because everything would be out in the open after that night. Everything was already out in the open between Kyle and Heather. Heather had broken off the engagement. What was to happen that night had nothing to do with Kyle or Heather. In fact, Annie was certain that Vanessa was looking ahead to her subterfuge with Max and seeing her participation as a seal to a bargain. She would make it possible for Jon to score off Max by making him appear drunk in a cheap bar. In return, Vanessa would achieve her goal. She would no longer be a secretary. Jon would leave Lillian and ultimately marry Vanessa.*

7. *The sense of danger that had emanated from the unseen figure in the hallway when she spoke with Maybelle. Two unmoving shoes . . . Annie felt a chill as she remembered that reflection. He'd been there. What had his face looked like when he listened? It was Jon that Maybelle saw staring at Vanessa with death in his eyes. Annie was sure of it.*

But every supposition was as evanescent as sea foam, gone when grasped, impossible to prove.

Annie finished packing one box with shoes, taped the top. The bedroom and closet done, she turned to the bathroom, quickly packed powders, makeup, odds and ends. The clothes hamper didn't harbor the diary. The bedroom and bath completed, she started on the living room. She began with the desk. She emptied the drawers, checked the bottoms, looked for false compartments. Turning to the bookcase, she checked each volume. She searched beneath the cushions of the sofa and chairs. She lifted the rug, peered behind the drapes, ran a hand atop the valances, in desperation thumped the wall for a hidden compartment.

Annie was standing in the center of the living room, glaring at the empty bookcase, when the phone rang. She started, swung toward the small maple desk. It rang again. She took two quick steps, picked up the receiver. "Georgia Lance."

"Ms. Lance"—the voice was high—"this is Esther. Lunch is ready in the breakfast nook off the terrace room. Mrs. Dodd thought you might want to join them."

Annie's hand clenched on the receiver. *Come into my parlor . . .* "Thank you, Esther. I'll be right up."

Annie turned off the lights, gave a final glance at the packed boxes stacked near the door and at the unrevealing living room. She was frowning as she hurried down the stairs and followed the path toward the house. The lagoon looked still and hot, the dark water scummed with algae near the cattails. On a far bank, a seven-foot alligator basked in the sun. Annie felt burdened by the sodden humid air and by her failure to find Vanessa's diary. Either she hadn't kept a diary or she had hidden it too cleverly to be found. Could she have hidden it in the house? Perhaps in the library? But there was always the possibility it might be found by a member of the family, and surely that was a chance she wouldn't take.

Annie reached the side entrance. She walked quietly up the hallway. The house now seemed oppressive despite the splashes of color in abstract paintings and the occasional tall blue vase with flowers. She reached the main hallway and was turning to her left when she paused. No one knew she had been searching for a diary. No one knew she had not found a diary.

No one knew.

She heard a murmur of voices. No one knew . . .

Annie reached the terrace room and moved purposefully toward a curved glass room at the far end. Jon Dodd rose as she entered. Lillian gestured toward the seat opposite her. Annie saw that only three places were set but she made no comment when she took her seat.

Lillian smiled. "I'm glad you could join us." She looked tired, her fine-drawn face lined. Her eyes were somber above her gracious smile, but Annie might have been a most welcome guest instead of an unexpected stranger.

Annie wondered where Heather was, if she'd withdrawn to her room, refused lunch.

A slap of shoes on the tiled floor and a squeak of a wheel on a cart announced Esther's arrival. "Ma'am, Maybelle had to go home." The cook's voice was vinegary. She placed a platter of sandwiches, a large salad bowl, and a soup tureen near Lillian.

Lillian looked concerned. "Is she sick?"

Esther stood with arms akimbo. "She's gone home with the misery, her eyes aflame and her hands shaking. I told her she would feel fine if she kept herself away from black magic and talk of the Evil Eye. I told her, 'Be sober, be vigilant; because your adversary, the Devil, as a roaring lion, walketh about, seeking whom he may devour.'"

Annie had a quick vision of the tips of two shoes. She looked under the table at Jon's brown loafers, rich cordovan, the tips she'd seen reflected in the mirror.

Lillian offered the platter to Annie, who took two crustless triangles of chicken salad and another of egg salad. Annie handed the platter to Jon.

Esther turned and walked majestically from the breakfast room, her dignity unimpaired by the slap of her shoes on the tiles.

Jon selected four halves. "Next thing you know," his tone was sardonic, "there will be eye of newt or chicken entrails served up with dinner if Maybelle has her way. I think it's time to let her go, Lillian."

Lillian's brows drew down into a tight line. "Oh, it doesn't really matter. She needs the job and I don't want to upset Esther. On the plus side, Maybelle is good humored and sweet and she works hard." She looked toward Annie. "Forgive us for airing our domestic problems." She gave Jon a tired smile. "Let it go. After all, we're leaving in the morning. Here, Georgia, have some gazpacho. Esther brings tomatoes and green peppers from home."

Annie smiled. "It looks delicious." She half filled her bowl with the bright red cold soup, always one of her favorites. She knew it would be a struggle to swallow. She was too aware of the man who sat opposite her, eating with gusto. As she spooned the gazpacho, she slid careful glances toward him. He was not strikingly handsome but he was attractive, with a well-shaped head, thick curly black hair, green eyes, a straight nose, strong chin, full lips. Sensuous lips. He looked rich, confident, and pleased with himself, his gray silk Italian polo perfectly fitted, his white slacks immaculate. Perhaps it was his king-of-the-hill aura that she found most chilling.

Abruptly his eyes met hers. For an instant she felt a cold and inimical gaze. Then, as he wiped a curl of mayonnaise on his napkin, his sensuous lips parted in a quizzical smile. "How is the packing up coming along?"

Annie seized her opportunity. She put down her soup spoon. "Oh, it's slow going. I had another talk with Ginny this morning. The police are really counting on my finding Vanessa's diary. They think she'll have written about the man she was seeing. So I have to take my time, look carefully. Ginny said Vanessa always hid her diary, didn't want anyone ever to see it."

"Diary?" Jon's hand closed around the tumbler of tea.

Annie looked at the strong fingers, tufts of hair growing between the knuckles. He was right-handed. He had gripped the tire tool with that hand, lifted it, battered the woman whose lips he had kissed, whose body he had known.

Annie felt a wave of nausea. She put down her spoon. She spoke, knew her voice was thin. "Oh yes, Vanessa kept a diary. Always."

Jon lifted the glass, drank, restored it to precisely the same place on the glass-topped table.

Lillian's spoon clattered on the tabletop. "Oh, it's all dreadful. I hope it's the man they have in jail." Fear was obvious in her drawn face. "It would be too awful—" She broke off.

Jon lifted a sandwich. "Stop worrying about Kyle. We've always known he was trouble." His gaze was vindictive. "The good thing is that now she's broken off with him, whether he had anything to do with Vanessa's death or not."

"I'm not worried about Kyle." Lillian's eyes blazed. "If he's guilty, I hope they catch him. It's what you might expect from a man who's unfaithful. There's nothing worse than a man who cheats on his wife. And nothing sadder than the fool of a woman who ties her life to an adulterer." She lifted a trembling hand to her throat. "I tried to warn Heather."

Annie suspected Lillian's fury was from pain remembered. What had been the reality of her marriage to Howard Whitman?

Lillian brushed back a wisp of hair, her look forlorn. "I hate seeing Heather so upset. She's devastated."

"Maybe he won't be so cocky when the police go after him." Jon ate with every evidence of pleasure.

Lillian looked outside toward the terrace and the sand dunes beyond.

There was silence. Annie forced herself to finish another half sandwich. She sipped iced tea and watched Jon over the rim of her glass. His cheeks were patched with red. Annie was aware of the bristly spring of his thick black hair, the close set of his ears to his head, the deep indentations that bracketed his full lips, the suggestion of a cleft in his rounded chin.

Lillian ignored her food. "I suppose they will. Anyone could see that he and Vanessa were involved, even though he tried to act like he wasn't interested."

For an instant Jon looked utterly satisfied. For that flicker of time, he gloried in his own cleverness. As quickly as it came, the expression left. "Of course he pretended she was coming after him. How else could he hope to hang onto Heather? It didn't fool anybody."

Lillian's mouth twisted. "I should have fired her. But that would have been humiliating for Heather. I didn't know what to do. And Vanessa was so arrogant. It seemed to me that she didn't care what I saw or did. It was as if she thought her place was secure, no matter what." She touched trembling fingers to her throat. "I'm sorry, Georgia. Sorry for everything. I'm sorry Vanessa died, but you might as well know the truth. I know she was your friend, but I have to tell you that I disliked her toward the end." Her gaze was defiant.

Annie put down her glass. "I appreciate your telling me. It makes everything much more understandable." Oh yes indeed, it certainly did. "I won't tell Ginny. I know this is hard for the family. I could tell last night that Heather was unhappy. Well"—Annie's voice was determined—"I'll keep looking for Vanessa's diary. For everyone's sake. We have to find out who the man was. I better get back to work." She pushed back her chair. "I'll let you know at dinner if I have any success."

Lillian fingered the blue ceramic necklace at her throat. "We're out this evening, Georgia. Esther will see to your dinner." She was distant, perhaps regretting her frankness.

Annie shook her head. "That's not necessary. I saw a restaurant at the marina this morning when I picked up the boxes. If I keep after it,

I'll finish late this afternoon. If I find the diary—well, I'd better keep it for Ginny. She's the one who should turn it over to the police if it comes to that."

She knew they were watching her as she left. Neither Jon nor Lillian called after her with encouragement for her search. Outside, she walked swiftly toward the cottages, welcoming the sun and heat. She carried with her that glimpse of satisfaction on Jon Dodd's face. He was pleased with the snare he'd laid, Vanessa dead, Max accused, Jon at risk, Heather brokenhearted. But there had been an instant of icy stillness when she spoke of Vanessa's diary.

Annie's hands closed into tight fists. She was going to smash his web of deceit, reveal him for what he was, a cruel, ruthless murderer willing to go to any lengths to hide adultery from a wife with bitter experience of infidelity.

Lou Pirelli drew noisily on the straw, sucking up the last bubbles of his chocolate malt. He dropped the plastic container into the wastebasket where he'd tossed the crumpled sack that had held a double cheeseburger and fries. He swiped greasy fingers on a paper napkin before he picked up the glossy photograph.

Henny Brawley spoke briskly. "Rita Powell's with Seaside Realty. She was at a going-away party for a secretary Saturday night at that new supper club that took over at Raffles. Now it's called Hallie's Hideaway. You know the place—"

Lou did. Billy had done good work in catching a murderer and art thief there when the restaurant was called Raffles.

"—and it's been redecorated with high-sided cozy booths and tables tucked behind fake palms. Dim lighting. A couple of phosphorescent waterfalls and a central fountain. Very hard to see anybody in there. The idea is that everybody's slipping away to a secret tryst with a lover. Cheesy, actually. I understand the food's mediocre, the drinks watery, and the tariff high. Rita was there with a gang from the office. They were crammed at some tables pulled together near the fountain. Her chair faced the last booth on the back wall. She didn't much like the gal the party was for and she wasn't paying much attention. She kept looking at the couple in the booth. She'll swear the woman was Vanessa Taylor. That's the man." Henny pointed at the photograph of Jon Dodd.

Lou knew Billy would be pleased at another piece of information linking Dodd to the victim. But . . . "No crime to take your wife's secretary out to dinner. Even if the guy was up to no good, why would he kill the girl?"

Henny dropped into a metal straight chair, her face thoughtful. "That's the rub, isn't it? Even if he was having an affair and didn't want his wife to know, why murder? Say Vanessa was getting impatient, wanted him to dump his wife, marry her. All he had to say was no."

Lou leaned back in his swivel chair. "Maybe his wife would have kicked him out if she ever knew."

Henny stared at him. "Out of the mouth of a young cop. Maybe Dodd knew his wife would kick him out if she ever knew he'd been unfaithful. Maybe Lillian Dodd can only be soft-soaped to a certain point. Maybe she holds the purse strings. That would be a motive. That's what we lack, a motive and some direct evidence."

Lou's face didn't change, but he thought about the tire prints, felt a glow of satisfaction. They were direct evidence, even though they still had to prove who had driven the car.

Henny got to her feet. She gave Lou an abstracted smile. "Thanks, Lou. I'll leave the photo with you. I wrote Rita Powell's name and address and phone number on the back. I've got some calls to make."

As the door closed behind her, Lou began to write a report for

Billy. He glanced toward the photograph. So this was the dude who owned the silver car.

Annie stood by the slatted blinds in Vanessa's living room. She looked out, watching the oyster-shell path. She would have plenty of warning should anyone approach from the house. She didn't expect Jon to approach the cottage by daylight. She'd have plenty of time to arrange everything. Then she would make one last search for the diary. She slipped her cell phone from her pocket, punched a number now familiar.

"Broward's Rock Police." There was a crisp, resistant tone to Mavis Cameron's voice.

Annie wondered how many media demands she'd fielded this day. "Mavis, Annie Darling. I—"

Mavis broke in, "Annie, I'm glad you called. Handler Jones is after us to find you. Please give him a ring as soon as you can. And, Annie"—her voice changed, the irritation dropping away—"he said Max is doing fine."

Doing fine . . . Shut away. Trapped. Accused. Charged. Doing fine . . . Annie would have cried, but she was past tears. She was past tact or cajoling or entreaty. "I'll call him. First, I need to talk to Billy."

"He's not back yet. He should get in pretty soon. I'll have him call you."

Annie gave Mavis the cell number.

Mavis sounded worried. "Where are you? Handler Jones says Max is afraid you are out trying to be a detective."

Annie looked across the lagoon at the Whitman house. "Tell Billy I'm less than a hundred yards from Vanessa's murderer." She clicked off the cell. That should get her a return call ASAP.

Annie was making a final check of the bookcases—she hadn't

packed the books, uncertain if they belonged to Vanessa—when her cell rang. She yanked it from her pocket, took a deep breath, answered, "Yes." She was marshaling arguments in her mind.

"Annie, that you?" Handler Jones's South Carolina accent was as soft as cotton candy, but he sounded tense.

She moved back toward the front window, once again checked the walk. It wouldn't do for this conversation to be overheard. "Yes. I was going to call—" There was a muffled exchange, a scraping sound.

"Annie"—Max's voice was sharp, urgent—"where the hell are you?"

"Max! I love you." Her voice wobbled.

"Don't change the subject. I've had Handler looking everywhere for you. I want to know exactly where you are and what you are doing."

"Don't worry." She tried to put certainty in her voice. "I'm working with Billy." That was almost true, would be true as soon as Billy called. "We're setting a trap for the murderer. Billy will be in charge." Certainly Billy would insist on that. "If everything goes well tonight, you'll be free in the morning."

His silence told her more than he would ever have said, how far he felt from freedom, how little hope he had, how deeply frightened he was.

"You will be free." She was fierce. "It's going to happen."

His voice was harsh. "You aren't taking any chances? Do you promise?"

She didn't hesitate. "Not a single chance. Billy will be with me."

"Annie, I'll—" A pause and sounds, perhaps a door opening. Max's words came from a distance. "Yeah, yeah, I'm coming."

Handler Jones spoke quickly. "Got to go now. Catch you later."

Annie ended the call. She felt as if she'd thrown a lifeline to Max. Now she had to make good on her promise. He would be hesitant to believe, but deep in his heart he would be counting the hours until morning.

Annie began to pace, waiting for Billy's call.

Henny Brawley wasn't using her cell phone. She sat at the desk in her lovely long house that overlooked the marsh. The late afternoon sun splashed into the room, pouring light as bright as molten gold. Henny cradled the portable phone, waited for the greeting to end, began her message: "Emma, see what you can find out about the finances of Jon Dodd and Lillian Whitman Dodd. Who has the money? Also, what's the financial state of his ad agency? See what you can round up."

She made a second call, smiled when Vince Ellis answered. "Hi, Vince. Henny. You know more than you ever print. You know secrets and scandals and chicanery. If you don't know, you know somebody who does."

Vince laughed. "You make me sound like a combination of Ann Landers and Rupert Murdoch. Would it were so." It was a disclaimer, but his voice was pleased.

Henny was abruptly solemn. "Vince, I want you to dig like you've never dug before. Here's what I need to know. . . ." When she finished, she waited for his answer. She pictured him at his beat-up old wooden desk—no modern, soulless gray metal desk for him—in the corner office of the *Gazette* newsroom. He had a habit of tugging at his curly red hair when he was working, so that he often looked like a Raggedy Andy by late in the afternoon. Now his freckled face would be drawn in a thoughtful frown.

"Pretty private stuff." His voice was serious.

"If there's nothing there, no harm done." Henny looked out at the Sound, at the far reach of water and a porpoise arching in a dive, wild and free. "If you find something, it may be the start of getting Max out of jail."

"A motive for murder." Vince cleared his throat. "Oh hell, yes. I'll try."

Billy Cameron didn't talk on a cell when he was driving. He heard the beep of his pager, unsnapped it from his belt. He glanced at the number, looked at the shoulder. Plenty of room to stop along here. He signaled, pulled off. The sun was slanting through the pines, dappling the hood with shade. He rolled down the windows, turned off the motor. In this kind of heat, he didn't intend to let his car idle with the air-conditioning running.

"Yeah, Mavis." He smiled. He felt like he'd learned how to smile the first time Mavis smiled at him. She'd been a battered wife, scared and hurt, running to safety with Kevin in her arms. One day not too long after they first met, she'd looked at him and the fear had left her face and she'd smiled.

"Annie Darling needs to talk to you." Mavis sounded worried. "She says she's a hundred yards from the man who killed Vanessa Taylor."

He wrote down the number, his face somber. Annie might be exaggerating. She might not. "Okay. I'll call her. Connect me to Lou."

Lou was finishing his report. "Yo, Billy." Quickly he outlined Henny's visit and the photograph. ". . . but hey, you don't go to jail for taking a woman out to dinner when your wife's out of town."

A ten-wheeler thundered by. Billy held the cell closer. "It's a start, Lou. How did the molds turn out?"

"Perfect." Lou was proud.

"Great." The molds had to be matched to the Lexus. But they needed more. And Annie was waiting for him to call. "I'll be there

in about forty-five minutes. We'll decide what to do. See you."
Billy ended the call, looked at his note, punched the number for
Annie's cell.

Emma Clyde's voice was almost admiring. "Certainly a lucky guess
on your part about Jon Dodd."

Henny Brawley could afford to smile, since she didn't have a cell
that transmitted photos. It wouldn't do for Emma to detect Henny's amusement. Emma wasn't quite able to bring herself to laud
Henny. After all, as the island's successful, indeed world-famous creator of tautly plotted mysteries, Emma prided herself on being the
most perspicacious in divining motives. Henny picked up a handful
of tropical-flavored jelly beans from the pottery bowl on her desk and
relaxed in her chair, prepared to enjoy listening to Emma.

Emma cleared her throat. "Yes. Everything I've discovered confirms your theory. Jon Dodd's ad agency would have gone down the
drain except for a healthy infusion of capital by his wife. Moreover,
she paid off the mortgage on his office building. The public perception is that he is quite well-to-do. Not so. The money all belongs to
Lillian."

"That's what I figured." Henny bit a piña colada jelly bean, but
the burst of flavor couldn't match the sweetness of Emma's report.
Henny glanced at a neatly printed sheet on her desk, all ready for Billy
Cameron's consumption. She'd add what she'd learned from Emma.
"You did a great job, Emma. I'll get the information to Billy along
with"—she didn't try to keep the satisfaction out of her voice—"the
lowdown on Lillian Whitman Dodd. Someone I know"—there was
no need to mention Vince Ellis, who had a reputation for keeping his
nose out of people's private lives unless there was a public impact—
"found out her first husband was a womanizer. She stayed with him

because of the daughter. A close friend said Lillian wished she'd left him and swore she'd never again tolerate an unfaithful husband."

"So"—Emma sounded as pleased as her celebrated detective Marigold Rembrandt when announcing the solution to a particularly knotty case—"he wasn't about to trade his cushy life as Lillian Dodd's husband for a girl without a sou. Goodbye, sex; hello, murder."

Annie answered immediately. "Yes?" Her voice was guarded.

"Where are you?" Billy Cameron was gruff. From what Mavis had said, Handler Jones was damn worried about Annie, which meant Max thought she was in over her head.

Annie took a deep breath and told him.

Billy managed to keep his voice even. "Let me see if I got it. You're staying in a guest cottage at the Whitman house under a false name. You have misrepresented your identity, assumed a disguise, gained access to property to which you have no claim, meddled in an ongoing criminal investigation, and possibly contaminated evidence. You could be charged with interfering with a criminal investigation, impersonation for purposes of fraud—"

Annie bristled. "I'm not trying to steal anything."

"Vanessa Taylor's belongings?" He'd made only a cursory inspection of the dead woman's living quarters. There had been nothing to tie her death to the place where she lived. Even if he'd looked, likely he wouldn't have found anything helpful. Still, Annie had no business there.

"All I've done is pack everything up. I'm not going to take the stuff anywhere. Billy, please. Let me tell you what I've learned. . . ."

Sweat beaded Billy's face, felt squishy under his collar. His shirt and pants clung to him. Billy assorted new facts in his mind. Heather Whitman had broken her engagement because of Vanessa. Kyle Curtis claimed he wasn't interested, but he had a history with women.

Sam Golden's wife was suspicious of Vanessa and her husband. One of Sam's photographs revealed Vanessa glorying in triumph. Was she looking at Jon Dodd or Kyle Curtis? Just how angry would Lillian Dodd be if her husband were proven to be unfaithful? He fitted these pieces to the picture of a silver Lexus following the red Jaguar.

"...and I know Jon Dodd is behind everything. You should have seen his face when they were talking about Kyle and Vanessa. He was pleased. Oh my God, he was pleased. He set it up. He told Vanessa to make a play for Kyle, knowing he was going to kill her. Vanessa must have thought Jon was going to dump Lillian and marry her. That's why she agreed to everything he suggested. Vanessa thought helping him fool Max would put Jon in her power even more. He convinced her to string Max along, drug him, then while Max was helpless, that's when he killed her. He took Max to the other cabin, knowing his disappearance would convince everyone Max was the killer. Everything was designed to make Max look guilty, but just in case, Kyle was the backup. Billy, he's terrible."

Billy wiped his face. Annie probably had it right. The pieces fit neatly along with the molds of the tire prints. "He's smart as hell, An-nie." His voice was grave. He felt grave. Annie was a hundred yards from a murderer. "I want you out of there. We're making progress—"

"I've set it up to catch him tonight."

10

The cell wasn't dark even though it was night. Dim lights shone every fifteen feet down the central corridor. Max stood to one side of the window, looking up and out. Through the bars, he saw a portion of the moon. The moon hung in a star-spangled sky. The moon had never before looked so lovely to him. At home, he and Annie often lay together in their hammock, watching the moon rise above the pines. Sometimes they talked. Sometimes they were silent, content with the night and each other.

Would he ever be with Annie again?

His mouth felt dry and his chest tight. Handler Jones tried to put a good face on everything. He'd insisted Annie couldn't be in danger, not if she and Billy Cameron were working together. Max wanted to know where she was. It was as if she'd walked away, her figure growing smaller as he watched, and disappeared into a swirl of fog and he couldn't find her. He wanted her with him, tight in his arms, safe.

He couldn't keep her safe. Instead, she was trying to help him, prove he was caught in a monstrous construct of lies. That search certainly could put her in danger and there was nothing Max could do to protect her.

Surely everything was all right if she was working with Billy.

He looked out at the moon, but he saw Annie's face, serious gray eyes and kissable lips, her flyaway blond hair. *Annie*—he breathed a prayer into the night—*be careful, be careful, be careful.* . . .

Billy Cameron occasionally whistled for an imaginary dog as he strolled along the beach. Who ever suspected a man with a dog of anything nefarious? He knew he was clearly visible in the white-gold radiance of the full moon. A half mile ahead he saw the pier Annie had described.

Billy looked beyond the sand dunes toward the houses. Lights burned in the second stories. It was just past ten. Too early for most people to retire, too early for a stealthy approach to be made to Vanessa Taylor's cottage. Not too late for a man to walk with his dog on the beach. The Spanish Mediterranean house with a tiled roof and stucco walls that looked like rich cream in the moonlight belonged to Sam and Martha Golden. Billy knew all about them, just as he knew all about Jon and Lillian Dodd. The Whitman house was next.

Billy ambled nearer the dunes. He reached the boardwalk leading over the dunes to the Whitman house. He looked back at the beach. A small form hunched near a tidal pool. Billy squinted. A faint splashing reached his ears. A raccoon scavenged for clams. Billy eased onto the boardwalk, scanning the dunes and the stand of pines beyond. Sea oats rustled in the offshore breeze. Frogs barked and yodeled in a lagoon. An owl swooped past, likely scooping up a cotton rat. The night was full of movement, the raccoon loping up the beach, a startled deer crashing away from Billy's presence, and sound, the boom of the surf, the sough of the pines and rustle of the sea oats, but no one else moved on the long ribbon of beach. Billy nodded to himself. He moved fast, running low just as he'd crouched when he'd carried the football long years ago, and with the same exhilaration. He reached the cover of the pines, walked to one side of the oyster-shell path. The pine straw was slick underfoot but he drifted forward, silent as a shadow. When he reached the path that led to the cottages—Annie's directions had been clear: the beach path went straight to the house, and the route to the cottage angled left—he moved even more cautiously.

When the path reached a spur from the main drive, he followed that, curling back toward the dunes, ending up behind the cottages. The parking place behind the second cottage was empty. Now he stepped from shadow to shadow, impossible to see in a long-sleeved loose navy shirt and black trousers with carpenter's pockets and dark sneakers. He wore a shoulder holster with his automatic beneath the loose shirt. His pager was attached to his belt, as well as a sturdy flashlight. A side pocket held his cell phone, turned off, and a small diary. The pager was set to vibrate, not ring.

When he was even with the second cottage, he waited for five minutes, eyes searching the shadows, ears straining to hear. Finally he crossed the parking place, visible for only seconds in the stark splash of moonlight. He slipped soft-footed up the wooden steps. On the porch, he darted to the second window, pulled out the unlatched screen, ducked beneath it, pushed against the sash. It slid up easily. Billy swung his legs over the sill, turned, shut the screen, closed the window.

Annie's whisper floated in the silence. "Thank you, Billy."

He waited until his eyes adjusted to the darkness. Enough moonlight spilled through the windows to illuminate a double bed, chest, vanity, an easy chair, and a chaise longue. Annie was curled in the easy chair, her face a pale blob in the darkness.

He walked around the end of the bed, sank onto the chaise longue. The room had a faint fragrance of violets. "How did you leave it?" His whisper was as light as hers, impossible to hear beyond the room.

Annie understood the question. "I called the house about nine, left a message on their voice mail, said I'd found the diary. I said I'd finished packing and had the boxes stacked in Vanessa's living room, ready to put in my car. I told them I'd put the diary in one of the boxes because Ginny had asked me to bring it to her. She wanted to read it before she gave it to the police. If it didn't have anything helpful to the police, she would keep it to herself. I thanked them for their help and said I hoped to say good-bye to them in the morning."

Billy looked across the room. "Does the bedroom door open directly into the living room?"

"There's a short hall. The bath is on the other side." As the night wore on, they'd crack open the door so they could hear Jon Dodd's entrance.

Billy thought about logistics. "Are the boxes stacked near the front door?"

"Yes. He'll probably step inside, use a flashlight." Annie shifted in her chair. "We should give him time to rip into the boxes."

"You don't have to be here." His whisper was firm.

"I think I do. I've had plenty of time to figure it out." She sounded determined. "Just catching him coming after the diary won't be enough. He could claim he was getting it to find out about Kyle. I'll have to face him." She took a deep breath. "Accuse him." She patted the pocket of her smocklike shirt. "I've got a tape recorder. I used it this morning when I talked to Kyle Curtis."

Billy frowned. He wanted to disagree. But he knew Annie was right. Yes, they had evidence, concrete evidence, in the casts of the tire tracks. If they were a match, the Dodds' silver Lexus would be tied to a parking place not far from the murder cabin and definitely linked to the cabin where Max was left. The real estate agent's claim that she'd seen Vanessa with Jon Dodd on Saturday night was simply a pointer, a break in Dodd's careful avoidance of public contact with Vanessa. Billy felt confident, thanks to Henny and her roundup of information, that Dodd had murdered Vanessa because he knew his wife wouldn't tolerate an affair and Dodd's business and lifestyle depended upon Lillian Dodd's money. But there was no proof. If only a diary actually existed, describing Jon and an affair and his collusion with Vanessa to engage Max on a fake search. If there was a diary, maybe someday it would be found. Maybe it would never be found. In any event, they had to move now.

Billy heaved to his feet. He looked at the luminous dial of his watch. "He won't come for another hour or so. He'll give his wife plenty of time to get into a deep sleep. I'm going to check out the living room."

Henny Brawley watched the moon rise higher, pouring creamy light over the dark Sound, emphasizing the black clumps of hummocks. The lights of jetliner made a steady path across the sky. She felt too restless to sleep. Billy Cameron had thanked her. That was all. Did he understand the importance of what she'd learned? Did he recognize Jon Dodd's unseen stage management? What was Billy doing?

Henny shifted in the canvas chair. She'd called Annie, left a message on her cell, but she'd had no response. In the morning, Jon Dodd would drive away with his wife, and Max would still be in jail. Max and Annie ... Henny treasured them. She took joy from their joy. Whenever she saw the special bond between them, she remembered Bob and the happiness they'd known if only for so short a while. He'd not come back from a bombing raid over Berlin, but she'd held his love close for a lifetime. That kind of love should not be cut short.

Henny pushed up from the chair. She'd not yet undressed for the night. It took only a minute to hurry inside, look up a number, and grab her car keys and purse.

Annie's eyes felt gritty and strained. She tried to relax, but her body was as tense as a coiled spring. How much longer would it be? What if he didn't come? That would be the worst, to wait and wait and wait until there was no hope and know that her trap had failed. But he'd sat so still when she mentioned the diary. He'd been shocked, she was sure of it. How could he afford to take the chance that Vanessa had mentioned him in her diary?

She almost asked Billy, but they had been silent for the past half hour as midnight neared. The door to the hall was slightly open so that they could hear Dodd's entrance. Billy's instructions had been firm. They would wait until Dodd came inside. Likely there would be the flicker of a flashlight as he checked out the living room. Would he be careful enough to search the entire cottage? As Billy warned, they had to take it as it happened. If Dodd discovered them, Annie would pull the diary Billy had brought from her patch pocket, tell him she'd found it. If he didn't search the cottage, they would give him time to open the boxes, then Annie would enter from the hall, turn on the light, hold up the diary. Billy would be hidden in the hallway, waiting.

What would Jon Dodd do?

Henny waited until the tower clock stopped chiming, then dropped the coins in the outdoor pay phone near the marina office. The breeze was freshening, sending water slapping against the pilings. Far out on the pier a couple walked arm in arm, enjoying the moonlit beauty of the August night. Otherwise, the boardwalk was deserted, the shops closed.

Henny punched the numbers, her thin face determined and intent. The phone rang. And rang. Four times. Five . . .

"Hello." It was a woman's sleep-befuddled voice. Lillian Dodd had answered the phone, not her husband.

Henny had been poised to speak a short quick sentence, "I saw you with Vanessa Taylor," then hang up. Her lips parted. She almost said, "Tell your husband I saw him with Vanessa." Her lips closed. Some risks cannot be taken. Jon Dodd was a dangerous killer. If Lillian confronted him, she would be in great peril.

Henny cut the connection. She was disconsolate as she walked slowly back to her car, her steps echoing on the wooden boardwalk. Who knows what difference it might have made, how much pressure it might have added, if Jon Dodd had answered the phone? Now the call was meaningless, a wrong number in the night.

Annie wondered if Billy was sleeping. She wondered if Max slept or if he lay staring into a frightful future in his cell. She was as far from sleep as she would ever be. She sat rigid in the chair, hands clenched, listening, listening.

The first sound, the creak of the front door, brought her to her feet, heart pounding, breathless and trembling. As they had expected, a beam of light moved swiftly, the brilliance shining for an instant in the hallway.

Billy was at her side in two great strides, a hand warm on her elbow. They moved nearer the door.

The second sound was startling, unexpected, a splashing and gurgle. A thump sounded. The stench of gasoline fumes flowed to them. Annie's nose wrinkled. Billy muttered, "Oh hell." He started for the door. Annie reached out, grabbed his arm.

As the front door slammed, flames flared. Within seconds, fire danced and spread, tongues flickering around the doorway. Billy took her hand, shouted, "The window." The force of the fire pushed the door open. The hallway was a maelstrom of fire. Smoke billowed into the bedroom, hot and choking. The noise was mind numbing, crackles and hisses, pops and creaks.

Billy's flashlight beam was lost in the smoke, but he pulled Annie forward, stumbling once against the chaise longue, and then they were at the window and he was pushing up the sash. He swept her up and over the sill, dropped down beside her onto the porch.

Annie gasped, welcoming the sweet pine-scented air. They pounded down the stairs as the fire poked through the roof. The wooden shingles flamed and the roof glowed, golden swirls of fire, filigrees of destruction.

Still coughing from the smoke, Billy was yelling into his cell phone. "Fire. Whitman residence. Two-eleven Tree Swallow Lane. Shore side. Rear cottage. Arson. Flames intense." He punched off the phone, yelled at Annie, "Stay here. It's probably too late but . . ." He plunged away from her, running hard toward the drive to the house.

Annie's stride was no match for his. She kept him in sight, forced her legs to pump and pump. Lungs aching, she caught up with him at the edge of the terrace. He'd stopped in the shadow of a live oak.

Billy's chest heaved as he tried to catch his breath. "No . . . sign . . . of . . . him."

Annie was too drained to answer. He'd outwitted them. Behind them, the cottage was ablaze. Ahead of them lights flickered on upstairs in the Whitman house.

"He'll be down here in a minute. Shocked. Upset. A homeowner with a great loss." Annie's voice was breathless, bitter. "Billy, we were so close. Now there's nothing we can do."

Billy sucked in air. "He doesn't know how close we are."

Faraway there was a sound of sirens.

Billy gestured toward her cottage. "Run like hell. Put on your pajamas. Start toward the house. The Dodds should be coming outside pretty soon. Tell them the fire woke you up and you ran to the front porch. Say you saw someone running toward the house. A dark figure." He took another deep breath. "Tell them you called nine-one-one. That will explain the fire trucks getting here so quick. We don't want him to know we're onto him, so I'll get out of here now. I parked a couple of blocks away. I'll get my car and come. We'll see what we find."

"He won't have left a trace." She heard defeat in her voice. She'd promised Max, told him they were going to find out the truth. Her hopes, her life were disappearing in the smoke that coiled, darker than the night, above the burning cottage.

"Get moving." Billy gestured toward the cottages. "Remember, you saw someone running toward the house." Billy ducked away into the shadows. She heard his thudding feet and then he was gone.

Annie didn't have the breath to run, but she walked fast. She didn't worry about the oyster shells beneath her feet. No one would hear that crackle in the hiss and roar of the fire. She stayed as far away from the blaze as she could and wondered if the embers swirling in the breeze would ignite the trees. Just as she reached the porch of her cottage, the sirens rose to a crescendo, and two fire trucks, lights whirling, jolted to a stop not far from Vanessa's cottage. The remnants of Vanessa's cottage.

Annie dashed into her cottage, hurried to the bedroom, pulling off her top and slacks, dropping them as she ran. It took only seconds to pull on her short blue nightgown. She kicked off her shoes, slipped into a pair of huaraches. She hesitated, then grabbed up a white cotton cardigan, pulled it on. Outside again, she shielded her eyes from the flames, started toward the house. She skirted to the far side of the fire trucks. Men in heavy yellow coats yelled, worked hoses. Water spewed in huge arcs to strike the disintegrating roof with a shocking hiss and turn to writhing curls of steam.

Another siren shrilled, cut. A Broward's Rock Police cruiser slewed to a stop near the trucks. Annie saw Billy climb out, move toward the fire chief's car.

Annie found Lillian and Jon and Heather on the terrace, watching the firefighters attack the blaze. Light flooded the back of the house and the terrace as well. Lillian wore an ankle-length cotton piqué robe. She brushed back tousled hair. Without makeup, her face was sallow, older. Deep lines flared from her lips. Jon was shirtless, barefoot. Cotton chinos sagged from his hips, revealing the band of red and green boxer shorts. He stepped toward Annie. "Thank God you're all right. We saw the flames and called nine-one-one." He sounded shocked and concerned. Heather looked young and vulnerable in a scanty pink gown. Her voice was high and shaky. "How can it burn so fast? What started it?"

Annie remembered, would never forget, the unmistakable odor of gasoline. "I heard something." There had been a pop and whoosh when the fire began. Was it loud enough to have carried to her cottage? Annie didn't care. She wanted to shout the truth. What if she faced Jon, accused him? *You threw gasoline on the boxes. You lit the fire. You killed Vanessa.* She knew the truth but she and Billy hadn't seen Jon. Damn him, they hadn't seen him. "When I came out on the porch, I saw someone running toward the house."

Jon's bland face stiffened. Light eyes watched Annie.

Lillian's head jerked toward Annie. "Who?" Lillian's voice was sharp.

Annie lifted a hand to her face. "I didn't have my glasses on. I only know there was someone running."

"Odd," Jon murmured. "I don't like the sound of that—"

Annie's hands clenched. Her nails gouged her palms. He wasn't worried. He was complacent, a surfeited lion at a bloodied carcass.

"—but it might have been a deer. Or you may have been mistaken." His voice was smooth, his glance at Annie dismissive. "In any event, I doubt there's anything we can do to help. It looks"—he gazed across the lagoon—"like the firefighters have everything under control. We're fortunate the pines didn't catch. Maybe I should go down. . . . Look, here comes somebody."

Billy Cameron strode toward them. Annie thought he had the look of an avenging Norseman, fair haired, strong, stern.

"It's the police chief." Lillian looked startled. "Why would he be here?"

Jon's shrug was relaxed. "I suppose a big fire brings out the police as well."

Billy reached the terrace. "Good evening. Mrs. Dodd. Mr. Dodd." He looked inquiringly at Heather and Annie.

Lillian quickly introduced them. "My daughter, Heather Whitman. Our guest, Georgia Lance. Chief Cameron."

Annie took this as her cue. She faced Billy. "I was in the next cottage. Something woke me up. When I went out on the porch, I saw someone running toward the house."

"Or the street." Jon pointed. "Anyone coming from the cottages would have to use our drive to reach the street. But I imagine Georgia saw a deer, something moving in the shadows. It's unlikely anyone would have been here. I would think even a trespasser would have the grace to report a fire."

"Not if they set it." Billy's stare was challenging. "The fire was started with gasoline."

Lillian gasped. She lifted a shaking hand to her throat. "Are you sure?"

"Yes." Billy looked at Lillian. "I'd like your permission to search the grounds, look in your garage."

Heather's eyes were huge. "Why the garage? Do you think the person who set the fire is hiding there?"

Jon lifted an eyebrow. "That would be a fairly mentally challenged arsonist, Heather." He sounded amused. "I imagine Chief Cameron will be looking for our gasoline tin. Tomorrow William can tell him where it is."

Billy was brusque. "There appears to be a burned gasoline tin in the living room area."

"Really. Clever of the firemen to find it. But"—a casual shrug—"it could be anyone's tin. If ours is missing, William will know. However, I should warn you, Chief, we never lock the garage." Jon was rueful, hands outspread, palms up. "I suppose that's regrettable, but we've never thought it was necessary. Until now. In the future, we'll be more careful." He turned toward Annie. "Georgia, it's a damn shame about the fire, whatever caused it. You've made your long journey to no avail." His frown looked genuine. "Chief, is it safe enough for our guest to return to her cottage?"

Billy looked toward the charred remains of Vanessa's cottage. Occasional tongues of fire erupted but the steady stream from the hoses were reducing the remnants of the fire to a smoldering mass. "Sure. The fire's almost out and there will be men here until it's completely extinguished. There's no longer any possibility it will spread. I'll be happy to escort Miss Lance to her cottage."

Jon smothered a yawn. "It's very late, Chief. Since there isn't anything we can do to help, we'd better try to get some sleep." His voice was firm. "We're leaving for the Cape in the morning and we have a long drive ahead of us."

Annie waited for Billy to announce that they weren't free to leave, that the arson investigation required their presence. He had to stop them. Surely there had to be a way to keep Jon Dodd from driving away in the silver Lexus.

Billy merely nodded, his face stolid. "If you'll leave us a phone number, we'll keep you apprised of the investigation."

Annie drew her breath in sharply. Was it going to end like this, Jon Dodd triumphant, Max branded a murderer?

Billy flicked a glance toward her.

"Certainly we'll do that. I'll leave the information with William." Jon was lord of the manor, distancing himself from an investigation that had no relevance to him. He touched his wife's elbow, glanced at Heather. "We'll say good night then, Chief. Thank you for your good efforts."

As they entered the house, Annie glared at Billy. "Are you going to let him get away?"

"He isn't gone yet. Come on, Annie, let's head toward your cottage. I've got some ideas." Billy led the way. He talked fast. When he left her at the cottage door, he had a final word. "Try to get some sleep. Mavis will call you at six. I'll have everything arranged by then. Alert me when the Dodds are ready to leave."

Max watched the window as moonlight gave way to the lighter dimness that preceded sunrise. Gray was followed by pink, then gold. Lights flared brighter in the corridor. A buzzer sounded. He rose and dressed. It wasn't until the cell doors were clicking open and prisoners assembling two by two to walk to the dining hall for breakfast that he gave up hope. Annie had said the murderer would be trapped during the night. If that had happened, if she and Billy had succeeded, they would have come for him by now. They had not come.

The line moved, the sound of shuffling feet a dirge in his mind. Max walked, head down, face bleak, hands balled into fists, disappointment and despair bitter companions.

———

Henny Brawley was a good actress. She had every confidence she could play any role demanded. She wasn't given to stage fright. Yet her hands felt damp as she punched the number. She had to succeed here. The phone rang.

A sleepy voice answered on the fifth ring. "Hello."

"Rita, Henny Brawley. I have some exciting news about your reward." Henny had no qualms about dangling bait. Moreover, she was sure the reward would be forthcoming. "Just a minor matter of making the identification. I'll pick you up in forty-five minutes. We'll have breakfast and then take a drive. I'll see you soon."

Esther Riggs finished reading the chapter in her Bible. Faithful unto life or death, she read a chapter to end her day and begin her day. The verse from Ezekiel echoed in her mind: "As it were a wheel in the middle of a wheel." She'd ruminated into the night about the policeman's request. He'd had a long talk with William after the fire was put out and he'd looked through the garage. She'd come down the steps of their garage apartment, been there when he came out of the garage with William. Esther wasn't surprised to learn the gasoline tin was gone and one had been found blackened into a heap in the burned cottage. That was when the policeman asked her to call Maybelle this morning, tell her to come. Esther told him she didn't hold with black magic, that it was an abomination in the sight of the Lord. "'Can two walk together, except they be agreed?'" The big young policeman had looked at her respectfully, said he understood what she meant. Then he said that even if the magic was wrong, Maybelle could make a difference in whether a good man went to prison and an evil man stayed free. Esther pursed her lips. The verse made it clear to her. One life touched another. Duty was duty. "'Pay to all what was due them.'" Stiffly, Esther pushed up from her knees. She reached for the telephone.

Lou Pirelli eased the crime van to a stop behind the cruiser, rolled down the windows, turned off the motor. They were around a bend in Tree Swallow Lane, maybe a hundred yards from the entrance to the circular drive at the Whitman house. Lou hoped Billy knew what he was doing. It seemed like a long shot to Lou. If Billy's plan didn't work, the mayor was going to be all over Billy, like an attack dog on a wounded stray cat. The mayor would fire Billy's butt, sure as shooting.

Lou tugged at his collar. It wasn't even ten o'clock but he was hot as a hush puppy in sizzling grease. Maybe it was the waiting and the worry as much as the temperature. He looked over at the plaster-of-paris casts in the passenger seat. Last night Billy had spotted that little tomahawk scar when he'd checked out the Lexus in the garage. So that was all right.

Lou moved restively in the seat. He glanced in the rearview mirror. There was Henny Brawley's old black Dodge. They were ready, all of them. How much longer would it be?

Billy Cameron's stomach roiled like he was out in the Sound in a Sail-fish on a stormy day. He wasn't a damn fool. He didn't ignore warn-ing flags. Not when he sailed. But now . . . Well, he was gambling his life on the island, a job he loved, his family's security, on the hope that successive shocks could crack a killer's varnish-slick confidence.

He knew the price if he failed. Max Darling would pay a grim penalty for a crime he hadn't committed. Billy would no longer be acting chief of the Broward's Rock Police Department. He stared grimly ahead, waiting for his cell to ring.

A bumblebee hovered near the pittosporum bush on the north side of the circular driveway. Annie smelled the sweet banana scent, ignored the threatening drone of the bee. She held a cell phone in one hand. She patted her pocket. Yes, the clothbound book was there. She was at one end of the shrub, out of sight but with an excellent view of the curving driveway and the front of the house. She saw the wide sweep of the front steps, the ornate wooden front door. The Whitman house drowsed in the morning sun, the stucco a soft gold. The silver Lexus was parked near the steps. Luggage was ranged in the drive near the trunk. The scene might have been a gay painting entitled *Ready to Go.*

The front door opened. Lillian Dodd was slim and elegant in a pale blue chambray slacks outfit. An oversize straw purse hung from her shoulder. She didn't look like a woman embarking on a holiday. Her face was pale and drawn. A tight frown might have reflected a dull headache or a persistent worry. She carried some magazines and a compact disc player.

Jon came down the steps after her, tennis rackets under one arm. He wore a soft slouch hat, white polo, khaki shorts, and running shoes. "I'll put the luggage in the trunk. Go ahead and get in, Lillian." He moved quickly, exuding a barely contained impatience. He looked over his shoulder, called sharply, "Heather?"

Lillian was nearing the passenger door. "She's coming, Jon. Let's not start off with any unpleasantness. It doesn't matter what time we leave."

Heather came through the door. Her blouse was a crisp white. Summer daisies were embroidered on her short cropped linen pants.

She could have been in a fashion shoot for a vacation getaway if her pale, unhappy face hadn't been twisted in a scowl.

Annie lifted the cell phone, punched the number.

The answer was swift. "Cameron."

Her mouth felt dry as she spoke. "Now." She ended the connection, dropped the cell phone into her pocket.

Annie waited in the shadow of the sweet-smelling shrub. The police cruiser came first. Billy turned into the drive, angled the car to block any exit. He stopped, turned off the motor. He stepped out, crisp and commanding in his khaki uniform, his captain insignia glinting in the sunlight, and walked toward the silver Lexus. The crime van rolled into the other end of the drive and stopped, blocking that exit. Lou swung down from the van. His uniform, too, was immaculate. He walked forward, his pace deliberate, a hand on the butt of the pistol in his holster, a plaster cast tucked under the other arm. The old black Dodge pulled up behind the cruiser. In an instant, the motor stilled and the doors swung out. Henny led the way, a woman in her thirties lagging behind her. The front door opened. Esther Riggs shepherded her niece outside. They stood on the top step, Esther staring down, face grim, arms folded, and beside her a wide-eyed Maybelle, twisting her hands around and around. William was a pace behind them, his face somber.

"What's going on here?" Jon Dodd no longer looked comfortable and at ease. His light eyes flickered from one face to another, came back to Billy.

Billy Cameron had never looked more like the cop that he was. There was no trace of fatigue or uncertainty in his face or in his stance. His thick blond hair gleamed in the sunlight. His blue eyes were grave and steady in a solid, dependable face. He stopped a scant foot away from Jon. "Jon Dodd." His tenor voice was stentorian.

"Chief Cameron, please. What do you want?" Lillian lifted a trembling hand in appeal.

Billy gave her a swift look, shook his head, turned his eyes back to her husband.

"Look here." Jon's cheeks flushed an angry red. "We're getting ready to leave town. Move those cars."

Billy pointed at the Lexus. "Jon Dodd, is that your car?"

Jon lifted his chin. "You know damn well it is."

Billy half-turned, gestured to Lou.

Lou moved fast, ignoring the exclamation from Lillian. Lou walked straight to the right rear wheel. He knelt, studied the cast, thumped the tire with a triumphant fist. "A perfect match." He rose held out the plaster cast to Billy. "This car was a half mile from the murder cabin Monday night. I took a cast of the tire print there. I also have a witness who saw the car. This car also left a track at the cabin where the man currently being held for the murder of Vanessa Taylor was dumped unconscious Monday night."

Henny came forward, a firm hand on the elbow of her companion. Her voice was loud and clear. "Don't be nervous. All you have to do is identify the man you saw with Vanessa Taylor."

Rita Powell looked straight at Jon Dodd. She stood stiff and straight, her eyes wide and staring. She pointed. "That's him. That's the man. I saw him."

"Oh my God." Lillian held her hands up to her face.

Dodd took one step back, another. "Cameron, I don't know what you think you're doing, but this is outrageous. I'll bring a lawsuit. I'm ordering you to get off this property."

From the top step, Maybelle's husky voice was a keen. "There's those that claim there's no such thing as the Evil Eye. They say"—her sidelong glance at her aunt was defiant—"they's no truth to potions and spells and such. But I can tell you that I know the Evil Eye when

I see it and he turned the Evil Eye on Miss Vanessa. I saw him. I saw Mr. Dodd and his face was all cold as the underside of the dark beyond and he was glaring at her and then she was dead. He had the Evil Eye."

Annie took a deep breath, pushed past the pittosporum shrub, moved swiftly to the center of the drive, only a few feet from Jon Dodd. She pulled the small book with the floral-patterned cover from her pocket. "You thought Vanessa's diary was in her cottage. I said I'd packed it away, but I didn't. I kept it with me. I wanted to read it, but I knew I shouldn't. I knew it should be left to Ginny. I put it in my purse. When the cottage burned, I knew it had to be because of the diary. When I got back to my cottage, I got the diary out and I read it." She held the book up. "It's all in there. How you promised Vanessa you were going to marry her. How you asked her to help you play a trick on Max Darling. How she went to his office and showed him a snapshot and said her brother was missing—"

Jon's cheeks flared red. Sweat beaded his face. He took another step back, another.

"—and how she wanted him to meet her at Dooley's Mine to hunt for him. It's all in there, how she pretended to be crazy for Kyle so that no one would know about you and her. How she thought it was funny to see Heather so upset and Kyle trying to tell Heather he wasn't after Vanessa and she wouldn't believe him—"

"Damn you, Jon." Heather's cry was one of sheer fury. "I should have known. You married Mother for her money and then you couldn't stay out of bed with that tramp. She thought the money was yours, didn't she?" Heather was derisive. "Big-deal Jon. Vanessa thought she was going to marry a rich man, but if you left Mother, it would just be you and Vanessa. You might have liked playing with her, but you didn't want to lose everything. You decided to kill her."

"Jon . . ." Lillian's voice shook.

Jon hunched his shoulders, stood like a bull tormented by ban-
derillas. "There's nothing to this. Nothing at all. They don't have any
proof."

His wife stared at him. "I saw you last night." Lillian's face might
have been chipped from marble. "I saw you coming back from Vanessa's cottage. The phone rang and woke me up and you weren't there.
I got up and the flames were already shooting up and I went to the
balcony to look out and I saw you coming back toward the house."

Esther Riggs's somber voice rang out. "'The heart is deceitful
above all things, and desperately wicked; who can know it?'"

Billy Cameron strode forward. "Jon Dodd, I arrest you for the
murder of Vanessa Taylor on the night of Monday, August 16 . . ."

11

Cameras clicked. Lights flashed. Tape whirred. Max was oblivious to reporters and onlookers, shouted questions, outthrust hands with microphones, television cameras. A car slid to a stop at the curb, Handler Jones driving, Max in the passenger seat. The passenger door opened and Annie was on the sidewalk, flying toward Max, arms wide. Her face had been scrubbed of the garish makeup, the wig and glasses discarded. They came together as if they'd never been apart. This moment was theirs alone, the world shut out. He buried his face in her sweet-scented hair; his lips moved against her cheek. "Oh God, Annie. I love you. I love you."

Tears streamed down her face.

"Don't cry. We're okay now. You saved me." He held her as if he'd never let go.

"All of us together did it, Max. Billy and Lou and your mom and Henny and Emma." She felt as if her heart was a balloon, bigger and bigger, filled with so much joy it must burst.

They held hands as they moved down the sidewalk, the questions following them. At the car, Annie was ready to climb into the back seat, Max close behind, when a petite TV reporter cried out, "Mr. Darling, don't you have anything to say to the world? It looked pretty black for you. Did you ever expect to be freed?"

Max stopped, his hand on Annie's elbow. He looked at the reporter, his blue eyes dark with memory. "I was innocent, but I didn't see how it could ever be proved. Do you know what happened?" A huge smile wreathed Max's face. "My wife and my friends and the police chief all set to work to find out the truth. I'm free because a first-rate police officer was too smart to be fooled by a killer. I'm free because I have friends who believed in me and worked for me. Most of all, I'm free because I have the smartest, bravest, most wonderful wife in the world."

Laurel Roethke smoothed back a tendril of white-gold hair. Her dark blue eyes gleamed with satisfaction as she bent close to Annie near the coffee bar at Death on Demand. "My dear, you are simply the cat's whiskers. Max has no idea about the party. I met the Stutz Bearcat man this morning at the ferry and that adorable car is now parked at Parotti's at the ready for the birthday festivities. That dear man may be back as well. I invited him." Laurel looked distracted for a moment, a smile curving her lips. She came back to the present. "The party Web site has been such fun I intend to maintain it. I've had several hits from Siberia. I believe I shall call it the merry-ever-after site. Of course, I'll feature the winners of our quiz. The table winners tonight will compete for a grand prize. Here's the question: Who sketched a design for a hovering machine that he called a helix pteron and when did he do so?"

Annie put a finger to her lips as Max approached, carrying a crystal plaque. "Later," she whispered to Laurel. Annie was as happy and frazzled as a mother duck ready to launch a brood on a triumphant sail. The wonderful week of Max's rescue was culminating in the best birthday party ever, though Max thought they were gathering at the bookstore to honor Billy Cameron. Indeed they were going to honor Billy, prior to departure in a double-decker bus hired from Savannah to convey the group to Parotti's.

Laurel turned. "Max, what a gorgeous plaque. Is Billy here yet?"

Ingrid Webb craned to look toward the front of the store. "Here he comes." The glad shout was raised by Henny Brawley, elegant in a pale violet georgette dress as summery as an August evening. Emma Clyde's orange and gold caftan swirled as she moved forward to greet the police chief and his wife.

The store was full of friends—Vince Ellis, Edith Cummings, Duane Webb, Pamela Potts. Standing near the coffee bar was Handler Jones.

Annie reached out, took the plaque. When Billy and Mavis reached the coffee bar, Annie held the plaque high above her head.

"Listen up, everybody." Max grinned and picked up a chair, stamped it on the floor for quiet.

Amid shouts and clapping, Annie held up the engraved plaque. "Billy, this is for you."

"I am thrilled to make the presentation." Henny Brawley stepped forward, glasses perched on her nose, and read, "To Captain Billy Robert Cameron, chief of police, in honor of his devotion to duty and determination to execute his responsibilities without fear or favor. Presented on this day of August 28 by grateful residents of Broward's Rock, South Carolina."

Billy's face burned apple red. "I just did my job." Mavis, lovely in a gentian blue dress, clapped loudly, eyes bright.

"That, dear Billy," announced Emma in her gruffest, deepest voice, "is the point. You did your job."

Max stepped forward, gripped Billy's hand. "If you hadn't"—and Max's voice was grave—"I wouldn't be here tonight. Thank you, Billy."

A cheer erupted.

Emma fluffed spiky orange hair. "Pass it around, Billy. I want everyone to see the mark in the right-hand corner, the mayor's stamp making this an official proclamation."

As the plaque went from hand to hand with appreciative oohs and ahs, Annie glanced toward Laurel. It was almost time to announce the arrival of the bus and their departure to Parotti's. Max was going to be surprised.

Laurel saw her glance, drifted near. "Leonardo da Vinci," she whispered. "In 1493."

Annie looked at her mother-in-law blankly. Had the moment come? Had Laurel's ever tenuous connection to reality been sundered? Had the trauma of this past week been too much for Laurel to survive?

Laurel gave Annie a sweet pat on her cheek. "My dear, the helix pteron. Now, isn't it time for us to leave?"

"Yes, but let's wait until everyone's spoken to Billy." Annie wanted Billy to have his moment in the sun, his well-deserved, well-earned moment in the sun.

Handler Jones paused near Annie. "Wonderful start to a wonderful night. And I'm glad to have a chance to tell you how much I like your store." He pointed toward the watercolors. "Neat idea. You can't beat suspense novels. Those are tops."

Annie recognized the tone of a mystery cognoscente. "Do you know them?"

"Oh, sure. *The Thirty-nine Steps* by John Buchan, *The African Queen* by C. S. Forester, *Thank You, Mr. Moto* by John P. Marquand, *Above Suspicion* by Helen MacInnes, and *The Light of Day* by Eric Ambler."

Annie grinned. "Pick a book, any book. Free coffee for a month, and"—she lifted her voice in a glad shout—"come on everybody. The bus is here. On to Parotti's. It's time to party."

Pink tendrils of sunrise graced the sky as Max turned the car into their drive. They'd laughed and sung, tangoed and marched, played games, hugged friends. Max had even managed a ragged "When the Saints Come Marching In" on a borrowed trumpet. As Max eased the car into their garage, Annie wriggled expectantly in her seat. She couldn't keep her secret any longer. "There's a special present for you upstairs."

Max turned off the motor. "The party was my present. And being with you." There was a world of gratitude and love and joy in his eyes.

"There's one more present in our room. The special one." Annie slipped out of her seat, called over her shoulder. "First one upstairs gets to open it."

They ran through the kitchen and terrace room. Of course, Annie let Max surge past her on the stairs.

Max stood in the center of their bedroom, holding a small, slender package wrapped in gold foil. He held it up, shook it. Something inside slid back and forth, made a thonking sound.

Annie hurried to stand next to him.

He ripped off the paper, opened the box, lifted out a worn black key. He stared at it in puzzlement.

Annie's smile was tremulous and loving and giving. "The key to the Franklin house. For you. For us. Happy birthday, Max!"